Miriam Coffin,

OR

THE
WHALE-FISHERMEN.

Miriam Coffin
First Published 1834

Historical Introduction
©1995 by Nathaniel Philbrick

Mill Hill Press
134 Orange Street
Nantucket, MA 02554

Library of Congress Catalog Card Number: 95-76873
ISBN 0-9638910-5-7

Manufactured in the United States of America

Mill Hill Press was established to preserve and record the history of Nantucket Island and the people who live by the sea—for therein lies, in great part, the story of America.

Hope you enjoy this offering from Mill Hill.

Albert F. Egan, Jr., Publisher
Mill Hill Press

Other Titles from Mill Hill:

Away Off Shore, Nantucket Island and Its People, 1602-1890
    by Nathaniel Philbrick
Early Nantucket and Its Whale Houses
    by Henry Chandlee Forman
Portrait of Nantucket, 1659–1890: Paintings by Rodney Charman
    text by Robert F. Mooney
Anton Otto Fischer, Marine Artist - His Life and Work
    by Katrina Sigsbee Fischer and Alex A. Hurst

HISTORICAL INTRODUCTION
by
NATHANIEL PHILBRICK

ON Nantucket Island the past is always with you. From the cobbled elegance of Main Street to the barnacled rubble at the end of Old North Wharf, you feel the tug of another time. And yet all the historic homes, museums, and walking tours that Nantucket has to offer can only take you so far. Even the many published histories of the island can only gesture toward that elusive sense of "what it was like" when Nantucket was the whaling capital of the world.

Short of a time machine, the novel you are now holding is probably the best way to experience the sights, sounds, and even the smells of Old Nantucket. Although a work of fiction, *Miriam Coffin, or The Whale-Fishermen*, first published in 1834, is a self-proclaimed "drama of Real Life" based on what occurred to the notorious Tory whaling merchant, Kezia Coffin (1723-1798), during the American Revolution. But the real focus of *Miriam Coffin* is not a single person; it is the island of Nantucket. From a 'Sconset fishing shack to the sheep shearing festival beside Miacomet Pond, from an Indian wigwam to a Nantucket sleigh ride, this novel brings the island's past convincingly to life.

In the last seventy-five years *Miriam Coffin* has been read by only a handful of academics primarily interested in tracing its now well-documented influence on *Moby-Dick*. But *Miriam Coffin* deserves to be read for its own sake. It was not only America's first whaling novel; it was also the first book to provide an in-depth account of Nantucket's history. Critically acclaimed in its day, it went into a second edition less than a year after its appearance. Indeed, if a white whale by the name of Moby Dick is what the American public now associates with Nantucket Island, in the nineteenth century it was an ambitious "she-merchant" named Miriam Coffin. It's about time her story was more widely known.

Joseph Coleman Hart (1798-1855), the author of *Miriam Coffin*, was a New Yorker with some major Nantucket connections. As his middle name might suggest to those familiar with the island's history, there was Nantucket blood (from his mother's side) flowing through his veins, and in 1832, according to William O. Stevens, Hart came to Nantucket to avoid the cholera epidemic then sweeping through Manhattan. That Hart looked to his island heritage with some reverence is indicated by the anecdote that while on Nantucket he saved (and later had framed) a shingle from the old Quaker Meeting House where his ancestor Elihu Coleman had once preached.

On an island where elderly people abounded (one visitor commented on the "many green old men"), the trail to Nantucket's Revolutionary past was still quite fresh. In fact, Hart was able to talk with several people who had actually witnessed the events his novel would describe. In the final chapter Hart assures us that "[f]iction has but little to do with our pages. The incidents and the manners of bygone times . . . are drawn from materials, which, if not altogether matters of record, still live fresh in the memory of a few persons, whose day of nativity dates near the middle of the last century." Given that tradition is as close as we can get in many instances to the facts of Nantucket's past, what Hart provides in *Miriam Coffin* is of immense historical value.

But a word of caution. This novel is more than one hundred and fifty years old. Although a best-seller in its day, it is a long way from Danielle Steel. It begins somewhat stiffly, with an account of Nantucket's unsuccessful attempts to solicit support from the federal government for a survey of the Pacific Ocean. Hart's attitude toward women (best if in the home), Indians (either stereotypically noble or depraved), and other native peoples—although the norm for his day—can get annoying; so, too, can his tendency to launch into lengthy philosophical asides. But despite its occasional lapses and absurdities, *Miriam Coffin* is well worth the effort. When Hart latches on to a descriptive scene (the arrival of a whaleship, for example) or an action sequence (an exciting "fight to the death" in the Pacific), the novel is surprisingly readable and fun.

Miriam Coffin properly begins on page xxxiv, when Hart takes us to the tiny fishing village of 'Sconset, circa 1832. It's the off-season, so all the shacks are empty except for one that is inhabited by a noted genealogist and slob. This character is based on the famed Benjamin Franklin Folger (1777-1859), who seems to have remained a font of knowledge on Nantucket well into the middle of the century, and Hart, appropriately enough, takes the opportunity to provide a thumbnail history of the island. Then, after Hart has established the premise that we are reading a manuscript provided by the Folger character, the story begins.

Although *Miriam Coffin* was destined to become a Nantucket sourcebook for other authors, Hart was not without written sources of his own. It's clear that he had access to the log and journal of Peleg Folger (1734-1789), who is, in fact, a character in the novel. But whereas the real Peleg remained unmarried and, after a career as a whaleman, became a school teacher and clerk of the Friends Meeting, the Peleg Folger of *Miriam Coffin* is an eccentric whale merchant and family man. His eccentricities, however, seem to have been based on the actual Peleg, who became something of a mythical character on the island known as "Uncle Pillick." And, in fact, after establishing Nantucket's role as the "American Island," Hart begins his tale with a scene right out of Peleg's journal: a Nantucket home in the midst of a terrible storm.

Yet another written source appears to have been Hector St. John de Crèvecoeur's *Letters from an American Farmer* (1782), of which roughly a third concerns Nantucket. From Crèvecoeur we learn of "Aunt Kesiah," the very same Kezia Coffin upon whom Hart's Miriam Coffin is based:

> *The richest person now in the island owes all his present prosperity and success to the ingenuity of his wife; this is a known fact which is well recorded, for while he was performing his first cruises, she traded with pins and needles and kept a school. Afterward she purchased more considerable articles, which she sold with so much judgement that she laid the foundation of a system of business that she has ever since prosecuted with equal dexterity and success. She wrote to London, formed connexions, and, in short, became the only ostensible instrument of that house, both at home and abroad. Who is he in this country and who is a citizen of Nantucket or Boston who does not know Aunt Kesiah? I must tell you that she is the wife of Mr. C——n, a very respectable man, who, well pleased with all her schemes, trusts to her judgement and relies on her sagacity with so entire a confidence as to be altogether passive to the concerns of his family.*

Hart, the novelist, inevitably takes some liberties with these facts. In the beginning, Miriam is just your ordinary, obedient Quaker wife. It is only after her husband Jethro exits for England that she begins to put in place the "schemes" Crèvecoeur describes. Instead of displaying a benign "sagacity," Miriam proves to be more of a diabolical Lady MacBeth, wreaking all sorts of havoc on her fellow islanders by striking up a private trade agreement with the British once the Revolution begins. Eventually, however, the island establishes its neutrality, which effectively robs Miriam of her favored status with the Crown, and her dreams of economic domination quickly come to an end. The islanders unite against her, and in no time she is bankrupt. Hart makes it clear that Miriam gets what she deserves. When her husband Jethro returns from England to find himself a ruined man, he shouts, "Get thee gone to thy kitchen, where it is fitting thou shoulds't preside:—Go—go—to thy kitchen, woman, and do thou never meddle with men's affairs more!"

Whereas the real-life Kezia and her husband John (1708-1788) had only one daughter (Kezia Jr. [1760-1820]), Hart gives them not only Ruth, but a son by the name of Isaac, who is destined to become the famed British admiral, Sir Isaac Coffin (1759-1839), to whom the book is dedicated. The real Isaac Coffin was born in Boston; but since he was one of Nantucket's biggest fans (in 1827 he endowed a school on the island that still exists today), he undoubtedly enjoyed being given Nantucket as a natal ground.

There is also a historical basis for the lawyer Grimshaw in Hart's novel. Phineas Fanning (1750-1798) was a Yale-educated attorney from Long Island who moved to Nantucket in 1773. Whether or not the pivotal scene in which Grimshaw draws up a power of attorney for Miriam ever did occur, we do know that Phineas Fanning represented Kezia before and after his marriage to her daughter in 1777. We also know that a document very similar to the one Hart describes (referred to as a "Mariner's Power of Attorney") was a commonplace on Nantucket throughout the nineteenth century. In fact, the dozen or so powers of attorney in the Nantucket Historical Association's archives correspond, almost word for word, to what Hart has Grimshaw draw up for Miriam. Were Kezia Coffin and Phineas Fanning, as Hart suggests, responsible for initiating a tradition that would enable generations of Nantucket women to transact business while their husbands were away on whaling voyages? In any event, the extensive use of these powers of attorney on Nantucket suggests that islanders had a good deal more faith in a woman's judgment than the author of *Miriam Coffin*.

Benjamin Tashima (d.1770), the "Last Sachem" and wise old Indian school teacher, was also a historical figure, but instead of living at Eat-Fire Spring, near the eastern end of Polpis Harbor (as Hart maintains), he lived to the south of Gibbs Pond at an Indian village site known as Occawaw. In this instance, the romance of the name "Eat-Fire" may have been too much for Hart to resist when it came to his use of Indian place names. In any event, upon his death Tashima's estate included twelve chairs used by his Indian "scholars"; his well-worn doorstone now rests in front of the main entrance of the Nantucket Historical Association's Fair Street Museum.

One of the darker subplots of the novel hinges on an Indian from the opposite side of Hart's moral spectrum: Nathan Quibby, an actual historical figure who was tried for murder in the Old North Vestry of the Congregational church and then hanged on May 26, 1768—the last execution on Nantucket. But where Hart has Quibby kill Ruth's whaleman suitor, Harry Gardner, the real Quibby allegedly murdered two fellow Indian crew members onboard the *Sally*, then murdered another Indian who was being held in jail with him. Although Hart maintains that half the jurors in the Quibby case were Indians (as had been common practice in previous Indian murder trials on Nantucket), the records prove that Quibby's jury was, in fact, all white, and that Quibby, who pleaded not guilty, was tried without the benefit of counsel. While it may have fulfilled Hart's conception of the Nantucket Indians as a "cursed" race, his claim that Quibby was the father of Nantucket's "last Indian," Abram Quary, cannot be substantiated; in fact, Quary seems to have been born several years after Quibby's death.

There are other instances in which Hart adjusts or combines elements from Nantucket's history for greater artistic impact. For example, his account of whaling is anachronistic: the large ships he describes were common in the nineteenth century, not the eighteenth. Although we follow Captains Macy and Coleman into the Pacific, it was only after the Revolution that Nantucket whalemen began to venture around the Horn. In this instance Hart utilizes his artistic license to combine Nantucket's two Golden Ages: that of the 1770s and 1830s. Another conflation: much of the political intrigue Hart describes concerning the island's response to the American Revolution more properly belongs to the War of 1812. The British vessel *Nimrod* did, as Hart maintains, come to Nantucket, but it was during the War of 1812, not the Revolution.

The *Leviathan*'s voyage to London and her crew's hilarious introduction to a Drury Lane theater is, on the other hand, faithful to the 1770s time frame of the novel. By this point Nantucket had established an extremely close (and economically successful) relationship with the English city, which is why many island whaling merchants (Kezia Coffin included) counted themselves Tories at the outbreak of the Revolution. Whether or not there ever was a Garrick-produced play subtitled "The Nantucket Adventure" (with, as Hart insists, music by Handel and a song by Samuel Johnson) has yet to be conclusively determined; however, Allardyce Nicoll's multi-volume *A History of English Drama* has no mention of such a production.

Although several Nantucket historians have discounted Hart's detailed account of Miriam's smuggling operation (especially the existence of a secret underground tunnel and warehouse) as purely imaginary, there is evidence that Hart based his description on some fairly reliable traditions. At the Nantucket Historical Association is testimony recorded in 1894 by the elderly Eliza W. Mitchell, who as a twelve-year-old girl talked with none other than Benjamin Franklin Folger—the 'Sconset historian to whom Hart attributes the text of the novel. Folger claimed to have been inside Kezia Coffin's subterranean warehouse in Quaise and told Mitchell, "In the center I could stand nearly straight. All was time-worn and very much decayed, but I saw what I needed to convince me she was a very capable woman but lacking very much in principle." Since Hart talked in detail with Folger, he undoubtedly heard a similar account of the tunnel story.

Another probable source of oral testimony concerning Kezia Coffin was William Coffin (1756-1835), a barber, wig-maker, and whale oil merchant, as well as President of the Coffin School and host to Admiral Sir Isaac Coffin when he stayed on Nantucket. Since Hart dedicates *Miriam*

Coffin to the admiral (whom he describes as his "friend"), it's reasonable to suspect that Hart also knew William Coffin, who as a younger man represented Kezia Coffin in some of her attempts to gain restitution for her losses during the Revolution. In any event, Hart's description of Miriam's rise and fall is very close to the known facts. Unfortunately, Kezia Coffin's two infamous homes (both of which still existed in Hart's time) are no longer standing.

Many of *Miriam Coffin*'s rewards are in the details, the individual facts and scenes that, taken together, provide an extraordinarily rich and textured portrait of Nantucket in the eighteenth century. Hart's description of the Brant Point lighthouse (which was blown down by what may have been a tornado or waterspout in 1774) is particularly interesting, especially his mention of a large sheet-iron windvane in the shape of a whale. Hart provides what may be the first published account of that New England institution known as a clambake; his recipe for quahog (or "pooquaw") chowder is also a first.

Reading *Miriam Coffin* we can begin to appreciate the rhythms of daily life on Nantucket: the familial agony and ecstasy associated with the arrival of a whaler, and how family alliances and rivalries touched almost every aspect of being a Quaker Nantucketer. Hart tells us how they dressed; how the young people—despite their staid upbringing—enjoyed such normal social outlets as dances (held surreptitiously in whale oil warehouses) and "dressing up." We learn of a "female combination" on Nantucket, a secret society in which island girls agreed to marry only men who had already killed their first whales. Hart slyly points out how these "female masons" were playing into the hands of the island's whaling merchants by ensuring a "monopoly of the trade to the island."

We get a sense of the bi-racial character of colonial Nantucket, of how Native and English Nantucketers interacted. Hart freely describes the island's system of Indian debt-servitude. Although it's easy for us now to deplore what became a veritable institution on Nantucket, Hart demonstrates that the English Nantucketers of the day may have disingenuously seen it as a kind of work-release program, an alternative to debtor's prison. At one point Peleg Folger explains, "To keep [the Indians] from becoming a charge to the town, when they refuse to work for the support of their squaws and pappooses, the s'lackmen send them aboard the whale-ships, where they are compelled to earn a share of the cargo equal to that of any other mariner afore-the-mast.…" Hart demonstrates that Indian wigwams on Nantucket were not necessarily the primitive, dirty dwellings white people often made them out to be. And in a wonderful anecdote worthy of "Bert and I," we learn about a "famous cow" that became a point of contention between an Indian and a retired whaling captain.

We also learn that English Nantucketers never saw themselves as part of the rest of New England. At one point Miriam's daughter Ruth delivers a blistering diatribe against the "Yankees" of the region and their Puritan ancestors: "I would deny my nativity in the Bay colony forever, if I thought we were to be classed, with any justice, with such a mean set of psalm-singing drivellers!" Nantucketers—Hart makes clear—were a breed apart, and yet, as he insists time and time again, a very American breed.

But, of course, any book about Nantucket must also spend a good deal of time afloat, and as the full title of the novel suggests, *Miriam Coffin, or The Whale-Fishermen* is also about whaling, taking us from Nantucket to the West Coast of Africa, then around the Horn to the Pacific. In fact, some have argued that it is Hart's sea passages that truly distinguish this novel. When he is writing about a group of whaleboats bearing down on a lone bull right whale, or a whaleship scudding through dangerous coral reefs under bare poles, Hart displays genuine descriptive talent. He also sounds like a man who has been there before, which raises the teasing question of whether Hart, like Melville, spent a part of his youth on a whaleship. Certainly his family connections would have steered him in the island's direction, and at one point in the novel, the narrator speaks convincingly of having seen the intricate beauties of a coral reef firsthand.

Unfortunately we know surprisingly little about Joseph C. Hart, in part because his whaling novel was published anonymously during his lifetime.

A New Yorker, and proud of it, he would publish another book, *The Romance of Yachting* (1848), a strange hodgepodge of a book that contains all of *Miriam Coffin*'s faults and few, if any, of its virtues. In fact, Herman Melville, who paid Hart's Nantucket novel the highest of compliments by integrating large parts of it into his own whaling masterpiece, called *The Romance of Yachting* "an abortion," adding, "And as for Mr. Hart, pen & ink should instantly be taken away from that unfortunate man, upon the same principle that pistols are withdrawn from the wight bent on suicide."

As revealed by the research of A. Stuart Pitt, we now know that Hart produced other works besides *Miriam Coffin* and *The Romance of Yachting*, compiling several widely used and extensively reprinted school atlases and geographies. At one point Hart was also a school principal as well as a practicing attorney. But by the 1850s he was, as stated in an appeal for a patronage job to the U.S. Secretary of State, "without adequate employment while surrounded by a large family." In 1854 Hart was appointed consul at Santa Cruz de Tenerife in the Canary Islands, but after only a few months on the job, he came down with a fever and died.

But if Hart slipped virtually unnoticed from this life, *Miriam Coffin* remained well within view, particularly on Nantucket. For years to come, the fictional names Hart assigned real-life people such as Kezia Coffin and Phineas Fanning became the names by which many Nantucketers referred to them. The owners of Kezia Coffin's property in Quaise remarked that they were sorry they had torn down the original house. So many people had come looking for "just a shingle or little trifle of what used to be Miriam's," that they were convinced they could have turned it into a profitable "resort."

Miriam Coffin also seems to have had an inevitable literary ripple effect. There is evidence that Edgar Allan Poe used it as a source for *The Narrative of Arthur Gordon Pym* (1838). Herman Melville not only borrowed much of Hart's information on Nantucket, he also integrated several of the novel's plot devices into *Moby-Dick* (1851), including a mysterious prophecy and the climactic destruction of a ship by an enraged sperm whale. *Miriam Coffin* also seems to have had an influence on Melville's other Nantucket source, Obed Macy's *History of Nantucket* (1835), published only a year after the appearance of Hart's novel.

Indeed, it is not entirely coincidental that two of Nantucket's most important works—Hart's *Miriam Coffin* and Macy's *History*—appeared within months of each other. The early 1830s were a pivotal time for the island. Just as the whale fishery entered its final "Golden Age," the island's Quaker establishment had fallen into decline. Nantucket was no longer the closely knit, overwhelmingly Quaker family it had once been. According to the Benjamin Franklin Folger character, "[N]ot a single custom of our ancestors is adhered to in its ancient purity, all—all is giving way before the spirit of innovation that now stalks abroad in the island,—prostrating all that is venerable for its antiquity, and good as being the delight of our fathers!" By preserving a past that was no longer, *Miriam Coffin* and Macy's *History* shared a certain similarity of purpose, even though they were two very different books. And they were not created in isolation.

Upon its appearance in the spring of 1834, *Miriam Coffin* won rave reviews in the Nantucket *Inquirer*, edited by Samuel Haynes Jenks. In the third article to appear concerning the new novel, Jenks wrote on July 16, 1834, that the anonymous author "has fabricated a tale of thrilling interest, out of materials intrinsically unimportant or mediocre. He has taken a mere skeleton, clothed it with beauty, and with more than Promethean success, given it the breath of life."

Meanwhile, Obed Macy and William Coffin, Jr. (son of the same William Coffin who may have provided Hart with material for his novel) were preparing Macy's *History* for the press. Coffin seems to have acted as a ghost writer and editor for the elderly Macy, and in an advertisement for subscriptions dated November 26, 1834, that would run almost continuously for a number of months in the *Inquirer*, Coffin states: "Some time in the Spring of the present year, I received a proposition from Obed Macy, to unite with him in preparing for the press, a History of Nantucket."

And so, as *Miriam Coffin* was winning praise for translating the "intrinsically unimportant or mediocre" history of Nantucket into something of "thrilling interest," Coffin and Macy were left with the burden of producing a straightforward history based on those same unimportant and mediocre facts. In what I take to be a preemptive apology for their *History*'s "dull monotony" (their own words) relative to *Miriam Coffin*'s "thrilling interest," Macy and Coffin would write:

> *It is said with some truth, that the history of our island presents little that is novel or interesting. . . . We look, almost in vain, for those apostrophes which enliven history, those little events which have their beginning, their middle, and end, within the narrow compass of a few years or months, without being attended with any consequences that can influence succeeding time. Yet we know that such events must have taken place, for the nature of man has ever been the same in all ages and countries. Hopes deferred, disappointed loves, and ambitious schemes defeated, expectations lively and cheering met by some melancholy or fatal reality,—these make the scene and drapery of the state of life. They are mingled with our blessings, they are the dates from which we mark the passing of our individual lives.*

Whether or not this wonderful passage was inspired by what modern-day criticism would call an "anxiety of influence" concerning *Miriam Coffin*, it provides eloquent testimony to why Hart's novel still deserves to be read. If we are to experience that intangible sense of "what it was like" to be alive in another time, we must enter an imaginative domain where fiction is welcome but history—if it is doomed to remain faithful to the facts' "dull monotony"—must fear to tread.

That is precisely why anyone with an interest in the history of Nantucket Island should read *Miriam Coffin*.

—Nantucket Island
March, 1995

PUBLICATION HISTORY AND TEXTUAL NOTE

Miriam Coffin, or The Whale-Fishermen was first published in two volumes by G., C. & H. Carvill of New York in 1834. A second edition, also in two volumes, was published by Harper & Brothers in 1835, which included several minor corrections to the first edition. A "New Edition—Two Volumes in One," apparently based on the second edition and billed as an "exact and unabridged reprint of the original work," appeared in 1872 under the imprint of H. R. Coleman in San Francisco, the adopted home of many Nantucketers. The "New Edition" assigned authorship to "Col. Joseph C. Hart." In 1969, MSS Information Corporation published a photographic reprint of the first edition with a foreword by Edward Halsey Foster. The Mill Hill edition of *Miriam Coffin* is complete and unabridged and based on the second edition, a copy of which was generously provided by the Nantucket Historical Association.

SELECTED BIBLIOGRAPHY

Crosby, Everett U. "Joseph C. Hart, Author of *Miriam Coffin, or The Whale-Fishermen.*" *Historic Nantucket* (October, 1956), 39-40. Claims that "it has always been understood that Mr. Hart was on Island for a time"; also states that the Nantucket Historical Association possesses a "colored print of Abram Quary published in 1839 on which is written, 'Presented by Col. J. C. Hart of New York.'" Unfortunately the print is no longer part of the NHA's collection.

Foster, Halsey Foster. Foreword in *Miriam Coffin*. Rpt. (New York: MSS Information Corporation, 1969). Very brief overview that discusses the novel as "a work of propaganda" written "to make Americans more aware of the national importance of the whaling industry and to acquire financial support for it."

Gaines, Diana. *Nantucket Woman.* (New York: E.P. Dutton, 1976).
A contemporary novel based on the life of Kezia Coffin that has almost as much historical detail as it has sex. With the possible excep-

tion of Kezia's super-heated libido, this account is surprisingly accurate and well-researched.

Howard, Leon. "A Predecessor of Moby-Dick." *Modern Language Notes* (May, 1934), 310-311. Howard, who would later write the definitive biography of Herman Melville, was the first twentieth-century critic to identify the relationship between *Miriam Coffin* and *Moby-Dick*.

Miller, Perry. *The Raven and the Whale.* (New York: Harcourt, Brace, 1956). Places Hart's novel in the context of the lively Manhattan literary world of the nineteenth century, which included at least two other best-selling novelists of Nantucket descent: Charles Frederick Briggs and William Starbuck Mayo.

Norling, Lisa. "'How Frought with Sorrow and Heartpangs': Mariners' Wives and the Ideology of Domesticity in New England, 1790-1880," *New England Quarterly* (September, 1992), 422-446. Begins with a brief comparison of Crèvecoeur and Hart's portrayals of Kezia Coffin.

Philbrick, Nathaniel. *Away Off Shore, Nantucket Island and Its People, 1620-1890.* (Nantucket: Mill Hill Press, 1994). Includes information on many of the "real life" characters behind Miriam Coffin: Kezia Coffin, Peleg Folger, Abram Quary, Benjamin Franklin Folger, Phineas Fanning, etc.; also mentions Hart's novel.

————. "'Every Wave is a Fortune': Nantucket Island and the Making of an American Icon." *New England Quarterly* (September, 1993), 434-447. Talks briefly about *Miriam Coffin*'s place in Nantucket's extensive literary tradition.

Philbrick, Thomas. *James Fenimore Cooper and the Development of American Sea Fiction.* (Cambridge, Mass.: Harvard University Press, 1961). Includes an analysis of *Miriam Coffin* as a sea novel. Philbrick praises "the vigor and sensitivity of Hart's concept of the sea."

Pitt, A. Stuart. "'A Semi-Romance of the Sea': *Miriam Coffin* as Precursor of *Moby-Dick*." *Historic Nantucket* (April, 1972), 15-30. Picking up where Leon Howard, Howard Vincent, and Thomas Philbrick left off, Pitt places Hart's novel in its historical and critical contexts, while arguing strenuously for its continued importance.

————. "'Last Scene of All': The Author of *Miriam Coffin* in the Canary Islands." *Historic Nantucket* (Fall, 1977), 9-13. Utilizing government documents from the National Archives, Pitt pieces together the last days of Hart's life.

Pollin, Burton R. ed. *The Imaginary Voyages of Edgar Allan Poe.* (Boston: Twayne, 1981). Suggests that Poe—just as Melville would do a decade later—integrated details and incidents from *Miriam Coffin* into his *Narrative of Arthur Gordon Pym.*

Stevens, William O. Nantucket, *The Far-Away Island.* (New York: Dodd, Mead, 1966). A popular history of the island that contains some very specific (and unattributed) information concerning Hart's visit to the island.

Vincent, Howard P. *The Trying-Out of Moby-Dick.* (Boston: Houghton Mifflin, 1949). A readable overview of Melville's many sources in *Moby-Dick.*

ACKNOWLEDGMENTS

The writing of the historical introduction was made possible by the financial assistance of the Egan Foundation. Research and editorial assistance were generously provided by Helen Winslow Chase, Peter McGlashan, and Betsy Tyler of the Nantucket Historical Association; island scholar Susan Beegel; Peter Gow, Beaver Country Day School; Thomas Philbrick, Professor of English, Emeritus, University of Pittsburgh; and Wes Tiffney, Jr., University of Massachusetts Nantucket Field Station.

Miriam Coffin

OR

THE WHALE-FISHERMEN:

A TALE

BY JOSEPH C. HART

Whilst we follow them amidst the tumbling mountains of ice, and behold them penetrating into the deepest frozen recesses of Hudson's Bay and Davis's Straits—whilst we are looking for them between the Arctic Circle, we hear that they have pierced into the opposite region of Polar cold— that they are at the Antipodes, and engaged under the frozen Serpent of the South. Falkland Island, which seemed too remote and romantic an object for the grasp of national ambition, is but a stage and resting place in the progress of their victorious industry. Nor is the Equinoctial heat more discouraging to them than the accumulated winter of both the Poles. We know, that whilst some of them draw the line and strike the harpoon on the coast of Africa, others run the longitude, and pursue their gigantic game along the coast of Brazil. No sea but what is vexed by their fisheries—no climate that is not witness to their unceasing toils!

Edmund Burke.

TO ADMIRAL

Sir ISAAC COFFIN, Bart.,

THIS TALE,

Founded on facts, and illustrating some of the scenes with which he was conversant in his earlier days, together with occurrences with which he is familiar from tradition and association,

IS

RESPECTFULLY AND AFFECTIONATELY

DEDICATED,

BY HIS FRIEND,

THE AUTHOR

INTRODUCTION

THE editor of the following tale feels it incumbent upon him to explain, in the outset, to the worthy Admiral to whom it is dedicated, as well as to the gentle reader who may deign to look into these legendary pages, how far he has been accessory in the production of this work.

During a tour to the eastward, several years ago, among the clusters of small islands which lie off the southern shore of Massachusetts, and which have proved the great nurseries of seamen devoted to the whale-fishery, it was our good fortune to sojourn for a season upon Nantucket. The principal object of our journey, at that time, being to obtain authentic information in relation to the actual state of that important trade, we embraced every opportunity of conversing with those who pretended to knowledge respecting it; and, in our necessary intercourse with all classes, it frequently happened that common sailors, who had spent their lives in whaling vessels, furnished the best sources of information—especially as we found many owners and captains who regarded us with shyness, whenever we broached the subject of the mystery of the trade "whereby they did live" and had procured their gains. Among other things we were anxious to discover by what means it had been brought to the present perfection in its management, and had maintained its prosperity under the absolute neglect of the General Government, whose province and whose constitutional duty it is to give facility to all our branches of commercial trade and navigation.

We were not surprised, however, at the discovery, upon our arrival at Nantucket, that its people had occasionally suffered from this neglect. We found that they had already presented a memorial to Congress, setting forth the great hazards and complaining of the unprotected situation of their trade, which they had for half a century prosecuted in the Pacific ocean;—where their ships were not only subject to dangers in navigation, from the uncertainty of the surveys, and the inaccuracy with which many islands had been laid down on the charts, but were constantly liable to vexatious detention and exactions from the authorities upon the South American Coast. The petitioners expressed their desire that Government would take the matter in hand, and fit out a small naval expedition which should be directed to cruise in the neighborhood of their whaling grounds; and otherwise be employed occasionally in making accurate surveys of new places, that were already, or might thereafter be discovered; as well as to ascertain the capabilities of the islands for affording those natural and necessary supplies, which all whale ships are in want of in the course of their long voyages, among numberless isles, where nature has been all-bountiful in the over abundance of her productions, but where the tenant of the soil is, in the same proportion, rude and inhospitable.

The short memorial of the Nantucket people, whose prosperity at home is so closely linked with the success of the whale fishery in remote seas, represents:—"That the intercourse maintained between different ports of the nation and the islands and countries of the Pacific ocean, has become a matter of public interest, and deserving the protecting care of the National Legislature. The fur business, and the trade carried on between the Pacific islands and coasts of China, have afforded rich returns, and increased the wealth of our common country. Besides this employment of national industry and enterprise, they would represent, that there are engaged in the whale-fishery, from various parts of the country, upwards of forty thousand tons of shipping, requiring a capital of three millions of dollars, and the services of more than three thousand seamen. Whether viewed as a nursery of bold and hardy seamen, or as an employment of capital in one of the most productive modes, or as furnishing an article of indispensable necessity to human comfort, it seems to your petitioners to be an object especially deserving the public care. The increased extent of the voyages now pursued by the trading and whaling ships, into seas but little explored, and to parts of the world before unknown, has increased the cares, the dangers, and the losses of our merchants and mariners. Within a few years, their cruises have extended from the coasts of Peru and Chili to the Northwest Coast, New-Zealand, and the isles of Japan. This increase of risk has been attended by an increase of loss. Several vessels have been wrecked on islands and reefs not laid down on any chart; and the matter acquires a painful interest from the fact, that many ships have gone into those seas, and no soul has survived to tell their fate. Your petitioners consider it a matter of earnest importance that those seas should be explored; that they should be surveyed in an accurate and authentic manner, and the position of new islands, and reefs, and shoals, definitely ascertained. The advancement of science, and not their private interest only, but the general interest of the nation, seem, to them, imperiously to demand it.

"They, therefore, pray that an expedition may be fitted out, under the sanction of the Government, to explore and survey the islands and coasts of the Pacific seas."

The public functionary who presided over the Department of the Navy at this period, and to whom this and other memorials, and the whole subject of the proposed expedition, were referred, by a committee of the House of Representatives, with a view to get his opinion thereupon, made a report to the committee of the House, which was alike creditable to his American feeling and his just perceptions of the merits of the case.

"I entertain," said that enlightened officer, "the opinion that such an expedition is expedient. My reasons are briefly these:—

"That we have an immense and increasing commerce in that region, which needs the protecting kindness of the Government, and may be greatly extended by such an expedition. Of the extent and nature of this commerce, it is not easy to write briefly; nor is it necessary. It is better known to none, than to some of the members of the Naval Committee in the House of Representatives. The estimate of its value has been much augmented in the view of the Department, by the reports which have been made, *under its orders*, by our naval officers, who have commanded vessels of war in the Pacific, and which are now on file.

"The commercial operations carried on in that quarter, are difficult and hazardous. They are correctly represented in the memorial of the inhabitants of Nantucket, to which I would refer, as well as to some of the many other memorials which have been addressed to Congress on this subject. It would seem wise in the Government to render these commercial operations less hazardous and less destructive of life and property, if it can be done by a moderate expenditure of money.

"The commerce in the Pacific ocean affords one of the best nurseries of our seamen. An expedition, such as that proposed, would be calculated to increase that class of citizens—an increase in which the Government and nation are deeply interested.

"We now navigate the ocean, and acquire our knowledge of the globe, its divisions and properties, almost entirely from the contributions of others. By sending an expedition into that immense region, so little known to the civilized world, we shall add something to the common stock of geographical and scientific knowledge, which is not merely useful to commerce, but connects itself with almost all the concerns of society; and, while we make our contribution to this common stock, we shall not fail to derive the best advantages to ourselves, and be richly paid, even in a calculation of expenditure and profit."

Among the documents to which the Naval Committee resorted for information, was one now on file in the Navy Department, which in warm language advocates the cause of the neglected whale-fishermen. Its authenticity and its general truth and force of reasoning are alike unquestionable.

We therefore make free in the insertion of some of its paragraphs, as follows:—

"The opening of the ports in South America, has already changed our course of trade in the Pacific greatly for the better, and will more and more benefit us, if we take care of our rights in those seas, and send a sufficient force to protect our commerce, which, no doubt, it will be the policy of our Government to pursue.

"To look after the merchant there—to offer him every possible facility—to open new channels for his enterprise, and to keep a respectable naval force to protect him—is only paying a debt we owe to the commerce of the country: for millions have flowed into the national treasury from this trade, before one cent was appropriated for its protection.

"The naval commanders we have sent into the Pacific, have done all that wise, active, and experienced men could do. They have not only taught the natives that we are a powerful people, and could defend ourselves in that distant country, as well as other nations, but these new states and empires which have arisen in South America, have been shown that we could punish wrongs and enforce rights, and had the good of mankind, as well as our own prosperity, at heart. *Power, judiciously exhibited, is the great peace-maker of the world*; and a people whose institutions are not yet thoroughly established, as those in South America, want looking after with a steady eye. In attending to these duties, it is impossible for our naval commanders to explore those seas for the purpose of discovering new places. Their duty is to watch the old; and this is a sufficient task for any force we can send there.

"The whale ships, having a specific object in view, and generally under strict orders, cannot waste an hour in the business of discovery; nor can they, consistently with their duties, stop a day to explore and examine what they may accidentally discover. The Northwest Coast trader, has, also, a specific object, and a more direct path than the whaler.

"It seems well understood, at this time, that it is for our interest and for our *honour*, to be well acquainted with the *capacities* of the globe; to see what resources can be drawn from that great *common* of nations—the *ocean*. The enlightened statesman therefore, surveys all parts of it, with the view of opening new channels for commerce and trade; and he does not refuse to advance them by a present expense, when coupled with the certainty of a future and greater good.

"And what place is left for us to explore but this Southern polar region? This has never been thoroughly done by any nation. It is almost an unknown region yet, and opens a wide field for enterprise for us, at a most moderate expense. There are more than a million and a half of square miles entirely unknown; and a coast of more than three hundred degrees of longitude, in which the Antarctic circle has never been approached.* There are immense regions, within the comparatively temperate latitudes, but partially known, and which deserve further attention; and, for aught we know, countries corresponding to Lapland, Norway, part of Sweden, and the northern parts of Siberia, in Asia, may still exist in the southern hemisphere.

"No one who has reflected on the vast resources of the earth, 'which is our inheritance,' can doubt that such a large portion of it contains many things which may be turned to good account, by the enterprise and good management of our people—and these are the true profits of commerce. The great mass of the intelligence of the country is for it, and is calling on the National Legislature for aid in the undertaking.

"The states whose legislative bodies have sanctioned it, are represented on the floor of Congress by one hundred and twenty-nine members,

---

*This assertion subsequently proved to be an error. It was not, we presume, known to the intelligent writer, when he made this report, that the 74th degree of southern latitude, as well as the icy barrier about the Antarctic circle, had been passed by an English navigator, by the name of Weddell. The Journal of his voyage was published in London in 1827; and its author declares that in the latitude of 73° South "not a particle of ice of any description was to be seen;" and further, that he "sailed to the latitude of 74° 15" South, and there left a clear and navigable sea." Capt. Cook, in his celebrated voyage of 1773–4, had been able to penetrate only as far as the 71st degree South, and was prevented from proceeding further by solid fields of ice, reaching, as he thought, to the pole itself.

to say nothing of the memorials from large cities and other places; and the aggregate of citizens of these states near six millions.

"It may be asked, if the navy and merchantmen are not to take this upon themselves, how is it to be effected? The answer is obvious to those who have reflected. Send out an exploring expedition, fitted and prepared for the purpose; not one that is to carry the majesty and grandeur of the nation, at a great expense, but one, the expenses of which shall be inconsiderable, but, at the same time, shall have the protection, aid, honour, and sanction of the nation, to give life, energy, and character, to individual enterprise. We have been an industrious, a commercial, and enterprising people, and have taken advantage of the knowledge of others, as well as of their trade: for although our entrance and clearance, without looking at our immense coasting trade, amounted to eight thousand seven hundred and sixty-six vessels, yet not one of these was sailed a mile, by a chart made by us, except we may suppose that the chart of George's Banks may have been used by a few of the navigators of these vessels. We are dependent on other nations for all our nautical instruments, as well as charts; and, if we except Bowditch's, we have not a nautical table or book in our navy, or amongst our merchantmen, the product of our own science and skill; and we are now among the three first commercial nations of the world, and have more shipping and commerce than all the nations of Europe had together when Columbus discovered this continent, but a little more than three centuries since; and our navy, young as it is, has more effective force in it, than the combined navies of the world could have amounted to at that period. Out of the discovery of this continent, and a passage to the Indies, grew up the Naval Powers of Europe. On the acquisition of the new world, Spain enlarged her marine; France and England theirs, to hold sway with Spain; and that of the Netherlands sprang from the extent of their trade, connected with the wise policy of enlarging and protecting it.

"Our commercial and national importance cannot be supported without a navy, or our navy without commerce, and a nursery for our seamen. The citizens of Maine, of New-York, of Georgia, of Ohio, and of the great valley of the Mississippi, are deeply interested in the existence of our gallant navy, and in the extension of our commerce, as they are interested in the perpetuity of our institutions, and the liberty of our country. Indeed, liberty and commerce have been *twin sisters*, in all past ages and countries and times; they have stood side by side, moved hand in hand. Wherever the soil has been congenial to the one, there has flourished the other also; in a word, they have lived, they have flourished, or they have died together.

"Commerce has constantly increased with the knowledge of man; yet it has been undergoing perpetual revolutions. These changes and revolutions have often mocked the vigilance of the wary, and the calculations of the sagacious; but there is now a fundamental principle on which commerce is based, which will lead the intelligent merchant, and the wise government, to foresee and prepare for most of these changes; and that principle consists in an intimate knowledge of all seas, climates, islands, continents, of every river and mountain, and every plain of the globe, and all their productions, and of the nature, habits, and character of all races of men: and this information should be corrected and revised with every season.

"The commercial nations of the world have done much, and much remains to be accomplished. We stand a solitary instance among those who are considered commercial, as never having put forth a particle of strength or expended a dollar of our money to add to the accumulated stock of commercial and geographical knowledge, except in partially exploring our own territory.

"When our naval commanders and hardy tars have achieved a victory on the deep, they have to seek our harbours, and conduct their prizes into port, by tables and charts furnished, perhaps, by the very people whom they have vanquished.

"Is it honourable for the United States to use, for ever, the knowledge furnished us by others, to teach us how to shun a rock, escape a shoal, or find a harbour; and add nothing to the great mass of information, that previous ages and other nations have brought to our hands?"

In obedience to the public will, which had pretty generally been expressed in favour of the proposed expedition, a small sloop of war was prepared in 1828, by direction of the President of the United States, which was to be accompanied by one or two smaller vessels, as relief-ships, in case of accident occurring. The language of the President, in his annual Message, communicated to Congress at the beginning of the session of 1828-9, is as follows:—

"A resolution of the House of Representatives, requesting that one of our small public vessels should be sent to the Pacific ocean and South sea, to examine the coasts, islands, harbours, shoals and reefs, in those seas, and to ascertain their true situation and description, has been put in a train of execution. The vessel is nearly ready to depart: The successful accomplishment of the expedition may be greatly facilitated by suitable legislative provisions; and particularly by an appropriation to defray its necessary expense. The addition of a second, and perhaps of a third vessel, with a slight aggravation of the cost, would contribute much to the safety of the citizens embarked in this undertaking, the results of which may be of the deepest interest to our country."

An accomplished navigator was selected from among our Nantucket commanders, to pilot the ships, and officers were named of approved courage and skill: several scientific gentlemen of high character, forming a small but efficient corps of naturalists, were anxious to seek greater reputation for their country and themselves, by accompanying the expedition; and a small amount, in aid of the project, was appropriated by the House of Representatives,—when,—to the surprise of every body, this wise and humane measure was arrested in the Senate, by the blighting interference of reckless, and, as they have since proved, faithless partisans, whose sole object appeared to be to thwart any and all measures of the executive. The steps already taken to send forth this little expedition, had been approved by all classes; and it had thus far gained a decided popularity with every real lover of his country. It was hailed in every quarter as the precursor of a new and brilliant career for our gallant little navy, in discovery; and regarded as the harbinger of great commercial advantage to the nation,—England and France had sent out various well-appointed expeditions on similar voyages of discovery, while we were talking about ours;—and, eventually, as may be already apprehended, the American expedition terminated in—*talk!*

A new administration now came into power, and the praiseworthy designs of the previous cabinet, in respect to the Southern Expedition, confirmed as they were by the popular branch of the National Legislature, were unceremoniously laid aside;— and for no other reason that has ever yet transpired, but that which the envy of little minds alone could suggest. The new incumbents, it is said, declared among themselves that all the honour of the measure would be reflected upon the originators, who had then gone out of office; and that not a particle of its glory would fall upon themselves. It was a damning sin to do good,—provided that good had been recommended by rival predecessors. It was thus, (posterity will scarcely credit it,) that a great national object was defeated, and the interests of an important branch of our commercial industry—to say nothing of the humane benefits which would undoubtedly have been conferred upon mankind,—were sacrificed to the pitiful considerations of political jealousy.

In this result, however, we may be taught a useful lesson. We may learn from the premises, how little practical philanthropy there is in the measures of mere politicians, and how selfish are all the movements of men who struggle in the political arena. But, as we do not pretend to fathom the gulf of cabinet trickery, we will dismiss all further reflections upon political profligacy, and come back to the information, which we intended to give the reader at starting, touching our agency in the production of the following Tale.

In a secluded quarter of the island of Nantucket, known by the name of Siasconset, there lived, a few years since, a singular being, whose mode of life, for several previous years, had been a mystery to everybody. To this individual, however, we had been directed for information on a point embraced in our investigations, respecting the state of the whale-fishery as connected with Nantucket. He had been represented by the people of the town as possessing a remarkably retentive memory,—particularly in what related to the early history of the island; and also that he was possessed of large stores of accurate statistical and historical information, which he had been many years in collecting and arranging: and furthermore it was reported, that in his person one might discover a walking genealogical tree, whose leaves and branches, so to speak, would unfold the birth, parentage and education of every resident of the island, from the days of the first settlers downwards to the time present.

There are now some three or four score houses at Siasconset, of one story and a half in height, erected on the margin of a high sand-bluff overlooking the sea. Some of these are very old, and built after a peculiar fashion which prevailed all over the island during the early part of the last century. It was then a small village, inhabited by poor fishermen, and the huts we speak of were their domicils. Latterly, however, these huts have been turned into summer residences for the wealthier townspeople;—and right pleasant lounging places do they make, for those who have leisure to enjoy them. If any of our readers should feel curious to see the style of building that prevailed one hundred years ago in the town which has since assumed the name of Nantucket, let him now pay a visit to Siasconset, and enter its dwellings, and regard attentively its pepper-box out-houses. He will there see how, of old, every inch of room was economized, and how sleeping chambers were scaled by perpendicular step-ladders, like those used to descend to the pent-up cabin of a fishing smack, or to clamber up the sides of a merchantman;—and how the best and most spacious room in the house is finished like the cabin of a ship, with projecting beams, whose corners are beaded and ornamented with rude carving, while the walls are wainscotted with unpainted panel work, and the oaken floors have grown alike brown by time, and smooth by a century's use. There is but one house in the whole village which makes modern pretension to fashionable exterior. It is the only innovation upon the

unity—the ancient *"keeping"* of the place;—and its projecter deserves ban-
ishment under the wise provisions of the time-honoured *"Laws of 'Sconset,"*
for presuming to make any change in the architecture of the settlement.

It was our fortune to make a pilgrimage to Siasconset at that season of
the year when its houses were tenantless,—its deserted avenues choked
up with sombre and lifeless thistles and decayed long grass,—and all as
still as the grave. Threading with uncertainty its narrow and silent lanes,
in search of the habitation of the veteran, we came at length to a hut
before whose door stood a car of fish, which had been recently caught
and wheeled up from the shore. The chimney top, too, gave evidence of
civilization and of the whereabout of humanity. A stream of blue smoke
issued forth and briskly curled up in the clear atmosphere. The sight of
the fish, jumping and floundering about in the little car, and the lively jet
of smoke overhead, was as welcome to us, at the moment, as a house of
"entertainment for man and beast" would be to a traveller in the desert,
or to a virtuoso, without corn in his scrip, exploring the mysteries and
antiquities of a city of the dead. We tapped lightly on the closed door of
the hut, and repeated the signal more than once:—but no answer from
the indweller bade us welcome to the hospitalities of 'Sconset.

"This is strange!" thought we,—"very strange, in a land proverbially
celebrated for the open door and the open hand!"

A thirst after knowledge, and a stomach yearning fearfully for a morsel
from the frying-pan or the fish pot, gave us the courage of desperation:
and thereupon we lifted the latch of the door,—for lock or bolt, or other
fastening, there was none,—and entered boldly into the main apartment
of the house. There we stood for the space of some minutes, silently con-
templating the furniture and appointments of the place. It was clear that
the hand of woman had not been there for many a day, though it was evident, from the arrangement of pots and kettles, and platters and frying-
pans, that attempts had been made, if not with female neatness, at any
rate with manly clumsiness and good will, to preserve a degree of cleanliness that was creditable to the owner of the mansion. Over the rude man-

tel hung an old-fashioned, turnip-shaped, silver watch, ticking loudly, and striving on in its daily race with the sun; and against the still ruder partition, which separated the larger room from a closet or small sleeping apartment, hung a heavy fowling-piece of most capacious bore: while underneath depended a well-worn shot-bag, and a powder-flask of semi-transparent horn. Around the room, somewhat in confusion, the implements of piscatory warfare were visible. Scapnets and fishing-lines, of various sizes and lengths, wet from recent use, were spread over the backs of chairs to dry, and indicated that their owner had but lately come from an excursion upon the sea.

There was no help for us but to sit down and quietly await the approach of the master, and the issue of our adventure. On coming to this very natural conclusion, we drew the only chair which was disengaged, towards the engulfing fireplace, and essayed to correct the chilled atmosphere of the room, by feeding the decaying fire with billets from a small heap of prepared wood piled in the corner, which, from certain appearances, had been gathered along the beach, and had once formed a part of some unfortunate vessel wrecked upon the shoals of the island.

There we sat, punching the fire with the tongs, and watching the sparks "prone to fly upwards," and wondering where all this would end. A dreamy sort of abstraction came over our faculties; and in this secluded spot we almost began to fancy that we were alone in the world. We felt some of those sensations creeping upon us, which one might suppose the *last man* would feel, who had seen all generations pass into the grave,—leaving him the sole tenant of the earth. The crooked legs and clawfeet of the little old-fashioned cherry table, multiplied a thousand fold in number and in crookedness, till we almost fancied it a huge creeping thing, with the legs and arms and claws of a dragon.

Presently an agonized groan escaped from the chest of some sufferer near at hand, and invaded the deep silence of the place,—which before had been rendered doubly painful by the distant monotonous roar of the surf, rolling and tumbling in upon the beach. We dropped the tongs in affright; and mechanically springing upon our feet, we were in the act of rushing forth from the cabin, to avoid the perturbed ghost which our imagination had conjured up to haunt the place withal.

"Who's there!" said a loud voice that appeared to come from the cockloft.

The charm was at once broken by the utterance of these words in the vernacular tongue, and our nervous sensations gave way before the idea of the utter ridiculousness of running away under such circumstances. We had always longed for solitude,—for "a lodge in some vast wilderness,"— but that charm, too, was broken; and we believed, in our very souls, that we had had enough of the eternal silence, which is too often hankered after by the "mind diseased."

"Henceforth," said we mentally, "give us the hum and the bustle of the world, and the sprightly chat of intimacy:—Solitude!—thus do we blow thee to the winds!"

We answered the hail from aloft, nothing loath; and begged the host to come down, as we had walked full seven miles to see and converse with him upon matters with which he was reputed to be familiar. The burly form of the man now darkened the aperture above, and he descended the step-ladder, with his back towards us, holding on for safety and letting himself down with both hands by two knotted cords,—such as are thrown over at the gang-way of a man of war, to aid the descent into the tiny cutter alongside. As he stood confronting us, we could not fail to observe that he must have seen many winters and some hardships. His face was much weather-beaten, and his head, bald in some spots, was here and there covered with long and thin tufts of whitey-grayish locks, standing up and streaming out in admirable confusion. Deep boots, resembling fire-buckets, together with drab small-clothes, encased his legs; while his upper garments were covered over with a huge shaggy wrapper, which sailors call a monkey-jacket. He looked at us keenly for a moment; but finding his craft fairly boarded and in possession of the enemy, he deigned to offer us a seat, and to utter an excuse for his absence by telling us that he had sought rest in his chamber after the fatigues of his late excursion. Moreover, he explained the cause of his fearful groaning, by giving a graphic portrait of the fiend-like nightmare which the falling of the tongs had scared away from his breast. We did not, upon the whole, find our companion as morose as we had been led to believe, by the description given to us of his habits. At any rate, he gradually became familiar, and undertook to find out for us, heaven knows by what intricate process, a collateral descent from the "*great Trustum Coffin;*" and, perhaps, to this circumstance, more than to any other, are we indebted for the favours, both of speech and manuscript, which he afterwards bountifully showered upon us.

"Odd's-fish!" exclaimed he of the monkey-jacket, breaking in upon a long historical descent, in the mazes of which he had involved himself while answering a casual question of ours; "Odd's-fish!—thou must have fasted sufficiently well by this late hour; and I will defer giving the remainder of the information which thou hast demanded, until our frugal meal is prepared and discussed. I have but few luxuries, friend—what didst call thy name?"

"Thompson, sir," said we at a venture, feeling for the present a desire to preserve our incognito.

"Thompson, is it?—I thought thou saidst but now it was Jenkins."

"Thompson, sir—a relative of the Jenkinses by the mother's side."

"Ah—well—I have but few luxuries, friend Thompson, to offer thee in this mine humble abode; but if, peradventure, thou art fond of fish, and bringest a good appetite, I will prepare thee such a dish as the townspeople can scarcely make without resort to 'Sconset." Whereupon our companion selected a large fish from his car, and in a trice disrobed it of its scales and disemboweled the intestines;—while, in order to gain some little credit for skill in culinary handy-work, and furthermore to convince him that we knew how to accommodate ourself to circumstances, (or that, in the words of a Jonathan in the east, "while in Turkey we could do as the *Turkeys* did,") we seized upon a bucket and filled it with the purest of water at the village pump;—and then we kindled up the fire anew, and made all things ready for the accommodation of the dinner-pot.

In due time, but not a minute too soon, a savoury dish of chowder came upon the table; and, such is the force of a good appetite, we did think that in all our life before we had never swallowed provender half so delicious. But, let that pass:—The reader, whose mouth waters, must go to 'Sconset for his chowder, if he would, like unto us, enjoy a superlative luxury compounded of simples.

As the clam-shell dipper, which had come and gone full oft between our pewter platters and the chowder pan, rested from its labours, the host pushed back his chair. Whereupon, lighting his pipe, and coming to an anchor in his easy chair in the corner, he cast his eyes up towards the well-smoked roof in a sort of thinking reverie, and at last broke silence as follows:

"As I was telling thee, friend Tompkins, the island that now bears the name of Nantucket, whose barren plains thou hast crossed in coming hither, was once a well wooded and well watered garden-spot. It was owing to the improvidence, or perhaps I might better say, to the lack of foresight of our ancestors, that every tree of native growth, save one or two little clumps of oak, hath disappeared from the face of our land. It is melancholy to think on't—for I love the sight of trees. The soil, however, friend Timpkins, as thou may'st have observed, is not altogether as sterile as the world in general imagine. But the cry of the *'sand heap'* hath gone out against us:—and herein I would say something to thee about evil speaking;—but of that hereafter, if we have time.

"To make a long story short, friend Timson," continued the narrator, "I will give thee merely the outline of our history, which, as time and opportunity serve, thou may'st fill up at leisure.—Nay—do not interrupt me—I will answer thee more at large upon any point thou may'st propose, when my sketch is finished. Being a stranger here, it may profit thee to know, that for a long time after the cession of the colony of New-York to Lord Stirling, the island of Nantucket, as well as all other islands on the

Northern coast, were claimed as dependencies of that distinct colony. It came to pass, however, that by peaceable negotiation, Massachusetts obtained dominion over the islands upon her shore, and Block Island fell to the lot of the Providence Plantations; while Long Island, with which Nature had defended the shore of Connecticut, continued the appendage of New-York.

"Touching the manner in which Nantucket was settled by the whites, I have authority for declaring that it was brought about by accident, as it were, and under peculiar circumstances. We, who are natives of the island, trace our descent to the Seceders, or rather to the Non-Conformists who dwelt in the Eastern part of the Massachusetts. They were principally of the Baptist persuasion; and, in ancient times, they were persecuted and hunted down by their Puritanic brethren, for opinion's sake. By one of those strange inconsistencies incident to human nature, the Puritans upon the main, who had themselves been the objects of persecution in England, began the same infamous and brutal career of intolerance in America, by establishing a code of revolting laws, which would have put a Herod to the blush. I thank God, my friend, that *I* am not descended from that vile fanatical race. Let others boast, if they will, of their Puritanic blood,—*mine* knows not the contamination!"

Here my companion rose from his chair, and opened a tobacco-closet in the chimney-side, from whence he produced a well-thumbed volume, and read as follows:

"No Quaker, or dissenter from the worship of the established dominion, shall be allowed to give a vote for the election of magistrates, or any officer.

"No food or lodging shall be afforded a Quaker, Adamite, or other heretic.

"If any person turns Quaker, he shall be banished, and not suffered to return but on pain of death.

"No Roman Catholic priest shall abide in the dominion; he shall be banished, and suffer death on his return."

"Such, my friend," continued our host, "were the laws of the Cameronians; and to their existence may be attributed the settlement of Nantucket, as thou wilt presently see. About the year 1659–60, while these and other fiend-like enactments were in force in the eastern section of the present United States, one Thomas Macy, a Baptist, who had come from England some twenty years previous, in search after a peaceful habitation in our Western wilds, and who had settled among the Puritans at Salisbury in the Massachusetts, committed a crying sin against the laws of the wrathful Cromwellites or Blueskins. And what think'st thou it was? He had dared to shelter some forlorn and houseless Quakers in his barn one tempestuous night; and for that offence was he doomed, by the Puritanic Roundheads, to undergo the signal punishment of stripes at the whipping-post! Before the day of its infliction arrived, he procured an open boat, or yawl, and with two companions, Edward Starbuck and a youth by the name of Isaac Coleman, he launched forth upon an unknown sea,— declaring that he would pull his barque to the ends of the earth, sooner than dwell longer among beings so uncharitable and intolerant.

"Macy and his friends arrived at Nantucket, where before the white man had never dwelt. At that time two hostile tribes of Indians inhabited opposite ends of the island, numbering altogether some three thousand souls. The new comers were received with kindness by the natives; and they obtained a great but honest influence over their councils. Thus commenced the settlement of Nantucket by the whites; and in the following year one Thomas Mayhew, having obtained a grant of the island from Lord Stirling, conveyed it, in fee, to ten proprietors, each of whom chose an associate from among his brother 'heretics;' and the whole company of twenty, with their persecuted families, immediately thereafter took possession as proprietors in common."

Our companion hereupon pulled forth a slip of paper from a long-worn pocket-book, from which we took the liberty of transcribing the names of the original settlers of the Island. Although some of the names are now extinct, we would preserve the remainder, if possible, to their posterity. Their industry, single-mindedness and perseverance are worthy of the admiration and the imitation of their descendants.

The first ten.	*Their associates.*
Thomas Mayhew,	John Smith,
Thomas Macy,	Edward Starbuck,
Tristram Coffin,	Nath'l. Starbuck (son of Edw'd.,)
Thomas Barnard,	Robert Barnard,
Peter Coffin, (son of Tristram,)	James Coffin, (brother of Peter,)
Christian Hussey,	Robert Pike,
Stephen Greenleaf,	Tristram Coffin, jr.,
John Swain,	Thomas Coleman,
William Pile,	Nathaniel Bolton,
Richard Swain.	Thomas Look.

Finishing the transcript of these venerable names, we handed back to our companion the original list. He took the paper between his finger and thumb, and with his nail resting on the third name from the top, he remarked, with a glow of pride, that the direct descendants of the senior Tristram Coffin had been computed at the enormous number of twenty-five thousand!—A prolific progenitor, and a goodly posterity, truly.

We now ventured to start a theme upon which our host dilated with wonderful fluency and apparent delight; and, in the course of a short time, we were made acquainted with the history of the rise and progress of the whale-fishery in these parts. But, as the reader may, in other places in these pages, find the subject touched upon by an abler pen than ours, and perchance derive an interest from the perusal great as our own, we will omit the detail here;—merely premising, however, that the daring natives of the island of Nantucket, in their frail canoes, first initiated the white settlers in the dangerous art of grappling with—

"That sea-beast
Leviathan, which God of all his works
Created hugest that Swim the Ocean stream."

But the ingenious whites, who in the beginning dared the perils of the sea in their little open skiffs, and dashed in among the huge game that then played about the island in troops, soon betook themselves to larger vessels, and made lengthened voyages upon the ocean, out of sight of the island. From such imperfect and perilous beginnings have they come to be the most hardy and expert whalers in the world.

Feeling anxious to ascertain by what means the first settlers had been converted from the faith of the Baptists to that of the Quakers, we gave a hint to that effect, and were enlightened accordingly.

"Quakerism," said he, "was not introduced upon the island until about the year 1701;—when John Richardson, an itinerant but powerful and accomplished Quaker preacher, came among the people. Mary Starbuck, eldest daughter of the '*first* Trustum Coffin,' was not only the first English child born upon the island, but the first convert to the Quaker faith. The other settlers gradually embraced the peaceful doctrines of Fox and Barclay as preached by Richardson, and eventually the Society of Friends became the predominant sect. To the introduction of Quakerism, and its unvarying customs, together with the unyielding manners of the Puritans to which the islanders had been accustomed, and which still lingered about them even after their change of faith, added to their isolated situation, is perhaps to be attributed the unchangeableness of the ways and habits of the Nantucket people. It is the last hold of the simple manners of our English ancestors in America. In this respect Nantucket is to the rest of America, what Iceland is to the Northern nations of Europe. For while all has undergone a change, I will not say for the better, in the continental countries, these two islands continue to exhibit the manners, customs, dress and language of their ancestors, in much of their pristine purity.

"The spirit of resistless change is, however, abroad in Nantucket;"

(here the narrator heaved a sigh, and continued,) "and I grieve to say the few years last past have worked a wonderful change in the people. The Indian prophecy hath come to pass in a shape which our fathers little dreamed of. Thou must know, my friend, that when the pestilence raged among the natives of the island in the year 1764, which reduced their numbers to a mere handful, but left the whites unscathed, the noble *Blue-fish,* such as thou this day hast partaken of, disappeared entirely from our waters. It is now more than three-score years since the species was thought to have become extinct. The superstitious natives looked upon the unaccountable disappearance of the blue-fish, which previously they had caught in immense numbers, as the sure forerunner of the total extinction of their Indian race;—and it was even so. 'But,' said they in bitterness, 'when our fire is extinguished, and our wigwams have become razed, then the blue-fish will return. Then let the shad-belly and the long-tail, (as they called the Quakers,) look out for *his* dwelling and his landmarks, and that the stranger wrest not his inheritance from him as he has wrested ours from us!'

"Now mark me, my friend," solemnly and slowly continued our companion; "mark what I tell thee in relation to the Indian prophecy:—The blue-fish *have* returned within the present year—the *last* Indian lingers amongst us without the hope of issue,—and the places of the wigwams of his fathers are only known by their desolated hearths. The lineal descendants of the original proprietors are scattered over the world, and are disappearing from among us before the face of the strangers who have come into the isle. Our broad corn-fields are trodden down, and our '*Shearing*' scarce deserves the name;—not a single custom of our ancestors is adhered to in its ancient purity,—all—all is giving way before the spirit of innovation that now stalks abroad in the island,—prostrating all that is venerable for its antiquity, and good as being the delight of our fathers!"

An honest tear came to the eye of the old man as he closed his historical details.

We confess that the ready information furnished by our host, had made the time pass away with unwonted celerity. With reluctance we cast our eyes out upon the sun, which was fast running down the West; and we reached for our hat, and held out our hand to take leave. Our companion gave it a kindly pressure, and followed us to the door with our hand folded in his.

"Stop!" exclaimed he suddenly; "do not go yet. Take it not as flattery, but I am pleased with thy curiosity and thy intelligence. I would fain bestow a mark of my favour upon thee; and the more readily and willingly because thy conversation hath been both amusing and instructive. I would crave therefore, a repetition of thy visit to this lone dwelling, from which the idle and the impertinent have been excluded for years."

While our kind host was once more engaged in ransacking his tobacco-closet, we endeavoured to recall the portions of our conversation in which we had conveyed the least information in the world, or in which we had rendered ourself at all amusing: but, certes, we could not recollect saying more than ten words at any one time,—and those were put in edgewise in the shape of questions; and truly do we believe that our host uttered ninety-and-nine full sentences to every monosyllable of ours. The thought flashed upon us that we had been an attentive listener, and the secret was out! Men given to be garrulous always praise good listeners.

Great was our surprise when our new-made friend approached and put into our hands a ponderous roll of papers, carefully tied up with a piece of tarred rope-yarn.

"There!" said our host of the monkey-jacket, "take it, friend Tinker," [this was the fourth time he had miscalled the name:] "take it, friend Tinker, and mend it if thou wilt:—Peradventure some pestilent printer, like him at the town, may use his types upon it, instead of printing essays upon schools and temperance, as *he* hath done, ('ad rat him!) to make children wiser and better than their fathers.* There is truth in every page of that

---

*We presume the allusion here made, was to Mr. JENKS, the spirited editor of the Nantucket Inquirer, whose faithful labours in the cause of education should be esteemed above all praise. His zeal may have given offence to some of the old-school gentlemen, who,

manuscript, my friend; and moreover something about the perils of the whale-fishery, which I have been a matter of twenty winters in putting together, after an experience and observation of more than sixty years:— and I have hoped the while, that it might some day be instrumental in bringing back to the people of my island, the recollection of the golden days of their ancient customs, from the which, alas! they have greatly departed of late, to cleave unto the fashions and vanities of the great cities. I have shaken the dust from my feet, in testimony against their multiplied follies, and have come out from amongst them, more in sorrow than in anger, to dwell here alone upon the seashore. But fare thee well, friend—how dost call thy name again?"

"Thompson, sir."

"Ah—Thompson!—I shall remember it when thou comest again. Once more, fare thee well!"

We now turned our back upon the little village, and made our way with rapid strides towards the town. The sun was sinking in the ocean as we commenced our retrograde march over the heath, and the full moon danced upon the waters ere we regained our hotel. In our eagerness to inspect the package so singularly committed to our charge, we thought

---

like our narrator, were opposed to innovation of every sort, and were content with the "humanities" as taught by such ancient dames as the "Widow Craddlers," and "Mary Gardner," and "Nabby Bunker," who, it is related, suffered their pupils to go to sleep comfortably throughout the hours of their school sessions. But they have been long gathered to their fathers. We have since marvelled why, in denouncing the "pestilent printer," he did not also give a thrust at Admiral COFFIN, to whom he had dedicated his work, and who had, previous to the above interview, established the foundation of the "*Coffin Grammar School*" at Nantucket, with a most munificent endowment out of his own private funds. It is a matter of wonder why he did not address the worthy Admiral in the words of *Cade:*

"Thou hast most traitorously corrupted the youth of the realm, in erecting a grammar school. It will be proved to thy face that thou has men about thee that usually talk of a noun and a verb; and such abominable words, as no Christian ear can endure to hear."

Posterity, however, will do justice to the motives of Mr. JENKS and Admiral COFFIN: and we greatly mistake if the present island generation do not regard their public labours with a proper appreciation. *Editor.*

not upon the weariness attendant upon a seven miles tramp;—and putting aside, rather unceremoniously, the cup of refreshing souchong tendered to us by the kind mistress of the mansion, we seized a lamp from the mantel and hastened to our chamber. We cut the matted rope-yarn, which secured the bundle, with an unskillfulness that deprived one of "Rogers's Best" of its keen edge, which half a day's friction upon the "Franklin Hone," and a faithful strapping upon the "Remedy for Wry Faces" to boot, with difficulty restored.

The severed string unfolded to our eyes the title-page of the following Tale; and upon the next leaf we discovered the Dedication which the reader has found prefixed to "this present writing." Following the Dedication, there came what we shall presently transcribe. Should some of our readers pronounce it a fault in us for having omitted sundry obscurities, and "ancient and fishlike" passages which occurred in the manuscript, or for reducing the antique spelling to the modern orthographical standard, or for amplifying all the y^es and y^ts and other elisions and short comings peculiar to ancient writers,—we must plead the license given by the donor in his parting words:—"Take it, friend *Tinker*, and *mend* it if thou wilt." But we can assure our indulgent friends that we have left the essence of the matter entire—having only dared to place a few scraps of poetry, by way of finger-posts, at the tops of the chapters, and otherwise to take upon ourself the office of the lapidary, who grinds away the rough corners of the diamond, that the superficial polish he bestows may the better show forth the inherent qualities of the brilliant.

NEW-YORK,
April 25th, 1834.

MIRIAM COFFIN,

OR

THE WHALE-FISHERMEN.

CHAPTER ONE.

Be it remembered, that we have not to compete with the old worn-out nations of the Continent: A new people—a few years ago *"in the gristle,"* but now *"hardened into the bone of manhood,"*—are our bold and adventurous rivals.

Oriental Herald.

THE great river of the West,—the Father of Waters, as it was called by the aborigines,—may be used as an apt personification of the power, the progress of change, and eventual destiny of the American people. Rising in the far wilderness, and taking its first impulse from a few trickling rills, it gathers in strength as it proceeds on its way, until, in its course of two thousand miles, it receives the contributions of those immense streams that spread out like the arms of a giant and embrace a whole continent;— grasping and binding together its remote corners, and conveying their tribute to the one great body, which thus becomes strengthened and invigorated by the aid of its natural members. With its power thus accumulated, the Mississippi moves on in the swelling majesty of its grandeur,

1

sweeping away with resistless force every opposing obstacle,—straightening and deepening its own mighty bed,—till finally pouring its volume of deep and rapid waters into the ocean, it mingles its turbid floods with the clear blue sea, and diffuses itself, as it were, in the immensity of creation.

It is even thus with the American nation. The remote and interminable wilds of the earth witnessed its birth, amidst forests boasting the growth of centuries, where, giant-like and unconquerable,—combining in its own elements and wisely directing its own energies,—it moves on surely and steadily to the accomplishment of a glorious and unequalled destiny.

It is not, however, our design to wander over an almost boundless continent, in search of the wherewithal to illustrate what is thus hinted at: It will be sufficient to select for exemplification quite an inconsiderable portion of the country—a mere speck of American earth,—and to point to it, as to a hive of industrious bees, for a miniature representation of the vast whole.

Near the coast of the United States of America, some ten leagues to the south of that part of Massachusetts which is called Cape Cod, the little sandy island of Nantucket peeps forth from the Atlantic ocean. Isolated and alone amidst a wide waste of waters, it presents to the stranger, at first view, a dreary and unpromising appearance. The scrapings of the great African Desert, were they poured into the sea, would not emerge above its level with an aspect of more unqualified aridity than does this American island, with the exception of a few small lakes, and swampy *oases*, nourished by an unwonted moisture, which, while they redeem the island from absolute sterility, rather serve to make the likeness to Zaara more complete. But few trees, and those, it is averred, not the natural growth of the soil, relieve the monotonous surface of the island. Scattered dusky patches of thin short grass, among which is included an unenclosed common of great extent, afford nourishment to droves of cattle and flocks of sheep, heedfully attended by a few shepherds or keepers during the seasons for browsing, which, be it known, are the same here as in other countries, namely, spring and summer. But, generally speaking, were it not for the moving things upon it that have life and activity, the island to most eyes would wear the face of utter desolation. Bleak and uninviting, however, as it may seem, it is the abode of much wealth and intelligence; and, from the nature of the tale which follows, we have constituted it the principal scene of our story. Though we may occasionally leave it for distant shores, the incidents of the tale will still be found divergent therefrom; and our *dramatis personæ* will perform their actions in direct reference to that little and peculiar world, though thousands of miles intervene between them and the common centre, from which they depart upon deeds of daring.

We love to linger upon this island. Perhaps there is no other place in the wide world of similar size and population, possessing so few intrinsic attractions, which has produced, under so many disadvantages, such an industrious and enterprising people as Nantucket. Though it is said to be literally sterile in the spontaneous gifts of nature, yet it is rife in the physical and intellectual vigour of manhood. For more than a century the islanders have exhibited the curious and unique spectacle of a thrifty community, bound together by a common interest as well as by a relative tie of consanguinity;— primitive though not altogether puritanic in their manners, as will be seen in the sequel,—winning equal respect for their virtues at home and abroad,—reaping harvests where they have not sown, and fishing up competency for their families from the unappropriated natural wealth in the depths of the sea.

We are not without fear of giving offense by denominating the Nantucketers an amphibious race. We do not mean *"half horse—half alligator,"*—for that is a distinction which the Kentuckians appropriate exclusively to themselves:—but we mean that sort of *half quaker—half sailor* breed, to be found nowhere else on earth:—the men spending the greater part of their lives upon the ocean, and the women, though they tempt not the dangers of the sea, oddly mixing nautical phraseology with that which landsmen are accustomed to listen to "all along shore." Nevertheless, tinctured as their conversation is with the technicalities of the quarter-deck and the forecastle, the females of the island are modest, virtuous, and agreeable, and thrive with a commendable industry at home; while the men are fishermen upon a grand scale, and pursue and conquer the monarch of the seas in distant and remote waters. At the present moment they, together with the whale-fishermen in their immediate neighborhood, are the lamp-supplyers to more than half the civilized nations of the globe. In the exercise of their hazardous trade they have become a bold and hardy race of men;—in danger, cool, collected and adventurous;—seldom or never indulging in the vices or evil propensities of the common sailor, but possessing all his generous and manly qualities, tempered with correct notions of economy and of the true obligations of society. We know not how we can better sum up their character than by giving them their own expressive title of AMERICAN WHALE-FISHERMEN; and adding thereto, that to the successful prosecution of their trade, the energies of all the inhabitants, both male and female, are constantly directed.

The town of Sherburne, when its people first undertook fishing for the whale with something like system, was but a small place: but, notwithstanding its insignificance, as contrasted with some of the continental towns, it shortly engrossed the oil-trade of America and of many of the European nations. It was long after the permanency of its trade was secured, that the eloquent Burke, in the British House of Commons, pronounced the eulogium upon the skill of the islanders which we have written upon the title-page of this tale; and he added that "Neither the perseverance of Holland, nor the activity of France, nor the dexterous and firm sagacity of English enterprise, ever carried this perilous mode of hardy industry to the extent to which it has been pushed by this recent people,—a people who are still, as it were, but in the gristle, and not yet hardened into the bone of manhood."

England, tying up her prosperity by granting a monopoly to the trade to a chartered company, had fitted out and abandoned her whale-ships in despair; the Dutch had been crippled in contesting the right of fishery with her formidable rival, and the ruder Norwegians, bordering upon the Icelandic seas, had as yet contented themselves with entrapping the monster of the deep, which, like the stultified Esquimaux, they valued chiefly for the greasy and unctuous blubber that the animal afforded for food.

It may not be denied, however, that the Northern nations of Europe, and principally the bold navigators of England, were the pioneers who opened the way of the whale-fishery to other people. In a long course of perilous and sometimes disastrous voyages of discovery in the Arctic seas, the English endeavoured to penetrate through a supposed North Western passage to the East Indies, and the Danes to regain a doubtful and almost fabulous settlement or colony, planted, as they believed, by their ancestors, somewhere on the coast of Greenland or Labrador.[*] Though their principal object was always defeated, yet science has been greatly benefitted by the devotion and personal sacrifices of such men as the persevering Hudson, Davis, and Baffin, and the patient, self-denying, and encouraging example of Hans Egede, the benevolent Lutheran. But the mariners of Nantucket were assuredly among the first to turn the labours, and, in some respects, fruitless discoveries, of those zealous and enterprising navigators, to good account.

At the commencement of our tale, which the reader will fix at a period antecedent to our existence as a distinct people, the Northern seas were covered with the whale-fishermen of most maritime nations. The field in the North had, at that time, as it was thought by American navigators, been well gone over and well reaped; and the precarious cargoes of oil obtained by all, warned them that the persecuted whales had been much diminished in numbers, or had betaken themselves to other and more secluded haunts. The explorations of Ross and Parry have since

---

[*]Hecker, a German author, translated by Babington, in treating of the history and causes of the "Black death" which raged in every part of Europe in the fourteenth century, thus alludes to this colony:

"The inhabitants of Iceland and Greenland found in the coldness of their inhospitable climate, no protection against the Southern enemy who had penetrated to them from happier countries. The plague caused great havoc among them. Nature made no allowance for their constant warfare with the elements, and the parsimony with which she had meted out to them the enjoyments of life. In Denmark and Norway, however, people were so occupied with their own misery, that the accustomed voyages to Greenland ceased. Towering ice-bergs formed at the same time on the coast of Greenland, in consequence of the general concussion of the earth's organism; and no mortal, from that time forward, has ever seen that shore or its inhabitants."

But this is mere conjecture in the German, with regard to the colony, and does not deserve a moments credit. Danish writers on this subject make no allusion to the German extravaganza of " the general concussion of the earth's organism!"

confirmed the latter opinion. Merchant traders, however, had in the mean time reported that a species of the whale, unlike the "right-whale" of the North, was sporting in great numbers in tropical regions, near the coast of Brazil and Western Africa; and some of our captains who had doubled "*The Horn*" told of immense "schools" of the valuable Spermaceti on the coasts of Peru and Chili, in the great Pacific Ocean. Thither we may take occasion to turn the attention of the reader, whilst we follow the new current of Nantucket enterprise.

Among the low, scattered, and unpainted buildings of the Quaker Settlement, which surrounds a small but commodious bay on the Northern side of Nantucket, and in the center of the ancient town of Sherburne, whose name has since given place to the unromantic title of the island, uprose the unostentatious mansion of Jethro Coffin, the Oil Merchant. Originally of small dimensions, it had increased with the gains of the owner, and now appeared a succession of unshapely buildings, of various orders of architecture and design, covering a goodly portion of ground. Uncouth as were these buildings, they were the storehouses of considerable worldly riches, honestly and laboriously gotten, yet never boastfully nor vain-gloriously displayed. Content and quiet were the inmates of Jethro's dwelling; and both wealth and comfort, as well as odd gable-ends and patch-like additions to the main building, increased with each arrival from the whaling-ground. Jethro Coffin was the sole owner of ships and smaller vessels; and had, besides, large interest in others wherein English merchants had invested capital. Wisely preferring to have their vessels fitted out at Nantucket, and manned and commanded by Nantucket seamen, the foreigners had appointed Jethro their agent and factor, and were well content, from time to time, to receive their gainful dividends through his hands—sometimes in cash, but most generally in shipments of oil and candles of sperm, which were regularly sent to the "mother country." It is worthy also of remark, that at this period nearly all the successful whale-ships sailing out of English ports, were commanded, and sometimes entirely manned, by Nantucket-men who were seduced from their native island by large bounties from the British government. In the end their skill and economy came to be imitated by the British; but

though they parted with the mystery of their trade, the merit of instruct-
ing that nation in the art of killing the whale with dexterity, belongs to our
own countrymen.*

Two of Jethro's ships were now at sea, and expected to arrive at Sherburne daily. Nearly three years had elapsed since their departure, and he
began to feel anxious for their return from the long voyage. One of them
had been spoken on the hither-side of The Horn near the Equator, deeply
laden with oil; and her consort was reported to be not far behind. The two
vessels were manned by nearly a hundred souls, selected from the hardy
populace of Nantucket; and every family on the island consequently felt
an interest in the successful termination of the voyage. Wives looked anx
iously and fearfully for husbands, too long absent from home;—affectionate parents for affectionate children;—and sisters for brothers long
parted. This intensity of feeling, wound up to a painful pitch by the protracted absence and uncertain fate of the vessels, had however been much
relieved by the report of a fast-sailing India trader lately arrived at Boston,
then the chief mercantile port of the colonies. The welcome news was in
due season transferred to Nantucket, and joyfully bruited on the Oil

---

*Mr. Jefferson, while Secretary of State, in 1791, goes into some detail in relation to the
whale-fishery of the island of Nantucket. He was unwittingly led into, and assisted materially
in propagating, the common error respecting the agricultural capabilities of the Island. He
speaks correctly however of the inducements held out to the islanders to emigrate to foreign
countries,—"But the people," he says, "especially females, are fondly attached to the island;
and few wish to emigrate to a more desirable situation." This attachment to the soil could
scarcely have existed if the island was so utterly barren as he would lead us to imagine by the
words of his Report, which are as follows:—

"The American whale-fishery is principally followed by the inhabitants of the island of
Nantucket,—a *sand bar*, of about 15 miles long and three broad, capable of maintaining by
its agriculture *about twenty families;* but it employed in these fisheries, before the war, between
five and six thousand (?) men and boys; and in the only harbour it possesses it had 140
vessels, 132 of which were of the larger kind, as being employed in the Southern fishery. In
agriculture, then, they have no resources; and if that of their fishery cannot be pursued from
their habitations, it is natural they should seek others from which it can be followed, and
prefer those where they will find a sameness of language, religion, laws, habits, and kindred.
A foreign emissary has lately been among them for the purpose of renewing the invitations
to a change of situation; but attached to their native country, they prefer continuing in it, if
their continuance there can be made supportable."—See Mr. Jefferson's *Report on the Fisheries,*
January, 1791.

'Change at Sherburne. The weathercock of the lighthouse, on, the sandy point at the entrance to the harbour, was, after this, more constantly watched than ever. The least unfavorable turn of the huge sheet-iron whale, swinging faithfully with the breeze at the top of the beacon-light, was sufficient, at this conjuncture, to produce sadness of heart in the multitude; but the chopping of the vane, when the breeze sprung up from the south, was the signal for renewed hope and cheerful confidence. Thus did the slight and inanimate fishlike profile, symbolical of the trade of the place, as it veered about under the impulse of the wind, become the lever to raise or depress the animal spirits, and to excite, alternately, the hopes and fears of a whole community!

Amidst the anticipations consequent upon the report of the Indian trader aforesaid, preparations were making for the far-famed festival of the "*Sheep-Shearing*." It is annually held about the middle of June.[*] The time set apart for the shearing was sacred to mirth and merriment among the young people, and strangers, in no moderate numbers, flocked to the place to participate therein; while the elders busied themselves in arranging the preliminaries of the festival, or in adjusting the graver matters of high concernment which gave occasion for the merry-making. This extraordinary jubilee had, down to the times of which we write, been held on the island from time immemorial, or, at least, dated its origin so long back that the memory of that wonderful personage, "the oldest man living," claimed not to run to the contrary thereof. It had always brought gladness and plenty, and revived old recollections, and united old friends:—but, alas! for the first time (we speak from having seen the fact upon record) it was likely to have an inauspicious beginning. A storm had gathered over the island and extended seaward, which, for violence and severity, had scarcely ever been paralleled in this temperate region, at a season which, in our latitude, is generally mild and balmy. The heaviest artillery of the gathering clouds, which lay darkly piled upon each other in triple array

---

[*]The celebrated *Sheep-Shearing* of Nantucket commences on the Monday nearest to the 20th of June. The ceremony of washing occurs on the preceding Friday and Saturday; the scattered flocks being previously driven from all parts of the island, and secured in pens on the borders of a pleasant little fresh-water lake, called by the Indian name "*Miacomet*."

in the heavens, ushered in the rain and the wind, and both continued increasing in violence, until the one became a deluge and the other a hurricane. The gale proved sufficiently powerful to decapitate chimneys and unroof buildings; while the floods, forming in small swift-running watercourses, did infinite damage to the lands of the settlement. A shudder thrilled the hearts of the islanders at every gust of wind. They knew their ships must be near at the commencement of the storm: and less furious gales had been known to strike down vessels at sea, as well prepared and well managed as their own.

Much to the annoyance and vexation of the expectant youthful merrymakers, the rain, in unremitting torrents, continued to deluge and gully the sands of the devoted little island, long after the thunder had ceased; and, when it had fallen prodigiously for two consecutive days, it is worthy of record that it gave occasion for that original and quaint remark for which Peleg Folger, of Nantucket, stands sponsor;—to wit, that "the storm was *likely* to turn into a *settled rain!*"

Jethro Coffin saw all this with dismay at heart, notwithstanding he was a member of that placid and "straightest sect," which in modern days are known by the denomination of Quakers, and are supposed to be incapable of strong emotion. He inherited his membership from birthright, and had long ago been taught, by precept and example, to hold his mind under the strictest discipline, let what would befall him.

If evil fell to his portion, no murmurings were heard; if good came, he tempered his rejoicing with meekness of spirit. Assuming a calm, outward demeanour, which but ill concealed the workings of his mind, Jethro sat himself down in a corner of his ample, old-fashioned fireplace, opposite to his wife Miriam, who, possessing one of those strong minds that sometimes fall to the lot of woman, was far less agitated both in reality and appearance, than her spouse. It was cold and damp, and required a fire within doors. A cheerful, blazing hearth will go far, at any time, to dissipate gloomy thoughts; and the comfort of a good fire is exquisite, while the rain is heard rattling against the casement, and the wind howling over the chimney top. There is no situation that sooner calls up the grateful incense of the heart.

But if a sensation of personal security, and assurance of present comfort came over the mind of Jethro at all, they were but momentary. He had ships on the coast, and his only son trod the deck, or perhaps "rocked on the giddy mast" of one of them. His thoughts were "far—far at sea." In the midst of his painful reflections, he frequently drew his breath hard; and; anon his lips uttered an unwonted sound, between a sigh and a groan, plainly denoting the agonizing of the spirit. Now, lighting his pipe, he smoked vehemently, but in silence; and then, resigning himself, with a desperate effort, to the trying emergency of the time, he leaned back in his chair, and no further betrayed the conflict within than by a convulsive nervousness, that showed itself in the clasped hands and the rapid twirling of his thumbs. Miriam, seated in the other corner of the fireplace, was absorbed in her own reflections, and plied her fingers zealously at her knitting-work. Ruth Coffin, the daughter, stood at a window looking out upon the gloomy sky, pouting with her pretty cherry lips, and ever and anon biting her finger-nails with sheer vexation at the weather.

"Heigh-ho!" exclaimed Ruth, as, half talking, half thinking aloud, her thoughts began to embody themselves;—"Heigh-ho!—will it never stop raining! Bless me, how it pours! Nothing but rain—rain—rain! We go to bed and it rains—we get up in the morning and it rains still. The shearing will come on the day after to-morrow, and there will be no going to the common, as I see;—and what use would it be if we did? Though the thirsty soil of Nantucket can drink up oceans of water, I dare say enough remains of what has fallen from the clouds to drown the flocks. There will be no occasion to wash the fleece before shearing, for the rain has done that all to our hand. Many thanks for the trouble it has saved the good people of Sherburne! Not a soul has come from the continent to see our doings, and we sha'nt have any body but the 'Tucketers to make merry with. Merry indeed!—very merry we shall be, truly, with the Folgers and the Gardners, and the Jenkinses and the Starbucks, and Colemans, and Macys, and Swains, and such like, that one sees every day from year's end to year's end, with their everlasting drabs and eternal Thees and Thous,— every one of them 'cousins' too, I declare. Vastly new and edifying it will be to hear their greetings:—'Cousin Macy, how's thee do?'—'Thank'ee, cousin Jenkins, how's *thee* do?'—'Quite well, all but the rheumatics, which plague me sorely as usual: How's thy father and cousin Miriam?' (Here Ruth spitefully repeated the names of a long list of Nantucket cousins.) 'When didst thou see cousin Mehetable Starbuck—and cousin Peleg—and cousin Joshua—and cousin Josiah—and cousin Obadiah!'—O how amusing!—dear me! Four days of constant rain—and this, the fifth day of outpouring; what an age!—and then, to crown all, the wind blows a right down 'harry-cane,' as cousin Peleg calls it, and as cold as mid-winter—ugh!—Father, didst thou not tell me that thy ship Leviathan was expected home shortly? and isn't the gale dead ahead from the north-east? Poor brother Isaac—I wonder if he is boxing about in this dreadful storm, and thinking of home!"

"Ruth," slowly answered Jethro, "thou talkest too fast and too much. Thou'rt sixteen years old, come the twentieth day of sixth month: thou hast been at Cousin Mary Gardner's seminary for seven years, and thy education in the great city of Boston hath cost me a sweet penny; but I don't see that thou hast mended thy ways in proportion to thy opportunities." As he uttered these words, Jethro compressed his lips, and coolly knocked the ashes from his pipe against the thick-lipped figurehead of the iron firedog, by way of giving emphasis to his admonition, and clenching the argument of his preachment.

"Well, but father," said Ruth, who already understood how to manage the kind-hearted Jethro, "here we've been pent up for nearly a week without setting foot out of doors, and the shearing is close by, and not a living being has yet come to the island to see us. Thou know'st, father, it's only once a year we have a shearing, and our friends are sure never to heave in sight at any other time."

"True, child," observed the father kindly, "but bethink thee, all things must have an end—the storm cannot last for ever. Thou must learn to take things as thou find'st them, Ruth, and not repine and worry when disappointment comes athwa't thee. The wind that's dead ahead to-day may be free to-morrow; for what saith the verse—

'Hoot away, despair!
Never yield to sorrow—
The blackest sky may wear
A sunny face to-morrow.'"

Here the conversation ceased. It was one of those short, pithy lessons, easy of application and abiding in the memory, with which the fathers of the Friendly Faith were wont to school their children. It is thus they regulate by degrees the outbreakings of the restless spirit in youth, and teach them to be passionless and long-suffering in years of maturity.

Jethro Coffin, however, though an exemplary man abroad, and stiff and straight as a handspike before the eyes of the world, was by no means severe in his household. Turning his eyes from the gloomy prospect without, and from the equally overcast countenance of his cherished and only daughter, they rested affectionately on the matronly form, and sedate, though majestic features of Miriam. His mind involuntarily reverted to the days of their youth, when, with a fervour incident to the first impressions of love, he passionately admired her. He remembered when, like his daughter now fast approaching woman's estate, they had set their hearts upon the junkettings and merry times of the shearing, and with what pride he harnessed his sleek but well broken colt to his calêsche, or little pleasure cart, and traversed the common, or peered into the tents of the victuallers, or vexed, by undue familiarities, the few Indian families whose dwellings skirted the confines of the common, upon that beautiful water sheet, Miacomet;—and how he drove, with censurable speed through the sands, to the Ultima Thûlé of fashionable drives—even unto the little fishing village of Siasconset, some seven miles distant from Sherburne, accompanied by the spirited and joyous Miriam, who in after years became his wedded wife. In this way, as his mind ran over the scenes of his youthful heyday, the waywardness of Ruth was soon forgotten or forgiven. His countenance gradually reassumed its accustomed placidity; but he twirled his thumbs again as the transition of his thoughts conjured up more serious subjects for contemplation.

"Tush!" exclaimed Jethro, communing with himself, while a chilly sensation fell upon his heart, and he wiped away the cold drops from his brow:—"Tush!—why should I fear:—the Leviathan is a good ship, and a stout one to boot—Seth Macy is an able commander—always on the look-out—vigilant, active, and nervy. His people jump like crickets when he gives the word; and if skill will avail aught, the property and the people will be preserved:—a valuable cargo beneath deck, if report speak truly:—seven-and-twenty hundred barrels of sperm are worth the toil of three years. Let me reckon:—twenty-seven hundred barrels of thirty gallons each—pshaw! I am quite forgetting the boy Isaac. After all, I do believe it is the thought of the lad that overcomes me. His safety is dear to me indeed; bone of my bone—flesh of my flesh—it would surely be unnatural not to care for one who derives his existence from me. He must be a stout boy by this time, and turned of fourteen. The lad had a strong desire to go to sea, and I instructed Seth to put him before the mast, and make a sailor of him;—but what if he should have transferred him to the Sea-Horse? Well, and what then ? She is a smaller vessel than the Leviathan to be sure; a trifle short of two hundred and fifty tons;—but what of that? She has a large tonnage as vessels go nowadays; and Jonathan Coleman, a light-hearted, honest fellow, will keep the deck as long as the planks stick together. But the Leviathan is the better sea-boat, and rides the waves without labouring. She measures three hundred tons, carpenter's measurement, and was thought a famous ship;—in fact, when despatched upon her first voyage, she was the largest whaleman known in these parts; and I remember, as though it was but a thing of yesterday, what an object of curiosity she was while on the stocks, and how at her launching a multitude of people attended; and how handsomely she slid off into her element—diving deep with her stern, and lighting up like a waterfowl as her bow made the plunge from the ways! We build ships larger now; for one generation always grows wiser by the experience of that which precedes it. The vessel which I expect in a few days from New-Bedford will surprise our nautical men. Four hundred tons—sharp at the bows below the water-line—bold above water—flush deck—clean counter—salted on the stocks—fastened and bolted with copper, and coppered to the bends:—verily she hath cost me a mint of money, and should be a capital craft. I wonder what Macy will say to her? He is particular in such matters, and people do say a little old-maidish. No matter; he shall command her. There is Jonathan Coleman, too—a queer fish—I misdoubt he will utter some jibe at her model; but I have good reasons for every thing new in her construction, and am pretty certain, though with much contention with the stiffnecked builders, of having a ship at last after my own heart."

It was after this fashion that Jethro's thinking ran from one subject to another. A great man has said that the step is but a short one from the sublime to the ridiculous. Another of less pretension has declared that the thickest darkness of the night immediately precedes the dawn of day. Certain it is, that the grave and the gay are apt to go hand and hand with each other, even as a tall man will sometimes select a short female for his companion; for—

"In joining contrasts lieth Love's delight."

Jethro Coffin was by no means an exception, in the composition of his temperament, from these general rules. He had forgotten the storm, and the ships at sea, and all on board; and the new ship of four hundred tons, "coppered and copper fastened," was now uppermost in his mind. The only difficulty remaining was to find a name for her, and sorely it did puzzle him to hit upon a good one.

"Let me think," said he, pursuing the present train of his thoughts; "what shall her name be? It is meet that it should be characteristic, and like unto her destined calling. There's the Leviathan and the Sea-Horse for the two ships—Industry and Hope for the brigs—Periwinkle, Nautilus, and Miriam for the small craft. The 'Sea-Lion,' or the 'Sea-Elephant,' would sound well enough for the new comer—but then already I have the 'Sea-Horse,' and the repetition of the word 'Sea' would lead neighbours to imagine my invention rather barren. Hercules—that's good, and betokens strength; but it's Heathenish, and I may not, even in the naming of my ship, offend the tender consciences of the brethren. The 'Thunderer' sounds well—but it won't do—it's Pagan. 'King Philip' or 'Anawan' might answer upon a pinch, but such titles savour of man-worship. 'The Grampus'—yea, that's it—I have hit it at last! Grampus—Grampus, ay, that will do. Her name is decided on. It shall be the Grampus, and her commander shall be Seth Macy. Jonathan may take the Leviathan for the next voyage; and Seth's mate, Nahum Bunker, shall command the Sea-Horse. The other vessels shall go as they are: Jerudathan Starbuck in the Hope; Pelatiah Gardner in the Industry; Joshua Jenkins in the Periwinkle; John Folger (rather a dull sailor) in the Nautilus, and Jeremiah Barnard in the little Miriam;—a smart, handy craft that of Barnard's—spins round like a top, and sails in the wind's eye, when moved thereto by the helm."

These important particulars, in regard to the ships and smaller vessels, being happily disposed of, Jethro sat awhile gazing vacantly at the red blaze upon the hearth; but presently his thumbs began slowly to revolve again, and he cogitated once more. A rupture between the mother country, as Great Britain was familiarly called, and her refractory, tax-burthened colonies, was beginning to be not only hinted at, but openly discussed by the colonists; and Jethro had lately read, with many misgivings, a powerful and well written pamphlet, which spoke of the absurdity of three millions of freemen running to the seaside, upon every arrival from England, to ask what measure of liberty was meted out to them by their haughty governors and lordly masters on the other side of the Atlantic.[*] He was perplexed as to the course it was proper for him to pursue, in case the colonies or the parent country should push matters to extremities; but he hoped for the best—for he was a man of peace, and eschewed quarrel and contention. He could not, however, shut his eyes upon the prospect before him, if war should grow out of the rebellious discussions of the colonists. Should he attempt to side with them, as he was secretly inclined, his property both at sea and on land—his ships and his sheep—would fall an easy prey to the British; and if he continued loyal to the crown, its power could not afford him permanent protection

---

[*]In reference to the ineffectual remonstrances of the colonies at this period, the author of "*Common Sense,*" the pioneer publication in the cause of American liberty, put forth about the year 1774–5, thus boldly spoke to his countrymen:—

"To be always running three or four thousand miles with a tale or a petition, waiting four or five months for an answer, which, when obtained, requires five or six more to explain it in, will in a few years be looked upon as folly and childishness:—there was a time when it was proper, and there is a proper time for it to cease."

against the saucy cruisers of the Confederacy, which, in all probability, would cover the seas within a month after the commencement of hostilities. Jethro would fain have determined to maintain an "unarmed neutrality," as it best suited the doctrines of that religious creed in which he had been brought up, and which breathes nothing but peace and good will to man. But there could scarcely be a neutral flag between belligerents; and his ships must either display the ensign of Old England, or that which the colonists should adopt as their own. There was, to be sure, no immediate cause for making the choice between them; yet, in looking attentively at the signs of the times, he discovered a lowering political horizon, and the absolute necessity, at no very distant day, of meeting the question, or embracing the alternative—

"Under which king, Benzonian? Speak, or die!"

It was true, he was exposed to the fires of both combatants; and, let him embrace either horn of the dilemma, danger and death might follow. Nantucket was assailable from every quarter, and alike subject to the violence of invasion from either side, as the inhabitants might determine where to bestow their allegiance, and provoke the vengeance of the rejected party. The only relief, under this view of the subject was the hope in which Jethro indulged, that both parties would mutually agree to regard the little, sandy, unprotected island, as the contending armies of old did the Wilderness City,—the "Tadmor in the Desert" of Solomon,—and spare it from spoliation, in consideration of the temporary rest and shelter it might afford to the wayworn and weatherbeaten.

"Mercy on us!" exclaimed Jethro, suddenly. A vivid glare of lightning, and a rattling peal of thunder, came simultaneously, and Jethro's dwelling shook to its foundation. This sudden interruption cut short the thread of his musings, and caused him to start upon his feet with an alacrity altogether unusual to his customary formality of motion, when rising from his easy-chair in the chimney-corner.

"Mercy on us!" repeated he, in great consternation: "I trust the house is not struck with lightning—and yet I scent a sulphureous smell—phew!—it almost chokes me. Wonderful! see—it has struck the vane and the lights from the beacon—the building is tottering—look, Miriam, look!—there it falls to the ground!"

"Nay," answered Miriam, calmly, "it is the strength of the gale that hath done the mischief: trust me, the lightning hath had no agency in the matter."

"What say'st thou?" said Jethro, putting his hand to his nostrils, "thou mistakest, Miriam; the lightning hath surely done the deed, for I smell the abomination of brimstone."

"The air may be filled with that unsavoury odour," replied Miriam, "and yet no harm be done by the electric fluid."

"Electric fluid?" rejoined Jethro;—"ah!—I remember,—thou art a true descendant of Mary Morriel,* who married the first Folger; and consequently thou'rt near akin to Benny Franklin by the side of the Folgers— and I suppose thou hast heard something from him about electricity, and the like, that makes thee so positive—"

"I spoke of the *negative,* Jethro," retorted Miriam, playing upon the philosophical signification of his last word. "Thou knowest, or ought to know," continued she, "that the glass which surrounded the lights is a non-conductor—and therefore, instead of attracting, it would *repel* the lightning."

---

*Mary Morriel, the great-grandmother of Dr. Benjamin Franklin, was maid-servant in the family of the Reverend Hugh Peters, one of the chaplains of Cromwell, who fled from England in the year 1662. Peter Folger, the first of the name that came to Nantucket, was passenger on board the same vessel, and became enamoured of the maid, who was a buxom, sensible lass, and won the heart of Peter by laughing at his sea-sickness, and betraying no fear of bilge-water. Peter admired the cheerful endurance of Mary Morriel so much upon the voyage, that he proffered his hand to the maid, and bargained for her with the greedy old hunks, her master, and counted out to him the enormous sum of twenty pounds sterling, all his worldly store, for the remaining term of her servitude. He forthwith married the lass, and apparently had no cause of repentance, for he always boasted afterwards of having "made a good bargain." The value and scarcity of money at Nantucket at the time, may be estimated from the fact, that when King Philip, as he was called, pursued an offending and fugitive Indian to Nantucket, in 1665, about three years after Peter Folger and his wife, Mary Morriel that was, had settled on the island, the Indian king consented to bury the hatchet, and let the offender go free, for the consideration of a present of wampum composed of a string of coins, in value nineteen shillings sterling, which was all that could be found in possession of the twenty original proprietors of the island, and Peter Folger to boot.

"That may all be true enough—*and,* if thou sayest it, I dare say it is so:—but," continued her argumentative spouse, who did not relish being beaten even by his wife,—"I recollect, Miriam, when the image of the whale, that swung aloft, and told the direction of the wind, was forged in the shop of neighbor Tinker, the smith;—and the rod upon which it turned was of iron also: now, thou wilt not deny that iron *attracts* the fluid, as thou call'st it?"

Miriam Coffin was a woman of sense and perception, and did not deem it worth the trouble to continue an argument in which she saw her husband was determined to triumph; but she intimated, by way of having the last word,—as all women, gentle or simple, will have—that if the destruction of the lighthouse had been accomplished by the lightning, it would have been shivered into splinters, and not fallen over upon its broadside. The conclusion that the gale had overthrown the light seemed to prevail among the inhabitants, upon a closer inspection of the premises after the storm had subsided; and Miriam's theory was confirmed by the majority. Now, who will deny that it argued well for the general prevalence of good sense and sound reasoning at Nantucket, that the popular decision, in this important matter, should have been a philosophical one? The authority of Jethro, touching the agency of the lightning, did not prevail, although he attempted to sustain his position in an argument of great ingenuity, which the lack of printing-presses at Nantucket has prevented us from handing down to posterity. The people *would* think for themselves; and they refused to look through Jethro's spectacles. It is a good republican example to bow to the will of the majority. But the majority, nevertheless, do not always decide well. We have seen many instances of crookedness in an American multitude, both in politics and philosophy. We have every-day examples of blind partisan zeal, which neither investigates cause nor consequence. It must have been after some expression of popular wrongheadedness that Horace exclaimed, in a fit of vexation—

"Odi profanum vulgus!"

and that Virgil turned up his magnificent nose at the uninitiated vulgar, in the line—

"Procul, o! procul este profani!"

    The old lighthouse upon Brant Point, remembered by few people at this day, was a wooden contrivance of inappreciable ingenuity. In shape it was like to an inverted leech tub, which is known to bear a considerable similitude to the frustum of a cone. It rested, without stancheons to secure its permanency, upon spiles or stilts, driven partially into the unstable sands; and the approach to the lights at its top was by a ladder placed on the outside. Elevated upon perpendicular timbers, it presented not only its sides, but an under surface, to the eddying action of the wind; and the reader will easily conceive the possibility of its taking a lee-lurch, when rudely assailed by a gale of such power as we have described. Wherefore, as between Miriam and Jethro and their several partisans,—though the point at issue was long contested, and remains "moot" even unto this day,—we do verily believe that Miriam was right in her "assignment of errors," and, *ergo*, Jethro in the wrong: and we pronounce judgment accordingly.

    It was whispered at the time, with many wise and portentous shakings of the head,—and the allusion to the "coming event casting its shadow before," was remembered long after the signal descent of the iron image, which erst had crowned the unfortunate building, that the glory of Nantucket and its commercial prosperity would depart for a season, as typically exemplified in the upturning of the beacon, and the consequent downfall of the symbol of its trade. Jethro Coffin and his wife Miriam, though they came of a sailor breed, did not enter into the superstition which prevailed in regard to the prostrate lighthouse: but this great misfortune gave them more immediate uneasiness on another score; for they dreaded the approach of the Leviathan at this particular conjuncture. There was now no guide to vessels making the island at night, and a dangerous shoal stretched out to sea for many leagues round the island.

    The art of navigating vessels over the pathless ocean had not reached that scientific precision which a later day has supplied. The admirable chronometer, which gives the longitude to the minute, was not dreamed of; and the brain of the sage, and the crazed skull of the visionary, were cudgelled alike in vain to produce an equable and perpetual motion, which, in all latitudes, should determine the eastings and westings of the navigator, with a certainty equal to that which a well-adjusted quadrant deduces for the latitude from the great luminary of day, whatever may be his declination. With no sun from which to take an observation, nor star to aid in the projection of a lunar, the unconscious Macy, feeling secure from the very absence of the accustomed night signal, might receive the first intimation of his dangerous proximity to land, by the striking of his ship upon the shoal, and the sudden breaching of the sea over his ill-fated vessel.

Amidst apprehensions such as these, which must be felt to be appreciated, the family of Jethro Coffin retired to rest at the close of this eventful day:—Jethro and Miriam to uneasy slumbers, and Ruth to dream of the enjoyments of the shearing. The thunder, which awakened Jethro from his revery in the chimney-corner, was succeeded by a heavy fall of rain, that proved, as the chroniclers declare, "a clearing-up shower." Before midnight the wind had changed to a favourable quarter, promising good weather. The thick darkness ceased to canopy the earth, and the stars, one by one, became visible, until the blue vault glowed with brilliants, obscured at intervals by the lessening and departing clouds.

$\mathscr{C}$HAPTER TWO.

But lo! at last, from tenfold darkness born,
Forth issues o'er the wave the weeping morn:
Hail, sacred vision! who, on orient wings,
The cheering dawn of light propitious brings:
All nature, smiling, hailed the vivid ray
That gave her beauties to returning day,—
All but our *Ship!*—

Falconer.

A sail!—A sail!—a promised prize to hope!
Her nation—flag—how speaks the telescope?

The Corsair.

THE bright streaks along the Eastern horizon at early dawn, and the small fleecy clouds, scattered and scudding over the face of the heavens, indicated that the storm, which had raged with such appalling violence

21

for many days, had passed off, and was about to be succeeded by a glowing sun, and the genial weather of the earliest summer month.

The sun had not yet risen to dispel the hazy atmosphere, that rested, like a thin mist, on the surface of the sea, when the indistinct figure of a man was seen moving to and fro on the beach, at the side of the island opposite to the town of Sherburne. The distance from the town to the Southern shore is not great—for Sherburne is deeply embayed in the body of the island; but he who sleeps in the town and finds himself on the Southern beach before sunrise, must have waked with the lark, and travelled with commendable speed.

At times the man upon the beach stopped and bent his looks earnestly upon the heaving ocean; and then slowly resuming his musing perambulations over the sands, the object of his coming seemed to be forgotten. In his left hand he carried a short spyglass, which afterwards, as he looked seaward, he applied occasionally to his eye, and carefully swept the whole range of the horizon. His right hand grasped a stout hickory walking-cane of great length, curiously carved by the jack-knife of some ever-busy whale-fisherman. It was wrought into diamonds and ridges, and squares and oblongs, like the war-clubs of the South-sea Islanders, and surmounted by the head of a grinning sea-lion, with a straight black pin of polished whalebone driven through its ears, and forming a guard to accommodate the gripe of the hand. This staff was armed at the smaller end with a pointed iron, from the side of which a short grapple turned upwards in the shape of a well-curved boat-hook. It is easy to conceive that the sharp iron point was used to render the footing sure in slippery places; but the utility of the hook could not be so easily guessed at. And how could he manage a walking stick reaching above his ears, and long enough for the tandem whip-stock of a first-rate whiskered Jehu? We shall see.

The dress of the lone pedestrian was such as the reader may still occasionally see in the habiliments of an aged Quaker in any part of Europe or America, or wheresoever else the society of the Friends is tolerated. Like the "last of the cocked hats," it is fast disappearing; and, in almost every other place in America but Nantucket, it may be pronounced rare and ancient. All travellers agree that whatever *is* rare and ancient should be faithfully described. *Imprimis:*—A drab single-breasted coat, with useless brass or steel buttons, of the size of a half-dollar piece, on the one side, and sham button-holes "to match," worked in worsted or mohair, on the other—meeting at a single point across the breast, and fastened by an invisible hook and eye—collarless, flapless and pocketless—skirts stinted in breadth, but of great longitude, and dangling below the calves of the legs. The chest of the wearer was left uncovered by the coat, but protected by an ample vest—drab in its colour, and buttoned close around the throat—collarless like the upper garment— embracing the body snugly down to the hips, over which depended immensely capacious pockets, covered by huge flaps—a single row of dark brown apple-wood buttons in front, marshalled regularly from the throat to the lower points of the jacket, which were snipped off, or turned under, so as to offer no impediment to the motion of the legs. As suspenders (a modern invention) were never worn with this dress of antiquity, a portion of the linen of the wearer was visible at the snipping, or at the place where the vest should come in contact with the waistband of the small-clothes in front. When seated, the deep flaps of the jacket served the purpose of curtains to the chair legs. The unmentionables, or tight smalls, (long togs or pantaloons, were never seen ashore at Nantucket,) were much the same as those of modern days, and consisted of drab cloth, like the other garments, and were tied or buckled with much precision at the side of the knee. A pair of homespun stockings for the legs,—blue woollen in winter, and unbleached thread in summer,—a string of a muslin cravat, white as driven snow, tied carefully in folds about the neck, so as to be equally visible behind and before—shirt collarless—knuckle-dabbers, or ruffles, over the hand—drab wool hat of immense dimensions in the brim— *e converso* as to the crown,—round and fitting the head closely, and displaying the convexity of the gourd-shell without its handle, the broad brim being looped up to the crown, *a la macaroni,* or brailed up *a la fantail* with cords resembling a ship's back-stays—shoes of neats-leather, finished in the grain, and saturated with bee's-wax and tallow to render them pliable, as well as to preserve the feet from wet, and clasped over the instep with tremendous buckles of steel or massive silver, as best suited the means of the wearer—and the costume of the solitary upon the beach, as well the *tout ensemble* of the once fashionable dress of the grown-up Nantucketers is completed.

The steps of the nameless stranger were suddenly arrested by the appearance of an ill-defined object, which floated heavily in the water close to the shore—approaching and receding with the surf, but evidently grounding as each successive swell sent it toward the beach. It came gradually nearer to the land, being buoyed up and impelled forward by the powerful rollers which beat on the shore, and spent themselves in foam and noisy spray, and then rapidly slunk away, but with diminished force and nearly level reaction, leaving the object for some moments visible and almost motionless.

The man hastily pulled a small cord from his pocket, and rigged a slip-noose at one end. He then cast it over the figurehead of his walking stick, and threw the coil, with the expertness of a sailor, far up the beach. Watching his opportunity, and taking advantage of a receding wave, he dashed into the water, and, in an instant afterwards, the hook of his cane was inserted under the ropes that secured the exterior of the package. A moment more sufficed him to regain the shore, with the cord trailing in his hand as he retired from the water. Bracing his feet in the sand, and surging gently upon the line whenever the surf lightened up the package, he drew his burthen to land, until it began to be partially buried in the sands of the undertow, where it was soon left, high and dry, by the receding tide. It was found, upon investigation, to be a bale of light fancy goods of great value, so thoroughly enveloped in tarred covers that the water had not penetrated within. Such valuable prizes were not uncommon after a storm, and the early riser was often repaid in this way, for deserting a comfortable bed betimes, and performing a morning's chilly ramble upon the beach. But the good luck of the islanders was never kept secret; nor the rightful owner, if he could be found, kept in ignorance of the whereabout of his property. In pursuance of this praiseworthy habit, the packet was afterwards advertised in the only newspaper published in the colonies—but no claimant appeared; and the fine dresses of some of the females of Sherburne, in due season, betrayed the fact that the ownership was considered vested in the finder.

"Good!" exclaimed the beach-walker, "a very good morning's work, I trow;—but at the expense of some foundered ship perhaps. Ah, the dangers of the sea! but stop a bit—I'll put my *waif* upon it, as they do upon the whales at sea, to prevent the lazy louts of the town from claiming it, until I return with a truck to carry it home, where I may examine the windfall or the waterfall more at leisure. Aha,—here comes an interloper, I dare say! Had the greedy booby come sooner he would have claimed half the profits of the salvage;—but he will be disappointed, if I do not mistake the virtue of a first discovery." So saying, the fortunate bale-finder pulled from his fob a little ticket, apparently prepared for such purposes, and fastened it with a string to the bale-rope. Relieving his hickory cane, which had done him such good service, and hastily coiling up his slender cord, he snatched up his spy-glass and took to the beach again, with his back turned upon the approaching stranger. He at once resumed his measured step and his musing; feeling perfectly secure that nobody would dare to remove his waif, or question his sole right to the prize he had left half imbedded in the sands, while that little talisman remained upon it.

The "*waif*" or target-shaped board, and sometimes a little pennon of bunting, fastened at the end of a slender pole and stuck into the body of a slain whale at sea, is sacred among the whale-fishermen of all nations. It happens frequently that the crews of several vessels are at once engaged among a "school," or troop of whales. When one is struck with the harpoon, and the death-blow is given with the lance, which brings his belly to the sun, the successful crew forthwith plant the waif-pole firmly and deeply in his flesh, and thenceforth leave the carcass in pursuit of other animals. When the work of death among the "gigantic game" is ended for the day, and the scattered fugitives are deemed beyond pursuit, the boats and the ships shape their course towards the slaughtered whales, and the property of each is easily made out by the peculiar mark of the waif. All dispute as to the identity of the animal is by this means avoided: the waif settles the question at once and for ever. The same principle guided the honest islanders in determining the right of property found astray upon the beach. If the mark of a discoverer was set upon it, the article might remain till doomsday without molestation from a subsequent finder. Our modern wreckers, along the seashore of Long Island and New-Jersey, are not so fastidious—as many an owner of a stranded ship's cargo can avouch, whose goods have been plundered and buried beneath the sand, until the hot pursuit of the Revenue officials is over; when the pilfering Arabs are left free to disinter their ill–gotten spoil, and to plunder, if they list so to do, from one another. These rascals are the only "thieves" in the western World without some touch of "honour" to redeem the infamy of their character.*

But let us resume. The stranger, a short, thickset, dapper figure, habited in the ordinary Quaker vestments of the island, had not yet caught sight of him of the hickory and spy-glass. Presently his eye turned upon the dark bunch upon the beach, and the unusual sight quickened his steps. Coming up with the black mass, he surveyed it round and round

---

*The editor of these sheets would not be without misgivings, if he should permit the dictum of the ancient writer of this memorial, regarding the exclusive honesty of Nantucket, to go without question. It may be true, as the author declares, that the bygone inhabitants of Nantucket were scrupulously correct in their treatment of wrecks and estrays; but, in later days, he is inclined to the belief that the island assimilates to all other parts of America having a seacoast. He is credibly informed, that when a vessel, laden with rum and sugar, from the West Indies, was recently stranded near the identical spot where Jethro Coffin found his valuable prize, many of the people were busy in appropriating portions of the cargo to themselves; and an anecdote is told of a couple of practical philanthropists, who laid siege to a hogshead of sugar, after this manner:—One had succeeded in landing from the wreck a cask of sugar, and had punched a hole in the head of the puncheon; upon this, the wight stretched out his legs like the Rhodian Colossus, and spread out a sack therebetween, with mouth prepared to engulf a goodly proportion of the saccharine mass, when, lo-and-behold, a new comer, upon the same errand, seeing how matters were going, and disregarding the "*waif* " of his neighbour, silently crept *par derriere* of the sugar abstracter, and placed his own sack in readiness for a grist from the same mill. The roar of the surf prevented detection; and while *Monsieur le premier* was filling his sack from the cask, *Monsieur le second* cut a hole therein, and scooped therefrom sundry parcels, enough to fill his own; wherewith decamping unperceived, the *waifer* was left in the purgatory of absolute astonishment at finding the cask one quarter *less,* and his sack altogether *minus* of its contents, after his fatiguing operation of excavation.

with commendable curiosity; and, as he guessed at the value of the god-send, he incontinently rubbed his hands with irrepressible delight.

"Minnows and Mack'rel!" exclaimed a shrill voice, "here's a 'bone prize' for thee, friend Peleg! It's an ill wind that blows *nobody no* good, sure enough. The storm, that capsized and smashed the lighthouse last night, hath sent thee this to help pay thy tax for a new one! I am ahead of thee now, neighbour Jethro, any how. Thou mayest brag and crack over the barrel of wine, which thou fished up and brought to land t'other morning, before I was stirring; but this time I am more fortunate than thou. 'Early to bed, and early to rise,'—that's what makes men's fortunes. A bale of silks, maybe—or of Flanders lace—who knows? Solid as a pump-bolt, I see; carefully swathed and bound up, and tarred, and lashed crossways, and lengthways, and 'down the sides, and up the middle,' as the profane dancers say —not a mark nor scratch upon it, to tell the owner's name, as I'm a living kritter. Eh!—minnows and mack'rel! what's this? 'Sdeath! it's the waif of Jethro Coffin, as I live!"

Turning his eyes coastwise, the chop fallen Peleg Folger did undoubtedly see Jethro Coffin in his own person, standing at no great distance like a statue, with the spy-glass to his eye, slowly sweeping the horizon as the sun sent his first level ray across the water.

"There he stands," said the belated Peleg, "peering into the sea with his glass, and trying to spy more bales and barrels, I s'pose. Some how or 'nother it doth seem that if I should sit up all night, in order to be first up in the morning, Jethro would contrive to be on the beach afore me. But I'll see what he's arter now; and,—minnows and mack'rel!—I'll be sure to share the next with him!"—

"Neighbour Jethro!" screamed Peleg Folger, at the top of his cracked, phthisicy voice; "Je—thro—Cof—fin!"—But Jethro Coffin, availing himself of the roar of the surf, did not choose to hear; or perhaps the abstraction of his thoughts rendered him deaf to the shrill seagull voice of Peleg. Yet the morning greetings of Jethro and Peleg were destined to take place; for the latter soon made the former sensible of his presence by the sound of an accelerated asthmatic wheezing, and a slight punch in the ribs that could not be overlooked. That Peleg had recently walked fast and far, was apparent from the staccato crack of his unmusical soprano voice, which emitted a peculiarity of sound that denoted the new-comer to be considerably wind-broken. Poor Peleg was one of those prying, good-for-nothing, meddlesome bodies that vex every community; and yet he was not vicious, nor would he designedly do an ill turn to his neighbour for the world.

"How dost do, neighbour Coffin?" commenced Peleg.

"Ah—it is thou, neighbour Peleg?" asked Jethro; "thou'rt come at last, I see."

"Besure I am—didn't thou hear me half an hour ago, calling thee at the top of my voice, as I came along the beach?"

"Nay, varily;—but now I bethink me, I did hear something like thy voice, though I mistook the direction, and thought it came from those screeching birds of prey that hover over our heads. Truly thy voice so much resembles the cry of the seagull, that I was deceived by the similitude."

"Thou art no flatterer, cousin Jethro," said Peleg, endeavouring to hide his chagrin.

"Nay, thou must not take any pride in what I say," said Jethro, repeating a saying old as the hills.

"Thou hast been lucky this morning, friend Jethro;—I saw thy waif upon the package. What dost thou think it is?"

"I know not," answered Jethro, evasively; "perhaps a bale of cotton, or some such light trumpery."

"Nay, nay; thou must not tell me that:—I felt the bale all over, and—"

"I warrant thou did'st," retorted Jethro; "and thou did'st think thou had stumbled upon nice pickings, until the waif fell into thy hands—eh, friend Peleg? Thou must rise earlier, friend;—thou sleepest too late a-mornings."

"Plague on't," said Peleg, wincing under the rebuke of Jethro; "I'll let thee see that I can rise as early as thou—and earlier too, for the matter o' that. Thou'lt find me wide awake as a black-fish hearearter, I tell thee."

"I should like to see it, friend Peleg," said the taunting Jethro: "But when did'st thou ever hear of a *Folger* rising before a *Coffin?* Never, surely, since the settlement of the island."

"There thou hast lost thy reckoning, at least," said Peleg, who stood up boldly for the blood of the Folgers, and because he understood Jethro not altogether in the literal sense of his words: "Beshrew me, thou can'st not claim precedence for the Coffins: —thou know'st, well enough, that the Folgers were among the foremost of those who settled the island, even while the Indian claimed dominion over the soil;—and thou should'st know that my great-grandf'ther was the first English child born on the island. I have the start of thee there, surely—*thou* must rise *early*, if thou attempt to controvert that truth. Get up early indeed!—Marry, when did a Coffin show a parallel to a Folger in ingenuity or forecast ? I should like to know *that*,—friend Jethro. Tell me of one of thy petulant race of

'The Coffins, noisy, fractious, loud—' *

(thou knowst how the verse runs)—that hath studied over the midnight lamp, or even at thy favourite dawn of morning, that can show the handy-work of my young cousin, Walter Folger, who, unaided by the lights of science, hath constructed a clock that will, by the slow revolution of its machinery, show a hidden wonder a hundred years hence, and that hath puzzled all the clockmakers of the land: or who of the Coffins hath had the gumption to turn the lightning from its direction, like the industrious

---

*There are some doggerel verses still current among the islanders, which, better than any thing now remembered, or to be discovered in the altered manners of the people, show up the ancient character and propensities of the then prevailing families, with much truth and freedom. They were written, it is said, by a young lawyer, who came to the island about the time we speak of, and who employed his pen in rhyming, for lack of briefs. Two of the verses run thus:

" The Rays and Russells coopers are,
The knowing Folgers lazy,—
A lying Coleman very rare,
And scarce a learned Hussey;

The Coffins noisy, fractious, loud,
The silent Gardners plodding,—
The Mitchells good,—the Barkers proud;—
The Macys eat the pudding."

Ben Franklin, who, as thou know'st full well, belongs to the race of the Folgers?"*

"Go to—thy history is lame, neighbour Peleg," retorted his opponent; "if thou wilt take the trouble to examine the records of the town, thou wilt find of a surety that a direct ancestor of mine was the first English child born on the island; and thy ancestor, that thou ignorantly speakest of, only the *sixth* who can claim the earliest nativity of this soil! Tut, man!— the Coffins had the start of thy progenitor from the beginning; and their posterity will assuredly keep ahead of thy slow and easy race, depend on't. The line thou hast quoted is matched by another from the same hand, wherein the author is pleased to call—

'The knowing Folgers—*lazy!*'

Thou canst repeat the lines well—and I marvel thou did'st omit the one about the Folgers. But enough of this: Go thy ways, friend, and let me finish my morning's labour without further interruption. Thou see'st I'm busy with the glass," continued Jethro, applying the instrument to his eye, "and I'm trying to catch a glimpse of the Leviathan, if peradventure she be near enough. Take to the left, an' thou wilt;—or to the right, if thou prefer it;—for, like the peaceful patriarch of old, I offer thee the choice, and will not dispute about the direction. I would be alone, neighbour Peleg."

Peleg was not to be flung off in this cavalier manner. He had hoped to share in some of the prizes of the morning, rightly conjecturing that the storm which had endured so long would do great damage upon the sea, and, as usual, cast some of its spoils upon the island. Besides, Jethro was brisker in his motions than his companion, and took to the water, as Peleg expressed it, "as nat'ral as life."

---

*The wonderful clock, referred to in the speech of Peleg, is still clicking behind the door of the maker; and the maker himself—the Hon. WALTER FOLGER, late a member of Congress—still living in the house of his fathers—a pattern of the gentlemanly manners of the old school—a profound scholar and mathematician, and the inventor and constructer of one of the most powerful telescopes ever known, and which Nantucket still has the merit of possessing.

"Minnows and mack'rel!" exclaimed Peleg, in an undertone; "I'm not in a hurry to go on my way, and I'll e'en abide with thee yet awhile:"—and then, modulating his voice to its most conciliating key, he observed aloud—"When thou hast done with thy glass, neighbour Coffin, if thou wilt lend it to me a moment I will take a look upon the waters."

"Thou art welcome to look as long as it pleaseth thee," said Jethro Coffin, in despair, as he handed over the glass to his persevering friend.

A new subject now engaged Jethro's attention. As his eye fell upon the surf a few yards from his feet, he saw, as he thought, a small barrel buffeted by the contending waves. Adjusting his cane once more, he hastened down the beach towards his object: but, by this time, Peleg had seen the barrel also, and determined to offer his assistance.

"Stop, neighbour Jethro, stop, I say!" shouted Peleg, "and I'll help thee to land the kritter—but mark what I tell thee, afore thou layest finger upon it—I claim the halves—"

"Thy greedy covetousness shall be rewarded with *the whole*," returned Jethro, as he hurled a ship's water bucket upon the beach with the hook of his hickory staff. The wet and pliant hand-rope twined round the legs of Peleg, in its landward flight and brought him to a seat upon his mother earth, as neatly as a South American cattle-hunter could arrest a wild horse in full career.

"Minnows and mack'rel!" shouted Peleg:—and thereupon his companion took up his glass, and unceremoniously departed; leaving his short-legged friend, whom, it is but justice to say, he had unintentionally brought down, to pick himself up, and gather himself together as he might.

Doubling a small point of the island, which effectually screened him from further interruption, and ascending a convenient bluff, Jethro again adjusted his glass, and busied himself in reconnoitering every fancied speck upon the face of the sea, and every little cloud which his imagination could torture into the appearance of a distant ship.

"It is in vain!" murmured Jethro, with a painful sigh, as he closed up the joints of his glass; "she comes not. The wind has been favourable since midnight, but the adverse weather of last week has, I fear, driven her off—may heaven forefend that she should have gone to the bottom! The sun is now well up, and my long fasting warns me to bend my course homeward. I will first secure my prize upon the beach, and then hie me home to my household, and, afterwards, look in upon the condition of the factory."

Jethro now descended from his elevation, and returned to his bale of goods. With but little exertion of strength, he rolled it out of reach of the coming tide. This done, he took his way toward the town by the shortest cut, mounting in his path a succession of sand-heaps, covered with a stinted growth of seagrass, which eventually landed him on the more compact, but scarcely more productive, soil of which the main body of the island is composed. Lingering a moment upon a little sandy eminence, he determined to take another and a last look upon the sea, as his present position allowed him to compass a wider range of the horizon. Accordingly, the glass was once more brought to its focus, and lifted to the eye. Steadily moving it upon the distant line, where sky and water appeared to meet, Jethro at last arrested its motion, and attentively regarded a tiny spot, which seemed to rise and disappear at short intervals. It cannot be doubted that Jethro's heart began to beat at this interesting moment, which succeeded to that of utter hopelessness.

"Can it be that I mistake?" asked Jethro, anxiously; "I had it but now, and it occurred to me that it might be the truck at the mast-head of some lofty vessel—perhaps the Leviathan's—would that it might prove her's! But where is it gone?—My direction was South-South-East, as near as may be—but I have lost it, or it may have been nothing after all. There—there it is again!—there—and there once more! It is surely a moving object, and rises upon the sight:—steady—once more I have caught it; how my heart flutters, and my hand trembles!—verily, I am nervous to-day. If it be a vessel, the breeze is fresh and fair for her, if peradventure she makes for our port. I'll hie me to my dwelling, and rest an hour, by which time her spars will come more distinctly into view. I will then mount to the top of the beacon light—pshaw! how my memory fails me—the light was levelled to the earth by the lightning, or by the storm, as Miriam contends—no matter which; I am sick at heart, and faint from long fasting and over anxious watching—how my head turns!—"

Jethro's knees smote each other, as he stood murmuring to himself, and gazing on the broad sea with a vacant stare. His body tottered, and he sank upon the ground, overcome with a sudden tide of contending emotions, in which joyful anticipations predominated, though not unmixed with a sickening sensation of fear of some indefinable drawback upon his vision of happiness. His vessels, and above all, his only begotten son—his dearly beloved—had been absent for three long years. Was the youth well? Was he alive? Had he prospered? Had he improved in knowledge as in stature and comeliness? These, and the like, were questions which Jethro often asked himself, without the possibility of a satisfactory reply. The moment when all would be answered, was probably at hand. The yea or the nay would shortly be responded to the anxious yearnings of his heart, which was now wound up to a tension of indescribable agony and apprehension. It was too much for Jethro, and it overcame him. He felt as a fond father would naturally feel, and as a man under such circumstances *should* feel.

Jethro was found in his recumbent posture, by his quondam associate upon the beach. Peleg Folger had got tired of the fruitless task of speering for windfalls alone, and had wisely taken the shortest cut homewards which his wiser neighbour had taken before him. As he mounted the sand-spits, with the only trophy of his laborious perambulations in his hand, with its "cable-tow" thereunto appertaining, he came plump upon the body of Jethro. Here was a sight calculated to startle even the firmest islander! What to do, or how to act in the premises, did not presently occur to Peleg Folger.

"Peradventure he only sleepeth," said Peleg, musing;—"nay—that may scarcely be voluntarily done upon this damp ground! Mayhap he is dead!—Of a verity it is not death—the spirit hath not yet departed from its tabernacle—the body is yet warm, and a slight pulse stirreth within his veins.—Minnows and mack'rel!—what a dunce was I, not to divine the true cause at once," exclaimed Peleg, grasping the bucket, and waddling with unwonted celerity to the shore. The bucket was dipped into the sea, and the cool liquid sprinkled, with no sparing hand, upon the pallid face of Jethro. His eyes opened languidly; and in a few minutes he was sufficiently recovered to signify his wish to proceed on his way.

"Lend me thine arm, Peleg," faintly spoke the invalid; "I am better—the air revives me—so—I am quite well again!"

*C*HAPTER THREE.

Yes—she is ours—a home returning bark—
Blow fair, thou breeze! she anchors ere the dark.
Already doubled is the Cape—our bay
Receives that prow which proudly spurns the spray:—
How gloriously her gallant course she goes!
Her white wings flying—.
Hail to the welcome shout!—the friendly speech!
When hand grasps hand, uniting on the beach;
The smile, the question, and the quick reply,
And the heart's promise of festivity!

Byron.

WITH the kind assistance of Peleg, Jethro regained his dwelling, and rest and refreshment operated beneficially upon his frame, and set him on his legs again, bolt upright, and as stout as ever. The Oil Merchant once more sallied forth, and took his position upon the highest point of the hills back of the town of Sherburne, which overlooked the sea in the direction of the approaching vessel. The islanders, who had heard of the strange sail in sight, were already assembled at various points of lookout upon these eminences, which, being studded with windmills, were, and still are, called the "Mill Hills." Groups of men, armed with all the spy-glasses which could be mustered on the island, had assembled together in deep consultation, and were speculating upon the probabilities of the ship proving the long-looked-for Leviathan. The industrious and the laborious had quitted their various occupations suddenly, deeming the approach of a whale-ship a sufficient apology for making a holyday. Women forgot their household affairs—preparations for their frugal meals were arrested at the news,—and the dinner-pot hung neglected over the fire; beds were left half made up, and rooms half swept; the wheel was stopped, and the distaff thrown by in haste. In the general joy of the town, all but the lame and infirm crowded to the hills. Even little children partook of the excitement, and wended their way with the rest;—and the aged, too, forgot their years, and slowly hobbled toward the point of attraction. The town was soon depopulated, and its thousands were assembled in groupings upon the hills, at once quaint and picturesque. The broad brims and precise costume of the wealthier classes, were contrasted with the close paper and velvet caps, and greasy over-dresses, of the workmen from the oil factories, who felt no inequality in presence of their employers; nor did it ever enter their heads that wealth could create any distinction between man and man. The plain Quaker bonnet and sedate countenance of the matron, and the somewhat tastier hat, half concealing the rosy cheeks and liquid blue eyes of the maiden, were sprinkled among the more common and less striking head-dresses of laborious housewives, who had hastily thrown a handkerchief, or the corners of their clean homespun aprons, over their heads, for protection against the rays of the sun. For a time after the reappearance of Jethro, the silence was deep and uninterrupted, and the gaze upon the waters intense. The compressed lip, the immovable body, and the steady look at a single spot in the ocean, which rivetted the gaze, and concentrated the thoughts of the assembled congregation, formed no bad picture of a conventicle of pilgrims worshipping in the open air, and paying silent adoration to the Deity.

The upper sails of the far-off vessel were visible to the unassisted eye. Those with glasses had already made her out to be a ship, but as yet no signal appeared, to bespeak her name or identity.

"She steers dead for the island," said one of the spectators with a glass.

"Does she make any signal yet?"

"None."

"Can'st thou see her foretopsail?"

"Not yet," was the brief reply.

"What dost make of her with the glass?" demanded the catechist.

"A large three-master, with heavy spars, and every rag of sail set aloft," was the answer.

"No vessel answering that description ever touches at the island, unless it be our own whale-ships," observed a bystander.

"She must surely be a vessel of the largest class," observed the speaker with the optical instrument, "and I judge from comparison, after this manner: When Captain Starbuck came home from a whaling voyage in the old Ocean, I recollect distinctly, that although she measured good two hundred tons, and had heavy sails and spars for her class, they did not seem so large as yon ship's at her present distance, though the day was clear as a bell, and the sun shone as bright as it does to-day. Now her topsail begins to show a little—there, it creeps up!" continued the speaker, bending his glass upon the ship; "there's something painted in the canvass; but I can't make it out yet."

Other glasses had, in the meantime, been levelled at the vessel, and Jethro's among the rest. He was the first to catch the upper outline of the figure in the foretopsail, and it appeared to him to resemble the hump of a whale which had been painted by a travelling artist, before the sail had been bent. The intention of that new conceit, which has since found its way into the signal-books of most maritime nations, was to furnish a picture emblematical of the name of the ship, and, at the same time, a permanent signal whereby she could be recognized at sea.

"I do verily believe it is the Leviathan!" exclaimed Jethro.

A hum of gladness and confidence ran through the crowd, and passed from group to group at the good tidings. It was the first general interruption to the silence of the multitude which had yet occurred.

"Neighbour Jethro," screamed Peleg at a distance, in his peculiarly shrill tone, "what makes thee guess it is thy ship? Thou know'st that friend Mitchell and myself have a vessel at sea nearly as large as thine;—peradventure it may be the Columbus. Take heed that thou art not too sure, friend; it may be *my* gain, and not *thine*, for aught thou canst tell."

This doubting annunciation of the asthmatic Peleg fell like a damper upon the spirits of a large portion of the people.

"And if it *is* the Columbus," retorted Peleg's old opponent, "I wouldn't give much for *thy* share of the cargo. She has been out but a few months, and, if she has returned thus early, the vessel must have put back in distress, and consequently thy venture is clearly as good as naught. Thou keepest a profit and loss account, I hope, after the Italian method? Thou well knowest on which side thy venture will appear, in that case?"

Peleg Folger did not relish this new view of the question, but nevertheless returned to the charge lustily.

"Thou forgettest, Jethro, that once in a while, a vessel lights upon a school of whales within a few days after leaving port. A captain in thine own brigantine returned with a hundred and fifty barrels of good oil, besides much blubber, in less than a month from the day he set sail."

"But not of the sperm, neighbour Folger,—not of the sperm; that sort of fish comes not so close to us, I ween. It was wrong for the commander thou speak'st of to return before he had accomplished his voyage, unless he had met with some accident beyond remedy at sea—and I told him so. Little thanks did he get from me or mine for departing from orders. Thou rememberest the old Nantucket saying:—'obey orders, though thou should'st break owners!' It is a wholesome motto for a sea captain, and thou may'st recommend it to the observance of thy skipper of the Columbus."

"A nimble sixpence is better than the slow shilling though, since thou art in the humour for old saws," said Peleg, with exultation; "and a single barrel of common oil, returning upon us once a month, is better than many of 'parmacitty at the end; of a long voyage."

This keen encounter of tongues was cut short by the rough

exclamation of a veteran boat-steerer from Cape Cod, made within hearing of the rival dealers in oil and spermacetti. He was perched upon an arm of a windmill, and gave the word from aloft—

"Belay there—the foretawpsil looms up a bit! Take a squint at that queer fish in the canvass, as she mounts the sea. Shiver my timbers, but that's a whale's back, as clear as mud!"

"Ay—there it is, sure enough!" said the exulting Jethro Coffin: "What hast got to say now, neighbour Folger?"

"Say? Why I'm not sure on't yet: Lend me thy glass, Jethro;—it's a leetle the best one on the island—though sometimes I can't bring it to the right focus, for the plaguy creases, and joints, and night notches:—Thou call'st that ship the Levi-Nathan, dost thou?"

"Ay, the Leviathan, to be sure:—and by what name dost thou call her?"

"I don't call her any thing yet, for I can't bring her to bear."

"Look South-South-East-half-East, and close thy left eye;—what dost keep both eyes open for?"

"Now I've hit her," said Peleg;—"don't talk to me; I can't see so well for't. Why, Jethro! The foretopsail's spick and-span new! Minnows and mack'rel!—that whale is painted too well to be daubed by any of the people aboard—and thou wilt not maintain that the sail is three years old, friend Jethro?"

"Yea, verily, it is full three years old," said Jethro, chuckling; "She had two suits of new sails, as is the custom, and both foretopsails were painted before she left port. I dare say that one of them bid farewell to the bolt-ropes and took sudden leave in the storm of yesterday. Nothing can be more natural than to bend a new sail when the old one is gone— eh, Peleg?"

"I give up the argument then," said Peleg. A hearty shout from the young men, and an ill-repressed titter from the maidens followed upon the discomfiture of the speaker.

The noble ship now came booming on under a press of sail. As she diminished the distance between herself and the land, and, as it were, overcame the rotundity of the earth, her lower sails and then her hull successively appeared, until she stood in bold relief against the blue sky—

a ship of three hundred tons, with every available sail set alow and aloft. It was a gallant sight! A pardonable pride (if pride *be* pardonable) took possession of the hearts of the islanders, as some sixty years ago, they saw the good ship Leviathan, a glorious specimen of the enterprise and prosperity of Nantucket, and, at that time, the largest and noblest of American whalers, careering with the speed of the winds over the sea,

"—Like a thing of life,
That seemed to dare the elements to strife."

The gallant ship now bore away to make her passage through the sound that stretches between the island of Nantucket and the main; and the scene necessarily changes to the bay opening from the town of Sherburne. But there was no diminution in the congregation of spectators. As the vessel rounded the headlands, and approached the haven, the people on board became sensible that they were the objects of the regards and solicitude of the assemblage upon the shore. A signal was run up at the fore, which Jethro Coffin, with some little difficulty, translated from his pocket-signal book, in the words and figures following, to wit: "*all well,—2700 barrels.*" The absorbing anxiety of the multitude, for they were all more or less interested, was relieved. "All in good health, and a famous cargo—sperm of course!" was repeated from mouth to mouth, upon the authority of Jethro's translation of the signal. Then came the hurried greetings of friends, and the gratulations of neighbours, and the dislocating, hearty shaking of hands, as after a silent meeting of a Quaker congregation, when all are right glad to be relieved from coventry;—and then—nature would burst forth, even among the staid Quakers of Sherburne—then uprose a shout that made the welkin ring. The cheering was rung out again and again from hundreds of mouths with hearts in them. The men doffed the Quaker and raised high their broad brims, and the women shook out the folds of their smooth 'kerchiefs, and waved them joyously to the wind, in token of welcome.

Silence was restored by common consent, and the multitude waited for some recognition from the ship. They did not wait long without a fitting response. The crew jumped to the shrouds, and displayed themselves upon the extremities of the sharply braced yards, and in conspicuous parts of the rigging. The Leviathan swept by, and at a preconcerted signal, a roar as hearty as the rough throats of fifty bold seamen could send forth, burst from the chests of the hardy whale-fishermen, and was renewed and repeated, while the stiff tarpaulings of the crew made the customary circles in the air! She then bore away to avoid a shoal, and the command was given to "take in sail." One by one, as if by magic, the pieces of canvass disappeared under the hands of the active crew; while the few glasses upon the beach passed rapidly from hand to hand, and the sunburnt faces of old acquaintances were easily recognized in the distance, as they successively showed themselves upon the yards, and were busied with the sails.

"Stand by the anchor!" shouted the pilot, as the ship approached the harbour. As she rounded to, the few remaining sails flapped in the wind.

"All clear!" was the instant reply.

"Let go!"

> "Hoarse o'er her side the rustling cable rings,"

and the heavy plunge from the bow denoted that the good ship Leviathan, Seth Macy commander, swung at her moorings off the harbour of Sherburne, whence, three years before, she had taken her departure upon the long voyage, followed by showers of blessings from separating friends.

The small craft of the town was now in brisk motion, and the ship's deck was soon crowded with eager and inquisitive visitors. Among the foremost, but with decent gravity of demeanour, came Jethro Coffin, the owner, in his light skiff.—

"Father!"

"Ah, my son!—is it thou?" were the short, but heartfelt exclamations of Jethro and his son, as young Isaac flew to embrace his parent at the gangway.

"Seth Macy, thou'rt welcome home again," said Jethro, passing on, and approaching the quarterdeck, where stood the captain, a pleased spectator of the warm greetings that were going on in every part of his ship, to the total destruction of all discipline. But the ship was safely anchored, and the sails that had so long stretched to the breeze, neatly furled: and that was enough for Seth, for the time being.

"Jethro Coffin!—I'm right glad to give thee a shake of the hand again!" shouted Seth: and then, in a subdued, but anxious tone, he asked—"How fare my wife and family—thou can'st tell me, Jethro?"

"Well quite—well," was the brief, but satisfactory answer.

"Thanks to Providence!" exclaimed Seth; and the tears unbidden started to his manly eye. "Pshaw! I am ashamed of this weakness—and before my people too,"—continued he, dashing the tears off with the back of his hand, and turning his face away from Jethro.

"Tush, man!—they do thee credit: I love the honest heart that feels and rejoices for the welfare of its kith and kin, though it do inhabit the rough bosom of a sailor. He must have a dull soul that would not honour thee for thy tears. What saith an approved writer? 'The tear of sensibility is the most honourable characteristic of humanity.' [*] Thy wife is well, and thy little ones are getting on bravely.—So," continued Jethro, after a fitting pause, "thou hast brought home a full cargo, friend Macy?"

"Enough for thee and me—for *me* at least," answered Seth: "I have made up my mind to cast anchor ashore for a season; and I'm thinking I shall not put to sea again for a long while to come, if ever. Thou know'st I've been somewhat active in my line of life for twenty years past, and I begin to feel the stiffness of premature age coming over me. Sailors, and especially whale-fishermen, do not sleep on beds of down at sea."

"Tut, tut!—Who would have believed that a man like thee, in the full vigour of life, would talk of rest! Thou art not over five-and-forty, and that age is the very prime of manhood; unless one should get the rheumatics, and then one grows old faster than common, sure enough. But plague take rest and rheumatics—I've got a noble ship for thee, Seth;—bran new—just off the stocks—coppered to the bends, and four hundred tons! What dost say to that, neighbour? Wilt thou have her?"

"I cannot answer thee," said Seth, "until I have seen my wife, and—"

"Oh—ah—thou must see thy wife for a time, of course. I forgot thou

---

[*]Juvenal.

had'st been absent so long. But when thou art satisfied, Seth,—thou understandest me,—then I will converse with thee more upon the matter. In the meantime, it may not be amiss to inform thee that her first voyage will be but a short one. I must perforce cross the Atlantic to arrange my affairs in the mother country, which are rather loose-ends between me and my English copartners in the whaling trade. Thou'lt have time enough to think of the proposal and I'll e'en leave thee for the present. When thou can'st spare Isaac, thou wilt let him come ashore; for there are those at home who are desperately anxious to see him."

Jethro walked forward among the crew, and gave a kind word and a welcome to each individual; and presently his skiff was seen touching the shore. Within an hour after the pilot restored the command of the ship to Seth Macy, the Leviathan was deserted, and the people of the ship, from the captain downward, were among the missing; leaving the tawny cook and a few nameless adjuncts shipkeepers for the rest of the day, and undisputed masters of the noble vessel, that, but a few hours before, was riding so proudly upon the sea.

Need we lift the curtain on those homely joys that succeed the restoration of long absent kindred? It is unnecessary: they are better left to the fruitful imagination of the reader, than to be spoiled, or come tardy off, by any effort of ours to embody or portray them.

CHAPTER FOUR.

The housewife waits to roll her fleecy stores,
With all her gay drest maids attending round.
Thomson.

—Travellers tell
That in "New-England" folks live well
On good fat pork and bacon hams,
On oysters, lobsters, crabs and clams;
Pumpkin pies, roast beef and mutton—
Enough to satisfy a glutton.
If folks live there so well, why may not I
Live there as well as they?—By George! I'll try.
Pindarics.

AN eager importance sat enthroned upon the countenances of the islanders, on the morning of the "Shearing," which followed the arrival of the Leviathan. Hundreds of curious strangers from the continent had taken advantage of the recent sunshine and favourable breeze, in order

45

to participate in the "doings." No one who has ever voyaged to Nantucket at this interesting period, has sojourned with regret, or gone away unamused or uninstructed. The Shearing, which lightens many thousands of sheep of their fleece, and adds proportionately to the wealth of the people, was celebrated with a "pomp and circumstance" before the Revolution that is, perhaps, not equalled by the parade of the present day. We are not among those who value the past at the expense of the present, and would fain assert that no unseemly innovation has been suffered to creep in upon this time-honoured festival,—nor to retrench the homely, but well ordered—nay, liberal provision, that of yore was furnished forth. It is not likely, however, that the festal day will ever be forgotten, though its splendours may be somewhat dimmed. At any rate, it is still kept sacred by the islanders, and the proper day of the month of June is regularly marked upon the calendar as the advent thereof.

It is remarkable that war, though it has more than once sensibly diminished the number of the flocks annually submitted to trenchant instruments of the island shepherds—and terrible and overwhelming as it has always proved to Nantucket especially,—it is remarkable, we repeat, that it has never put its extinguisher upon the merry sheep shearing. Amidst sufferings the most intense, and privations the most appalling, it has been kept as a holyday season for more than a hundred years, and without the interregnum of a single year. Its undoubted antiquity thus carries it back to a period long prior to the existence of the Republic; while its observance, both ancient and modern, has been as regular as that of the national jubilee. It is a rational holyday of labour and recreation—of toil and profit—of enjoyment, unsullied by dissipation or excesses. Long may it endure—and long may it prove the source of happiness, and of increase of store to the worthy island dwellers!

By early cockcrowing, the plain, or common, which we have elsewhere spoken of, was ornamented with its yearly complement of camp tents and awnings of canvass, marshalled in approved array, and skirting the area in the vicinage of the sheep-pens. The flocks scattered here and there since the shearing of the previous year, had been carefully collected, and after the inspection of the marks of the owners, and the customary washing in the limpid waters of Miacomet, had been folded in temporary enclosures. They were thus kept in readiness for the operation of shearing. The poet Thomson gives a vivid description of a sheep-washing in his own land, and has saved us the trouble of entering into the same preliminary particulars:—

"They drive the troubled flocks
To where the mazy running brook
Forms a deep pool; this bank abrupt and high,
And that fair spreading in a pebbled shore.
Urged to the giddy brink, much is the toll,
The clamour much, of men, and boys,
Ere the soft fearful creatures to the flood
Commit their woolly sides. And oft the swain,
On some impatient seizing, hurls them in:
Emboldened then, nor hesitating more,
Fast, fast they plunge amid the flashing wave,
And pant and labour to the farthest shore.
At last, of snowy white, the gathered flocks
Are in the wattled pen innumerous pressed
Head above head: and, ranged in lusty rows,
The shepherds sit and whet the sounding shears."

By sunrise the selectmen, or magnates of the town, dressed in their "best bib-and-tucker," were seen moving towards the common in a body. The solemn importance of the office, and the magnitude of their calling, were observable in their prim and sedate carriage, while acting in their official capacity of umpires or judges in the division of the fleece, or in determining the ownership of the sheep whose marks had been obliterated or defaced. Next came the inhabitants and their guests— staying not for precedence, or the order of going forth—but bending their hasty steps to the common. These were immediately followed by a train of carts and calêches, or those little two-wheeled vehicles peculiar to Nantucket, and adapted, by their uncommon lightness and small friction of the hub and axle to the sandy soil—if such may be dignified by the name of soil which forms the super-stratum of the island.[*] The heavier and more capacious carriages were laden with the profusion of good things, carefully provided against the great day by every family, and destined for the comfortable refreshment of the body during the progress of the shearing. Each family had reared its own tent, and now garnished the suburban board with its choicest provisions. With some, the savings of a whole year were liberally and anxiously appropriated to furnish the various appointments of tents and camp equipage, and the other paraphernalia of meats, bread stuffs, and vegetables. The rare teas of the East, so shortly destined to provoke a bloody quarrel between Great Britain and her stubborn daughter; the confectionery of the West Indies, and the substantial *et cetera* of their own island and adjacent coast; foreign wine, of generous vintage—seldom used except upon rare occasions, by these people of simple habits; home-made fermentations and pleasant beverages; the freshest produce of the domestic dairy, in all its variety of rose-impregnated butter, yielded by means of the tender herbage of June; pot-cheese, curds and cream, and the venerable cheese, which in distant countries would pass current for "Parmesan;" pies of dried fruit, custards,

---

[*]It is to be feared that the good people of Nantucket have but a poor notion of the capabilities of their own soil—for there are but few attempts made to cultivate it. Yet, whenever the attempt is made, the crops are found to be abundant.

"The island of Nantucket," observes Mr. JENKS, in a late address to the people, upon the anniversary of the Declaration of our national Independence, "has been spoken of as '*a barren sand bank*:'"—and he adds—"those who come hither with this impression, however, depart with exclamations of pleasure and surprise upon their lips, at the utter disproval of their prejudices."

Still, we must say, this disproval does not appear from any great exertion which the inhabitants themselves have made, to convert the apparently sterile, but in fact productive soil, into farms and garden spots. They must be insensible to their own agricultural advantages, or they would not have merited the following gentle rebuke of their public spirited orator:—

"I have already hinted at the opinion usually held by strangers abroad, touching the supposed sterility of our soil. From this opinion, every individual who has inspected the qualities, and studied the capabilities of that soil, will at once dissent. An intelligent gentleman, learned in agricultural science, recently passed a few days upon our island, and acquainted himself particularly with its topography. In the course of his examination of our lands, and his inquiries in regard to their products, he expressed his surprise at the little

and tarts of cranberry; cakes of flour, mixed up with ginger and treacle, and the more costly and ambitious poundcake, stuffed with raisins, and frosted over with an incrustation of sugar, resembling ice; puddings of bread, of rice, and of Indian meal, enriched with eggs; pickles of cucumber, beans, beets, and onions;—these and all the other eatables and accompaniments, which a prudent and well instructed housewife can imagine, or put down upon a catalogue, after a week's thinking and preparation, were plentifully provided, and importunately—after the good old American fashion,—piled and pressed upon the pewter platters of the thronging guests, as long as the shearing lasted, or a hungry customer could be found.

While the tables beneath the tents were spread with snow-white linen, and decorated with the choicest and best provisions by the matrons, the sturdy and vigorous men were hard at work among the sheep. It was the pride and boast of these people, in that day, to rear the best sheep in the colonies;—and wool as fine, though without the Merino cross, and mutton as fat as any found in America, were the produce of the excellent breed possessed by the Nantucketers, whose flocks in the aggregate numbered some twenty thousand head. It was, therefore, no trifling job to shear the fleece from so many animals; and, although a day of leisure

---

comparative attention paid to the cultivation of the soil. 'There is scarcely an acre,' he remarked, 'upon the face of your little world, which is not capable, by judicious management, of being converted into farms, more profitable, by far, than very many at the East, or in the famed West.' Farms derive their value chiefly from contiguity to a ready market; and this we have at all times. Most of the productions of our soil are known to excel greatly in quality similar articles raised in other places: for example, our corn, and garden vegetables generally. The husbandman may *here* reap the fruits of his toil as fully as elsewhere: so that whether we plough the land or the sea, we may as safely calculate on adequate returns. One observation made by the friendly visitor to whom I have alluded, I feel tempted here to repeat—since it expresses not only a high opinion of the physical properties of our sequestered isle, but conveys a delicate compliment to the moral qualities of its inhabitants:—'You require,' said he, '*nothing*—positively nothing, but trees and tillage, to make Nantucket an earthly paradise.'"

Plant trees, therefore ye Nantucket people! or render yourselves obnoxious to the imputation of Dean Swift, who says that "no man is a *good* citizen, unless he can boast of having got children,—built a house,—and *planted trees!*"

Editor

and pastime to most of the islanders, especially the females, it was to the men a busy and laborious season, and, at the same time, to strangers a curious and highly gratifying display.

> "—The glad circle round them yield their souls
> To festive mirth, and wit that knows no gall.
> Meantime their joyous task goes on apace:
> Some, mingling, stir the melted tar, and some,
> Deep on the new-shorn vagrant's heaving side
> To stamp the cipher, ready stand;—
> Others th' unwilling wether drag along:
> And, glorying in his might, the sturdy boy
> Holds by the twisted horns th' indignant ram.
> Fear not, ye gentle tribes!—'tis not the knife
> Of horrid slaughter that is o'er you waved;
> No, 'tis the swain's well guided shears."

It was not, however, the congregation of the flocks, and the temptations for the appetite, that solely constituted the interest of the scene. The shearing, as it is called, is seized upon, also, as a fitting occasion for the free interchange of those friendly courtesies that so signally distinguish and cement the families of the island, whose pursuits and whose gains,—whether on land or on sea,—are in a measure common to the whole. The success of one is sure to bring gain and prosperity to his neighbour. Their sheep and their cattle feed and herd together on the same unenclosed pasturage, which of itself is owned in common by the islanders, and denominated the property of the town. The success of a whaling ship at sea brings joy and worldly store, not only to the owners, but to the crew and their families in their due proportions. The people are thus linked together by the strongest ties;—by a sort of community of interest. The failure of pasturage, or blight in the flocks, curtails the enjoyments of all; and a disastrous voyage affects, in the same degree, the property and happiness of all the members of the little community—

—"If there is sorrow there,
It runs through many bosoms;—but a smile
Lights up, in eyes around, a kindred smile."

But there are other considerations that weigh with the inhabitants, and mark the wisdom of the founders, if so they may be called, of this annual festival. Friends and relatives, long sundered and kept apart by a wide expanse of water, now make it a point to cross the Sound which divides them; and a pretty general assemblage upon the island at the shearing, though but for once in the year, compensates in a considerable degree for the long separation, and for the slender and unvarying amusements of the isolated settlement. The reunion is not unlike that of the aged grandfather who assembles his children and his grandchildren, during the Christmas holydays, at his own festive board; and, by promoting general hilarity and exciting the buoyant mirth of his youthful descendants, adds thereby to his own happiness, while he contributes to that of those who surround him.

The hour of eating approached, and was welcomed by the worshipful Selectmen, "and all others in authority," as well as by the industrious clippers of wool and the gadders after amusement; who all sat down, as they could find places in the tents, and intermingled without ceremony. It may perhaps be a work of supererogation to inform the reader that, thus circumstanced, they fell to work upon a substantial and "glorious breakfast." To attack and demolish huge mountains of toast, vast broiled slices of the unequalled salmon, caught by the Indians and brought in cars from the waters of the wild region of the Penobscot, cutlets of veal, slices of mutton, ham boiled and peppered in various dark spots, and garnished at intervals with cloves, beefsteaks swimming in butter, the finest flavoured fish which but an hour before were sporting in the sea,— but which now appeared in the various garbs of "roasted, baked, and boiled, and brown:"—we say, to attack and demolish these comfortable appliances, and to wash them down with a strong mug of coffee or tea, was but the work of a few minutes; for the Americans are quick eaters, and the invigorating air, and the morning's exercise had whetted the appetite of the multitude. And yet there was enough for all, and many baskets to spare, without the imputation of a miracle.

The savoury and hearty meal was further supplied, or we may say "topped off," with amazing quantities of a species of animal called by the islanders the "*Pooquaw,*"and sometimes by the other Indian name of "*Quohog.*" These are found in great numbers on the sandy shores of the island; and, but for their great plenty in the northern parts of America, they would be esteemed a delicious luxury.

Lest we may not be well understood while we speak of the inimitable quohog, and, by our obscurity, engender doubts of its inexhaustible abundance, it may be well to inform the gentle reader and enlighten his understanding. Its aboriginal name, and that which it still holds in the oldest parts of America, is just as we have written it down. Nevertheless the "*quo-hog*" hath neither bristles nor tail, nor is it a quadruped, as its name would seem to import; but it is in truth a species of shell-fish, which naturalists, in the plenitude of their lore, denominate *bivalvular*. It is grievous further to say, in explanation, that its original and sonorous name, and that by which it is still known in Nantucket, has been made to yield, by the pestilent spirit of innovation in the middle states, to the flat, insipid and unsounding title of—the clam! Spirit of the erudite Barnes, the conchologist—spirits of Sir Joseph Banks, and Sir Humphrey Davy— Spirit of the learned Mitchell—could you not, in the course of your long and well-spent lives, hit upon a more expressive and euphonious jaw- cracker for the persecuted quohog, than the abominable name of "*clam?* "

The manner of cooking the quohog in the most palatable way at the "*Squantums*" of Nantucket, as oracularly given out by the knowing Peleg Folger, was resorted to on this occasion, to eke out the foregoing meal. Even unto this day, some of the eastern people adopt the same method, to "stap the vitals" of the quohog at their "roast-outs " or forest junketings. As to the peculiar mode of cooking, we adopt the argument of Peleg, even as he learnedly discussed the matter while arranging a bed of the aforesaid bivalvular shell-fish on the morning of the shearing. Imprimis— The quohogs were placed upon the bare ground, side by side, with their mouths biting the dust. The burning coals of the camp-fires, which had done the office of boiling and broiling, were removed from under the cross-trees, where hung the pot and tea-water kettle, and applied plentifully to the backs of the quohogs. In a few minutes after the application of the fire, the cooking was declared to be at an end, and the roasting of the quohogs complete. The steam of the savoury liquor, which escaped in part without putting out the fire, preserved the meat in a par-boiled state, and prevented it from scorching, or drying to a cinder, and the whole virtue of the fish from being lost. The ashes of the fire were effectually excluded by the position in which the animal was placed at the beginning; and the heat as completely destroyed the tenacity of the hinge which connected the shells.

"And now," said Peleg, "take a few on thy platter; remove the upper shell, and apply a lump of fresh butter and a sprinkling of pepper and salt." Our blessings on thee, Peleg Folger. The morsel, if taken hot, might be envied by an eastern emperor, whose palate is pampered by bird-nest delicacies;—or by the exquisite gourmand of any nation. But in America, who eats a clam or a quohog? None but the wise—and that includes a majority of the people;—the fashionable, never—more's the pity.

"Just in time for the quohogs, eh?" exclaimed Peleg Folger, as, blowing like a porpoise, he ran his head under the tent of Jethro Coffin;—"A meal without quohogs goes for nothing with me. But, minnows and mack'rel! as near as I can make it out, I've come behind the feast, and I'm in a fair way to have the quohogs served up without the meal;—and it all comes of my running after the rascally ram that jumped over the shear-pen, followed by the other four-and-thirty imps of Sathan, that the S'lackmen put under my charge to gather wool from. Cousin Miriam,—a cup of thy tea,—ah, it's always the best on the island; where did'st thou light on it, pray ?—a slice of that ham, Jethro—a little toast and a few of thy pickles, Miriam,—and then—I shall be ready for the quohogs. Whew! I'll just throw my coat on the bench, and hang my wig on the peg of the upright there;—now then for a morsel to stay my stomach. I hope thy tea is hot, Miriam, for I'm summat warm with running; and hot tea, thou know'st, cools one so nicely."

Thus warbled the musical Peleg, as, with the utmost nonchalance, he took possession of a seat at the board of Jethro. It was nevertheless no intrusion;—he might have done the same thing with impunity at any other table on the common. His own tent, had he sought it among the many similar temporary shelterings, he would have found occupied by some of his neighbours and friends, who cared as little as himself where they sated their hunger or slaked their thirst. When both these had been reasonably appeased, and Peleg began to be afflicted with loss of appetite, he came to discover that other persons besides himself were in the tent;— though Jethro and Miriam had made their escape, leaving Ruth and Isaac to do the honours of the morning to Peleg. Between the pauses of his slackening efforts at mastication, he found leisure to address himself to the persons present; for when not employed in eating it was painful to restrain his tongue.

"So, Isaac, thou hast found thy way to the shearin' again," said Peleg: "How didst thou relish the sea?—rather sickish at the stomach once-in-a-while, eh? Didst thou strike a whale, Isaac?"

"Besure I did," answered Isaac, with the proud bearing of a young whaler: "Dost thou think I would be gone three years, and not use a harpoon on a whale?"

"But thou'rt quite young, Isaac, and hardly strong enough to do execution on a 'parmacitty."

"Young or old, cousin Peleg, I've done the deed more than once, and have fairly earned my share of the Leviathan's cargo."

"I warrant me," said Peleg, with a knowing wink,—"young as thou wast, thou hadst some damsel in thine eye, who told thee not to come back without killing a whale, under penalty of losing her favour. Thou hast heard of the female combination at Sherburne? Thy sister Ruth can tell thee all about it, and translate to thee the meaning of my words."

We must deter the explanation of the allusion here made by Peleg, to the next chapter.

CHAPTER FIVE.

The world is in pain
Our secrets to gain,
　　But still let them wonder and gaze on:—
They ne'er can divine
The word nor the sign
　　Of a free and accepted Mason.

Burns.

Lawyer. You have broken the thread of my discourse.—
Cobbler. Wax it then.

Old Play.

WE have the best authority in giving the following details which go to unravel the hint that Peleg gave at the conclusion of the last chapter, about a combination of women at Nantucket. We hope the reader will not skip over what we are now going to say, because he will find, hereafter, that it has an important bearing upon the actions of more than one

55

character who will be found figuring in our veritable pages.

Peleg Folger, no doubt, alluded to an association of females which existed about this time, and perhaps still exists, at Nantucket, who had constituted themselves a secret society, after the manner of the Freemasons. Some of the male islanders had established a masonic lodge at Sherburne, under the belief that it would prove beneficial to them, while pursuing their profession abroad upon the seas. A striking instance of its utility had been quite recently experienced by one of its members, which, perhaps, more than anything else, had contributed to the recent rapid growth of the fraternity.

A Nantucket captain, of the race of the Colemans, as the records of the lodge inform us, sailing a colonial vessel,—or, in other words, an American ship under the British flag,—had been met at sea by a French cruiser. England and France, those near neighbours, but inveterate hereditary enemies,—were then at war,—as indeed they had been, with but little intermission, for seven centuries or more. The colonial vessel was compelled to heave to, within reach of the Frenchman's guns, and the captain was commanded to go on board with his papers. With a desponding heart, the American mounted the side of the man-of-war, expecting nothing but confiscation and imprisonment. As a sort of desperate resort, little dreaming of its efficacy in this instance, the Nantucketer carelessly made the mystic sign as he approached the French commander, who at once gave a recognition! and, instead of being turned over to the inferior officers of the ship, or left to amuse himself as he might, while his papers were undergoing scrutiny, the Nantucket captain was courteously invited into the cabin, where a confidential intercourse was soon established between them, which ended in the dismissal of the American, with his papers untouched. A supply of fruit and wines, had, in the meantime, been deposited in the boat alongside, by order of the generous Frenchman. As the American was handed over the side, with the neat and becoming ceremony of a man-of-war, his extraordinary host whispered in his ear—"Prenez garde à vous, mon capitaine:—Peut être, si nous avons à faire ensemble une autre fois, vous ne me trouverez pas si bon enfant:—adieu!"

"Christmas!" exclaimed the Nantucketer, as he filled away;—"If that *an't* an escape? Well, who would have thought it? I should have no objection to meet just such a chap once a week at least. So much for masonry:—the women may jibe and jeer at me as much as they please when I get home; but if masonry can save a ship and cargo for my owners, and my own precious body from the dungeons of a French Bastille, and get me three dozen of wine and a basket of grapes to boot, why, 'egad, I'm strongly tempted to believe there is more in it than a name!"

The impulse given to Free-masonry upon the island, when this transaction became known, made the institution a favourite with all classes of the men, and especially with the seafaring portion of the inhabitants. The women, too, who in all ages have been supposed to be constitutional contemners of secrets and secret societies, abated much of their opposition to the masonic association; and some of them went so far as to urge their husbands to become familiar with its mysteries. But, out of this situation of affairs, a rival society sprang up among the women; and the tables of secrecy, with all the attendant winks, and nods, and significant looks, archly implying—"*we* know a thing or two," and "*we* understand,"—were retorted upon the men, with a laughable, and sometimes irritating, effect.

The spirit of anti-masonry was thus abroad among the females of Nantucket; and it may hereafter furnish the subject-matter of grave disquisition for prying antiquarians in political matters, and lead to the discussion, if not the settlement, of the important question, whether the origin of the party called "*anti-masonic,*" which now seeks to control the political destinies of some of the most populous states of our Republic, may not be fairly traceable to the opposition first made to the institution by the Nantucket women; and not, as some imagine, to the abduction of William Morgan.

It was never fairly understood what were the secret obligations of these female masons; and it was even doubted whether they had any "secrets worth knowing,"—inasmuch as no important operations, either of good or evil tendency, were known to be put in practice in the little town of Sherburne, or to disturb the world at large. This much, however, came afterwards to be divulged:—An obligation, if not under the solemnity of an oath or affirmation, was at least assumed by the novitiate under the charge of the officiating mistress, that she would favour the courageous whale-fisherman, under every circumstance, in preference to a stranger and a landsman, if the alternative should ever occur. The letter and the spirit of this charge, were for a long time pertinaciously adhered to by the unmarried members; and some of them were known to carry it so far, as to make it a *sine qua non* in permitting the addresses of their suitors, that they should have struck their whale, at least, before the smallest encouragement would be given, or a favouring smile awarded as the earnest of preferment.

It has been shrewdly suspected that the chivalric ordeal thus enforced by the fair maidens of the isle, was set on foot by some of the patriotic whale-fishermen and oil merchants of the place, in order to perpetuate a nursery of peculiar seamen: while, in doing so, they were sure to secure valorous husbands, and a certain competency for their daughters, as well as a monopoly of the trade to the island. The intermarriage of so many whale-fishermen with the daughters of whale-fishermen, until almost all the inhabitants did, in reality, claim near relationship, and call each other "cousin,"—at all events would seem to point that way, and, to favour the presumption. Certain it is, that the daughters of some of the wealthiest men of the island, had already formed a compact not to accept the addresses of sighing swains, much less to enter into the holy bands of matrimony with any but such as had been on a voyage, and could produce ample proof of successfully striking a whale; and among the rest were Ruth Coffin,—a girl, as we have elsewhere taken occasion to observe, scarce sixteen years old,—and her bosom companion at school,—the amiable and lovely Mary Folger, about her own age, and the daughter of our friend Peleg;—who, with all his peculiarities, be it said, *en passant*, was a man of substance, and of good mercantile repute.

It would seem, then, that the determination of his daughter Mary, or, perhaps, the general determination of the young females of the island, was familiar to Peleg, by the manner of his intimating to Isaac Coffin that, young as he was, he had sought the favour of some fair mistress, by venturing to approach within striking distance of a whale. Certes, the saying of Peleg has carried us away from the natural flow of our discourse, and brought on this long episode, which, we hope, will be tolerated by the reader, as explanatory of Peleg's allusion in the last chapter, when bantering young Isaac in regard to his prowess. We will again take up the thread of the narrative.

"Nay, Cousin Peleg, the sea is *my* mistress," answered the son of Jethro; "the girls do not trouble my head at all, I assure you:—but, if they did, you will acknowledge that I am duly qualified to make pretension?"

"Yea, verily; but, with all thy freaks upon the whaling ground, I fear the damsels will question the growth of thy beard:—get me a platter of the quohogs, Isaac, and the butter also, and the pepper and salt likewise— there,—thou may'st go now, and try the virtue of thy beard upon the cherry-cheeks of the young maidens, provided thou can'st catch them."

Glad to escape from the service and annoyance of Peleg, Isaac forthwith departed to join the merry lads on the common,—several of whom were his messmates in the Leviathan. Ruth still remained to keep him company, and to replenish his platter. It was now *her* turn to undergo a questioning; but she did not suffer the infliction with the most exemplary Christian fortitude.

"Ruthy, my dear; why art thou not out upon the common, with the other youngsters?" commenced Peleg.

"To speak the truth, Cousin Peleg," answered Ruth, half vexed by the prolonged meal of her tormentor, "I should have been there long ago, if thou had'st not made such desperate love to the quohogs."

"Ah, Ruthy, Ruthy, thou must not be so snappish with thy Cousin Pillick:—I've got so'thing to tell thee that will pay thee for waiting on me;—a few more of thy nice quohogs, Ruthy. What dost think?—While I was giving chase to that wayward and most 'cursed ram, I met two young strangers who had just landed."

"Did'st thou measure the prints of their feet in the sand, Cousin Peleg, as the Coofs* say we do those of all strangers?" asked Ruth, not being able

---

*"Coofs,"—"Off-islanders,"—or people living on the continent:—a term of derision, or reproach.

to discover any thing particularly amusing in the twaddle of Peleg, and wishing to cut short the sitting which abridged her morning's ramble.

"Nay, child, I did not think of that;—though I have done so before now when I've seen strange tracks on the beach, in order to satisfy myself whether they were the steps of a new-comer, or the prints of a new pair of shoes. For the matter of that, Ruthy I know all the shapes of the neighbour's feet, and can easily find out by the impression in the sand who has been travelling. Some are long and slim,—some short and dumpy,—some turn their toes in, like our Indians,—some turn them out,—some make long steps, and some,—like thyself, Ruthy,—mince their steps a little. Everybody has a peculiarity in the placing or the shape of the foot, which an observant man, like myself, can easily distinguish. But that is not what I want to tell thee, Ruthy. Listen now—wilt thou?"

"Well, Cousin Peleg, I'm listening;" said Ruth, as she sat down, and prepared for a long story.

"Thou must know, then, that as I was chasing that 'tarnal ram, I met the two strangers."

"Thou hast said that afore, Cousin Peleg," interrupted Ruth.

"Did I?—Then thou'lt remember it the better for repeating. The two young strangers, seeing me hot foot in chase arter the infernal ram, stood stock still ahead of the kritter. 'Stop that ram!' says I,—'I can't,' says one on 'em; 'I've got no stopper.' 'Turn him, then,' says I, *turn* him!' 'He's *right* side out already,' says he. But the kritter *did* turn short about, notwithstanding; and, finding no escape, he bolted right at me:—so, in trying to avoid a punch in the stomach, I gave a spring into the air, and threw out my legs to let him pass through—but, would'st thou believe it?—instead of clearing the imp of Sathan, I landed stem to starn smack upon the back of the abomination! Off went my hat, and in it my best wig that hangs on the peg yonder. 'John Gilpin, by Jove!' exclaimed one of the youngsters. 'You're right,' says the other—

> 'Away went Gilpin, and away
> Went Gilpin's hat and wig;'—

and then they both roared out in an unseemly horse-laugh at my misfortune. But who is that John Gilpin that they mistook me for? Dost thou know him?"

"Not I, as I'm a sinner," said Ruth, convulsed with laughter at the picture of a flying Cupid which Peleg drew of himself.

Peleg now came to the conclusion that there must be something ludicrous in his misfortune, by its making everybody laugh who heard of the odd mishap; and, hastily betaking himself to his trotters, he retreated to his sheep-pen of "four and thirty imps of Sathan," which had been placed in his charge by the "S'lackmen." He stopped a moment at the entrance of the tent, to don his coat and wig; and, like Grumio while consoling the "good Curtis," he took his leave with a significant shake of the head, and a determined rap upon the crown of his enormous drab sombrero, and muttered as he went:—

"Thou'rt not over-mannerly, Ruth, to laugh so immoderately at my adventure with the ram. If thou hadst maintained a becoming gravity, I would have told thee more of the two strange gallants, which would have made thy ears tingle again; but—minnows and mack'rel!—thy ears may itch with curiosity for a season, before I scratch them for thee!"

Ruth now departed to seek her companion Mary, with whom she had agreed to commence a tour of that sort of inquisitive inspection among the tents, which of late years is better understood by the polished expression of "making a few morning calls;" or in plainer phrase, prying into the domestic economy of one's neighbours.

The timely arrival of the Leviathan, and the recruits from the continent who had lately come to the island, contributed in no small degree to people the common, and to give life and animation to the scene. The broad plain, which, on every other day in the year, presented a quiet and uniform appearance, sprinkled with small droves of sheep and a few neats-cattle peacefully cropping the short grass, now showed unwonted signs of activity and gayety, mixed up with more or less of the bustling importance of the middle-aged, and the stalking gravity peculiar to the habits of the older inhabitants. The young men and maidens, in their gayest attire, began to mingle in groups on the plain, or to fill up the little two-wheeled cars, to make a drive round the circuit of the grounds marked out for the encampment.

The young men, who had met Peleg Folger while in pursuit of the refractory ram, had visited the island as total strangers, being enticed thither by the reputation of the shearing and the hope of beguiling a few hours among the throng. What sort of reception they should meet with did not give them any uneasiness. They were on the *qui vive* for pleasure and pastime, and they trusted to circumstances to make themselves acquainted with the "natives." Strangers, unheralded, were not closely scrutinized upon occasions like the shearing; and it was sufficient passport to the hospitality of the friendly islanders, to come among them at a time like this, simply with the appearance of respectability and civility of behaviour. The breeding of the strangers could not be gainsayed or questioned by any person except Peleg; and, it appeared, they had suffered but temporarily in his good opinion, as Ruth would have been presently informed, had she listened patiently and soberly to the detail of his rencontre with the pugnacious ram.

When they discovered that Peleg had been unceremoniously capsized by the horned animal, and that he lay motionless after his fall, they checked their ill-timed mirth, and hastened to his relief. Raising him carefully and attempting to seat him upon the ground, they surmised that he had either been much frightened, or considerably injured by the violence of the tumble, as animation was entirely suspended, and not the slightest indication of the pulse perceptible. The younger of the two, assuring himself of the condition of the patient by application of his fingers to the wrist, hastily drew a case from his fob; and, thereupon, winding a ligature round the arm of Peleg, which had previously been stript of its covering, he selected a lancet and made an incision in a vein. The blood flowed, and with it returned animation to the body of Peleg Folger. The bleeding was soon stanched, and the unfortunate man was well again. Falling in the loose and yielding sands, he had escaped bruises or wounds; and as it happily proved, he had been only prodigiously frightened. Peleg felt no inconvenience from the loss of blood, which had been inconsiderable; and he rose up, adjusted his clothes, and brushed the sand from his coat and breeches, while his companions replaced his wig and hat.

"Friends, you are welcome to Nantucket," said Peleg, in a tone which evinced his solicitude to do the honours of the day and the place with dignity. "But pray what is the matter? what has happened to me? I was but now astraddle of a run-away ram—"

"Yes, Mr. Gilpin—"

"Thou mistakest;—my name is Pillick Folger."

"Indeed!" ejaculated the man of the lancet;—"you so much resembled a friend of mine by the name of Gilpin,—'John Gilpin, of credit and renown'—that I did not hesitate to call you by that name. But I beg pardon, Mr. Fogrum, if that be your title—"

"Pillick Folger, men call me, my friend."

"Your fall from the beast, Mr. Folger, was like to prove unlucky for us; for without you we should have been destitute of a responsible person to introduce us to your good people. We are told you make merry to-day on the island; and so, as we found you in rather a sad pickle, and in want of a little professional aid, while we at the same time were in want of a pilot, I made bold to drive a lance into a vein;—you understand the rest."

"Thou art a physician, I s'pose? And yet thy red coat doth not betoken thy professional acquirements."

"I am, notwithstanding, a bit of a doctor, sir."

"And your friend here in the black coat is—"

"A limb of the law, sir;" answered the doctor.

"A what?" asked Peleg.

"A lawyer, sir."

"And what sort of trade is that?" demanded Peleg, who had never heard of a lawyer before.

"It is an honourable profession, sir," said the doctor;—"one that 'doth make the meat it feeds on,' and therefore a very economical and profitable trade, sir: it first makes mankind miserable, and then humanely puts them out of their misery; and thus it has the advantage over mine own humble profession, which is only instrumental in putting those out of misery who suffer under the dispensation of Providence. Pray, Mr. Folger, have you never heard of a land-shark among the deserts of Nantucket?"

"Nay, verily," answered Peleg, in the honest simplicity of his heart; "the animal, if it be one, hath never been found on these shores—but our mariners tell of a ravenous speshy of fish, which swims around the carcass of the whale, when it lies by the side of the ship, and the people are slicing away at the blubber. Wo betide the man that loses his foothold, and slips into the sea:—he is seized in a twinkling by the greedy *man- shark!*"

"The *man-shark!*"—that's the animal, sir, and a most dainty fish it is;—man, and man only is his prey. 'There be land-rats and water-rats,' Mr. Folger; and the man-shark is to the sea what the lawyer is to the land. Both lie in wait for the unfortunate man who loses his foothold—and then farewell to the poor devil!"

"And dost thou call the trade of thy friend *honourable?*" asked Peleg, casting a terrified glance at the law expounder.

"Nay, Mr. Folger," observed the man of sheepskin, "my friend, the doctor, is quite too severe upon the profession of which I have the honour to be a member. We are simply the agents who appear in the courts, to settle controversies according to the laws of the land, and—"

"And, to gain your point," interrupted the doctor, "you strive to make the worst appear the better reason, and prove to us that white is black, and black is white. It is an easy thing, Mr. Fulcrum, for a lawyer of skill to whitewash a character that is darkly stained; and still easier to blacken one that is stainless. Have you none of the tribe on the island?"

"The 'Tucketers would have no use for such an animal," said Peleg.

"And how do you get along without such necessary evils! Have you no justices of the peace? Do you never quarrel upon Nantucket?"

"Of a verity we do not quarrel," said Peleg, seriously; "and if at any time we have cause of difference, touching the straying of our sheep, or the division of our oil, we choose our arbitrators and our umpires, and sometimes we go before our s'lackmen—"

"*Slackmen?*—Oh, I understand—they are the drones of the town, I suppose," observed the man of physic.

"They are chosen once a year by the people, from among the wise and the upright," said Peleg.

"Good qualifications, those; and does not King George send a magistrate or a governor to lord it over you?—Strange, that he should not have planted one of his minions or bastards here, to save you the trouble for thinking for yourselves. By-the-by, it would be difficult for so tender an exotic to thrive in this sandy soil of yours. Whew!—Knee-deep, by Jupiter!"

The knight of the lancet, unused to the heavy sands of the island, now called a halt, to breathe a little, and Peleg continued:—

"As I was telling thee—sometimes we choose our arbitrators indifferently, and sometimes we go before the s'lackmen, whenever we differ among ourselves. Our nay is nay, and our yea is yea, always;—the story is soon told,—but no man ever forgets himself so far as to exaggerate;—nor does he attempt to make white appear black, as thou say'st. We ask for no man to lay down the *law* for us;—it is *justice* between man and man that we're arter. Why, minnows and mack'rel!—it is not once a year we have an arbitration; and an expounder of the laws—psha—he would starve among us—of a verity he would not make salt to his porridge! As for justices of the peace, we have heard of *them*, nay, now I think on't, a justice did come over here once upon a time from the continent, (we are under the government of the Bay Colony, thou know'st;)—'Squire Thomas I think they called him—but it's a long time ago, and I'm not sartin as to his name. Old Captain Macy, father of Seth Macy, who came home yesterday in the Levi Nathan, lost a noble cow one day from the common, and it was thought wonderful strange what could ha' come on her. We all gi'n her up for lost, and made up our minds that she had got drowned, or some sich thing, when, lo-and-behold, a neighbour of ours, Judah Swift, afterwards Captain Swift, was fishing and digging for quohogs (we call them *pooquaws* sometimes) off the other end of the island one day, and what should he see but the identical self-same kritter that belonged to old Captain Macy, drinking in the edge of the water on the beach—the kritters love salt once in a while, thou knowest. Judah Swift knew her by her stumpy tail, and because one of her horns twisted down towards her eye. The old captain had sawed off the tip, thou see'st, to keep it out of the eye, for in a month or so it would have steered smack into it;—as it was, however, it made her squint pretty considerably. She was a famous cow, with a bag as yellow as gold;—and that's always a sign of a good cow. What does neighbour Swift do but slip a knot over the cow's horns, and arter hauling his boat upon the beach, he led her, nothing loath, towards home. He hadn't got a hundred yards, before a 'tarnal Indian,—one of the tribe of lazy scamps on the island,—came up and claimed the cow as his'n. Swift knew better; but as the Indian insisted on't, he untied her and went back to his boat—well knowing that the kritter couldn't leave the island without the knowledge of the owner. Captain Macy went the next day, and demanded his cow; but the Indian still said she was his'n, and told a cock-and-a-bull story about dreaming for a cow, and how the Great Spirit had sent her to him. 'I'll spirit thee, thou thieving skunk—if thou don't spirit my cow back again,' said Captain Macy;—but all would not do. So he went over to the continent for a justice of the peace and a constable, who soon settled the hash, and restored the cow to the captain; and then the 'squire ordered the constable to give the copper-coloured thief forty lashes, save one, with the cat-o'-nine tails. The whole tribe of Indians was called together on the common by the s'lackmen, to witness the punishment of the offender, which old Tashima, the chief, said was just and right enough. But the captain begged the Indian off—and arter he got him clear, he brought his cow up, and said to the fellow: 'There, thou scoundrel,—take her! I'll let thee know that justice can be had on the island! The kritter has been proved to be mine, and that's all I care about. Take her, and carry her to thy wigwam—but never steal thy neighbour's property again.' That Indian affair was the first and the last business that ever required the presence of Justice Thomas and the constable at Nantucket."

"Are there many Indians remaining on the island?" demanded the doctor.

"A hundred, perhaps, and all told," replied Peleg; "and they are pretty well managed by old Tashima, who preaches to them on the Sabbath or First day, and keeps a school for the little Indian children on the other days of the week. They are a poor, spiritless, thieving race, and abominably treacherous withal. To keep them from becoming a charge to the town, when they refuse to work for the support of their squaws and pappooses, the s'lackmen send them aboard the whale-ships, where they are compelled to earn a share of the cargo equal to that of any other mariner afore-the-mast. They possess a dogged disposition, and will endure much hard labour at sea without complaining. To be sure, they skulk a great deal; but, in pulling the oar in a whale-boat, when the eye of the mate or the boat-steerer is upon them, they do their duty well enough. Thou canst see, from this little elevation, the tops of some of their wigwams at Miacomet; and there is another settlement of the lazy varmints at Eat-Fire. As thou art a stranger here, (which one may well imagine by thy flaming dress,) thou wilt be welcome at the hamlet; and, besides, thou wilt be amused by calling on the old chief, and inspecting for thyself the economy of the tribe."

CHAPTER SIX.

No plumed cap was on his head—
  No sword was at his thigh—
And of the band which erst he led,
  Not one was standing nigh;
    His hour of pomp and pride was o'er,
    He was a battle-chief no more—
    His friends—his followers—were gone,
    And he was left to die alone!
Ah me!—it is a bitter thing,
When those, to whom in joy we cling,
Forsake us in our withering!

Miss Pardoe.

PELEG FOLGER now hastened towards the enclosure of the tents upon the common, and introduced his guests to Mary, though with scant ceremony, by reason of not yet having ascertained their names. Of their quality he had, to be sure, already had a taste. The advantage of knowing Mary and the other inmates by name, was all on their side; while they, without other titles, were introduced by Peleg simply as "friends" from abroad. Nevertheless, they received all the attention due to strangers from a hospitable people. The flock assigned by the Selectmen to Peleg's management, so thoroughly engrossed his thoughts, that, without waiting to break his fast, or to see his visitors well bestowed, he vanished from the presence of the lawyer and doctor immediately after their installation. An unavoidable detention at the shear-pen, made it too late to return to his own tent in time for the morning meal; and therefore, taking advantage of the nearest opening, where the unremoved apparatus gave prospect of good cheer remaining, he darted, as we have already seen, into the tent of Jethro Coffin, and solaced himself with the latter end of the feast, consisting principally of quohogs or pooquaws.

Ruth Coffin, after the departure of Peleg Folger, overtook his daughter Mary on the plain, and found her, much to her surprise, under protection of the stranger visitors. It was incumbent on Mary, after the introduction by her parent, to make her guests acquainted with "the qualities o' the isle;" and accordingly, though under much restraint from the novelty of her situation, she undertook to show them the lions of the encampment. To relieve herself in part from the arduous task, she determined to seek out Ruth, and to request her to share the Herculean task of guiding the two young men. The damsels fortunately discovered each other midway on the common. To introduce the gentlemen properly, was an affair of considerable moment; and how could it best be done? They were nameless, so far as the knowledge of Mary extended; and it was altogether a thing not to be entertained for a moment, to ask them for their titles. The introductions were accordingly made in the best way that suggested itself to Mary; and she simply mentioned the name of Ruth to her companions, and left the gentlemen to enlighten them both as to their own, if they chose. The doctor came opportunely to her relief, and observed that—

"As Mr. Folger had omitted to declare their names, when they had the happiness to be introduced to Miss Folger, he trusted they would pardon him for announcing his friend—Lawyer Grimshaw!"

"And, ladies," said Lawyer Grimshaw, taking the hint from his associate, "allow me to make you acquainted with my friend and companion— Doctor Imbert!"

The ceremonious starch of the little party was effectually destroyed by the oddness of the introduction; and a smile of good nature lighted up the countenances of the whole. They were at once at home with each other: and the obligation seemed mutually imposed to utter small talk, and to make the agreeable in a thousand little ways. Our heroes and heroines were so well pleased with each other, that the lapse of a few minutes only sufficed for the projection of a tour round the camp, and elsewhere, as circumstances might invite. The necessary arrangements ware soon made;—and now behold them seated in a calêche, jolting over the common, the gayest among the gay, nodding to cousin This, and saluting cousin That,—threading their way among the tents and sheep enclosures, and passing in their route the numerous merry groups collected at various points, or sprinkled at short intervals over the plain. A visit to the little village of Miacomet, or Indian settlement, then in sight, was proposed, and agreed to; and from thence they wended their way to the main settlement at the spring of Eat-Fire. While on the road, a short historical account of the tribe was furnished by Mary to Imbert and Grimshaw.

The history of the aborigines of Nantucket is the history of every tribe in America;—except that, in the instance before us the withering influence of the whites was in no wise prematurely assisted by the intoxicating draught, "whose every ingredient is a devil." From the moment that the natives felt the ascendancy of the "Yenghese," or "Yankees," on the continent, the spirit of despair, and the consciousness of inferiority, unnerved the red warrior, and prostrated his wild and savage nature. The presence of the whites seemed, of itself, to blast the Indian with mildew, and to seal up the source of procreation to his sable race. The command to "increase and multiply," applied no longer to the savage. A deep and abiding, though unwritten curse, appeared to rest upon them;—it was the curse of inherent self-extermination—gradually, but surely, drying up the springs of prolific vitality, until the last vestige of Indian originality, and every lineament of the American aboriginal should fade away into nothingness. The memory of the race is destined to be saved, if saved at all, only by miracle. Already the flame flickers in its socket;—its fading rays linger only on the pages of romantic fiction. The night will come, and the sun will go down upon the Indian for ever! Even so let it be. They have ever shown themselves cruel and blood-thirsty, with scarcely a touch of humanity in their composition sufficient to redeem them from their native and indisputable brutality.

Relieving the horse from the calêche, and securing him among the tufts of wild bushes which grew near the Indian settlement at the spring, the little party proceeded cautiously to reconnoitre the neighbourhood— not wishing to intrude unceremoniously upon the domestic privacy of the inhabitants. This settlement consisted, perhaps, of a dozen circular huts, bearing the outward appearance of the Indian wigwam. The rudeness of the architecture was, however, by no means to be compared with that of the natives in the interior of America; for the intercourse of the tribe with their ingenious white neighbours, had greatly improved their condition, and initiated them in many of the arts of civilized life. The wigwams were surrounded by small garden patches, filled with culinary vegetables, whose neatness of cultivation was the more remarkable, as being the work of the laborious squaws.

Near to the hamlet, the "Eat-Fire Spring" of the Indian,—a living fountain of the purest water,—gushed forth from the sands, forming the source of a crystal stream, scarce a yard in width, which trickled over the white, rounded pebbles of its bed, and finally found its way to the sea. Over this little "Diamond of the Desert," inclined the graceful branches of a single American willow, preserving, by its impenetrable shade, a refreshing coolness to the waters of the spring, at the same time relieving the monotony of the arid prospect, and forming, with the little bunches of wild shrubbery before alluded to, the scanty *Oasis* of the surrounding desert.

It is worthy of a passing observation, that the springs and small water-courses of America are often adorned with clusters of the weeping willow—than which nothing can be more appropriate, or more in keeping with the delightful coolness which one is apt to associate with the purity of a natural fountain in a sultry clime. The weeping willow peculiar to this country, is rapid in its growth, and, unlike most other trees, it does not need to be transplanted with the root. It is sufficient for its culture, to insert a branch, or slip, in a moist soil, where it quickly takes root, and puts forth vigorous branches. It is, of course, mostly used for ornament, as the texture of its grain is not sufficiently close for many mechanical purposes. The body of the tree in a short time arrives at considerable magnitude; while its branches, numerous, slight, and flexible, droop over from the parent trunk, and fall, with graceful curves, towards the earth— sweeping it, almost, as they depend from the body, and kissing the bosom of the stream, as they wave gently to and fro in the wind. Among all the trees of the forest, or of the cultivated vales of America, there is not one so pleasant to look upon as the inimitable willow. There are those, it is true, that strike the beholder, by their extraordinary size or elevation, with awe and wonder—but none so agreeably and soothingly as the willow—or whose incomparable shade is sooner selected for reflection and repose.

On the margin of the little spring, and beneath the willow aforesaid, Mary and her companions were assembled in consultation, as to the best means of gaining entrance to the wigwams, and obtaining the favourable notice of the old chief. Most of the males of the tribe were assisting at the shearing, for which ample remuneration was promised by the whites. The huts were consequently solely tenanted by the squaws, who were busily engaged in their domestic concerns; while the old and benevolent chief, to whom all paid the greatest deference, had assembled the children of the hamlet at the school-house. Not a soul was stirring abroad of whom to make inquiries, or who could be secured as a guide for the party. It was finally determined that the doctor should pioneer for the whole; and he forthwith proceeded to explore the nearest hut. At the entrance he was arrested by a sight so unlooked for, that it fixed him to the spot in mute curiosity. Expecting to be greeted by the filthy remains of the last meal, or the stench of raw and uncooked vegetables in process of decomposition; with dirty blankets strewed over the floor, and shared by naked pappooses, grunting pigs, and ferocious dogs,—Imbert was agreeably surprised and disappointed at the extreme neatness and exact order of the hut—so unlike any thing he had ever heard of as appertaining to an Indian wigwam. Against the partition, which separated the inner from the outer apartment of the wigwam, was erected a dresser, or a succession of pine shelves, white as soap and sand, and the boonder could make them. On these were arranged, with the approved exactness of a thrifty and exemplary housewife, rows of vessels, consisting of mugs, pans, and platters, of tin and pewter,—all glistening with a brightness that might have been coveted by the daintiest knight-errant of olden time, for the stainless polish of his steel armour. On the lower shelves were secured, in the same ambitious mode of display, upright and on their edges, wooden bowls and kids of red cedar, together with pails and buckets of native manufacture, vieing with the metallic utensils in speckless exterior. A loom, at which the sole inhabitant was seated with her back to the entrance, occupied a recess in the apartment; and the process of weaving a species of cloth called "linsey-woolsey," (the making of which formed the first attempt at manufacturing of woolen in America,) was going on. The noise of the machine prevented the female within from observing the approach of Imbert; but the tying or adjustment of a thread requiring a pause in her labour, her visitor's presence within the apartment was discovered.

"*Aw-ooh!*"—exclaimed the squaw, with a strong guttural accent, surprised by the sudden entrance of Imbert, whose dress and appearance were so dissimilar to those of the islanders. She rose quickly from her seat, and turning to Imbert, confronted him with a broad stare, which the unpractised physiognomist would have hesitated to designate as the glare of disapprobation, or the look of wonderment. Imbert, too, gazed for a moment at the bright vision of a handsome, well-formed Indian girl, now standing before him; but, lifting his hat and bowing courteously, he pointed to his companions beneath the willow, and asked for a cup wherewith to dip water from the spring. The request was understood, and instantly complied with. As she handed him one of the burnished pewter mugs from the shelf, the young woman spoke a few words in her native tongue, in a tone so musical and so different from the harsh salutation which had escaped from her when Imbert was first discovered within the hut; that he might well have mistaken it for the sweet undulation of the Spanish, when uttered by the soft voice of a Castilian maid.

Imbert retired with his glittering trophy, which he held up to the sun as he came towards the spring, exclaiming, in exultation, as he approached, that he "had never seen anything so bright and beautiful before!"

The eyes of Ruth and Mary met as the exclamation was made by Imbert, and an arch glance of peculiar intelligence passed between them. Their own habits of neatness and cleanliness prevented them from discovering any thing extraordinary in the brightness of the pewter vessel which he brought in his hand; and perhaps it would not have elicited any remark from Imbert, but for its unexpected association with an Indian wigwam, where a conch, or a rude horn drinking-cup at best, might have been looked for. The girls, however, mistook, or pretended to mistake, the allusion of Imbert; and Mary "guessed" aloud, that "the doctor had been smitten with the *bright eyes* of Manta."

"Manta!" repeated Imbert.

"The same," answered Ruth; "The girl you have seen is the daughter of the old chief, Benjamin Tashima; and prides herself much in being the first woman of the nation."

"Indeed!" exclaimed Imbert. A dark thought entered his mind as he received the intimation of her parentage; and an embryo design was formed within him, which the arch fiend of hell only could have prompted.

"An Indian princess!" thought he; "she is the more deserving of my favour for being above the common herd, and I like her the more for pluming herself upon being the daughter of a chief. It is a sort of kingly paternity."

After slaking their thirst at the spring of Eat-Fire, Grimshaw proposed that they should go to the wigwam in a body, to obtain, if possible, a closer inspection of the hamlet, and an interview with the aged chief, in whom though unseen, he began to feel a deep interest. The Indian girl observed their approach, and received them with a grace and courtesy which, elsewhere, might have been looked for in vain among Indian women. A conversation commenced immediately between Manta and the girls, in a sort of *Lingua Franca*, in which a few English words were observable. But although Manta could not speak our language fluently, she knew enough of the tongue to convey her meaning in proper words; and the rest was easily supplied by her auditor. If she was not a ready speaker of English, she was the next best thing in the eyes of those who are given to the *cacoethes loquendi,*—and that is, a good listener. She inclined her ear gravely and attentively while others spoke, and understood well the purport of what was said.

"Look!" said Imbert to Grimshaw, in an under tone; "here are the paraphernalia of a kitchen which might grace a drawing room. Do you observe the neatness with which everything is arranged? By Jupiter! the bright sun himself is scarcely more dazzling than the tin and pewter before us. I should like to take a peep into the rest of the establishment, to see whether the appointments of the inner temple answer to those of the vestibule. I'll wager a crown that she is like all the rest of woman-kind, and has a regular set of lumber-holes, in which to tuck away the duds and the dirt. I have always found women guilty of that hypocrisy;—and you may be sure the best foot is now foremost."

The keen black eyes of Manta glanced repeatedly at the speaker, while she listened, or appeared to listen to the prattle of the young women by her side. She had heard enough to gather the meaning of Imbert; or perhaps she judged by his gestures of what was passing between him and his friend. Approaching the aperture which led to the interior of the wigwam, she drew aside a curtain that served the purpose of a door; and, as she passed from their sight, the apartments became visible which overlooked the garden spot behind. If Imbert was gratified with what he saw in the outer apartment, he was no less so with that exhibited within. A neat withdrawing room, with a sleeping closet on each side, was now subjected to the scanning of his critical eye. The furniture of the first was of that simple kind, which a woman of good taste always knows how to select according to her station in life, and to arrange with becoming skill. There was none of that slovenly heaping together of the useful with the ornamental, nor the piling of ornament upon ornament, which betrays vulgarity of taste. There was but little of the Indian garniture about the wigwam. The only things which in any way betrayed the nationality of the indwellers, were an ancient calumet or council-pipe, crossing the stem of a rude arrow, tipped with a sharp angular piece of semi-transparent stone; and both were secured against the slight ceiling over the mantel-piece. These relics were the fabric of a powerful tribe, then almost extinct, which more than two hundred years before had exercised sovereignty over the island of Nantucket; and indeed they were the chief naval power of the northern and eastern tribes. Their canoes were the largest and most numerous of any nation at the north, and their warriors the most athletic and skillful. No war among the tribes upon the main was entered upon without seeking their alliance, and no peace was agreed to without their concurrence.

Manta, the last representative of the princesses of the tribe, now appeared in the passage between the rooms. She had adjusted her dress, and placed a smart bonnet upon her head; and signified that she was ready to conduct her visitors to her father. Lingering for a moment in the doorway, with somewhat of indecision in her manner, her pride, or her vanity, which had been piqued by the curiosity of the gentlemen, induced her to invite the party to look at her garden;—in doing which they necessarily passed through the inner room we have spoken of. The curtains of the sleeping apartments were drawn aside; but whether accidentally or purposely was not apparent. A glance sufficed to show that the beds were covered with sheets and counterpanes of incomparable whiteness, a little turned down from the equally snow-white pillow. The arrangements for making the toilet were also in everything complete. The covering of the earthen floors, throughout, was woven of the broad flag-leaf found in all swampy grounds. The pale green colour of the carpeting, lighted up and relieved the different apartments, from much of that sombre appearance which a floor of heath or of well-trod earth, would naturally present.

Passing into the little garden, the same neatness was observable in the arrangement of the beds, and the training of the bushes and vines. It was yet too early for fruits or flowers in any great variety; but it was evident that both would be forthcoming in their proper season. An arbour, too, had been erected, which in due time would derive its shelter from the green leaves of the prolific hop-vine. And who had done all this?—The youthful Manta, with but very little aid from her father. Her taste and her economy were patterns for both of the Indian villages of Miacomet and Eat-Fire, and they were not without a salutary influence. Every Indian family had its culinary garden, and its improvements upon the uncomforts of Indian rudeness.

Imbert and Grimshaw were observed to stoop, from time to time, and to gather up from the beds and pathways a number of small stones of an unusual shape. They had noticed the same remarkable stones in various parts of the island: some they had found turned up in the furrows of the ploughed common, where immense fields of the Indian corn had been planted; others they had seen exposed on the surface of the sandy roads as they progressed about the island. The shape was entirely different from the small granitic masses, or globules, that are invariably found mixed with the sands of the sea-shore, or with the soil of the contiguous upland—which, from such appearances, may be supposed to have been once washed by the sea. The little stones, which excited the curiosity of the visitors, were evidently of a silicious nature, sharpened like the modern gun-flint, with a thin triangular appearance, and sometimes with a stem projecting from the side opposite to the sharpest angle.

"What can these be?" asked Grimshaw.

"Egad! I was about asking the same question myself," replied Imbert:— "I have a handful of them here that are as nearly alike as one pea is like another. From these indications I imagine the soil of the island, which is not reputed over-rich at any time, must have been occasionally manured with a cargo of gun-flints! They can scarcely be the *debris* of the island rocks—for I have not seen a large stone in all the land."

"Perhaps the young lady with the brown skin can tell us," observed Grimshaw. "They may be Indian ornaments, or Indian antiquities.—Pray do you not know the origin of these queerities?"—demanded he, addressing himself to Manta.

"They are the arrow-heads, used in the wars of my ancestors!" answered she, while her dark eyes flashed and her form dilated. The words and the manner were not lost upon the auditors.

"She answered you like a queen!" whispered Imbert to Grimshaw; "at it again, and bring her out—will you!"

"No," replied Grimshaw; "she has already spoken volumes in that little sentence; and I would not destroy the impression it has made upon me by further converse. It was indeed spoken like a queen."

"Let us on to her father, then," said Imbert; and they moved from the garden.

We cannot say why it is—but since our arrival at years of maturity, we have never entered the doors of a school-house with pleasurable feelings. We have moreover doubted the truth of that verse of Thompson which pronounces "teaching the young idea how to shoot"—a "*delightful task.*" Depend upon it, there are not five schoolmasters in America who will agree with him. The sensations of a faithful teacher of youth are anything but delightful, when he quits his stifled schoolroom, at the close of a hard day's mental and physical labour. If he feels delight at all, it is because he has seen the last boy depart; and because he looks to the short interval of repose which succeeds as to a blessing. Do the pale, attenuated features of such a man speak of the pleasures of his calling? Does the hand convulsively pressed upon the bosom, as he leaves his refractory charge, to rest his "listless length" at home, betoken the delights of buoyant health? What candid man will say that the task is a pleasant one, who has witnessed the deep anxiety of a teacher as he endeavours, but with small success, to inculcate the truths of morality and science upon the minds of the stupid, or the perverse, or the inattentive? And then, after his conscientious duties are most scrupulously discharged, who but the teacher can tell of the ingratitude of children, the querulousness of unthinking and unreasonable parents, or the tyranny and pretension of ignorant and self-sufficient trustees! With all these the teacher has to deal—all these he must contrive to satisfy—and for what?—For a paltry stipend, grudgingly yielded, that in nine instances out of ten, will hardly keep soul and body together. It is thus, however, that this species of talent is rewarded in many parts of America:—yet, while teaching is looked upon as one of the learned professions, the professor himself is rated in society below his employer, and his emolument is that of the veriest slave.

The station and the salary of the priest are princely, when compared with his; and the income of the lawyer and the doctor, who batten upon the miseries and misfortunes of mankind, places them above the reach of want, while their titles alone are passports to refined society. But while these flourish in sunshine, the poor contemned pedagogue—who should be "right honorable," and above them all,—ranges below zero, and perishes in the bleak shade. We cannot imagine any thing more beneficial to society, or deserving higher consideration, than the labours of the faithful man, who devotes himself to the cultivation of the youthful mind, and prepares it alike for social intercourse with the world, and for immortality hereafter. It rests with the schoolmaster—as everybody will acknowledge—to bend the twig in the way it should incline. What a pity, then, that in a country where intelligence is the best safeguard of its liberty, the "school-master," as he walks "abroad," (to quote the words of HENRY BROUGHAM—that greatest of men, and the firm friend of school-masters,) should not be fully appreciated, and fostered with kindly care by all the people! But, gentle reader, as the world *now* goes with us, and honourable as we deem the labour, may Heaven preserve both you and us from engaging in that—

> "Delightful task!—
> To teach the young idea how to shoot!"

May it keep us, now and for ever, from that profession, whose every classical recollection, how beautiful soever, (as we have elsewhere seen it better expressed,) is marred by some scene of sighs and tears, or painfully associated with images of perversity, ugliness, ingratitude, and contumely!

With this short sermon at the threshold, let us enter the humble Indian school-house. The introduction of the strangers was made by Manta to the venerable Benjamin Tashima; and they were at once struck with his dignified manner and the commanding intelligence of his features. There was very little in them, except the swarthy colour of the skin, which betrayed the Indian. But for this, and the prominent cheek-bones, and the deep sunken eyes, the *caste* would not have been discoverable. Though of the true breed, and in his youth a wild ranger of a continental forest, subsequent education, and conformity to the habits of civilization had wrought an agreeable change in his person and demeanour. He had long been looked up to as the father of the tribe, which was now a fast-fading remnant. The last children of the race were before him; and, like a good man and a good Christian, he was endeavouring to smooth the way of their destiny. He was their lawgiver, their preacher, and their schoolmaster. He inculcated, both by precept and example, sound morality and the religion of the Saviour of mankind. He was honest and benevolent; charitable and humane. His people loved him, and feared his displeasure. By his persuasion, the bane of the Indian race was banished from the little hamlet, and a drunkard was only seen at long intervals. Industry was encouraged, and always met with its reward. It is difficult, however, to change the skin of the Ethiopian; and it did, sometimes, happen that the dogged and loose propensities of the Indian would break forth as of yore. Sullen laziness, drunkenness, petty theft, and cowardly violence—inherent qualities of the race—would prevail for a time among a few of the more dissolute; but the correcting hand of the old chief was instantly laid upon them, and the salutary discipline of the whale-ship was their punishment. A long life of vigilance and kindness he had devoted to the tribe: seventy winters had already passed over the head of the venerable Tashima, and he had, in the time, seen generation after generation of his people pass away. His red companions had dropped one by one around him, and none came to supply their places. The good old man felt melancholy at the sure indications of withering decay, which had caused his people to dwindle to a mere handful of the once terrible lords of the American forest, leaving him to stand,—solitary and alone, without the prospect of succession,—like the riven and mutilated trunk where the blasting hurricane had been busy. The LAST CHIEF of a once great and powerful nation was here; and but little more than half a century was destined to see the total extinguishment of the island race!

A portion of the industrious life of Tashima had been devoted to study; and he had succeeded, with infinite labour, in adapting his literary acquirements to the language and capacity of his tribe. He had nourished the vain hope of preserving the nation without a cross in its blood, and the language of his people in its pristine purity. It was a magnificent conception! The design was worthy of the last, as he was the greatest, chief of the tribe. He was the last, because none succeeded him; he was the greatest, for he was the most benevolent.

Seated before him, in his little wigwam school-room, were some twenty Indian boys and girls. A gleam of intelligence shot from their dark eyes, which spoke nothing of the savage glare that is so remarkable a trait in the wild Indian when agitated or enraged; and it was equally unlike his stupid, lack-lustre eye when at rest. It was plain that "the schoolmaster had been abroad" among the tribe. Each of the little urchins was provided with a convenient board upon which a paper had been pasted, containing numerous combinations of words in the Indian tongue. These were illustrated by sensible signs or pictures. This method of delineation was an elaboration of a mode of expression already in use among the tribes of the interior, who, in all their treaties with the French and English, and, of later years, with the United States, drew, for their signature, the outline of some animal, or other object, which they had adopted for their title. Thus the "*Black Hawk,*" whose depredations upon our frontiers, with less than five hundred followers, have recently called forth the merited chastisement of our government (in a campaign which has cost us more than a million of dollars, and a sacrifice of two men for every live Indian,)—makes his mark by the strange outline of a pouncing vulture; the "Great Snake," by a coiled viper, &c. It may be apposite here to remark, that Bell, the contemporary and successful rival of Lancaster, took the hint of his plan from an inspection of similar modes of conveying instruction in India, where the pictorial method of teaching has been in use time out of mind.

The characters adopted by Tashima for the instruction of his pupils, were, in addition to his pictures, the Roman letters; and the alphabet, so far as it was necessary for conveying Indian sounds, was substantially the same as our own. The combinations of letters were, however, quite remarkable, and exhibited frequent groupings of the vowel sounds. The letter O, in duplicate, and even triplicate consecutive arrangement, frequently occurred in the lessons, and was perceptible in the deep guttural sounds which predominated in the language of Tashima. The utterance of the Indian is slow, but by no means sonorous or agreeable: yet the voice of the female, when giving vent to feelings of admiration or of pleasure, will sometimes ascend into a modulated *alto,* that falls quite musically upon the ear.

Tashima's numerous books and lessons were all in manuscript; and it is to be regretted that the printer was never called in to aid in their preservation.[*] They would have furnished delicious *morceaux* for the literary wranglers and philologists of the present day; but, at the time we write of, a printing-press was unknown at Nantucket. Even in Boston, which some of its people still insist upon calling the "Literary Emporium," that persevering printer, Benjamin Franklin, could scarcely find support for his little "Weekly News-Letter."

There are a few aged people still living at Nantucket, and elsewhere, and we might include the gallant old Admiral to whom these pages are dedicated, who remember the old chief Tashima, and will attest that there is but little romance in the faint outline here given of his occupations. But his efforts were all in vain! The aged patriarch, after a well-spent life, was shortly gathered to his fathers. Although full of years, and ripe for translation, his death was no doubt prematurely hurried on by a melancholy event connected with this history, and in which one of the characters, already introduced to the reader, had but too intimate a participation. The generation he had undertaken to instruct, grew up, and forgot the knowledge he had imparted. Their parents, no longer under his wholesome restraint, soon relapsed into the beastly habits of the Indian; the loom and the spinning-wheel were cast aside, and intemperance and abject poverty and destitution, succeeded to sober and industrious habits. A few years more, and every vestige of the race must become extinct! A solitary Indian, claiming kindred with nobody living, still wanders over the island, and must shortly sink into the nothingness

---

[*]Since the above was written, the editor has learned that the Massachusetts Historical Society has preserved a translation of a portion of the Bible, in the Indian tongue, which was used at Nantucket in the time of Tashima. It is most probably a translation by Elliot, the missionary, and was in fact the first Bible printed in America.

of his fathers. But shall the memory of Benjamin Tashima, the virtuous and the good, be also buried in oblivion? The pages of a tale like ours are too ephemeral to warrant that it will prove otherwise. It is to be hoped that some permanent memorial will preserve to posterity the estimable name of Tashima; for no man better deserved to have his virtues emblazoned in monumental marble.

The example of such a man—such an Indian, if you please—is worth more to posterity,—and,—the philanthropist will say,—should be dearer to it, than all the savage glories of a thousand Philips or Tecumthês, whose claims to admiration rest upon countless deeds of blood and rapine, and a very questionable valour displayed in the slaughter of women and children. May God forgive the uncharitableness!—but of such a race of miscreants we are almost ready to say—"Perdition catch their souls!"—as, like the ghosts of Banquo's line, the red visions of their cruelties rise up before us:—But to the manes of such a truly godlike Indian as Benjamin Tashima, we would say with fervour—

REQUIESCAT IN PACE !

CHAPTER SEVEN.

So withered and so wild in her attire,
Who stopped their way upon the blasted heath,
With strange prophetic greetings.

◆　　◆　　◆　　◆　　◆

Ye black and midnight hags!—What is't ye do?
Macbeth.

It's all done by shuffling and dealing!
Tom and Jerry.

ON leaving the Indian school-room, the guests returned with Manta to her paternal wigwam, where they partook of some slight refreshment which she voluntarily provided; and then, proceeding together to the fountain, they drank again from the waters of the spring of Eat-Fire. The day was now past its meridian, and they set out to return to the dwelling of Jethro Coffin. The little Indian village was still in sight, though at considerable distance, and their new route, which was taken by a circuitous path, lay in the direction of a miserable hut, standing alone in the midst of dreary sands. It might easily have been mistaken for the deserted hovel of some poor fisherman; or, as is most likely, it was one of those ancient huts which skirt the sea-shore, erected by the humane islanders, at intervals of a mile upon the coast, for the reception and shelter of shipwrecked mariners. Not the least sign of vegetation grew near it, and in everything it was the opposite of the carefully repaired wigwams and neat garden patches of the Indian hamlet. Like the Upas, it seemed to have blasted by its presence every green blade of grass and every shrub, for half a mile around it, and nothing could be more desolate and forbidding than its cheerless look. In the doorway stood the tall, bony figure of a woman, apparently past the middle age. Her tattered dress and haggard features betrayed her extreme poverty, and marked her for the tenant of this abode of wretchedness. Long and coarse black hair, high cheek-bones, and swarthy complexion, bespoke her Indian origin; and yet the lack of the squat figure, and the waddling gait, and the total absence of the parrot-toed planting of the foot, showed plainly enough that the breed was spurious. It was owing perhaps to this circumstance that she was disowned by the tribe of Indians as well as by the whites. Certain it was she could find fellowship with neither. An outcast in the midst of society, she wandered over the island, a poor neglected object;—sometimes subsisting upon charity, and at others gaining for herself a scanty meal by an idle profession, which was far from being reputable in the eyes of the ever-busy and industrious islanders. In process of time Mother Quary came to be the terror of all naughty children, and was looked upon as but little better than a dealer with the evil one. Her fame as a successful fortune-teller had of late received considerable accession; inasmuch as she had told Jerusha Starbuck where her long-lost silver spoons had been mislaid through excessive carefulness; and she had predicted good fortune and a safe return to several of the crew of the Leviathan. Some of the thoughtless, or superstitious, had even ascribed to her an interposition in saving the ship during the late terrible storm—as she was seen wandering on the beach beneath the cliffs at nightfall of the day previous to her arrival, drenched with rain, and muttering strange words; while ever and anon she stopped and made fantastic gestures as if commanding the sea. She had moreover gained great credit with Peleg Folger, who had the misfortune to lose a pet sheep, which she was the means of recovering, by pointing in the direction where it might be found. It was found, sure enough, in a sort of deep pit-hole, originally excavated by the island sportsmen, or gunners, for concealment from their game, and into which it had accidentally fallen and was unable to extricate itself. But whether her wandering mode of life had made her better acquainted with the by-places of the island than Peleg, and had suggested the pit-fall as the most likely place to find the animal, does not appear.

Under all these circumstances, and possessing much natural shrewdness and ingenuity, which had been sharpened by poverty and neglect, it is not wonderful that Mother Quary should have made up her mind to prey upon the community that had cast her forth from its bosom; nor that she should lay to the charge of that same community all the sin of her practices of deception.

"Live she must—and live she would!"—she was heard to exclaim, as she screwed her mind up to the necessity of making hay while the sun shone, by taking advantage of her rising fame; and in truth she might well have uttered in her wrath, had she known the text,—

"Since the Heavens have shaped my body so,
Let Hell make crook'd my mind to answer it!"

"What scare-crow is that?" demanded Imbert of the girls, as they approached.

"It is the fortune-teller;—poor Judith Quary," answered Ruth, with a touch of pity in her tone.

"*Sancta-Maria!*" exclaimed Imbert; "I thought she looked like a dam of Satan;—See, she holds out her hand;—I suppose we must stop and cross her palm, or she will send after us one of her blessings, seething hot from the cauldron of Belzebub."

The calêche was accordingly halted before her door, and Imbert and Grimshaw assisted the young ladies to alight.

"Your servant, gentles!" said Judith, as she dropped a curtesy to her visitors; "I knew you would not be likely to go past without stopping to notice poor Judith. A busy day this on the common!"

"How comes it that you are not at the Shearing?" asked one of the gentlemen; "there are some good pickings there for you, Mistress Quary;—you are too modest by half, to conceal your attractions at home, on such a day as this."

"Ah!" said the hag, "you don't understand looking into the stars as well as I do, or you would discover that the proper place for me to-day is here at home. This is the receipt of custom on such a holyday as this. Those who wish to see me, do not like to have their destiny foretold before a crowd of people:—they'll be along directly, gentle and simple, to speer out their fortunes, I warrant ye."

"I dare say they will," observed Imbert; "but the Selectmen and you are no great friends, if I have heard aright; and I'm told they interfere with the regular course of your vocation."

"May my curses light on them for it!" grumbled the fortune-teller, "and on you too for your taunt, ye viper!"

"What do you say?" asked Imbert.

"My prayers for the prosperity of the Selectmen," said the sibyl, aloud.

"Prayers indeed!—Do you say them forward or backward?" demanded he, with a sneer.

"Why, that's just as suits the time and my humour," answered she; "but the day *you* commence saying them, there will be a man less in this breathing world."

"Fairly hit," said Imbert; "but a truce with bantering. Come, give us a taste of your trade;—there is a piece of silver for you. Be at it quick, old 'un—*tempus fugit*—out with your glasses and tea-cups, and all the rest of your jack-o'lantern flummery."

"I must shuffle the cards first," said the woman. "Did you talk about the *jack-of-lanterns*, sir?" continued she, with affected simplicity:—"I sometimes turn up *jack* when I deal the cards, but I have none with *lanterns* on them; nor do I remember ever having seen any with that device."

"I suppose not; for such folks as yourself, old mother, have very little to do with the *lights* of knowledge; I take you to be one of the tribe who prefer the darkness rather," observed Imbert.

"Well, well—come in, and you'll see," said the hag, not altogether pleased with some of her guests. She had seldom dealt with those who spoke and acted so boldly and familiarly with her as Imbert. "Come," she continued, pointing to several dilapidated benches, "sit down round the table, while I close the shutter and shuffle the cards.—Who cuts?"—

"Oh—no matter who," said Imbert impatiently;—"here—the pack is separated;"—and he slapped the portion he held in his hand down upon the table, with a force and quickness that startled his companions.

"How you frightened me, doctor!" exclaimed Ruth, as she almost jumped from her seat. Everything within the darkened hut looked so gloomy, and she had heard so much of the necromantic skill of the fortune-teller, it was not to be wondered at that she did not altogether feel at ease.

"A doctor!" thought the old woman, as Ruth repeated his title, "I wonder who the other is? Never mind—I'll give them a 'screed o' doctrine' at a venture."

"By-the-by, Grim, what is the penalty of the law which the wise ones of your profession award to the fortune-telling tribe? Don't they condemn them for witches in Connecticut?" asked Imbert, carelessly.

"A man of the law too!" exclaimed Judith, mentally: "I am highly honoured truly. A lawyer and a doctor, forsooth! They give pain and trouble enough, in their day and generation, to us poor bodies:—It's *my* turn now—and if I could only contrive to scare them—"

"I believe," said Grimshaw, "they bind them hand and foot in the Connecticut colony, and throw them into a horse-pond; where, if they sink, it is proof of their innocence; but if they swim, it is proof positive against them. In either case they get a passport to the other kingdom."

"A wise law,—that of the blue-bottles!" said Imbert; "That's what you and old Coke-upon-Littleton would call a 'contingent remainder, with a double aspect,'—a sort of two-edged sword, cutting right and left. I've heard of the 'glorious *uncertainty* of the law;' but I suppose the horse-pond cooling may be quoted as a worthy sample of the *certainty* of its punishment. But what is the old woman about?—Deal me a good trick, my good dame, and spell me out a fair fortune,—or I'll have you transported to Connecticut, and punished for suspicion of contumacy of the laws, and a bad translation of my fortunate horoscope. Come—begin!"

"There!" said the fortune-teller, dealing the cards to each individual, with the backs uppermost; "and now be silent!"

> "The cards are dealt, and the fortune sped,
> And weal or wo be on thy head!"

"Come!—that's something for our money," said Imbert; but without regarding him, the fortune-teller placed the cards more carefully against the rim of the little round table, opposite to each person; and, waving a wand, the top of the table began slowly to move on its centre. Presently it acquired an accelerated motion, of such swiftness that the bunches of cards became indistinct, and finally seemed to form a continuous marginal belt of white. During this surprising manœuvre, which, in such a place, could only be accounted for upon the principle of Redheiffer's perpetual motion, or the Automaton Chess-player of Maelzel, the fortune-teller continued to wave her wand, and to chant in a measured cadence—

> "Tell now, ye fates,
> What doom awaits;
> And silent speak,
> To those who seek
> To win your favour here.
> Turn—turn again!
> On!—circling plane!

> Cease—cease ye now:—
> Come weal, come wo—
> Appear!—Appear!—Appear!"

The motion of the board gradually became less rapid, until, as the chant ceased, the card-packs again rested opposite to those who were sitting round the table. A deep curiosity, approaching to solemnity, began to take possession of every mind. The woman now continued her incantation, which she delivered with impassioned *onction*, while she pointed upwards with her wand—in which direction she also turned her deep-set eyes, that glowed like balls of fire in the gloom of the chamber:— the spirit of prophecy was come upon her.

> "Ye spirits of the upper air,
>   And ministers of earth and sea,
> To these weak mortals lend your care,
>   And their sure fortune tell to me!
> Give me to know their various fate,
>   Or smooth or checkered here below;
> Protect the good—and turn your hate
>   On such as merit only wo!—
> The cards are dealt, and the fortune sped!
>   Come weal, come wo,
>   Appear! Appear! Appear!

Mother Quary, as she repeated the last words of her wild invocation, took up the cards from before Imbert, and examined them attentively. He began to feel less at ease than when he first encountered the fortune-teller: he tried to smile as usual, but it was a faint effort, and he did not succeed. A superstitious awe had crept over him. So much for the effect of the *manner* of the fortune-teller. Manner is every thing—matter comparatively nothing. Nobody could possibly believe less in the power or prescience of fortune-tellers than Imbert; yet now he was painfully listening to what fell from the lips of the half-breed, Judith Quary. She fixed her fierce eyes upon his countenance, but the colour had fled from it. In an impromptu she thus "redde" the stars to him:—

> "With the eagle's soar thou'rt aiming high—
>   But the dazzling sun shall pain thine eye:
> When with wearied wing thou tri'st to fly,

> And thou seek'st some friendly haven nigh,
> Then, no resting place shalt thou descry,
> And they fondest hopes shall droop and die!—
> Like to passion's slave I see thee yield,—
> And the sullied spot comes o'er thy shield!"

"Enough!—enough of that!" exclaimed Imbert—"In heavens name, pass on to the next?"

"Have I brought you down—my lark!" mumbled Judith, between her teeth; "a prick of a lancet, sharp as your own, will bring health to you, and mend your manners, my jeering gentleman!" She cast the cards into the centre of the table, and took up those before Grimshaw. A moment's reflection, while looking at the cards, enabled her to send another harpoon in the direction of the lawyer. She continued thus, and was listened to with breathless attention by her auditors:

> "Slow draws the curtain from my sight,
> And dreamy mist obscures the light;
> Dimly shines out thy natal star,
> That looks o'er shadowy forms afar!
> The cloud clears up!—I see thee now,
> With deep design upon thy brow!
> Thy struggling victim too is there—
> Thy hand is grappled in her hair!
> Another form, with matron zone,
> But heart within as cold as stone,
> Stands gazing, passionless, while thy
> Victim begs in her agony
> For help!—Where is that loved one now
> Who should redeem his plighted vow?
> Lo, there!—the monster's gaping jaws
>   Show a deed of blood,
>   Far,—far o'er the flood!
>
> ◆   ◆   ◆   ◆   ◆
>
> The sick'ning heart has need of pause—."

Without waiting to notice the effect of this upon the stolid Grimshaw, Judith snatched up the remaining cards, which had fallen to the lot of Ruth and Mary, and, seemingly absorbed in her prophetic vision, hastily glanced at them, and proceeded:—

> "See the cypress wreath, of saddest hue,
> The twining destiny threading through;
> And the serpent coil is twisting there—
> While, regardless of the victim's prayer,
> The fiend laughs out o'er the mischief done,
> And th' canker-worm makes the heart his throne!"

A scream from Mary, as the door of the hut slammed to with a startling noise, and shut them up in total darkness, cut short the further experiment of the fortune-teller. The young women rushed out, followed by Imbert and Grimshaw, nothing loath. In a moment afterwards they were seated in the calêche, and driving rapidly away from the fortune-teller.

"There they go," said Judith, as she looked after them with her gaunt form half projected from the doorway of the hut—"there they go, like frightened wild fowl on the wing—and a precious fortune I have foretold for them! They will not soon forget old Judith Quary, I trow. Out upon ye—fortune-hunting knaves, as ye are! I pity the poor young things of girls there, if they have any thing to do with you! Jethro Coffin and Peleg Folger had best look after their daughters, while such ill-favoured sharks as they are prowling about the island. I should be loath to predict harm to the gentle young creatures—they are always so kind to me, when I'm hungry and cold—but it did almost seem to me that my words would prove prophetic. I saw it all as plain as day, and,—it's wonderful to think on't,—I never had so little trouble to make rhymes before! Well, well;— I am but a humble instrument in the hands of Him who created all things; and, sinful as I am, I may have been chosen to speak the words of fate. Poor things—how they trembled, and turned pale with affright!— Ah—here comes 'other-guess' company, who will take every thing for granted I choose to tell them, in plain prose, without cudgelling my poor brain for verses."

The hut of the fortune-teller was soon filled with idle lads and lasses, who came to have their fortunes told; and Judith received money enough, in the course of the day, to place her above want and the fear of the Selectmen, for half the year to come.

"How that old hag made my flesh crawl!" exclaimed Imbert, as he slackened the rein to let the horse breathe;—and, faith, she made tolerable verses too. She's a shrewd thing! I thought she would but look at the lines in one's hand, or turn a teacup, or the like, to give colour to her trick,—and then tell us all a good story about prosperous journeys, pleasant voyages, happy matches, and so forth:—but,—blast the old shrivel-skin!—she made me fly in the air, like Noah's dove, without a resting-place, and then gave me a bad name—a spotted escutcheon,—bad luck to her! By-the-by, Grim, she gave you a heavy wipe too—something about seizing a victim by the hair, and so forth."

"What a dreadful verse she told over for us!" said Ruth to Mary; "Ugh!—my blood runs cold when I think of it."

"Let me console you with the butt-end of an epigram," said Imbert; "it is applicable to all rhyming fortune-tellers, and others who derive their poetic license from his Satanic majesty. It runs thus:—

> "—The gods in blank verse rule the skies,
> While in *rhyme* speaks the Father of *lies!*"

"God grant she may have shadowed forth nothing but lies," observed Mary; "but the fearful woman sent a withering chill to my heart, that I am sure can be equalled only by the icy coldness of death!"

The business of the shearing was now nearly over, and most of the islanders, with their guests, began to wend their way into the town, and the flocks of sheep, shorn of their fleece, to scatter freely over the extended common. Ruth pointed out the house of her father to Imbert, and he accordingly drove up to the door; where the calêche and the animal were discharged for the remainder of the day. Imbert and Grimshaw were introduced to Jethro and his wife, and were received with that quiet welcome of hospitality which is characteristic of the people. An early tea soon made its appearance upon the table; after which the young ladies retired, to make preparations for an evening's amusement, of a kind which is never enjoyed by the Quaker youth except by stealth, and after great precaution, and dexterous hoodwinking of parents.

While Ruth and Mary were making their toilet, Jethro and Miriam set themselves at work, by a peculiar process of questioning and cross-examination, known only to inquisitive Americans, to ascertain all about the connections and professional business of their guests. Imbert acquitted himself to their satisfaction; and they came to the conclusion, that a doctor of physic was a useful animal. Grimshaw did not come off as well, and Jethro looked upon him with suspicion.

"No good can come from a visit from a lawyer," thought Jethro.

His wife Miriam thought otherwise; for she shortly afterwards, invited him to take a seat by her side, apart from the rest; and, in a mysterious conversation, which lasted more than an hour, Miriam and Grimshaw came to a good understanding with each other, and from that moment were the best of friends. The house of Jethro Coffin from that day forth was the home of Grimshaw; and it was thought, when the extraordinary character of Miriam afterwards became more fully developed by the circumstances of the times, that she had made up her mind as to her future course, and taken counsel for her first measures, at this unaccountable interview.

$\mathcal{C}$HAPTER EIGHT.

—The joyful maid with sprightly strain
Shall wake the dance to give you welcome home.
The Shipwreck.

WE have often thought that parents must have managed their children erroneously, when they have failed to secure their confidence in all their little concerns,—however unimportant some of them may have appeared. It is undoubtedly an error not to enter into their amusements. Forbid a child the privilege of going to a ball, or to the theatre, under proper protection, and you may be sure that the desire to enjoy the forbidden fruit will increase an hundred fold. Depend upon it, the march *will* be stolen, and perhaps the double sin of disobedience, and prevarication, if not downright falsehood, will be added to whatever of evil there may be in the amusement itself.

As a general rule, we have found it to prove infinitely more satisfactory to both parties, for parents to gratify the inclination of their children for such innocent amusements, when they cannot be denied without giving pain or disappointment. They at once obtain and secure the undisputed right to select the places of resort; and can easily assure themselves of their respectability. There are undoubtedly assemblies well conducted in most populous places; and none will deny that dancing is a healthy, as well as a graceful exercise. If, therefore, our children were less restrained, and more generally encouraged in this particular, we should not only produce in them habits of vigorous muscular action, which every physician will declare is requisite for the promotion of health, but they would also acquire a graceful carriage;—the lack of which among us is remarked upon by intelligent foreigners.

We love to look upon a French woman when she moves: there is grace in every step, and even poetry in her motion. The French are a dancing nation, and none are more cheerful in their dispositions, or more healthy in body. The amusements that conduce to their happy temperament should, therefore, not be contemned for slight cause. But touching theatrical displays, we are not so great sticklers as for those other amusements that assist in promoting the mind's cheerfulness.

Every man, it is said, must "eat his peck of dirt;" and the sooner he does it the better. In these degenerate days, when Punchinello and gorgeous pantomimic spectacle usurp the place of the intellectual and "legitimate drama," the sooner we take our children by the hand and feed them the peck of trash, so much sooner will they become sated with the dexterity of the scene-shifter, and the whistle of the prompter;—for these personages, be it known, are by far the most important characters in a modern melo-dramatic play, which, without much essential variation, begins and ends after this fashion:—

"'Act first—scene first—moon scene behind a cloud;'—enter Count Traveliero, as large as life,—(only twice as natural,)—disguised in a slouched hat and heavy whiskers; legs encased in enormous jack-boots; armed with a broad-sword and blunderbuss;—walks rapidly up and down the stage, and then across;—stops short in the middle, and—says nothing!—a crash of discordant music from the orchestra, and a peal of thunder from a Chinese gong—and—the curtain falls amidst the most deafening applause from the audience!"

Such are the amusements of a modern play-house. But enough of this:—Let the hint for reformation be taken, if it will, and we shall be satisfied.

The twilight of an evening in June began to gather, and the hum and bustle of the sheep-shearing revellers was fast subsiding in the streets and public places of the quiet town of Sherburne. The wind from the sea freshened into an unpleasant chilliness, and Jethro Coffin with his guests retired from the piazza which overlooked his garden enclosure, (for even the deep sands of Nantucket may be brought under cultivation,) and all but Ruth and Mary were assembled in the comfortable parlour. "Comfortable" it was not altogether, at the present moment, by reason of the fact above stated; for the windows of the parlour being open, the sea air, which is republican in its nature, had equalized the temperature within and without. But in the general, Jethro's dwelling was comfortable. It was substantially built, and might even defy the violence of a hurricane. Its furniture and appointments were convenient, and Miriam and Ruth were ever on the alert to keep the apartments in order. But Miriam was somewhat of a royalist in her sentiments, and had but little sympathy with the familiar liberties taken by levellers. She therefore ordered the sashes to be closed, to check the rude and impertinent advances of the chilly air, and fire-wood to be deposited in the fireplace.

"Where can the girls be gadding?" inquired Miriam. She was fond of paying proper respect to all guests who were admitted to her hospitality; and from the unusual stay of Ruth and Mary above stairs, she was half inclined to construe their protracted absence into a designed slight of her visitors. Here, however, she was wrong in her surmise. The gallants of the town, uniting with the officers and most of the crew of the Leviathan, had made arrangements for a ball: and Ruth and Mary were among the invited. This *fête* was considered by the younger folks, as an appropriate finale to the shearing; besides, it would serve the additional purpose of a *réunion*,—a bringing together of many who had been so long separated, that they had become almost, if not entirely estranged. And then there was the prospect of seeing the new faces, both male and female, which were sure to be there. In short, it was an admirable eking out of the festival, which could by no means be foregone by the younger people; although such "doings" were contemned and discountenanced by their elders.

A ball,—or a dance, if you will have it so,—came but seldom, at Nantucket. Indeed we have heard, (though we hope the report of the result is a slander,) that a concert of instrumental music, which is accounted not half so wicked as a dance, was proposed to be given to the inhabitants of that place, not many years ago, as the best and most acceptable return that could be made for hospitality shown to a numerous cargo of fashionables, who had been landed by one of our splendid floating castles, or steamers,—and was defeated by the stiff-necked perversity of the Selectmen. A celebrated musical band accompanied the steamer, and they proffered a display of their talents at the townhouse, for the gratification of the townspeople. It is related that the towncrier had sounded his bell, and cried his "*oyez* three times," at the corners of the streets, to warn the good people (we give his identical words) that "A celebrated consort of vocal and instrumental music would be given by the celebrated Bostin band at the townhouse; and the ladies and gentlemen were invited to attend punctually, free-gratis-for-nothin', at six o'clock, P. M. in the afternoon!"—Again came the "*oyez*"—"three times and repeat," at the next corner, until all the town was duly notified. Hearts beat high with expectation, and dresses and ribbons, and bonnets and curls, were in a pretty considerable state of readiness to make a due degree of display at the townhouse. But,— alas!—The towncrier, with sadness in his heart, and bitterness in his speech, was obliged to retrace his steps, and tinkle his bell again, and cry his *oyez*! to another tune:—"Ladies and gentlemen," cried he, "I am sorry to inform you that the celebrated consort, by the celebrated Bostin band, which was to be given free-gratis-for-nothin', at the townhouse, at six o'clock, P.M. in the afternoon, is *postponed!*— because, ladies and gentlemen, the S'lackmen will not open the townhouse—unless the Bostin band pays them *ten dollars!!* "

From the foregoing fact, (if fact it be,) the belief may be entertained that half a century's lapse has made but little difference in the habits or tastes of the islanders. Dancing and music, then, may be set down as abominations at Nantucket. Abomination, or no abomination—to the ball of the shearing Ruth and Mary were invited; and to it they intended, by hook or by crook, to go. Being a sudden thing, and "got up" at short notice, it became no small matter of concernment to the girls, how they should dress, and get ready in time for the occasion. There was the curling of the hair, (another abomination,) the assortment of the silks and the brocade, the trimming of ditto, and the lacing of stays,—not stays like the body-killing corsets of the present day—but stays made of some fitting material of great strength; and sometimes faced with a bright satin, purposely to show its colour through a thin muslin over-dress. Whatever was the material selected, it was invariably sherred all round, at intervals of an inch, with thin whalebone, to give ease and elasticity to the garment, and comfort to the wearer.

Such were the stays which our mothers and grandmothers wore at Nantucket, even while they were children, and, when they grew up, they were the best shaped and most graceful women in America—rounded, but not cramped or "collapsed" at the waist;—with prominent hips and chest, and a fullness of the bosom, like most English women who have been well nurtured. Hauling taught upon the strong plaited clewline, which was rove through the grommets of the Nantucket women's whalebone stays, was to them a comfortable operation—not metaphorically or ironically, like the skinning of eels, when an eel-woman peeled their jackets off, and said—"Lord bless your soul—they likes it!—they loves to be skinn'd!"—but literally, in point of fact—an agreeable operation. With the quantity of whalebone about them, which it was then the fashion to wear, there was not the least danger of too great compression of the body. The long waisted sort of court-dress of the females, (such as may be seen in the pictures of the full-dressed belle of the time of Louis XIV.,) ornamented with a neatly stitched and pointed stomacher, of satin or brocade, always sat well and looked well over such admirable stays; and the position of the wearer, whether standing, walking, or sitting, were greatly improved by their use. While wearing the by-gone stays of whalebone, with the broad busk, no fear needed to be entertained of pulmonary disease being contracted, by the leaning posture of the body in sedentary employments. They were the "preventer-braces,"—the panacea for consumption,—and not the promoters of it. Would that Mrs Cantelo, and the other *marchandes des modes*, would revive the whalebone stays of our grandmothers, and furnish the fashionable lady with a grateful pressure for the body, instead of the pinching, crucifying, squeezing bandage, called a corset! We do not despair, after this, of hearing the delicate city dame making inquiries after a comfortable "*Miriam Coffin*," in the warehouses of sherring and padding, or wheresoever else the priestess of fashion presides.

"Where can the girls be?" repeated Miriam; and stepping to the stairway, she called out—"Ruth, where art thou?"

"I'm in my chamber, mother," answered Ruth, from above.

"What art thou doing aloft so long?"

"Nothing in particular," answered Ruth.

"What's Mary about, then?" asked Miriam.

"She's helping me," returned Ruth.

Imbert and Grimshaw burst into a fit of uncontrollable laughter, at the *naive* dialogue which had been going on between the mother and daughter; and the former felt himself called upon to explain away his rudeness, by the remark that he had been reminded of the current sea-story of the captain who called out to Tom and Jack, in the maintop, to ascertain what they were doing, who answered much after the manner she had been replied to by her daughter Ruth.

"I am also reminded of this little incident," continued Imbert, "that there is a singular habit prevalent among the females of your island, which I have never observed elsewhere."

"And what is it, pray?" asked Miriam good humouredly.

"I have noticed," answered he, "that they constantly interlard their conversation with sea-phrases."

Miriam shook her head in doubt; but before she had framed a reply, denying the truth of the assertion, the young ladies entered the parlour, and the current of conversation was turned.

"Well, upon my word!" exclaimed Miriam, addressing Ruth, "thou'rt trick'd out mighty fine, to be sure!—Why hast thou changed thy dress? Thou know'st it is e'en a-most time to go to bed, and thou hast taken a deal of trouble for nothing."

"Why, mother, I want to take a short walk," answered Ruth, with an awkward attempt at indifference of manner.

"Where would'st thou go at so late an hour?" asked Miriam.

"Over to cousin Peleg's, with Mary," replied Ruth.

"What would'st thou do there, that thou canst not as well do at home?" again questioned Miriam.

"Nothing much," said Ruth; "I'm tired of staying at home forever—and—I want to *go out*," continued she, with impatience.

"Go out!" repeated Miriam, suspiciously; "thou hast been '*out*' enough to-day, and I don't approve of girls gadding about so much. Thou may'st take off thy bonnet, Ruth;—thou can'st not go. Pretty respect thou'rt paying to thy company, to '*go out.*'"

"They may go along with us, if they will," said Ruth, grasping at the last chance of escaping from her mother.

"Certainly!" said Grimshaw.

"Most undoubtedly!" said Imbert, jumping up with alacrity, and reaching for his hat.

"Nay—nay;"—said Miriam, "that may not be:—Not that I object to thy friends walking with thee, Ruth; but there is some junketting going on down below there, as I hear, and thy stay at Cousin Peleg's will be very short, I warrant thee:—Thou wert going to the dance, Ruth:—Put up thy bonnet—I forbid thee stirring tack or sheet."

Ruth did as she was commanded, but tears came into her eyes at the disappointment. Mary also dared not to go, now that Ruth was forbidden, for fear that her father should make the discovery, and be displeased with her. A disagreeable silence ensued; but after the awkward interval of a few minutes, Miriam resumed her conversation with Imbert:—

"So," she said, breaking in upon the pause, "thou thinkest our women use too many words of the sea?"

"Every female I have conversed with to-day, has said something of that sort, in the course of her speech, so very broad as to excite my remark upon the fact. I have never, in any other place, observed the females make use of so many sea-phrases in common conversation. I confess, however, that I do not at all wonder at it," continued he; "for the male population, being quite actively and constantly engaged in the business of the whale-fishery, have acquired the technical mode of conversing upon the sea. The customs of the sailor, like all other acquired habits of long duration, are not put off at pleasure, nor can he leave them at will on board the ship. They travel with him, and acquire the force of habit. Now as all habits, whether of manner or conversation, are caught imperceptibly from those with whom we are on terms of intimacy, and, in time, by repetition or frequent indulgence, become a second nature, it is not surprising that your females should be found in the habit of using sea-phrases."

"Thou mistakest altogether, friend Imbert; I have never observed the practice; and, speaking for myself," observed Miriam, "I can assure thee, thou wilt never discover the habit in *me*." This observation was accompanied with a self-satisfied toss of the head.

"It may be that I never shall be able to detect a sea-speech in your conversation, Mrs. Coffin; but I can scarcely believe you form an exception to the general rule. I am so certain that you do not," said Imbert, "that I will venture to make a hazardous bargain with you."

"Let me hear thee propose it," said Miriam.

"The hazard shall be equal," said Imbert, "and the forfeit must be scrupulously yielded by the losing party. On my part, I will stake you a satin bonnet of the newest Boston fashion, and throw my character for acuteness of observation into the scale;— and on your side, there shall be hazarded a free consent (which, if you lose, shall be granted at once) for the young ladies to go to the ball to-night;—and that which shall determine the wager is this—that in the course of twenty minutes' conversation, you do, or do not, utter some palpable sea-phrase. *I* take the affirmative, and *you* the negative side, of course."

"Agreed!" said Miriam; "your bonnet and your character will strike the beam, depend on't—Jim!" continued she, addressing an Indian servant boy—"why hast thou not made the fire? I told thee to build one long ago;

and thou hast left the wood carelessly thrown down upon the hearth. Come,—stir thyself, and make up the fire; and then do thou get the broom, and brush up the dirt thou hast made."

Now Jim was an obtuse, dogged, matter-of-fact fellow, and never exceeded his orders; and he ventured to contradict his mistress. "You on'y tole me to bring a wood—never tole me to make a fire," said Jim, as he began to arrange the back-log in his clumsiest manner.

"Psha!—How awkward thou art," said Miriam; "take up the log again, and place it—mark what I tell thee—place it *fore-and-aft* the fireplace!"

"Victory!—I've won the wager!" exclaimed Imbert;—"Put on your bonnets again, girls, and let's to the ball!"

The girls *did* put on their bonnets, without waiting for a second bidding, and tripped it off to the dance,—well pleased at the stratagem that procured them the enjoyment of the forbidden pleasure; while Miriam, as she detected the slip of her tongue, bit her lips with chagrin, and hastily left the room, to conceal her discomfiture.

CHAPTER NINE.

"The Manager's Last Kick!"

Burlesque Play.

Merrily danced the Quaker's wife,
And merrily danced the Quaker.

Old Song.

THERE are, or were, no ball-rooms in Nantucket; and it was with dismay that the committee of arrangement, on the morning of the shearing, reported progress—if being foiled at every turn in obtaining a room suitable for dancing, and finally being beaten to a stand-still, may be so reported. The cards of invitation, or rather "*invites*" by word of mouth, slily whispered, with an injunction of secrecy, by way of *nota bene*, were given out; and it now became an affair of honour, as well as of credit, to make the invitations good. What was to be done? Several of the empty warehouses, or oil-stores, could with but little preparation be put in order

107

for the reception of the company; and it was a matter of perfect indifference, as to the appearance of the place, if a spacious room could be obtained where dancing could be going on with comfort:—but such a place was not to be had for the asking, nor for love;—much less could it be obtained for money, when the object was made known. The bare proposition to any of the owners would have defeated the whole scheme, and rendered any subsequent attempt to get up a ball abortive; for the opposition and the ire of the Selectmen would have been roused,—and then—"good night to *Marmion!*" Secrecy was, therefore, the watchword; and he or she who could not keep the secret was unworthy of dancing. Ulysses gave a similar intimation to Telemachus, when he whispered in his ear—"*Quiconque ne sait pas se taire, est indigne de gouverner.*"

The second story of Jethro Coffin's storehouse, situated near the wharf, had been cleared of its contents for a considerable time, in anticipation of the arrival of his ships. Nothing but the intervention of the shearing had prevented its being filled to overflowing with oil-barrels from the Leviathan; and the following morning was set apart for breaking bulk, and for the transfer of a portion of her cargo to the building. The situation was sufficiently remote from the habitations of the uninitiated islanders; the noise of the fiddle would scarcely be heard in the town, and Jethro would retire to bed early—and so would doubtless the rest of the *magnates*, after a day of toil upon the common. The young men were desperate—it was noon of the day—a place *must* be had:—Jethro Coffin's loft was a good loft—a capital and capacious room—he would surely know nothing of its occupation until all was over,—and *then*, what if he did?

Thus pushed to extremities, there appeared no alternative but to take possession of the empty store-room; and the committee forthwith agreed among themselves that Jethro's loft should be the ball-room, and that young Isaac should be called in as an adjunct committee-man;—and this for two reasons:—first, because he might otherwise feel himself neglected, and so blab of the base uses to which the premises of his father were about to come; and second, because certain keys, to which Isaac could have access, were necessary to unlock certain doors of entrance and egress. Violence would scarcely be tolerated; and indeed it could by no means be resorted to. A convenient flight of steps led to the second story from the outside; and the drawing of a bolt would give them admission, without the necessity of passing through the lower apartment, which was stowed with barrels, cordage, sea-stores, and apparatus for whale-fishing; and withal was by no means a pleasant entrance for the revellers. Isaac was therefore hastily sought out, and the project was warily proposed to him.

"Neighbour Isaac, how dost thou do?—Fine sport this, once more, after thy three years' absence!" said one of the managers to the lad, as he found him strolling among the shear-pens, munching a huge piece of gingerbread.

"To-be-sure!" said Isaac; "nobody enjoys it more than I do."

"Art thou going to the dance to-night, Isaac?"

"I should like to go very well, but I've got no *invite*":—answered he.

"Oh, that's easily managed," replied the manager, "and we've put thy name on the list. Thou must not miss coming by any means;—I hear there are a number of smart little girls from New-Bedford, with black eyes and rosy cheeks, who are setting their caps for thee—and they will all be at the dance to-night:—so thou see'st that thou'rt expected."

"Indeed!—I'll come,—thou may'st be sure on't," said Isaac, "but where dost thou hold the dance?"

"Why, to tell thee a truth, and a secret to boot, we have not yet made up our minds as to the place. Canst thou not put thy wits to work, and help us in our extremity? There's Peleg Folger's shanty—but we don't like it altogether; its rather old, and the floor is none of the best—and then he's had the cooper at work for some time, and it might be dangerous to carry lights in among the shavings:—then there's neighbour Hussey's store-house; but it's full of tar and grease, and the try-kettles are in the way. What dost think of thy father's loft?"

"There's not a larger nor a better place on the island," replied Isaac, upon whom the invitation of his seniors, and the story of the New-Bedford girls, with black eyes and cherry cheeks, added to the morning's lecture of Peleg Folger, had their full effect.

"Well, then, suppose thou should'st take a turn with us down to the landing, and help us to arrange a little; thou'rt not particularly engaged, I see?"

"Not in the least," replied Isaac; "I'll give thee all the assistance in my power to set the dance a-going. Truly a shearing without a dance would be a new thing with us. But it is time thou should'st be at thy preparations, if thou dost intend to have anything but bare clap-boards and shingles to look at."

"Thou art right, friend Isaac; and we are well reminded that it is time to be stirring. By-the-by, thou has'st better run and get the key of the storehouse, and we will meet thee at the door. Hark, in thine ear,—there's no particular necessity of telling thy father about the affair. He will know all about it in due season, thou know'st."

"I understand," said Isaac, winking and placing his finger knowingly by the side of his nose;—and away he scampered for the key.

"There—that's well got over," said the manager, "and our propsects begin to brighten up apace."

"But," observed another committee-man, "suppose we should be thwarted in obtaining possession—or suppose, after we do effect a lodgement, and all is arranged for the dance, that neighbour Jethro should get wind of the trespass, and come in and order us away—eh? What say'st thou to that?"

"Never fear—never fear; he'll be none the wiser till it is all over. The chances are in our favour, in consequence of the delay in making preparation. I'll tell thee how we've managed such things before. A sentinel must be posted to give us notice of interlopers, and the cabin of some convenient vessel, with a strong padlock for security, will serve to imprison a spy for a time;—or, for lack of a cabin, I would consent to head up the ill-natured fellow in an oil-cask, sooner than be defeated after all this trouble. Jethro Coffin was once a young man himself, and is up to all these tricks;—so that if he does get information of the dance, he will be wise enough to go to bed quietly, and forbear to thrust his head into the lion's mouth."

"Thou are a veteran, and a daring manager, truly," replied his companion; "and I will follow in thy wake with the obedience of a pupil.

But Isaac comes,—and see!—he holds the key up in token of his success."

Isaac now made his appearance, and applied the key to the yielding lock. Having admitted the managers through the inside passages to the loft, the door opening upon the outer stairway was unbolted, and the trapdoor over the store-room secured against intrusion from below. The committee-men were soon reinforced, and they went about their task in good earnest. Jethro's key was shortly afterwards hanging in its usual place at his dwelling-house, over the mantel-piece. The reader will pardon us for being thus particular about small matters, because we are anxious to show what pains were taken, by the young men of the time, to hoodwink the authorities, both legal and parental, in a community that was once, if not now, accused of being Puritanic and over-strict in their manners and habits.

Many hands make light work, they say: and some twenty young and athletic men soon completed the decorations of the loft. The beams and the rough siding were quickly covered with the spare white canvas of the neighbouring vessels—the festooning of which was easier and better accomplished by the sinewy hands of the sailor-managers, than it could possibly have been by the delicate touch of a modern upholsterer. It is said that the Grecian architect took the hint of his capital, from a bush of acanthus drooping from a flower-pot; and why should not the sailor learn the art of festooning from the brailing of a sail, or from the graceful appearance of a half-flowing sheet when he is reefing? There are more natural folds in the drapery of a ship's canvas on various occasions of enlarging or taking in sail, than a landsman would dream of. Therefore, let the fresh-water critic put a stopper upon his smile, if, haply, one should light up his vinegar countenance, at the idea of a sailor turning upholsterer.

Flags of every description, and eke of every maritime nation extant, were procured from the same source that yielded the canvas. The stripes and the stars,—handsomest of national emblems, were then not in being. The grouping of the party-coloured bunting upon the white ground of the canvas, and the festooning overhead to hide the rafters of the building, were not so soon arranged as the ground-work. But by dint of putting up, and taking down to alter for the better, and a deal of consultation upon every point of the display, it was at last agreed that the ornaments could not be improved in arrangement, nor be placed so as to present a more finished *coup d'œuil* to the spectator.

The lighting of the apartment next claimed the grave consultation of the committee. But how could that be a subject for long consultation, when oil of the best, and candles of the whitest sperm, were the staples of the island? There were ship-lamps to be had for the asking; and the lamp apparatus of the light-house, which still lay untouched and uninjured where it had fallen, was to be had for the trouble of picking it up.— Chandeliers, to be let down from the peak of the roof, were easily supplied, by boring holes in barrel heads, and suspending them with light cordage, from which the incomparable sperm-taper would send forth its clean light, as well as from a more costly piece of workmanship. A dressing-room for the ladies at one end of the apartment, and a closet for refreshments at the other, were prepared by stretching sails across the room, whose blank and bald appearance was relieved by festooned flags, and bunches of party-coloured signals, fancifully grouped. Benches placed round the entire space of the ball-room, covered with clean ravens-duck, unrolled from the bolt, furnished seats for at least two hundred guests. These arrangements being completed, the floor next claimed attention. The holy-stones of the craft in the harbour were put in requisition; and a vigorous application of these abominations of the sailor, over a plentiful supply of soap and sand, soon reduced the asperities of the planking, and rendered the floor sufficiently smooth on the surface for dancing. The trundling mop did the rest, and put the finish to the arduous duties of the committee-men;—who now, with arms a-kimbo, surveyed their handiwork with no little pride and exultation.

"We have two hours yet to sundown," said one of the active managers, "and have barely time to spread the information among those who have received invitation to the dance. Let us retire; an ablution, and a change of dress, will do some of us no harm—particularly those who have scaled the rafters among Jethro's cobwebs."

The door of the ball-room was carefully closed, and the managers went into the town. Presently young men and women might be seen scudding from house to house, where a nod, and a wink, and a whisper, or a telegraphic signal from the fingers, told the news that all things were prepared for the dance. The information spread, also, among the young folks who yet lingered on the common; and by sundown all the *invitees* were rigged out in their best, and ready to steer for the metamorphosed store-room of the unconscious Jethro.

The secret was well kept as to the place of meeting; and even Miriam, and the other staid dames, could only conjecture that a dance was on the carpet, by the unusual attention of their daughters to their personal appearance, after the amusements of the day were supposed to be over. By a species of management, which the young ladies of Sherburne were obliged to resort to, and which is well understood by all other females who are bent upon the gratification of their wishes, they slipped off under various pretenses,—such as a walk, or a visit to a neighbour,—in company with their favoured swains; and when evening began to gather, the ball-room began to fill. The young damsels were delighted with what they saw, and they took every opportunity to praise the zeal and taste which had been exerted, "at the shortest possible notice," in their behalf; and they essayed to recompense, by their smiles, and their cheerful behaviour, the projectors of the entertainment which would wind up the festivities of the Island Carnival. Who, but a sour old hunks, would put his veto upon an amusement so congenial to the buoyant feelings of the young,—especially on a day like the shearing!

But alas!—what a short-sighted animal is man! How small a thing is sufficient to disperse his visions of glory, and becloud the bright colours of the rainbow! Napoleon, it is said, would have gained his last battle, and riveted the chains of Europe, but for a trivial accident; and Columbus would have missed the discovery that gave him a deathless fame, except for the appearance of a few straggling spears of seaweed, as he was on the point of putting his ship about to return homeward. The great machinery of life—as well as that which brings happiness to mankind, or gives peace and plenty to a nation, is equally dependent upon trifles for its nice adjustment and regularity of motion. The drawing of a bolt or a pin, which a man may move with his little finger, will set an entire establishment at work, which gives bread and employment to a thousand human beings; and—for further illustration—the scraping of a single bow upon the strings of a fiddle will set a whole ball-room in active motion.

In the hurry of "getting up" the preparations for the dance, not a thought had been bestowed upon the fiddler—the very main spring of the great movement! Certes, it was a most unfortunate oversight; for some five score of dancers were already assembled, and stood on tiptoe with expectation, and waited, with beating hearts and anxious palpitations, for the signal to begin. But if the dancers appeared with beating hearts, how much more did the hearts of the managers beat with anxiety and throb with dismay!

"We are all aback!" exclaimed one, as with blanched cheek he hurriedly gathered some half dozen of his coadjutors into a corner; "devil a fiddler have we provided for, and not a man is there on the island who can draw a bow!"

"The devil!" exclaimed the rest, in concert.

"What is to be done?—I would give a barrel of the best sperm, if Captain Jonathan Coleman was here. He doffs the Quaker, and plays the fiddle, at sea; although he wears his big beaver and shad-belly when ashore. We might press him into the service, if Jethro's other ship had arrived;—zounds! was there ever any thing so unfortunate!"

"What's the matter?" asked a manager who had just come in; "why a'nt you on the floor, jigging it away to some lively tune?"

"Matter enough, my friend!" was the reply, "we have no tune to jig to— *no fiddler, d—n it!*"

"*The devil!*"

"We have called upon that gentleman often enough, and I don't see that he is forthcoming to aid us in our strait:—But hist—listen!—what is that? Speak of the devil, and straightway his imp appears! There is a fiddle a-going somewhere in this vicinity, or my ears deceive me. Don't you hear the squeak? Come!—let us follow up the sound in a body; and be he man, or devil, forth he shall come,—unless he be too unsubstantial for our grasp."

"Ay—ay!" exclaimed another, "I'll lend a hand to bring him, will he, nill he:—at all events, he *shall* fiddle for us, 'whether he will or no—Tom Collins!'"

The affair did not brook delay, and forth rushed the managers in pursuit of the fiddler,—exciting, by their conduct, no little wonder in the ball-room. They traced the sounds of the scraper of catgut, until he was fairly made out to be the black cook of a sloop, that had lately arrived from New-York, and was waiting for a cargo of oil. The negro was the sole tenant of the little vessel, and was amusing himself in the cabin, during the absence of the commander, by running over his short catalogue of dancing tunes, which he played "*by ear*;" that is to say, mechanically, without knowing one note from another. He was now playing them for the thousand and first time, and had, of course, by much practice, got them well established in his memory. He was one of that numerous tribe of self-taught violin players that inhabit the Dutch neighbourhood, along the shore of New-Jersey, and in sight of the city of New-York. The spot most prolific in such ebony artists, is familiarly known by the name of Communipaugh.

The black, who was now sawing away for his own edification, had played many a night, and all night, at the frolicks in and round about the little village of Bergen, while the untiring Dutch girls and their athletic admirers "stomp'd it down" to his rattling music. He was just the man for the dance at Jethro's storehouse; and, as time developed, proved no mean professor in his way.

"Hillo-there!" exclaimed a voice at the companion-way of the sloop; "come up here, thou man of the fiddle!"

"Hello-dere, yoursef!—what a want wid a nigger, massa?" demanded the black.

"Come up here, thou gut-scraper, and bring thy fiddle along with thee;" said a committee-man;—"thou'rt wanted ashore, to play for the folks."

"I can't leave de sloop;—massa cap'n gone ashore, and nobody here. What you gib a nigger, if he go;—heh, massa?" demanded the negro, thrusting his curly pate through the companion-way.

There was no time for parley nor bargaining; and he had no sooner shown his body halfway above deck, than he was seized by four gentlemen in drab, against whom he found it useless to contend, and was quickly trundled ashore; while a fifth descended into the cabin, and captured his instrument. A few steps brought them to the foot of the stair at the storehouse. Here, putting down the black, who was sorely frightened at the unceremonious usage of his abductors, they addressed a few words to him, of the following effect:—

"Now, friend, thou'rt to understand that there is one of two things to be done—and that quickly. Mark!—we will have no words—either thou must go up, and fiddle for the dancers until midnight, for the which thou shalt be well rewarded,—or thy fiddle shall be broken into shivers over thy pate; and perhaps a ducking alongside the wharf will be thrown into the bargain. Choose, and be quick!—Yea, or nay!"

"Well, but, massa—."

"Not a word more—be quick, or I'll try the strength of thy instrument on thy head!"

"Stop! massa—stop!—don't smash a-fiddle, massa. I s'pose I *mus* go; but you scare a-nigger so—you 'mos make 'em turn white!"

"Never care for that;—up stairs with thee!—and a noggin of strong waters shall restore the tone of thy stomach, and the Egyptian darkness of thy complexion. March, march!" And up stairs went the unfortunate fiddler, attended by the honourable committee as a rear body-guard. The bareheaded professor was quickly "ensconced behind the arras," and a full half pint of "raal ginniwine Jimmecky," without dilution, was poured down his throat, by a desperate tormentor.

"Hah!—dat smacks!—Yah—yah—yah! I t'ink I feel 'mazin better now," said the black; "I don't care if you scare a-nigger agin, if you treat him *arter* wid good likker like dat."

"Thou feel'st much better—dost thou ? What's thy name?"

"Pete Schneiderkins, massa."

"Where art thou from?"

"I comes from Communipaugh, in de Jarseys."

"Well, then, Mr. Pete Schneiderkins, of Communipaugh, thou wilt be pleased to take thy station, and strike up." The managers' edict having gone forth, Pete was introduced to a little bunk, or raised pulpit, at the side of the ball-room, where he began to tune his instrument;—and the dancers took their places.

Scrape—scrape, jangle—jangle, twang—tang,—went Pete's fiddle, as he screwed it up in the tuning;—but he screwed up the string too much; and then he let down the peg too far. Between his flats, and his sharps, and his scrapings, the restraint of the dancers began to wear off. The glee and the good humour of the managers returned, now that they had secured a fiddler, which ten minutes before was considered a hopeless thing. The incident was buzzed about, while Pete was trying to hit the happy medium of the strings; and it caused no little merriment among the dancers. The relief did not come a moment too soon; for that something was out of joint was manifest to the girls; and the absence of all the active managers, at a time when dancing should have been under way, threw an awkward chill over the spirits of the assembled guests. All was now right again!—and so determined were the conductors of the revel that there should be no other vexatious interruption, that, had the meddlesome Selectmen made their appearance in a body, it would have been only a "*hey—presto—bygone!*" operation, to have bottled them up in their own oil-casks.

We find it recorded among the papers of Peleg Folger, who amused himself, at an advanced age, in writing an unpublished history of his time, that "Certayne Yuthe nott having ye feare of God afore theire Eyes did sorely grieve ye S'lack Menn by their Doings, and did threaten most contumashusly and with a high Hand to bungg ye afore said Magistrates up within certayne Ile-Casks—ye which would indubitably have proved an unsavoury Operation and a most unChristian Trespasse upon the Libertys of ye Subjecte." We are thus fortified by the authority of a writer of antiquity, whose lucubrations no contemporary worthy of notice has dared to controvert; and we may therefore venture to publish the fact to the world, that the managers of the ball afore-said, did actually prepare "certain oil-casks" for the reception of the intruders, provided the Selectmen had made the anticipated onslaught.

But let the dance proceed:—scrape—scrape, again sawed out the violin of Peter of Communipaugh, and a short prelude upon the strings announced that his instrument was in perfect tune. The precision with which an ignorant Communipaugh fiddler will attune his strings, has often excited the astonishment of the scientific professor; and a violinist of repute, who had witnessed their displays, was once heard to assert, that not one player in a hundred who make pretension to skill, ever equalled the sable Dutch fiddlers of Bergen in nicety of ear in the detection of discord.

Peter Schneiderkins of Communipaugh gave the signal, and a country dance was led off. Vigorously did Peter play that night, and well did he sustain the musical reputation of the Dutch neighbourhood, which the inimitable Deidrich Knickerbocker, the American Herodotus, informs us may be distinguished from all other places, by an overshadowing cloud of tobacco smoke. The sweat rolled down the ebony face of Peter, while labouring at his instrument, and keeping the time with the heel of his iron-shod brogan of horse-skin and ben-leather. And lightly tripped the cheery-cheeked damsels to the music of the ebony Peter; and never has Nantucket seen a sprightlier dance nor a better arranged ball-room;—nor an assemblage of fairer women, nor a more robust, active, and intelligent set of young men, than were then gathered together, by stealth as it were, to partake of an innocent amusement.

Imbert, accompanied by Grimshaw and the young ladies, entered the ball-room in the midst of the first dance, but stopped for a moment at the entrance, where the powerful light, and the novel arrangement of the drapery of the room, burst upon their sight like a picture of enchantment. The moving, graceful figures of the females completed the magic scene. Ruth and Mary were handed to the dressing-room of the ladies; from which, after certain modifications of gowns and adjustment of curls, they reappeared just as a new set was called, and in time to take the head of the next country dance.

It was not until some few years afterward that the admirable *cotillion* was introduced into this country. The French officers, who came with Lafayette and Rochambeau, in the early part of the Revolution, were the first to teach the Americans the mystery of that agreeable and rather ceremonious dance; and Rhode Island was the foremost to give currency in America to the quadrilles of France. Heretofore the *contra-danse* and the Scottish reels were only understood and practised, and, perhaps, they were altogether sufficient for the taste of the country, for refinement in amusement was not then deemed necessary for enjoyment. The hearty exercise of the latter species of dancing, was nearly allied to those habits of activity and industry which pervaded every portion of America at that time, and which contributed so materially to the bloom of the countenance and the flexible and rounded forms of the women. The progress towards wealth, and what is termed refinement, has somewhat abated these; and we are, at this day, too apt to discover in their stead an alabaster complexion, and a slightness of frame, which denote the reverse of rosy health and bodily exercise.

The ladies, some sixty years ago, danced in full dress, and high-heeled slippers; and Ruth and Mary were not out of the fashion. Their trailing gowns, to be sure, if suffered to float off at full length, would be rather out of place in the dance; and their broad hoops would undoubtedly be voted a great bore by the present generation, if it were not for the prevailing fashion of cording the petticoat to an extent of unseemliness even more inconvenient than the ancient hooped under-dress. The remedy for the flowing trail was a natural one. The *danseuse* would simply secure it in the left hand, or cast it over the arm, which added a swimming grace to her movements, as her dress—balloon-like,— caught the inflation of the breeze; or, if the extension of both hands was required, as in the changes of the reel, a pin would secure it to the girdle without deranging the folds of the drapery. This peculiar manner of tucking up, or accommodating the exuberant length of the dress, was styled the "*trollupee*," and sometimes the "*negligee,*" but these terms, though appropriate and applicable to the ancient court-dress of the female, as was also that of "*knuckle-dabbers*" to the hand ruffles of the gentlemen, which were much worn formerly, will be sought for in vain in the "Belle Assemblée," or in the modern vocabulary of fashion. But how shall we explain away the encumbrance of high-heeled shoes? Yea, in good sooth, slippers with heels an inch and a half or two inches in height! What!—did our mothers dance in these? Truly they did—and danced well, too. They tripped it on the light fantastic toe with the heeled slipper, as adroitly and gracefully as a modern *demoiselle* with the heel-*less* apology for a shoe, which now graces her delicate foot;—even that foot which seems almost

> "*Too delicate* to touch the ground!"

There was nothing clumsy in the ancient slipper, neither:—there was no accumulation of leather about the heel, like that upon the hindermost part of the brogans of an Irish bog-trotter. It was a slipper, as light and handsome,—as "narrow in the shank,"—as beautifully Corinthian,—as any which we now see worn by the women; and far more costly than the satin or prunelle sported by the exquisites of the sex. A light, symmetrical, wooden heel, carefully shaped by a *pedemestrian*,[*] (we give the word as we once saw it on the sign of a last-maker, beneath the window of a classical school,) was inserted at the back part of the sole, and covered with delicate kid, or glistening goatskin from Barbary. Being neatly fitted and stitched with rows of white silk thread, it was finished by a cap, or single overlay of sole-leather, of the size of a shilling, and nearly as thin, at the place forming the bearing part of the heel. That these were pretty things to look at, cannot be denied:—but that they were precisely "*the thing*" to

---

[*]And why should not the manufacturer of *lasts*, smelling daily of the ancient dust of a classical seminary, coin an expressive word to suit his necessity, as well as Doctor Johnson, who saw the poverty of our language, and gave to the world a similar term. Let us hear Peter Pindar, in his satire of "*Bozzi and Piozzi*," upon this subject:—

"BOZZI.

"When Foote his leg by some misfortune broke,
Says *I* to Johnson, all by way of joke,
'Sam, sir, in Paragraph, will soon be clever,
And take off Peter better now than ever.'
On which says Johnson, with hesitation,
'George will rejoice at Foote's *depeditation.*'
On which says *I*, (a penetrating elf!)
'Doctor, I'm sure you coined that word yourself.'
On which he laugh'd, and said I had divin'd it,
For *bona fide* he had really coin'd it:
'And yet, of all the words I've coin'd,' says he,
'My dictionary, sir, contains but three.'"

dance in, we are not prepared to aver. Nevertheless, they were used in the dance before and after the introductlon of the quadrilles; and their slight clutter upon the floor was far pleasanter to the ear than the sharp rattle of the Spanish castanet, which we sometimes see brought in to give distinctness to the measure of the music.

The costume of the stranger gentlemen, also, was not without its peculiarities. While Grimshaw appeared in plain habiliments of black, as became his profession of the law,—Imbert, who regarded not the attendant honours of the doctorate, which are frequently shadowed forth in a dress of sables,—had donned the fashionable garments of the period, and came forth, the very pink of dressy gentlemen, in a coat of bright red broadcloth with buttons of silver; small-clothes of white cassimere, with polished steel buckles at the knee, silk stockings, and shoes of sealskin; while his own incomparable hair of jet black was covered with a tailed wig, with pendant curls, over which he sported his beaver, or three-cornerd "*fantail macaroni;*"—a name, by the way, given to the jaunty cocked-hats of the last century.

And now behold our young ladies winding in the mazy dance on the floor of the ball-room—(the place of all places best calculated to discover beauties or faults in a woman) with their rich rustling brocade dresses fitting over their whalebone stars enchantingly; with trails, and hoops, and trollupées, and negligées; high-heeled shoes, stitched to admiration; bright eyes, glossy ringlets, clear skin, and faultless forms; with slender feet, that the longskirted dress permitted once in a while to show forth, as they dodged backward and forward, like Sir John Suckling's "peeping mice,"—a simile applied to a modest woman's feet, when she dances, which Sir John expresses very prettily in his couplet :—

> "Her feet, beneath the petticoat,
> Like little mice, peep'd in and out,"

And then sprinkle among these enchantresses a corresponding number of good-looking men,—some with unromantic drabcoloured, single-breasted coats, and small clothes; and here and there a smart sailor jacket, (adorned with double rows of gilt buttons,) surmounting white ravensduck pantaloons;—and the rest of the men-kind dressed, knuckle-dabbers, red coats, tailed wigs, and all, like the rest of the world,—and a picture as characteristic as can well be painted of by-gone times in America, and of Nantucket in particular, will present itself to the mind's eye, and require but little aid from the imagination to fill up and render complete.

Imbert selected, by right of being her *cavalier servente* for the time, the gentle and amiable Mary for his partner in the dance; while Grimshaw, with becoming solicitude, sought and obtained the hand of Ruth. The dance proceeded, and Imbert acquitted himself marvellously well. There were none who excited more admiration for agility and grace than the couple who led off; and it may not be denied that Mary was a good deal envied in the possession of so handsome and so fashionable a partner as Imbert, who attracted all eyes, and was most critically scanned both by males and females. Ruth was less fortunate in her partner; and she was deeply mortified by the mistakes and general awkwardness of Grimshaw, who was, in truth, no favourite with the graces. His long legs got entangled in the dresses of the females, and created sad havoc among the satins and brocade of his neighbours; while, like a raw recruit under the hands of the drill sergeant, he invariably turned to the right, when he should face to the left. A general titter followed all his essays at agility, and completed his confusion, as well as the vexation and shame of Ruth. Deep burning blushes overspread her face; her black eyes flashed, and a curl of contempt set upon her lip. It would have been too much for the endurance of a spirited girl like Ruth, but for an accident which happened near them, and turned the laugh upon other objects. A neat girl had been "trotted out" by a tall young sapling, in Quaker costume, and both met with an unpleasant discomfiture as they were sailing down the dance together at too rapid a pace. The foot of the gentleman slipped, and he fell sprawling before his partner; while the damsel was forced to make a flying leap over his recumbent body. Her foot tripped, and lo! they were seated, face to face, upon the floor. The effect was ludicrous enough, and thereupon, instead of exciting commiseration, a hearty laugh ensued, which luckily drew off the attention of the dancers from the odd manœuvres of Grimshaw. However unfortunate it might be to others, it was at any rate a great relief to Ruth in the further prosecution of the dance.

There are few things that have a more abiding continuance in the imagination of a young and elegant female, than the awkwardness of a partner in dancing. She can forgive and forget anything but the clumsiness in her attendant, which, by contact and association, brings ridicule upon herself. It will be sufficient for the present to say, that the seeds of dislike to Grimshaw were already sown in the mind of Ruth; and we shall afterwards see what fruit they will bring forth.

There were other eyes this night that looked with pleasure upon the countenances of Ruth and Mary, besides those of Grimshaw and Imbert. But, if the whole truth be told, the strict attention of these gentlemen to the daughters of Jethro and Peleg had also excited the observation and displeasure of several sighing swains; and among others were Thomas Starbuck, the admirer of Ruth, and Harry Gardner, who in childhood had been the playmate of Mary, and of late years affectionately attached to her. Both these young men had followed the sea, though in a humble capacity, and were not much over eighteen years of age. The girls themselves were two years younger; and, of course, all the parties were too seriously juvenile to make and receive visits in the fight of professed lovers; much less could they allow the world to believe that they were affianced. Young men at eighteen are supposed to be a greater distance from that arbitrary period of maturity, when they are accounted capable of taking upon themselves the cares of a family, than young women at sixteen, who at that age are frequently made the objects of particular attention of men much further advanced in years. Nevertheless, soft words had passed between them; and Harry and Thomas felt themselves privileged to hope that, when they should come to the age of manhood, and parents should give consent, they might successfully prosecute their respective suits. It was, therefore, with anxiety and alarm that they saw their favoured ones gallanted all the day by strangers, and as pertinaciously danced with at night by the same intruders. Causes slight as these have, before now, strung the bow and shot the arrow of jealousy; and that the poisoned shaft was rankling in the bosoms of these young men was most certain. But, before the evening closed, it was equally certain that the wounds were half cured; for Thomas had danced with Ruth, without entangling her dress like his fancied rival, Grimshaw; and Harry led his Mary gaily through a reel; and the touch of her soft hand, and the glance of her blue eye, almost convinced him that he had not been supplanted by Imbert.

The evening began to wane, and the dancers to tire. Refreshments suitable to the occasion, were handed round, and the young women were waited upon by the beaux with a devotion that did credit to their gallantry. A set or two more, and a promenade to the music of Peter Schneiderkins, of Communipaugh, brought the hour of midnight; and, by common consent, the amusements of the dance and the shearing were declared to be ended.

We have thus given the outline of a festival which was no new thing at Nantucket sixty years ago; and which, from every indication, will not probably change materially for sixty years to come.

CHAPTER TEN.

Then as we watch the ling'ring rays,
  That shine from every star,
I'll sing the song of happy days,
  And strike the light guitar.
                              Barnett.

IMMEDIATELY after the termination of the ball, the decorations and embellishments of Jethro Coffin's store-room were removed. To give an adequate idea of the despatch with which they were displaced, it may be only necessary to say, that they were swept away with as much facility as a child's house of cards, with its gingerbread ornaments, could be prostrated in ruins. Of the tapestry of canvas, ornature of bunting, and candelabra of barrel-heads, not a wreck was left behind, to tell the tale, within a short half hour after the company had dispersed:—so much easier is it to pull down than to build up. The holy-stoned floor, alone, remained a monument of the sinful excesses of the night, and was a puzzler to Jethro for many a day afterwards. But how fared the sable knight of Communipaugh? Let us "put out the light, and then" let the following dialogue upon the wharf tell the tale:—

"Well, massa! I hope you satisfy wid my 'zertion for de benefit ob de lady and de gentimen?" said Peter, as he carelessly thrumbed the strings of his violin, to call attention to his vocation: "Shall I call to-morrow on Massa Jeter Coffy for de pay?"

Peter, amidst the hurry and bustle of removing the trappings, had been unintentionally overlooked. He felt the neglect; and knowing that Jethro Coffin was the last man in the world whom his kidnappers would wish him to call upon, he had framed the question for a little retaliation.

"'Sdeath!—call on Jethro Coffin for thy pay indeed! Let me catch thee at it, and thy Ethiopian hide shall be flayed,—thou impudent skunk! What is thy demand?" asked the manager.

"I dont 'zactly know, massa," said Peter, scratching his head, in doubt whether to be reasonable or rapacious; "sometime I git more—sometime less—jis as I can ketch it. When I play fiddle for de Bargen gals, I stop in de middle ob de dance, and gib rap on de fiddle wid de fiddlestick; and den de men sing out '*de fiddler's dry!*'—and den, massa, I hole out de hat, and git shower ob sixumps:—but when I work by de job, I sometime git six shil'n, and sometime seben shil'n. I tink, massa, about seben shorn for de long job, and anudder dram for de scare, which almos make white man ob me, be about 'nuf for de nigger, massa."

"There's twice seven shillings for thee; and here is the liquor;—take it, bottle and all, and decamp. Dost hear?—Begone!—Vanish!"

"Yes a-massa!—Tank a-massa—I'm off in de nex bote,—yah—yah—yah!—chaw!"—and away went Mr. Pete Schneiderkins, of Communipaugh, chuckling and laughing, loud enough to be heard a mile off, at the folly of his paymaster, who had given him a month's wages,—that is to say, at hoeing corn,—for fiddling half a night.

"D—n the nigger!—will he never cease laughing?" was the exclamation of the last of the Quaker managers, as he turned a summerset over the low fence of his father's garden, to obtain entrance at the back door of the dwelling, which had been slily unfastened by a friend within, after the family had gone to rest.

It is to be regretted that the foregoing is the last and only blesssing we have to record, as being invoked upon the head of Peter Schneiderkins, of Communipaugh, "professor of dancing, and all other sorts of music;" and sorry are we that we can follow his fortunes no further, except to tell the reader, who may be curious to trace out his lineal descendants, that Peter begat ten strapping sons, black as the ace of spades, and these ten begat near a hundred more; a majority of whom turned out to be fiddlers of the first water, and are now scattered in and about Communipaugh. They all remember their grandfather's version of the scene at the Nantucket storehouse, and give accurate imitations of his never-ending chuckle, whenever he repeated the story about the young Quakers "stomping it down."

A short walk, after the dance broke up, brought Ruth, accompanied by Mary, who intended to stay with her cousin for the night, to the door of her father's dwelling. They were attended by Grimshaw and Imbert. The seats of the "*stoop*," as the New-Yorkers call it, (or "*porch*," as the Pennsylvanians have it, who, by the way, should call it *stoop*, for they are more Dutch now-a-days than the New-Yorkers,) seemed to possess considerable attraction for the gentlemen; for they came to an anchor thereupon, and were quite desirous that the girls should do the same, to keep them company. It was too late to invite them to enter into the house; and a sense of propriety made it obligatory upon the young women to abridge the sitting, as soon as an opportunity offered to give a hint to that effect. But the time slipped on:—one o'clock in the morning found them still chatting, in half whispers, at the door, and indulging in a recapitulation of the incidents of the day, and of the entertainment which had just terminated. The lively fancy of Imbert, to say nothing of the occasional efforts of Grimshaw, easily invested each occurrence, and each prominent actor, with the reality of new life and animation: his colouring was so fresh and natural, and his caricatures so quaint and amusing, that daylight would have found them still at the door, had not a voice from within sounded over the threshold, and warned them to retire.

"Ruth!" exclaimed the watchful Miriam, from her chamber.

"It is the voice of my mother! Friends,we must bid good night; or, if the time was truly told, perhaps good morning would be the better bidding."

The gentlemen made their adieux, and retired to the boardinghouse of a neighbour, where they had arranged to sojourn for a season. The invitation of Miriam, however, had changed the intention of Grimshaw, and the morrow was destined to see him seated at the board of Jethro Coffin. Imbert placed his arm within his companion's, and a silence of a minute or two succeeded. Each seemed to have "hung up his fiddle," after the exertions of the day, and to be wrapped in his own reflections, while pacing through the heavy sands.

"Grimshaw!" exclaimed Imbert, at last.

"Well, doctor?" was the short reply.

"I have been ruminating upon your good luck; and thinking what devilish fine quarters you are about getting into at Coffin's. The old woman seems to have taken a fancy to you. I should like to know why she preferred you,—a silent, plodding fellow,—before me, who have so frequently found my account among the women for an exhibition of good nature, and a deal of rattling nonsense. Explain, will you, Grim? Tell us a little about your 'drugs and spells,' and give us a gliff of that immensely long talk that you and she had together in a corner."

"It was professional; and therefore must remain a secret," answered Grimshaw, after a little hesitation.

"Close as oak, I perceive," replied Imbert; "I suppose," continued he, "you intend taking her bright-eyed daughter off her hands one of these days, by way of fee for your professional services."

"Such a thing may be within the range of possibility," carelessly answered Grimshaw.

"I should think it by no means impossible, nor improbable," returned Imbert, "if your zeal continues as it has begun. 'Sdeath! man—you stuck to her to-night like a burr. Go on and conquer, my boy; you will feather your nest well, if you succeed, for old Coffin is worth his tens of thousands. But what think you of my laying siege to the blue-eyed beauty?—She hath indeed—

> —'An eye,
> As when the blue sky trembles through a cloud
> Of purest white!'"

"Do you mean Miss Folger?"

"The same. She is just such a confiding, flexible, kindly being as I should desire to cling to me. There could be no danger of rubbers in after life with a woman of her happy temperament; but the devil may take the woman who would refuse to twine her will with mine, and to bend to the wish of her lord and master. I have no notion of allowing a female to imagine herself the oak, around which the man may twine as the ivy; nor would I, for the riches of Crœsus, lay siege to a termagant like—"

"Like whom?" demanded Grimshaw, observing that Imbert hesitated.

"No matter whom," said Imbert; "I was only thinking of a scene at the dance. By the way, Grim, did you notice Miss Ruth while you were dancing? 'Egad! I thought she would have run you through the gizzard while you were entangled in her skirt."

"I was, it is true, somewhat unfortunate with her long dress; but, bating that, don't you think I got on pretty well, for one who is not a professed dancer?"

"Um!—so so—a few lessons from Flurry, the Boston dancing master, would do you no harm."

"How much does he charge?" asked Grimshaw, who was a lover of pence; "I wouldn't mind taking a little '*tuition*' in that way, if it won't cost too much. These dancing masters and musicians are extravagant fellows in their charges:—Only think—it cost me five silver crowns, besides a world of pains, to learn to play the flute."

"The flute —Did you bring it with you to the island?"

"Yes."

"And luckily I have brought my guitar, which an old uncle, who resided many years among the *Senors*, taught me to thrumb passing well. I was not sure what sources of amusement we should meet with in this vile *terra incognita*, and so I tucked it into the berth of the packet. No doubt it has been transported to the boarding-house with our luggage; and, if you like, as the moon is up, we will return and surprise the girls with a serenade. What say you to the project?"

"Agreed! But what can we play together? My musical vocabulary is none of the richest; and, but for the assortment of psalm tunes which I play, will be found like my wardrobe—consisting only of a few pieces."

"We will think of that—and, as we come along, I'll give you a new lesson. If you have a good memory, I can teach you the music of a little Spanish serenade, which I wot of, in five minutes, and as I will either say or sing the words of the song myself, my unmusical voice will cover the defects of your playing—if so be you do *not* play well, of which you must be your own judge. So—*allons!* "

Ere Ruth and Mary laid their heads upon the pillow, they also had compared notes; and Imbert and Grimshaw, and Harry and Thomas, were severely passed in review. Disrobing themselves of their heavy gowns, and quilted petticoats, and unlacing their whalebone stays, the girls gave a glance at the mirror, and took a last survey of the devastation committed by the midnight dews upon their ringlets.

"What a fright I look like!" exclaimed Ruth.

"Fright, indeed! Lawyer Grimshaw did not appear to think so," returned Mary; "his eyes glared and gloated upon thee the whole livelong evening."

"Don't mention the hateful creature!" cried Ruth;—"Didst thou ever see such an awkward lout in all thy life? I have just learned from mother that this lawyer Kick-shaw will take up his abode with us for the future. Didst thou not think it strange, Mary, that such an ungain being should have made so great an impression upon the good will of mother?"

"I own I do," replied Mary, "but the man can't help his awkwardness; and I think thou art far too severe upon him, when thou callest him out of his name."

"Oh, as to that, one name is as good as another," said Ruth;—"Grimshaw or Kick-shaw,—both are applicable to the long-shanked animal. Dost thou remember with what agony he got through the dance?—how he stuck out his fins, and stiffened his fingers, till they looked for all the world like tallow candles?—and how he set his teeth as if he had the lockjaw, when he trundled his legs into the skirts of the girls' dresses? In good sooth his name doth not belie him. He looked *grim* as a giant; and, that he can *kick* like a restive mule, the girls at the dance can bear witness. Grimshaw or Kickshaw,—it is immaterial for us which name he goes by;—to-morrow he quarters upon my father. The Yankee starveling will haunt us for a season—heaven knows how long, since mother is his friend—and I dare say he will stick to us, like a Portengal leech, until he falls off from repletion!"

"*Yankee*, didst thou name him? How fiercely and immoderately thou talkest, cousin Ruth;—something has gone wrong with thee to-night."

"To be sure!" replied Ruth, "I did call him a Yankee: he comes from Connecticut, depend on't;—for that's the only place for slab-sided, long-legged, tin-peddling, leeching *coofs* like Grimshaw. The Yorkers call all the people of the eastern colonies '*Yankees:*' but it's right down ungenerous to do so. I would deny my nativity in the Bay colony forever, if I thought we were to be classed, with any justice, with such a mean set of psalm-singing drivellers!—For the matter of our yankeeism, thou knowest, Mary, that our island once belonged to the colony of New-York; and though in fact our ancestors did come, in a manner, of the ungracious Puritans, we have abjured their intolerant faith, and claim no affinity whatever with the race of bigots who still linger in Connecticut. It is the last hold of their blue-laws, persecution, and selfishness; and I will have to do with none of their offspring. Yankees, indeed!—Let the Yorkers look to their own colony, that it be not shortly overrun with the vermin!"

"Dearest cousin Ruth, how canst thou declaim against an honest, industrious, and enterprising portion of the American people!"

"*Honest*, indeed!" replied Ruth;—"Hast thou never heard of the duration of their honesty?—Nay—then I will tell thee. In the days of their witchcraft, the genius of Connecticut bestrode a broom, and rode through the air over the whole colony, to hear the complaints of the poverty-stricken people: but every snivelling varlet received from their genius in reply to their complaints, an answer in the words—

'Work or die!
Work or die!'

But behold, it came to pass that the genius relented, when she saw the misery and starvation that, notwithstanding, followed upon the feeble efforts of their constitutional laziness. Mounting the broomstick once more, and flying again over the colony, she shrieked out in a loud voice—

'Cheat and lie!
Cheat and lie!'

and ever since that time, they have lived up to the command of their colonial genius. Their *honesty* and *industry* consist in making ash pumpkin seeds, wooden nutmegs, and horn gunflints, which they meanly palm upon the unsuspecting for the genuine productions of nature;—while their *enterprise* consists in mounting a peddler's cart, and driving into the other colonies to vend their tin notions, wooden clockery, brooms and cheaterie.—Bah!—I despise a Yankee!"

Here was a breeze!—and while Ruth worked herself into a passion, her face became flushed, and her black eyes flashed lightning. Mary had never before seen Ruth so excited; but on the contrary she had usually displayed much good nature, and a cheerful countenance. She had, however, seen Miriam when under the influence of deep excitement, and was struck with the palpable resemblance the mother and daughter bore to each other on such occasions. Miriam, however, was seldom thrown from her balance, although a woman of strong passions. When offended, her eyes took the semblance of the basilisk's; her form dilated, and she would plant her feet firmly, and poise her body in an erect and haughty posture, as if defying "the world in arms;" her lip would curl, and her proud eye would bend contemptuously upon the object of her disdain. But Miriam was no shrew, nor did she descend to utter womanish invective. Her displeasure was felt the keener because she spoke but little when she was angered; but what little she did speak in wrath was the concentration of venom.

"Would'st thou believe it," continued Ruth, "the fellow had the assurance to press my hand, and put his arm around my waist, as we came home! I did not strike him in the face, for presuming upon the civilities we have shown him as a stranger; but I wished for a man's strength, to lay him prostrate in the sand! Oh—if I should whisper this to Thomas, the island would be too small to hold them both!"

"Harry Gardner and Thomas Starbuck," observed Mary "were at the dance, and I think they looked with jealousy upon our gallants. In future they will not be so shy as they have been heretofore, if I may judge by the satisfaction they seemed to take in being permitted to dance with us."

"To tell thee the truth, Mary," said Ruth, "the only pleasure I had was in dancing with Thomas; and I am sure he must have discovered it in my conduct towards him. He is a noble-hearted young man; and a hair of his head is of more worth to me than fifty such suitors as Grimshaw. But thou hast not said a word about Imbert? What dost thou think of him?"

"He seems to be a gentlemanly, lively, good-natured person," said Mary; "but our acquaintance has been too short to warrant me in passing judgment upon him."

"Thou art cautious in confessing," retorted Ruth; "trust me, a young man with the agreeable qualities of Imbert, both mental and personal, will stand a fair chance of rivaling Harry in thy good opinion,—or I miss my guess. He is fairly caught with thy blue eyes, and that pensive, intellectual look of thine. Go to, Mary; he has made a successful impression on thy heart; and Harry must keep a bright look-out for breakers ahead. Is it not so, coz?"

"How strangely thou talk'st, Ruth; it was but now thou spoke of Thomas with commendation;—dost think thou art the only person in the world who can be faithful to old friendships!"

"Come, confess, coz," replied Ruth, in a bantering tone "did not Imbert talk agreeable nonsense to thee as we came along? I saw you incline your heads together, as if thou and he were afraid the night should get wind of your sayings."

"Well, I may as well repeat what he *did* say to me; for I plainly see thou canst not rest till thou know'st it all. He said," continued Mary, "that the satisfaction he had received in being in my company would not easily be forgotten; and, with respectful demeanour, though I confess with something more than the tone of ordinary compliment, he asked permission to visit me while he remained on the island. Thou knowest it would have been prudish and impolite to deny him; and, besides, our company is not so varied, nor so over agreeable, as to refuse ourselves the opportunity, so seldom offered, of having somebody to enliven our time with a little chat now and then."

"Ah, I thought it was so," said Ruth; "but, come what may, thou must not forget thy compact with me, Mary. After what I have seen of the conduct of Imbert towards thee this day, he will propose himself as thy suitor, depend on't,—and why should he not?—but thou must insist on his earning thy favour by a display in killing the whale, like the other island suitors. We must give no advantage to continental admirers; else in time we may run the hazard of being contemned by both. Remember thou didst put the task on Harry; and Thomas already understands that he must never talk of—thou knowest what—until he has fairly sped the harpoon. They have both been a short voyage to the Brazils; but, being new to the seas, they have not yet been intrusted with the command of a whale-boat. I am told that they go out in the next ship, and are both determined to tell a whale-story when they return. O, if Mr. Grim-dragon there would only dare to speak out, and tell *me* a tale of love,—as Imbert will to thee,—how quick I would despatch him on a three-years' voyage, and pray to the saints the while that he might ride on the back of a whale for a century! How it would convulse me with laughter, to see him uncoiling his long joints in the bow of a whale-boat, with a spermacetti under the prow! What a figure he would cut, to-be-sure, poising his harpoon, like grim death in the primer!"

How much longer this confidential conversation might have continued, it is impossible to say, had not the chamber light sunk into its socket, and left the young women in darkness. They hurried into bed, and soon lost their senses in that quiet repose to which they were fain to address themselves, and which is so charmingly expressed in the invocation of the Latin poet, thus rendered into the best of English:—

"Come, gentle sleep, attend thy votary's pray'r,
And, though death's image, to my couch repair:
How sweet thus lifeless, yet with life to lie;—
Thus, without dying, O how sweet to die!"

The light tinkling of a stringed instrument under the window of the bedchamber, and the soft breathing of a prelude from a tolerably well played flute, awoke Ruth and Mary from their half-dreamt dreams of youthful delights. Some moments elapsed before they were well aware whether notes so unusual at Sherburne, were the vivid remains of their dreamy impressions, or in very deed the reality of sound produced by earthly agents. Who has not felt himself transported to the third heaven of Elysium, if we may so speak, while, with the delusion of a dreamy indistinctness he has listened in the dead hour of night, when not a leaf was stirring, not a foot-fall broke upon the ear, to the soothing music of some kind serenader? And who has not felt regret, as the strain and the delusion ceased together, in the soft cadence of a dying close, to be renewed no more!

A deep, well modulated, manly voice, now rose on the ear; and a guitar, (the first, and, perhaps, the only one, ever heard on the island,) gave a softened melody to the song; while the flute filled up the breathing harmony.

Many years ago, while sojourning at Nantucket, the little air was hummed over to us by a venerable and aged lady, whom we suspected of having been participant in some of the scenes of this tale. The melody, with some difficulty, has been preserved, and is herewith imprinted for the benefit of modern serenaders. Why should not the pages of a tale be illustrated by the music type of a song, as well as by the graver of the artist? If we contrive to please the hearing organ, in the place where that of sight only has heretofore been courted, it cannot surely be said that we are gratifying one sense at the expense of the other; but, on the contrary, that we have made a useful discovery,—and, to change the simile, have found out the art of making "two blades of grass to grow where but one grew before." The words of the song have entirely escaped us; but, as far as memory serves, we can assure the reader that the loss is more than compensated by those supplied below from the pen of Sheridan. The old lady was much agitated as she repeated the strain—

"And sung the song of happier days;"

and a tear was detected stealing down her cheek, at the reminiscence of her youth, which the air no doubt revived.

THE SERENADE.

I.

Too late I've stayed—forgive the crime!
　Unheeded flew the hours:—
How noiseless falls the foot of time,
　Than only treads on flowers!

II.

Ah! who, with clear account, remarks
　The ebbing of the glass?
When all its sands are diamond sparks,
　Which glitter as they pass!

III.

Then, dearest, oh! forgive the crime,
　For roseate were the hours;
I lingered—and the foot of time,
　Stole lightly o'er the flowers!

SERENADE.—By the Author of Miriam Coffin or the Whale-Fishermen.—Words by Sheridan.

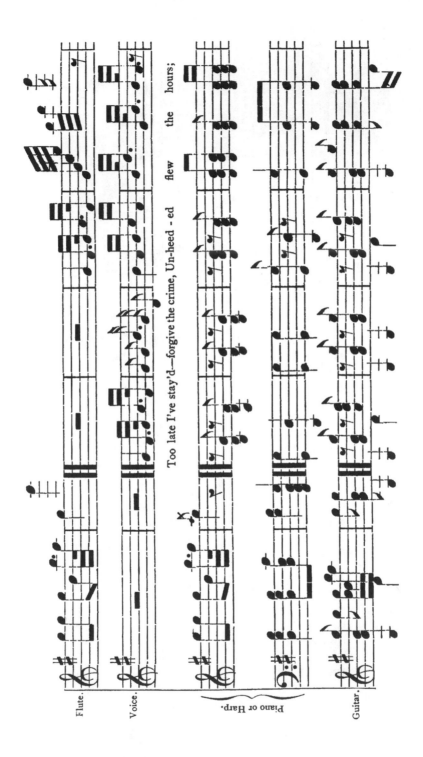

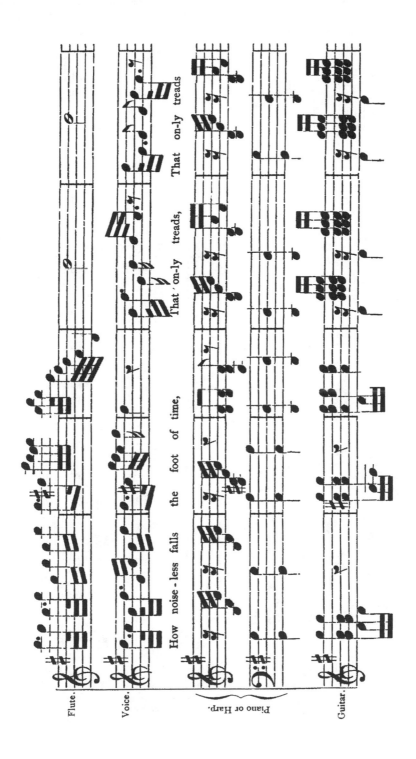

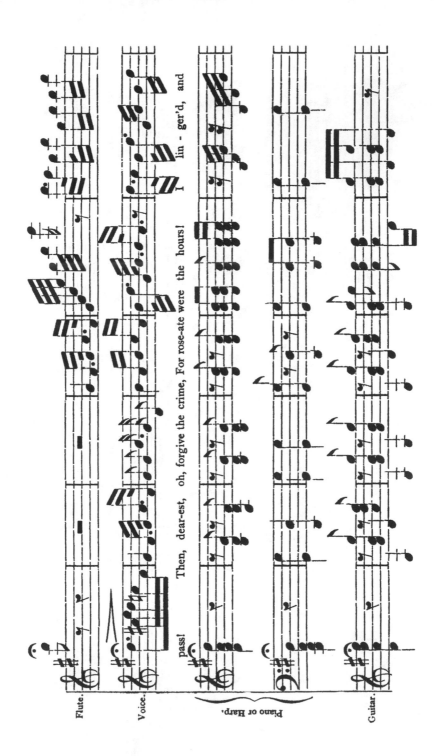

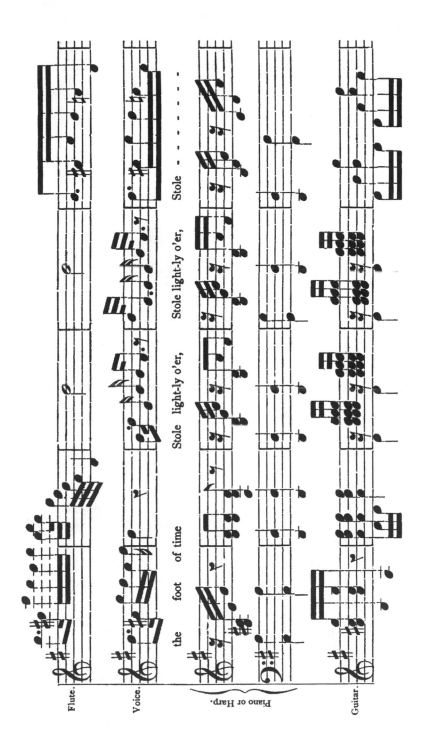

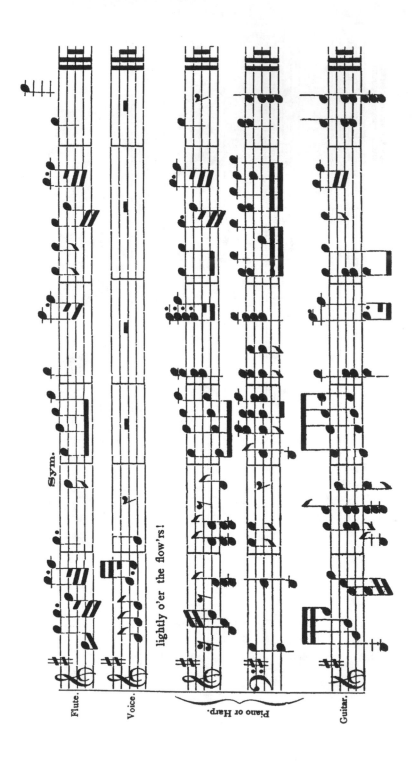

CHAPTER ELEVEN.

Our mountains are crowned with imperial oak,
Whose roots ages have nourished.
Robert Treat Paine.

And one beneath his grasp lies prone,
In mortal grapple overthrown.

◆   ◆   ◆   ◆   ◆

Miscreant!—while lasts thy flitting spark,
Give me to know the purpose dark
That armed thy hand
Against offenceless stranger's life!
Walter Scott.

It was as if the dead could feel
The icy worm around them steal,
Without the power to scare way
The cold consumers of their clay.
Byron.

IF there be no other excellence to which the Americans can lay claim, (and there are those who cavil at nearly all our pretensions,) there is at least *one* which will not admit of question:— *videlicet*, we build the finest ships in the world. In combining elegance of model, and swiftness of sailing, with capacity for burthen, we have distanced the clumsy floating castles of Europe, and furnished its shipwrights with models for imitation. England, opinionated, and therefore slow to imitate the excellencies of other nations in the arts, has at last been compelled to admire and to copy our naval architecture;—France has seized upon the hints we have given her, in our fleet vessels of war;—Russia has coveted and obtained our models, and even Turkey has, at a late day, opened her sluggish eyes in wonderment at our superiority in this respect.

The middle states of the union are, at the present day, the best ship-builders, and New-York the very best; while the south bears the palm for the swan-like floating of her smaller craft. The eastern states are reputable in naval architecture, but confine themselves principally to the structure of the burthensome class of vessels, which are most in demand for the carrying and coasting trade; but, at the time when our tale commences, Massachusetts was the great ship-builder of America.

We are possessed of an immense seaboard of several thousand miles;— of rivers of great depth and extent, which shame the diminutive though boasted rills of Europe. Our river-banks at the north are lined with forests of the white oak, cedar, and locust; and at the south with the matchless pine, and the incomparable and undecaying live oak,—all furnishing the most desirable materials for ship-building, within the easy grasp of a people, whose enterprise is proverbial, and whose expansive genius aims at, and will eventually secure, the dominion of the seas.

It is not strange, therefore, that at an early period in our history, we should have become conscious of the means by which a great national destiny might be accomplished, and set to work to apply the resources that abounded so plentifully.

Nor is it surprising, that America,—by which term we allude more particularly to the best portion of the western continent, namely the part now known as the United States,—should have furnished the means of carrying a large portion of the produce and the manufactures of other nations; nor that the American flag should be found proudly and broadly displayed in all ports open to commerce in the wide world. Nor is it at all surprising, that other nations should build ships in American ports, where materials are cheap, the workmen expert, and their ingenuity, expedition, and improvements in the construction of water-craft, beyond all praise.

The large whaleman, which Jethro Coffin had built at New-Bedford, was the admiration of all the accomplished skippers who had noted her just proportions. Yet she did not pass under the criticism of some of the veterans of the sea without many qualifying objections. He had most audaciously discarded the high and lumbering poop, which disfigures the quarter-deck of any vessel, and impedes her sailing; the quarter-galleries, which, though considered an ornamental finish to a tapering stern, are nuisances in a storm, and act as a drag to the ship in a heavy sea, were omitted in the construction of the Grampus; her bows were sharper than common beneath the water-line, but above it she swelled out in the fullest proportions, and her bulwark forward corresponded so nearly to her rounded stern, that to an uninitiated spectator, placed suddenly upon her clear flushed deck, it would have occasioned a momentary indecision whether he should walk forward or aft to find the cabin gangway. Her tall masts, as she swung at a single anchor in the inner harbour of Sherburne, appeared, in consequence of the absence of her deck-load of unseemly cabin-trunk, and unsightly cambouse, to rise above her deck with a length disproportioned to the compactness of the hull, that, in the unusual absence of the high quarter, assumed a neat though diminished form by no means common to a ship of her tonnage. When looked at singly, she would scarce have been pronounced a craft of four hundred tons; and it was only by comparison with the other large vessels in the harbour, that her great length and extraordinary bulk could be discovered. Her sails were neatly furled, and her appointments being complete in every respect, her novel outline, as she lay broadside to the town, drew upon her the gaze and the admiration of the islanders.

The last of the cargo of the Leviathan had been discharged, and barrels of oil were rolled promiscuously upon the wharf, ready to be hoisted into the loft of Jethro's warehouse, when two men came sauntering down upon the quay, and seated themselves upon the casks, so as to have a full view of the bay; while the unladen ship, at a trifling distance, was working over the bar with a few sails set, and a light breeze, favourable to entering the harbour. The individuals seemed lost in contemplation while watching the manœuvring of the whale-ship, and comparing the new fashioned rig and cleanness of hull of the Grampus, with those of the Leviathan, which were less modern.

"What dost think of her, Seth Macy?" said Jethro Coffin, as he pulled a few pine pegs from the deep gulf of his ample waistcoat pocket, and began with his jack-knife to whittle them into spiles for the use of the ship's cooper. "Will she answer for a voyage across the Atlantic, think'st thou?"

Before answering the questions of Jethro, the skipper of the Leviathan brought forth *his* knife, and, placing one leg over the other, he strapped the blade carefully on the upper leather of his shoe. Reaching over to Jethro, who understood the motion instinctively, he obtained a handful of the rough pine splints, and began whittling after the fashion of his companion. This was the signal for a long conversation: and as the ever busy Nantucketers deemed it almost a crime to remain idle for any great length of time, they frequently resorted to this simple method of producing something that might turn to good account, while wordy discussions were going on;—even as the women ply the knitting needle most zealously, while their precious confabulations are in a state of progress. We do not mention this little trait in the character of the islanders to excite ridicule. It is praiseworthy in itself, and deserves commendation. The fashioning of spiles and barrel-bungs with the jack-knife, to fill up the gap in one's time during a long talk, is worthy of the reputation of a Franklin, who never suffered a moment of his life to go unimproved; and we are now writing of a community who boast blood-relationship with that great man. There are many industrious Franklins, under other names, in Nantucket, who, if he were alive, would salute him by the title of "cousin."

We have somewhere read of a great banker, who, upon receiving his letters from abroad, quietly tore off the envelope, or spare leaf, and laid it by in his portfolio for future use in his counting house; and, upon being stared at by a young nobleman who handed him a letter of credit and introduction, and saw the saving operation of tearing off the flyleaf of his perfumed billet, he took occasion to observe that to this attention to small matters he owed the great bulk of his fortune; and his hearer, being a sensible, discreet personage, afterwards acknowledged the force of the practical lesson, by saying that he thereby fully comprehended the philosophical secret of making up an aggregate mass from particles. Even thus does the making of pine spigots and stoppers for oil casks help amazingly towards the increase of the oil-merchant's wealth. It is, to be sure, a small trade, and full easy of comprehension; but when it is known that many precious hours of the ship's cooper are saved to the owner, by having the spiles and the bungs carefully fashioned, and smoothed, and tapered off in an idle hour, and made ready to his hand, it may easily be conceived that the fortune of the oil-merchant becomes enhanced in proportion to the time saved to that useful appendage to a whale ship. Besides this, whittling sticks is a better and more amusing habit, by far, than sitting cross-legged after dinner and twirling one's thumbs, or folding the arms to rest. It is an active employment, and therefore promotes digestion, and saves one from the horrors of dyspepsia.

"To tell thee the truth, friend Jethro," replied Captain Macy "I do *not* admire the rake of the masts; or, rather, I would be understood as finding fault because they do not rake at all, but approach so much to the perpendicular, that they seem to lean forward."

"I see how it is, neighbour Seth; thou hast the Indian's reed in thine eye, which thou hast heard was so straight that it bent t'other way. But the masts of the Grampus are not stepped over the center of gravity without design. I will teach thee the philosophy of this thing. I grant thee, that for a fore-and-aft vessel, the rake of the mast should be well aft—the more the better—for in such case, there being but a single stick in the mast, the wind acts upon the broad sheets of canvas, which form the fore and mainsail of the schooner, after the manner of a lever; and it lifts her from the water, instead of pressing her under at the bows, as the effect would be if her masts were stepped in the perpendicular.* With the square-rigged vessel, where there are several pieces in the mast which give it greater length, the case is different. The sails act independently, and they never can be sheeted home so thoroughly, nor drawn so flat to the mast, as to act upon her bow like the canvas of a schooner. Consequently, there is no occasion to rake a ship's masts aft their center; besides, thou seest, if the masts should rake unnecessarily, the rigging could not be well set up so as to sustain the spars in the pressure of a gale. But, above all, the wind, which always acts horizontally, would lose the force of its action, in proportion to the inclination of the sails to the mast."

"Thou speak'st truly, I do believe," answered the captain; "but what hast thou done with the poop-deck? Would'st thou crib the people up in a narrow and confined cabin, without the convenience of ventilation?"

"Nay, verily," observed Jethro; "thou speak'st of a minor and imaginary evil, and dost wrong to my intentions. I would relieve the ship from the weight of the sea, when it breaks over her; for thou know'st that when she plunges, as it were, beneath the mountain wave, the bulk-head of the poop receives the shock of the surge, and the helm for a time becomes useless, while the strain is injurious to the timbers of the quarter. There is danger of foundering at a time like that; but a clear deck makes clear work, friend Seth; and the invasion of a heavy sea need not be dreaded, when nothing interposes to retain its force."

"Thou art right again, neighbour Jethro," said Seth, as conviction began to work on his mind. "The bow of thy vessel hath, however, a curious and unseemly shape, which, I fear, thou canst not as well explain away."

"Of what dost thou complain?" inquired the owner of ships.

"Why, without making any specific objection, I observe that thou hast departed from the approved method of graduating the bows from the

---

*The editor does not hold himself responsible for the opinions of the author, whose outline of this work was penned a long time ago: but he is well aware that the opinions above expressed in relation to the rake of a vessel's masts, prevailed, many years since, among the judges of well-rigged craft, and do still prevail in a great degree;—and that intelligent commanders are even now at variance in their estimate of the efficacy of Jethro Coffin's dogmas. Some, indeed, have discarded his notions altogether, and insist upon it that they should be pointed out as vulgar errors. We must leave the doctors to settle the question.

keel upwards; and it doth appear to me that thou hast given an unnecessary sharpness below the waterline, while the swell becomes too suddenly bold after leaving the water."

"I have fashioned her after the body of the duck, in some respects, friend Seth; for I hold it better to follow nature, than the arbitrary rules of art, which are often erroneous."

"If thou wert obliged to tow a log in the water," asked Seth, with an argumentative design, "which end would'st thou fasten thy line to?"

"To the butt-end, surely," answered Jethro; "for the water being once broken, the whole mass moves easily, and the reaction of the flood upon the sides of the stick assists the motion thereof; while the contrary would be the effect, if the small end were towed foremost, as it would be impeded by the wedgelike motion of the timber through the water. The same doctrine may be applied to the towing of a whale."

"Thou hast hit it," said the captain, "and hast given the identical reasons why the duck-like shape of thy vessel about the upper works of the bows, is misplaced. Thou hast put the sharp end of the log below the water, and hast unfortunately opposed the butt-end to the wind."

"There thou mistakest," answered Jethro, as he comprehended the objection of the captain. "Seest thou not that the breasting of the wave commences after the sharp wedge of the bow has opened the way, and rendered the water quick ?—And that the boldness of the bow, above the waterline, assists in turning the water off, even as the flare of the ploughshare overturns the sod? Thou wilt find no laborious ploughing of the Grampus with a heavy bone in her mouth, I warrant thee. Trust me, when I assure thee she will ride *over* the water, so to speak, and not labour *through* it as a dense mass, like the Leviathan, and the other vessels of the port. The force of the surge, instead of being directly ahead, will be carried off at the sides of the ship; and the eddy, whirling the closer to the vessel, will act the stronger under the clean taper of her stern. Thy objection as to the action of the wind upon the full bow above is easily met. Would'st thou not rather breast a thin fluid, like the wind, than the palpable resistance of a mass of water? Try the difference of thy speed, friend Seth, in making thy passage against a gale, and afterwards observe thy progress, body deep, in the water. To be sure, I might have continued the sharpness from the water upwards; but the gain in opposing the wind with a sharp bow, would never compensate for the loss of burthen, and for the wet jackets of the people!"

"There is reason in what thou sayest," answered the captain, "and I begin to think better of thy ship."

"Well, then," said Jethro, "as thou hast been ashore long enough to see thy friends, whom thou hast found in good health, and in prosperity, (how could they be otherwise upon our thrifty island?) what say'st thou to a voyage across the Atlantic? Would'st thou not like to see the wonders of London, that queen of cities, as people call her? Thou shalt command the Grampus, if thou wilt; and afterwards, if she is found to work well, and sustains the character of a good seaboat, thou may'st take her upon the long voyage, and mend thy fortunes among the spermacetti. What say'st thou?"

"I did not intend to try the sea again, friend Jethro; but it is dull work lounging about ashore, and I begin to tire of inaction already. So I shall be with thee, whenever it may suit thee to sail."

"Let us then," said Jethro, as the parties put up their jack- knives and wooden pegs, "let us take passage to the Grampus in the small skiff before us, and ascertain what is lacking to fit her out completely for the voyage. I shall fill her with a cargo of oil, and try the market of London with the commodity."

Jumping into the little boat, and unloosing the fastenings, few strokes of the paddles brought them to the side of the noble ship, which lay but a cable's length from the wharf. Macy, on gaining the deck, surveyed her various appointments with the practised eye of a sailor; and while he stood upon her ample flushed quarter, casting his looks alternately from the deck to her taper yards and towering masts, the novelty and beauty of her proportions filled his eye so satisfactorily, that a professional feeling of pride and pleasure was visible in his countenance, as he began to realize the idea of commanding a vessel, which was by far the largest, and, as she now seemed to him, the most beautiful craft of any he had ever seen in America.

A violent splashing in the water, in a shallow part of the harbour at no great distance, disturbed the silent reflections of Jethro and the captain. A full grown Indian and a lad were bathing in the neighboring water, which covered the shelving shore of sand, that in some places inclines so imperceptibly towards the sea, that, before one gets shoulder-deep in the water, he is a furlong from its margin. At most times the frolic of the swimmers would have excited no attention from such men as Jethro and his companion, who were accustomed to such scenes. The islanders are proficient in the invigorating art of swimming, to the exercise of which they are invited by the facilities at their very doors; and, as whale-fishermen, they often find their account in this accomplishment, when, as is frequently the case, they are spilt from a boat into the broad ocean, by the resistless struggles and dangerous flounderings of a wounded and angry whale.

The play of the Indian and the boy was, however, of the roughest kind; and it seemed to the two spectators, as they leaned over the quarter of the Grampus, in doubt whether to interfere or to resume the inspection of the ship, that the Indian, who was powerful and muscular, was taking undue advantage of his youthful companion. Both were in a state of nudity, and were interlocked in each other's arms. It was apparent that the Indian was fast overpowering the boy, and at one time he caught him in his arms and buried him for a moment in the water; but the lad, by a dexterous manœuvre, slipped from his grasp, and rising suddenly, sprang at the Indian's throat. The native staggered back a few paces, but saved himself from falling by his proverbial eel-like agility. His eyes now glared with savage ferocity, and he gathered himself for the spring of the tiger. With a single leap, half swimming, and slightly touching the hard sandy bottom with his foot, he struck the unresisting boy down into the water, and in an instant one hand was grasped tightly in his short hair, while with the other he pressed the body of his victim under, with the face downwards.

Nothing was now discovered but the bent body of the Indian, as he held the boy beneath him with a firm clutch; the agony of his struggle was scarcely perceptible upon the surface, and it was evident the poor fellow was fast relaxing his efforts, by reason of strangulation. A half minute more, and his body would float a lifeless corpse!

"Thinkest thou it is foul play?" said Jethro, as he moved with hasty steps to the gangway of the Grampus.

"It doth appear so," said the captain; "that copper-coloured rascal would murder his fellow creature for the pleasure of the thing. It is the nature of the savage: no kindness can tame him—no art can civilize the brute. It is but a short distance to where he stands, and as he has not yet discovered us, we may steal upon him unawares, and prevent mischief."

So saying, the captain pushed the light skiff from the side of the vessel with the strength of a Hercules, and it shot out in the direction of the combatants with the speed of a race-horse. Jethro and Seth quickly seized upon the sculls, or paddles, and, standing erect, they propelled the skiff silently, but swiftly, after the manner of the Indian, who faces the prow, but never uses the rowlock, or thole-pin.

"Give way!" whispered Jethro, in a husky undertone; "It is for life—for *life*, Seth!"

"Or perhaps *death!*" groaned the captain, as he plied with all his strength.

Cold chills came over Jethro, and his flesh began almost to crawl, at the idea of murder being perpetrated before his eyes. The agitation of his mind became visible in the unsteadiness of his stroke, and it was evident to Seth, that, before they could reach the Indian, the deed would be done, and the immortal part of the youth sent by unhallowed means into eternity. As the efforts of Jethro became weaker and more unsteady, the little boat sheared and yawed about, being strongly urged on one side, and not counterbalanced by similar power on the other.

"My God!" exclaimed Jethro, wildly, "must the boy perish? Hellhound—let go thy hold! See—the savage stands erect!—but where is the boy? Does he retain the unresisting body beneath his foot?"

"Damnation!" exclaimed Seth, incontinently, as both he and Jethro ceased rowing, and stood gazing at the Indian, without the power of further exertion. They had not yet approached half way to the scene of action. "Take to thy oar again, Jethro," continued the captain, "take to thy oar—give way—quick, or all is lost! Hah! see—he is safe!—the boy's head peeps from beneath the water to breathe—there he dives again to elude his pursuer!"

The boy again stood upright in the shallow water; and, reaching its rippling margin, and casting a quick glance behind him, he saw the Indian making towards the shore in pursuit. Neither of the combatants had yet discovered the men in the skiff; and, without the knowledge of the succor at hand, alarm began to show itself plainly on the countenance of the boy, while that of the Indian swelled with the workings of unsated revenge. The speed of the youth was no match for the fleetness of the native, and he gained upon him at every step. Suddenly the little fellow wheeled about, and planted himself before the Indian in the attitude of desperation. A bound or two brought the latter full upon his youthful antagonist, and his brawny arms were already extended in anticipation of his prey. But there are slips between the cup and the lip! The Indian was too eager, and entirely off his guard. Life was at stake with the lad—not a soul was near to protect him from the brutal fury of his swarthy opponent. Summoning all his strength, which had been almost exhausted in the water, and concentrating his resolution for the desperate effort, he dealt the Indian a blow on the temple that felled him to the earth. It was now the boy's turn to triumph. Ere his antagonist had well made the shape of his body in the sand, or could attempt to recover his foothold, the victor's knee was planted upon his breast, and his grip firmly fixed in his throat.

"Bravely done, my little fellow!" exclaimed Jethro.

"Throttle the scoundrel!" vociferated Seth.

The applause of Jethro and the advice of Seth were alike unheard and unheeded by the boy. Panting with fatigue, and desperate in his intentions, he held the Indian motionless beneath him. It is characteristic of the race, when they find themselves conquered, to yield quietly to the necessity of the case, and trust to other opportunities to accomplish their purposes. No distance of time can blot from an Indian's memory an injury; it is indelible and enduring as the mind itself. Years of quiet and peaceful demeanour,—years of apparent kindness and willing courtesy— are counterfeited, to deceive the victim against whom revenge is nourished in secret, until the unsuspecting individual is lulled into complete security. Beware of yielding confidence to the Indian! For an imaginary injury done to his remote ancestor, and handed down to him by tradition, he will wreak vengeance upon some innocent descendant of the wrong-doer, even to the fourth generation. He will steal upon you at midnight, or strike you in the back, when the way is open to him, and the fear of detection is removed from his mind.

"I have thee now, Quibby," said Isaac Coffin,—for it was he who bestrode the Indian;—"I've got thee safe; and, but that I would not commit murder, which thou did'st come near dealing unto me, I would meet my thumb and fingers through thy windpipe, in requital of thy good intentions towards me. Nay—stir not!—I shall hold thee to the earth, depend on't!"

"Ugh!" groaned the Indian, "my throat—my throat—not so tight—strangle—strangle!"

"Aha!" said Isaac, "thou feelest the pleasure of being strangled, dost thou? Well, then, since thou sayest so, the score is balanced; and I'll let thee up, if thou wilt promise not to molest me more. Say,—wilt thou keep truth?"

"I will; I swear by the Great Spirit—ugh!"

"Swear not!" said Isaac, "it gives no force to the promises of an Indian with me. I know thee and thy race to be a deceitful and bloodthirsty set of fellows; and if I let thee go now, depend upon it, I shall keep a bright look-out for thee in future. There—thou jail-bird,—thou mayest rise:—but first tell me, before I lose my hold, what is the cause of thy enmity against me? Have I ever crossed thy path in anything?"

"No,—your father!" muttered the Indian.

"My father, sayest thou?—and what of him?"

"He made my brother go to sea in whale-ship, for getting drunk," answered Quibby, doggedly.

"Is that all?"

"Yes!"

"And for that thou hast sought revenge upon me, who am but a boy, and do not possess half thy strength. Take that,—for thy good will,—thou cowardly assassin!" said Isaac, as the blood mounted to his face, while he clutched his fingers the closer about the throat of the Indian, and dealt him a blow that the vulgar pugilist would have called a "*gall-burster*," which, when duly delivered, is apt to make the recipient sick at the stomach.

"Ugh!" grunted the Indian.

"Begone from my sight,—imp of Satan as thou art!—and thank the Great Spirit that I have left life in thy carcass. Away with thee!"

The Indian rose slowly from the sand. As he gained his feet, he cast a glance of contemptuous defiance at his young opponent, but did not think it advisable to renew the combat. He had apparently got "glory enough for one day." Turning his back upon Isaac, he soon disappeared behind one of the storehouses near the beach, and the victorious young Quaker, feeling his strength returning, and elated with his good fortune, again took to the water, and soon forgot the affray which had come near costing him his life. Jethro and the captain, who were unable to reach the scene of action in time, seeing how matters had terminated, doubled a projecting pier with a few strokes of the boat-paddles, and remounted the side of the Grampus.

"What think'st thou, neighbour Coffin," said Seth, as they reached the deck;—"never, in all my life, have I longed for anything so much as for a good rifle, to wing that copper-head withal, as I saw him thrusting the boy down, with savage exultation!"

"It was an unchristian spirit that stirred within thee, captain Seth," answered Jethro; "thou knowest that we are forbidden to take up arms against our neighbour."

"But," replied the captain, "we are justified in buckling on our armour against the fiends of hell; and if yon athletic figure of bronze is not a devil incarnate,—then there's no snakes!"

"I will inquire into the cause of the fracas when we go ashore," said Jethro; "and if I deem the native dangerous to the community, I will recommend his removal to the Selectmen."

"Speaking of fire-arms, neighbour Jethro," said Seth, "I was about to give thee a little advice, thereunto appertaining, when we were interrupted by the Indian and the boy. Thou knowest that the English Channel is full of French privateers, and such like piratical traps, which are let loose upon the commerce of the mother country; and a colonial ship runs no better chance for escape than a vessel registered in London."

"True—but we must take our risk with the rest. The fleets of England are numerous, and may clear the way for us," answered Jethro.

"Nay," said the captain, "I have had some experience with such fellows, as well as with the Caribbean freebooters. They are easily scared by a row of teeth. Indeed, I have kept off many a picaroon in the West India seas, by rigging out a few well-painted Quaker guns, as they called the wooden barkers, which we sham for the sake of appearance. Mark me, Jethro, thou wilt not regret the purchase of a few six-pounders for thy ship. With four of them, and thirty stout seamen, I will make assurance doubly sure, and warrant to take thy vessel safe into the Thames."

"I will have none of them," said Jethro; "my ships shall sail under the protection of Providence and the colonial flag: I will not be instrumental in lifting the murderous hand against my fellow man, even to assure the safety of my property,—peradventure even of my life. Thou forgettest the peaceful doctrines of the sect which claims us both as members."

"I have seen much of the manner of doing things at sea," replied the captain; "and, in most instances, have found that 'might makes right.' I have, therefore, long ago come to the conclusion that all lawful means may be used for the protection of one's property, or one's life,—which, at sea, are not unfrequently invaded and jeopardized at one and the same moment. But hist!—seest thou that lurking rascal, prowling stealthily around the warehouse?"

"Ay—'tis the same that had to do with the boy just now: and see,—the lad is again gamboling in the water. Let us keep an eye upon him."

The Indian soon afterwards deposited his bundle of clothes between two oil-casks, and dropped silently into the water, from the side of the wharf next the Grampus. He disappeared beneath the surface, as he doubled the corner of the pier, which had previously hid him from the sight of Isaac, who was carelessly and boyishly turning summersets in the water—sometimes floating like a sleeping animal upon its surface, and then diving like a waterfowl, and reappearing, after a half minute's absence, a long distance from the place of his exit.

It was necessary for the Indian to breathe more than once before he reached Isaac; and he did so with the dexterity worthy of an Indian, by turning on his back and merely projecting his nose for an instant above water. Jethro and the captain watched the wary approach of the Indian to the vicinity of the unsuspecting boy, until they had satisfied themselves of the ulterior design of the assailant. The skiff was again in motion. Assailant and assailed had both disappeared;—the first to ferret out his intended prey, and take him by surprise; and the other, without a thought of what was about to ensue, to try the length of time that he could remain beneath the water without drawing breath. Presently two heads appeared simultaneously above water, confronting each other; and two long breathing sounds, like the blowing of a porpoise, accompanied by a hurried ejection of water from the mouth, freed the lungs of both the swimmers at the same moment.

"The demon, Quibby, again!" exclaimed Isaac, as he dashed forward in the water.

A strife of breasting the waves again ensued, which betrayed the earnestness with which each sought to outdo the other. In every thing, physically speaking, the Indian appeared to be superior to the boy. His sinewy frame, broad chest, and flat feet, were the identical requisites for a swimmer; while the undeveloped form of Isaac, and his protracted exertion in the water, unfitted him for coping with his athletic opponent. But though he was not the equal of the Indian in strength of limb, he was superior to him in stratagem, which the aquatic disciples of Franklin, who, in his time, was a practised swimmer, know so well how to execute in the water. Quibby had several times nearly overtaken Isaac, and had stretched forth his hand to secure his prey;—but the little fellow eluded his grasp, and slid away from him under the water, in an opposite direction, which left the Indian completely at fault. Though the scoundrel was baffled time after time, he returned to the assault so often, and so unremittingly, that he succeeded at last in tiring the boy down. Isaac made his last dive;—but the Indian anticipated him, and pounced upon his back, as he was repeating for the fifth time, the trick of passing under his opponent; and thus, by a well managed feint, drawing his attention to a point, towards which he appeared to be steering while his head was above water, but which he changed to a different direction the moment his body became submerged.

The greatest captain of the age ceased to be victorious, after he had taught his enemies the trick of his art, by beating them in a hundred battles. The obtuse intellect of the Indian, (they have thick skulls, like the African negro,) at last comprehended that the little Quaker meant to go South, below the surface, when his head was driving North above. But he had him now,—and dearly did he intend to repay the gripe of the throat and the punch in the stomach which Isaac had administered. Take thy last look upon the sun, brave boy!—The demon of the island has fastened upon thee, and it will be a miracle if thy spirit is not soon winging its flight to eternity.

It is said that the struggles of the drowning man, in the possession of all his faculties, are irresistible; and that no human hand can grapple and master his, without the sinews of a giant are brought to try the issue of strength. It was the demoniacal intention of the Indian to drown the boy forthwith, let the consequences be what they would. He had Isaac's neck between his legs, depth of several feet beneath the surface of the water, where he held it immoveable; while, with his hands, he pressed the body again strongly to the bottom. One minute in this position is an age!—It is an eternity of time! The death-struggle was again come upon the poor little fellow, and the fiend was once more exulting over him! He felt the blood of his whole body rushing to his brain—imagined loathsome snakes twisting about his neck and brow, and his body assailed by frightful sea-monsters. A streaming gush of water poured into his ears and mouth. His reason was on the point of giving way, in the agony of gasping suffocation:—but, for a moment, it rallied—and that moment was his salvation!

Isaac, without being aware of the fact, had, in his struggles been working himself, as well as his opponent, into deeper water. The murderer was obliged to discontinue his endeavours to press the body of the boy downwards, from the necessity which required that he should keep his own head, particularly his mouth and nostrils, in the free air. By this means the limbs of the boy were left at liberty, and he was enabled to brace his feet firmly upon the sandy bottom. His hands were also free; but heretofore he could do nothing with them, while his feet were *hors du combat.* But now he gathered himself, instinctively, for a desperate effort; and locking his arms around the legs of his foe, and planting his feet strongly beneath his body, with one mighty surge he raised the Indian from the bottom, and pitched him headlong into the sea! The relief thus gained was but just in time. A moment more would have closed the mortal career of the boy. But the advantage thus acquired was not to be lost. Isaac sprang after his enemy with the agility of a dolphin—and, ere he could regain his balance, his young hand, still nerved with the desperation of one battling for life, was firmly twisted in the lank black hair of the Indian. He avoided the experiment, which the native had tried, to conceal the struggling of his victim, and contented himself with holding the head, face downwards, beneath the water, at arm's length,—caring nothing for the splashing and floundering of the foe,—which the Indian, while he held the lad, was anxious to conceal, for fear of attracting notice from the shore.

"Perish!" exclaimed Isaac, in accents not loud, but deep;—"Perish!— thou black-hearted savage! Ay—kick if thou wilt—struggle on, monster!— It is my turn now:—I owe thee no mercy,—and die thou shalt the death thou hast twice essayed to bestow upon me, for the alleged sin of my father. Ay—sprawl—bite—scratch—it will require something more than human interposition to save thee from the death!"

"Boy! what dost thou do?—Release the Indian, and we will protect thee:—Release him, I say!" repeated an authoritive voice, close to the ear of Isaac.

"I am not deaf, good friend; I shall release him in a minute or two, but in my own discretion. The peril be mine—keep off—meddle not with this quarrel—I am desperate! I was but now dying in the grasp of this hell-hound:—twice within the hour has he given me a taste of the other world; and it shall go hard but I requite the favour. Keep off, I say!—By the heavens above us, I will serve thee after the same fashion, if thou darest to come between me and my prey!—Away!—I have said it—he shall die the death of a dog!—There—all is over now!"

The limbs of the Indian became relaxed and quiescent. The tide of life had withdrawn to the citadel whence it sprang;—the body floated for a moment, without convulsion, on the surface of the water, and then settled away gradually from the sight. Isaac had loosed his hold, and he stood gazing with stupid wonder upon the water.

"Isaac, my son, what hast thou done?" demanded Jethro, in a choked but fatherly voice, as, sorrowfully, he reflected on the termination of the violent and tragic scene, and marked the wild and altered looks of his son.

"Father—is it thou?—Oh, save me from the fangs of that dreadful Indian!—But where is he?"

"Where—indeed!" responded the father, mournfully.

Macy plunged into the water after the drowned body. He found it without difficulty, for the water was shallow, and not more than half-body deep. The captain placed the Indian carefully in the boat, across a seat in the stern, with his mouth downwards, to give the water egress from the stomach; and then, quickly seizing the oars, he pulled for the shore with all his strength, leaving Jethro and his son wading in the sea. The case of the Indian would not brook delay. The gaze of poor Isaac was fixed and vacant, while Jethro, taking his passive hand in his own, led him gently towards the beach. Exhaustion had rendered him powerless; and perception and memory had fled. The faculties of his mind were sleeping, curtained by what seemed to be a horrid dream,—but which partook too nearly of a tragic reality.

END OF VOLUME I.

OR

THE
WHALE-FISHERMEN.

VOLUME II

$\mathscr{M}$IRIAM $\mathscr{C}$OFFIN,

OR

THE WHALE-FISHERMEN.

$\mathscr{C}$HAPTER ONE.

Now art thou my lieutenant!
Shakespeare.

THERE are but few women of perception who are unable to estimate their own attractions, and to set a just value upon their power. Personal vanity, to be sure, is frequently betrayed to excess, in the exhibition of the thousand little arts to which females resort, to catch the eyes, or to rivet the chains, about the hearts of the men; but most women know the best way of managing these things, and how to adorn themselves for conquest. It is a lamentable truth, however, that many of the gentler sex draw off their light artillery at a time when it behooves them to play their engines most skilfully, and to keep up a constant and well-directed fire. How truly this may be exemplified, the attentive observer may determine for himself, by looking into the conduct of most females after marriage. The bright eyes and wreathed smiles of the maid, when she met her lover, are changed to lacklustre orbs and forbidding soberness in the matron

165

towards the husband; and, at times, to pouting peevishness, or dinning invective. The blessing of the parson, is, alas, too often the signal for letting down the pegs of the instrument, that before had discoursed the pleasantest sounds in the world; and if its strings are afterwards touched, they are sure to jangle inharmoniously.

This broad rule is not without its exceptions. The picture has its bright sides, and the desert its sunny spots. There are thousands of instances, we dare engage, wherein wives forget not the arts or accomplishments that won their husbands; and who, to the latest day of their lives, practise those kindly little attentions, that lose not their charm by repetition. They are jewels of wives, and crowns to their husbands, who, having won, continue the ways of winning, in order to keep the pure flame of early affection constantly burning in the bosoms of their helpmates. Verily they are not without their reward. We never knew continued and undeviating kindness in the wife to go unrecompensed. A peaceful household betokens holiness in the intercourse of its members; and be assured that happiness is there, in as great a degree as humanity can lay claim to, amidst the unavoidable vexations, which, like the scum of the cauldron, boil up full plentifully, whenever we have to do with the world. "Let there be peace at home," saith the child's book;—and that there may be peace around our own fireside,—where, of all places in the world, we should strive most for its maintenance,—we have only to will it, and it is ours. And most of all doth it rest within the power of the wife to keep her household in good humour, and to make the stream of life run smoothly, by pouring oil upon its troubled waters.

Among the arts least resorted to by married women to please their husbands, is that of personal attention to dress, before appearing at the breakfast table. The morning meal, of all others, is the dullest;—and it is made so by circumstances completely within the control of the one who presides at the table. The men of America are devoted to business; and unceasing toil and activity in their vocation are characteristics of the people. We will not stop to discuss the question whether, in comparison with other nations, they are deficient in many of the observances which appertain to the enjoyment of the elegancies of life, and which, in the present age of refinement, are supposed to contribute to the happiness of mankind. But we are not surely created for business alone,—nor predestined to delve, grub-worm-like, at the unvarying labour of hoarding up money;—unless, perchance, the curse attending the invasion of Eden by the wily serpent, and the punishment of the original sin of transgression committed by Adam, be visited upon his American posterity in particular, and they alone should, by any exception, be doomed to earn a hard subsistence by the "sweat of the brow."

There must be hours for relaxation and enjoyment, or we shall become sordid and sinister. The time before the morning meal, and at the breakfast table, may be converted, with the greatest ease, to the especial purpose of our highest enjoyment, instead of being aimlessly spent in stupidity; or, what is equally bad, in bustling anxiety to be off and about our business, or in a hurry to be mingling with the jostling crowd. Why not begin the day with cheerfulness and equanimity of temper in the midst of our families, instead of postponing our pleasures until the day and its cares are over? Little do some women dream that they are the principal cause of the quick despatch of the morning meal, and the unsatisfactory and often mortifying hurry of their husbands to escape from the duresse of the family circle, before their toast and coffee are well bolted!

What is the secret, pray?

It is nothing more nor less than neglect of those little duties about the house—that legitimate empire of woman,—and about her person;—both of which are put in the best possible array for the reception of strangers—but, good Lord! what woman cares a pin for her husband in these respects? A littered room—disordered furniture—stained tablecloth—negligent arrangement of the table—a slouched morning dress—hair unbraided and uncurled—slippers down at heel—a melancholy countenance—uncombed and unwashed children—all these are good enough for him to look at in the morning,—and no wonder he is off like a rocket! The wonder is, that he does not go *before* breakfast, and be somewhat tardy in returning.

Now Miriam Coffin and her daughter Ruth were very pinks and patterns of women. The sun never had the start of them in the morning

They were stirring with the lark, and their work was out of the way, and all their thrifty dispositions made about the house, before our moderns think of beginning the daily crusade of the broom and the scrubbing brush. The toilet was made, too, before breakfast; and when Jethro sat down to partake of his early meal, he found his wife and daughter in all their fresh and blooming looks, and in their clean and becoming attire, ready to sit down with him. The very appearance of his household begat an appetite within him, and gave a zest to the enjoyment of the good things of life. He lingered about his home for the very love of it; and he loved Miriam the more, because she studied to make his home pleasant to him.

Isaac, from the excitement and exhaustion of the previous day, did not appear at table, but confined himself to his room. He had, however, already recovered from his partial mental aberration, and the complete restoration of his bodily health was shortly anticipated. The worst that came of the rencontre with the Indian was a slight illness to himself, and great fright and solicitude on the part of his relatives. As for the Indian, he fared full as well as he deserved; and he was brought to life again by the severe, but old-fashioned ceremony of rolling his body upon a barrel, until all the salt water was ejected from the stomach, and respiration was restored to his lungs. Humane societies, with their well-adapted apparatus, lodged at the corners of streets, near the wharves of maritime towns and cities, for revivifying drowned people, were not as yet constituted. So the Indian underwent a sort of purgatory of existence; and, with a shadowy perspective of an hereafter, he opened his eyes to greet the sun once more, and was thus preserved for a time, to fulfill his destiny. Jethro had already made his arrangements with the Selectmen, and Quibby was declared a fit subject for the discipline of the next whale-ship which should depart from the Island.

If they dine at meridian at Nantucket, so do they breakfast, at a corresponding hour of earliness. Six o'clock, ante-meridian, found Jethro and his family surrounding the low, old fashioned, crooked-legged table; and they were on the point of depositing their bodies in their high-backed settles to attack the provision of the morning, when a knock upon the outer door arrested their further proceedings. Miriam answered the summons, and ushered in "Solomon Lob and his portmantle" in the person of Timothy Grimshaw, Esquire, with a small bundle of duds beneath his dexter arm. Jethro was discomposed at the sight of the lawyer; and Ruth impatiently curled her lip, and bridled up, and scarcely deigned to notice the intruder. Grimshaw could not fail to observe the coolness of his reception; but, feeling confidence in the protection of Miriam, he deposited his bundle in the corner of the room, and made an awkward obeisance to his unwilling host. Miriam hastened to his relief, and bade him welcome. Turning to her husband, she said—

"I have invited friend Grimshaw to take up his abode with us for a season, not doubting that thou wouldst be pleased to extend the same civility, seeing that he is a stranger among us." Without waiting for the answer of Jethro, she placed a chair for the new-comer at the table, and requested him to be seated. The breakfast proceeded in silence, relieved only by the occasional attempts of Miriam to put her visitor at ease. But not a solitary compliment did Jethro bestow; and Ruth was resolutely and deeply engaged in everything else but ministering to the comforts of the man whom she cordially disliked.

"Ruth," said Miriam, "help thy friend to the buttered cakes; Jethro, the cold mutton is before thee—why dost thou not put a slice upon thy neighbour's plate?"

"The custom of my house, thou knowest full well, Miriam, is for everybody to help himself. I am not given to urge visitors to eat—but our provision is spread out, and he is welcome to help himself."

Jethro, like the Southern Nullifier, threw himself upon his "reserved rights," and would not lift a finger at the hint or bidding of Miriam. Had it been anybody but the lawyer, his plate would have been piled up before he could have well seated himself at the table. Miriam, however, did her best to dispense the hospitalities in a creditable manner; while Ruth, with mischievous intent, became all at once exceedingly "helpful," and contrived to draw a circumvallation of edibles around the plate of Grimshaw, until he was fairly flanked by breastworks of toast, and rolls, and meats, and sweet-cake. He looked up in doubt and wonder, as dish after dish came to his aid; but Miriam regarded her daughter with an eye of reproof.

"Let those laugh who win," said Grimshaw to himself:—"there are some folks who will tire of officious insincerity, before I, Timothy Grimshaw, shall get weary of good provender. I am too well backed here by the women, to fear a continuance of the hostility of the other members of the family."

The breakfast over, Jethro hurried from his home without the ceremony of leave-taking. He was thenceforth vexed, he scarcely knew why, at the presence of his visitor, whom his wife had evidently taken under her patronage. Jethro was unaccountably harassed in his waking dreams with visions of law-suits; and his dreams by night were of the same texture. His aversion to Grimshaw was none the less because his image was always associated with a long perspective of writs of attachments, and ruinous proceedings at law, which were conjured up, unbidden, to his fancy, whether waking or sleeping.

Matters went on much in the same way, day after day, until the Grampus was ready for sea, and on the eve of departure; but Jethro was always filled with distrust in the presence of Grimshaw, and received his advances towards intimacy with shyness. Ruth made no concealment of her dislike, and repulsed his overtures to better acquaintance with an open honesty bordering upon rudeness. But Grimshaw bore it all with Christian fortitude and resignation. Week after week, duly as Saturday came, he planked his two silver crowns to Miriam, under pretence of discharging the cost of his entertainment; but it was observed that he always made his payments rather ostentatiously in presence of Jethro or Ruth, and he thus acquired with the former a character for independence, and ability to pay his way, which half reconciled him to his visitor. But Ruth, whose suspicions were excited by several trivial occurrences, such as an unaccountable increase in the wardrobe of Grimshaw, and an appropriation of some of the best hose and neck-cloths of her father to his use, did not hesitate to doubt the profundity of his purse; and, in spite of her mother's deep-laid plans, she set herself to scrutinize his weekly payments. Her doubts as to his pecuniary ability, and of her mother's disinterestedness, were entirely put at rest, when she saw a silver crown, of peculiar identity, paid over for the second time to her mother by Grimshaw. The nicking of the edge betrayed the unfortunate coin, which on the preceding week had been deposited in the pocket of Miriam; and before it had well got warm in its nest, had been refunded privately to the briefless lawyer, to perform the same service over again on the coming Saturday evening. Jethro did not discover the cheat of the transfer of his own property, and the nicked crown-piece escaped the notice of Miriam, who was intent only on the outward means of keeping up appearances, and satisfying her husband of the honourable conduct of Grimshaw. Ruth, however, marked the circumstance, trivial as it was, and treasured up the discovery to be used thereafter, as occasion might require.

Miriam had her long cherished designs to carry out, and she found it necessary to consult a legal adviser. Grimshaw had come opportunely to her aid; and in order to avail herself of his exclusive services, inasmuch as he was the only lawyer then likely to take up his abode upon Nantucket, she was determined to secure him at any reasonable cost, and thought the tax a cheap one which attached him to her fortunes, for no other compensation than entertainment at her house, and a small pecuniary supply. In return for these favours, which consorted well with the indolent propensities of 'Squire Grimshaw, he was not slow in giving his advice whenever asked, and in time ingratiated himself securely in the confidence of Miriam.

"It is now time," said Miriam to Grimshaw, while they were sitting together of an afternoon in the parlour,—"It is now time that thou should'st give me a substantial cast of thy profession. Thou knowest that my husband will shortly sail in the new ship for the mother country, and that the duration of his absence will be uncertain. He has as yet spoken nothing of his intention to appoint an agent at home, to manage his affairs while he is abroad;—and, though I doubt not that his eye will naturally turn to me for counsel, and, perhaps, the sole management of his business may be placed in my hands, yet I am anxious that no stranger shall be nominated to share in the labour. I would be uncontrolled in this matter,—in short, I am determined to be left the free and untrammelled disposer of his means. I have set my heart upon it, Grimshaw; and I must be clothed with written authority that none may gainsay. And now that thou knowest my wishes, I desire thee to contrive a method by which I may maintain the undisputed ordering of his affairs the while."

"What, Mrs. Coffin!" exclaimed Grimshaw, in surprise, "do you feel yourself, woman as you are, equal to the task of fitting out his ships, and superintending the details of his trade?"

"Do I, indeed! Let me but obtain the command I covet, and thou shalt see," answered Miriam, with an air of self-confidence, that set the question at rest.

"If thou hast well resolved upon it," replied Grimshaw, after turning the question in his mind, "I know of but one way to secure authority in the premises that shall not be questioned in the law."

"Name it," said Miriam.

"If your husband could be brought to execute a letter of attorney, such as I will prepare, your design will be accomplished."

"About it straight!" rejoined Miriam; "and do thou make it binding to the uttermost power of words. If thou doest this well, thou may'st name thy reward."

"I would that I might name a reward," answered Grimshaw, with some hesitation, "which you would find it as free to bestow, and as easy of accomplishment, as the draft of a perfect power of attorney will be from my pen."

"Speak it!" said she;—"thou wilt not name a thing unreasonable?"

"It is the hand of thy daughter," said Grimshaw. He watched the countenance of Miriam as he spoke the words. The effect was electric. She raised her eyes to his face in astonishment, and returned the look of her companion with a long gaze.

"Art thou in earnest?" demanded she, after a pause.

"I am."

"Thou throwest for a high prize," returned Miriam; "but it may not, perchance, be easily won. Thou canst not be serious in thy demand, surely! The extreme youth of my daughter will scarcely admit of the thought. She hath but just turned her sixteenth year, and I fear much that her wayward and girlish fancy cannot be secured for *thee.*"

"Time, Mrs. Coffin, and patient assiduity will, I hope, accomplish what I most ardently desire. Give me but your consent to try the experiment, together with your good word of recommendation, opportunely poured into her ear, and I will trust the result to future fulfillment."

"I confess that I am doubtful of the issue—but I give thee leave to undertake the conquest for thyself—nay, if thou dost wish it, thy endeavours shall not lack for my friendly countenance. But set about thy task, for it will not brook delay. Produce the written instrument which shall delegate to me the power I seek,—and this very night—if success attend my design with Jethro—I will strive to do thee good service with Ruth."

Miriam motioned with her hand, to cut short further conversation; and Grimshaw, elated at his unlooked-for good fortune, retired to frame the legal paper.

"And now," said Miriam, as Grimshaw disappeared, "now are my resolves taken: my purpose shall not be turned aside for small obstacles. The time has arrived; I have set my fortune upon a cast; and, spite of womanish fears, and what men call womanly propriety, I will run the hazard of the undertaking. I have waited long and anxiously for an opportunity such as this, to throw off the shackles which have bound me to duties with which other women are content. But what," continued she, "what will the generations that come after me say to my bold conduct?—No matter what! My womanhood, however, shall not be a reproach to my descendants, but my example shall be one for imitation rather. Must we, because we are women, for ever be confined to the distaff and the spinning-wheel—to the nursery and the kitchen? Pshaw!—I will assume such a front and presence as may become a woman with a masculine spirit. Men shall point to me, and cry out as I pass—'*That* is Miriam—Miriam Coffin!'—and children shall remember my greatness, and hand down the record of my actions to their latest posterity. I will be remembered for ever upon the island of Nantucket; and the race of the Folgers, from which I sprung, shall be proud to name me as their kin. Thus far have I been wary, and have obtained, by every means that assumes to the eyes of men a natural shape, a strong ascendancy over the mind of my husband. My counsel, kindly asked, and disinterestedly given, has thus far helped to swell the fortune of

Jethro, until but few in the colony may compete with him in extent of possessions. But I would be second to none—and it will be a miracle if I am not shortly the first in the colony in power, and in wealth and magnificence. Power is consequent upon wealth—then wealth must be sought by every channel, until it flows in constant and unremitting streams into my coffers. Let me but be firmly seated in the saddle, and I will ride such a race as shall make men—ay, the boasting men—stare with unfeigned wonder!"

Here Grimshaw entered, and handed his draft of the power of attorney to Miriam. Her previous train of thought had given a loftiness to her manner, and she reached out her hand to take the paper much in the way of a minister of state, full of his ideas of greatness, when he receives despatches from his drudging under-clerk, to approve and to sanction them by his signature.

"It is well!" said she, casting her eyes over the contents, which were formally expressed, and gave her unlimited control over the estate and affairs of her husband. "Take it back, and make a fair copy—and be sure thou forgettest not the seal. It is a fast-binding appendage, and may not be omitted. Do thou have it ready, when I give the word to produce it, for the sign-manual of Jethro."

Evening came. It was the evening previous to the contemplated departure of Jethro Coffin; and his family were assembled in the parlour. Jethro and Miriam maintained a sort of confidential conversation together, while Grimshaw attached himself closely to Ruth, who deigned only at times to look up from her needlework, and to answer him in crusty monosyllables. She took no pains to disguise her aversion to her would-be suitor, and, ever and anon, spoke to him so snappishly, that the countenance of Grimshaw fell with mortification and chagrin. Young Isaac, too, was there, and lingered about the room evidently full of some design as yet undeveloped.

"Father!" said he at last, breaking in upon his speech with Miriam— "Thou leavest us to-morrow!"

"I do, my son," said Jethro, affectionately, "and I leave thee behind to assist thy mother in the weighty matters that will engage much of her attention while I am gone."

"O, father, may I not go with thee?—I have many good reasons to urge in that behalf—and not the least is the fear of mischief from the hand of Quibby. Believe me, it will be unsafe for me to remain at home when thou art away; and I am sure my days will be spent in anxiety and peril here."

"Give thyself no uneasiness, my son, on the score of the Indian. I have obtained his commitment to one of my whale-ships, which will depart hence in a few weeks; and, therefore, thou wilt be at thy ease for three years to come, at the least."

"Three years, father!"

"Thou hast truly repeated the word. The Grampus will stop at her destined port for a season, until the Leviathan can refit at home; and I have arranged with the commanders of both vessels, that after I am left in London, they shall meet at a certain rendezvous at a given time, and thence proceed upon a whaling voyage to the Pacific Ocean."

"And may I not again accompany one of the ships upon the voyage?— I am weary already of remaining inactive upon this dull island. Give me thy consent, father, to follow the seas for a time—for I know I shall be unhappy and unoccupied at home."

"Not *unoccupied,* I trust," replied Jethro; "for thy mother will need thy active assistance. She is but a woman—"

Miriam smiled proudly and scornfully, but unperceived by her husband, as he gave out this insinuation, touching the weakness of her sex, and of herself in particular.

"She is but a woman, my son," continued Jethro, "and thou wilt now have a good opportunity to turn thy attention to mercantile affairs, and cannot fail to promote thine own and thy father's prosperity the more, by aiding and assisting her in all that appertains to my business. Thou did'st but now speak of the dangerous presence of the Indian, and, in the same breath, thou appearest willing to take thy chance with him at sea!"

"Nay," answered Isaac, who found himself unable to parry this thrust of his father, "nay, take me with thee in the Grampus, and let the Indian remain at home—or e'en suffer him to go in the Leviathan, as thou hast arranged it:—it matters not about *him,* so that I am permitted once more to try the sea—"

"Thou hast said enough, Isaac," replied Jethro, firmly and decidedly; "thou canst not go to sea again until my return, which will be within the year, if Providence speeds me. Let me hear no more of thy request."

Isaac, abashed, quitted the apartment; and Miriam, intent upon carrying *her* point, took up the parole:—

"Thou hast not, Jethro, come to a final determination, in regard to thy agent for conducting thy business during thy sojourn in a foreign land."

"The hint is unnecessary, Miriam. Thy discreet conduct heretofore is sufficient guaranty for the safe ordering of my affairs; and I leave them all to thy control. The burthen will prove somewhat weighty; but it is fitting that I confide in thee, for thou hast ever proved an able and efficient helpmate, in the honest furtherance of my fortunes. To whom, therefore, but to thee, could I leave the management with such assurance of fidelity and watchfulness?"

"Nay," said Miriam, and her eye sparkled while she spoke, "if such be thy will, I am content. But am I to receive no letter of instructions?"

"Thou needest none, surely: to one of less experience, I might leave instructions—but thou, Miriam, with thy well disciplined mind, wilt require only the promptings of thy own good sense, to teach thee how to act in all emergencies. The advice of friends may always be had when thou hast occasion for it; and I will speak to thy near kinsman, Peleg, about doing thy behest, when thou art in any strait. His experience and practical knowledge may advantage thee in matters of trade; and, though somewhat odd in his ways, he is very honest and sincere in his intentions."

"But," said Miriam, "suppose men should deny my authority?—Thou knowest the wife cannot bind the husband in mercantile trade;—and thy business, else, while thou art away, may suffer in consequence thereof. There are times when money or credit is not to be had without a pledge;—and surely none would take a warranty, of any magnitude, from a woman, without the consent of her husband. I prithee think of some method whereby the difficulty may be avoided."

"For thy satisfaction, then," replied Jethro, "I will adopt a course to which none upon the island will take exception. I will forthwith seek out the largest dealers, and say to them that my affairs will be henceforth, for

a time, conducted by thee; and that if pecuniary assistance be necessary—
and I cannot perceive that thou wilt need any, for our means are
abundant—but if assistance be lacking, I will request them to grant thee
any facilities thou may'st desire, upon my sure verbal pledge to restore the
borrowed sums at my return."

"Do as seemeth thee good," said Miriam, "but I would recommend a
present consultation upon this subject with friend Grimshaw."

"I like not the appeal, Miriam," whispered Jethro;—"he is not to my
taste. I would not, upon any account, be the first to break in upon our
ancient manner of conducting business, by adopting the technicalities of
lawyers. Whenever the hand of a man of the law appears, it throws
suspicion upon the minds of plain matter-of-fact people, like our straightforward, single-minded island race. Nevertheless, for thine own
satisfaction, let us hear what he will propose."

Grimshaw was accordingly appealed to, and, having his cue from
Miriam, he proposed, after much well-feigned thought, that a paper
should be executed, under Jethro's hand and seal, constituting his wife
agent for the transaction of his business.

"I will," said he, with well-enacted deliberation, "step to my chamber, and
prepare a letter of attorney, and forthwith submit it for your perusal. It is
the only safe way to give a permanent character to your affairs, or validity
to your wife's transactions as your representative." With this he departed;
and in proper time returned with the warrant of attorney, and placed pen
and ink before Jethro, in readiness for the due execution of the paper.

"Thou hast a clerkly and expeditious hand," observed Jethro, as he
glanced his eye upon the paper;—"but before I sign, I will read and
ponder upon the contents." Jethro then read as follows:—

"To all to whom these presents shall come: Know ye; that I Jethro
Coffin, Oil-Merchant, of the town of Sherburne, in the island of
Nantucket, colony of the Massachusetts, commonly called the Bay Colony,
send greeting:—Whereas I, the said Jethro, am about to depart for a
season from the colony aforesaid, and for divers other good causes and
considerations me hereunto moving, by these presents do make, ordain,
authorize, nominate, constitute, and appoint my beloved wife, Miriam

Coffin, my true and lawful attorney, to ask, demand, recover and receive all sums of money and debts to me due and owing of whatsoever nature, and to take all lawful ways and means for the recovery thereof: and further, generally to transact my business and carry on my trade, and to manage and dispose of my estate, and to contract debts in my name, either by bond, bill or otherwise, and to do all other acts concerning the premises, in as full a manner as I myself might or could do were I personally present at the doing thereof; and attorneys one or more under her, the said Miriam, for the purposes aforesaid, to make, and again at her pleasure to revoke: hereby ratifying and confirming, and by these presents allowing whatsoever my said attorney shall in my name do or cause to be done, by virtue of these presents. In witness whereof," etc.

"Peradventure, thy friends, as I have before said, may not have confidence in the management of a woman," observed Miriam, when the reading of the document was finished; "but in this warrant there is 'confirmation strong' of thy intentions. It would, therefore, be well for thee to sign the paper, lest accident should occur, or thy honest views should be misapprehended or thwarted by thy neighbours."

Jethro disliked the paper—not because it delegated power to his wife—for no man could repose greater confidence in woman than he placed in Miriam;—but because the lawyer had been at work. His wife reached him a pen, and he signed the paper reluctantly. It was then witnessed by Grimshaw, who, without saying "by your leave" to Jethro, delivered it over to Miriam.

"The deed is accomplished!" exclaimed Miriam, mentally, as she safely deposited the paper in her escritoire, and turned the key upon it: "The deed is done which makes or mars my fortune for the rest of my natural life!—Grimshaw!" added she, aside to him, "thou hast done well—and now will I redeem my promise, and bestir myself in thy behalf."

For the remainder of the evening Miriam and her daughter were left alone in the parlour. Jethro retired to continue and conclude his arrangements for his departure on the morrow, and Grimshaw absented himself, under the belief that his suit would be urged with more freedom and effect in consequence of his absence.

CHAPTER TWO.

Be kind and courteous to this gentleman:—
Hop in his walks, and gambol in his eyes.
Midsummer Night's Dream.

Sall never berne gar breif the bill,
    At bidding me to bow.
Mourning Maiden.

Anglice: —No one shall enrol the summons, which shall force me to yield to his suit.

MIRIAM was too well acquainted with her daughter's temperament to omit taking her measures warily, in approaching her upon the subject which Grimshaw had committed to her management. It was indeed a delicate task; and she feared that a proposition suddenly made, and boldly advocated, might frustrate the plan, which, with greater probability, would prove successful by a gradual development of her designs in favour of the lawyer. But a spark will spring a mine as easily as a brand.

"Why is it, Ruth," said Miriam, interrupting a long silence in the parlour, where both mother and daughter were intent upon their needlework,—"Why is it, that to all the world else, thou art obliging and courteous in thy speech and manners, while to Lawyer Grimshaw, the inmate of our house, thou art unkind and distant—nay, almost churlish?"

Gentle as was this first demonstration of Miriam, an indefinable suspicion came over the mind of Ruth, upon the utterance of so unusual a query; and the keen glance of her eyes sought to penetrate the ulterior tendency of her mother's speech. But Ruth discovered nothing in Miriam's countenance indicative of any latent design: it was calm and unruffled as usual; and Lavater himself must have used a lense of more than ordinary power, to detect the secret workings of her schooled mind upon her brow, or the trace of plot or scheme in her unbetraying eye. She contrived, however, carelessly to throw a sidelong glance at Ruth, while bending her head to bite off the thread of her work, in order to estimate the effect of her first attempt at breaking ground.

"Why dost thou ask that question, mother?" demanded Ruth, who was impressed with a vague belief that Miriam intended more than met her ear.

"Thou takest a curious method of replying to my question, by proposing another," said Miriam; "but I will answer thee;—nay thou dost even now curl thy lip, and contract thy brow at the very mention of his name. For shame, Ruth! Hath he not ever treated us, and thee in an especial manner, with becoming civility?"

"A plague on his especial civilities!" said Ruth;—"the man annoys me over-much. I cannot endure him. If thou art curious to know some of the grounds of my dislikes I am free to say that he hath neither the grace nor the spirit of a man, or he would cease to haunt my steps, and to vex me with his drawling importunities to enter into conversation with him. Let me go where I will, he is sure to intrude his unwelcome presence. In company he is always at my elbow; if I move away from him, he follows me; if I speak he is sure to put in his oar; at the meeting house he places himself in a position to pester me with his staring saucer eyes; and at home he bores me to death with his twaddle upon the state of the weather;—in short, mother, he is *particularly* disagreeable."

"For my part," replied Miriam, "I can discover in all this nothing but a desire to render himself acceptable. Thou hast yet to learn, I perceive, that a professional man, like friend Grimshaw, may claim superior consideration in society; but instead thereof, thou hast uniformly treated him with rudeness and contumely. His attainments, which so much exceed those of thy other young acquaintances, should entitle him to thy respect at least; and, above all, while he is our guest, the bounds of hospitality ought not to be infringed in thy behaviour to him, lest the world should say that we do not practice common courtesy to strangers. It would be a grievous thing to hear our family alone censured for a departure from propriety of conduct in this particular. I do not ask thee to be overstrained in thy manners towards him, for that is a fault which savours of insincerity and hypocrisy: but I pray thee to be more civil in thy speech and conduct than thou hast heretofore been. It may profit thee much hereafter."

"Mother," replied Ruth, "thou hast always taught me to be honest in my speech, and I will not now commence playing the hypocrite by deceiving thee. However favourably Grimshaw and his pretensions may appear in thy sight,—with me neither his person nor his profession can have the least influence. His manners do not please me,—though that may be matter of mere taste,—but I am sure that his professional abilities must be far below mediocrity, or he would not think of remaining at Nantucket, where his light must be for ever dim, for lack of the wherewithal to nourish the flame. Mother!—there is more in this than thou speakest. Thou hast hinted that it may profit me hereafter to alter my demeanour towards Grimshaw: prithee tell me wherein it may advantage me, to change my manner towards one so unworthy of a moment's notice."

"Thou speakest unadvisedly, when thou sayest he is unworthy of notice. The graces of his person do not commend themselves, I grant thee;—for he is plain in all that may be termed outward comeliness:—but dost thou estimate the cultivation of the mind as nothing? Doth not a learned profession, as it were, ennoble the possessor? I will be serious with thee, Ruth. All women, at some period of their lives, think of marriage. Thou art yet young—but I have known younger women than thou to change their estate. When the proper time comes—or rather, when the proper person presents himself, it is not meet to forego the opportunity and the advantage, which may never again occur. Thus to throw away a pearl of price, is a wicked slighting of the gifts of Providence. The young often look through a false medium in these important concerns, and suffer a wayward fancy or a childish conceit to control their election of a partner for life. The lights of age and experience should always be brought to their aid; nor ought they, by any means, to be slighted,—for they show the way to permanent happiness and worldly honour. Grimshaw, though he be ten years thy senior, is the man whom I would select for thee—"

"What dost thou say—did I understand thee aright, mother!" exclaimed Ruth, in consternation.

"Hear me to the end. I would select him for thee because of his station in life. To be the wife of *Lawyer* Grimshaw, would give thee an ascendancy in society which thou canst never hope to obtain by uniting thy destiny with any of the islanders. His title alone, to speak nothing of the wealth thou would'st bring him, would place thee upon an enviable eminence, to which, in our simple community, all men would look up with respect and envy. What honour could a whale-fisherman bring thee?—"

"Enough—mother!—I have heard enough! And is it for this thou would'st have me change my bearing towards him, and turn courtier to a spiritless fortune-hunter! And dost thou say that a whale-fisherman cannot bring honour? What! Not he that, in noble daring, challenges the world in emulation, and braves the dangers of the deep?—he that outstrips, in very deed, in the hazard of grappling with the giant of the seas,—the vaunted, fabled champions of olden time? Mother!—thou doest wrong to their hard-earned reputation, by comparing the gallant whale fishermen (who, in every encounter, peril life itself,) with such a crawling thing as Grimshaw. He must first try his prowess upon the seas, before may dare to mate himself with *them* in honour or attainments!"

The eloquent blood of Ruth mantled her cheek, as she pursued the theme with honest enthusiasm. Miriam was fearful that she had gone too far:—but it was now too late to recede, if she hoped to carry her point. She therefore changed her ground of attack.

"Thou hast answered me too hastily, Ruth. Reflection will come to thy aid; and I am sure, eventually, thy good sense will prevail over thy prejudices, and bring thee to think with me."

"NEVER!" said Ruth, with energy. "I can never hesitate a moment, if the alternative should be presented, in my choice between this starveling lawyer and an honest islander. I pray thee, let us drop this odious subject;—and, as thou lovest me, never again revive it."

"Nay, child, I speak but for thy good. Hear me yet awhile:—If, in thy cooler moments, thou shalt find reason in what I have said, and thou conformest to my wishes, thou shalt have a fortune set apart for thy dowry that thou little dreamest of."

"Talk not to me, mother, of a possibility of change in my thoughts. My mind is made up—and, once for all, I tell thee, in all honesty, I will not grant encouragement to Grimshaw, though the mines of the Indies were given me for my portion of worldly riches. I am irrevocably and unalterably resolved. Much as I respect thee, nay *love* thee, mother!—devoted as I have always been to thee, and submissive in all things,—I cannot promise thee obedience in this matter."

"Thou knowest my desire, Ruth, on this head; and for the present it is sufficient. Time may bring about a better state of mind within thee. Good night to thee, Ruth!"

The daughter of Miriam Coffin closed not her eyes the live-long night. Her pillow was wet with tears. These were the first sorrowing hours of her life.

*C*HAPTER THREE.

All hands unmoor!

Falconer.

The helm to his strong arm consigned,
Gave the reefed sail to meet the wind;
    And, on her altered way.
Fierce bounding forward sprung the ship,—
Like grayhound starting from the slip,—
    To seize the flying prey!

Lord of the Isles.

—Deep and dark blue Ocean!—
They sink into they depths, with bubbling groan,
Without a grave—unknell'd—uncoffin'd—and unknown!

Byron.

"GIVE way, my lads—give way!" exclaimed the first officer of the Grampus, in the sailor phrase of encouragement, to his boat's crew, as they

185

hurriedly pushed off from the wharf at Sherburne. The oars were briskly plied;—and soon rounding the extremity of Brant Point,—the little sandy arm that embraces the harbour,—the clinker-built whale-boat was brought to head in the direction of the ship in the outer roadstead.

"Give way, my hearties—the breeze freshens—and see!—they are sheeting home the topsails, and loosing the courses and topgallantsails. She is a-stay-peak, and we have no time to lose.—Give way merrily, and with a will!"

The men stretched to their oars in good earnest: the light boat skimmed over the water,—the spray parting and curling at her bow in white crested foam.

"Pull—ye lubbers—pull!" shouted the skipper, impatiently, through his trumpet, from the quarterdeck of the ship: "We are losing this fine breeze, and all for your having tarried too long!"

The sharp whale-boat sheared up on the lee-side of the vessel. The oars were instantly unshipped, and snugly piled; and the bowman with his boat-hook caught hold of one of the eye-bolts on the side of the Grampus. The mate sprang into the chains, and the boat was veered aft under the lee-quarter. The boat-tackles being ready overhauled, the little craft soon dangled from the davits. The topsails were now hoisted up—the head-yards braced one way, and the aft-yards the other. The windlass was manned; and after a few hard tugs at the handspikes, and a few rattling clangs of the pawls, the anchor was tripped, and presently the stock was seen above the water.

The jib was now run up, to pay off the ship's head; and that done, the captain gave the commands, in quick succession—"Fill the head-yards"—"Hard up the helm"—"Board the fore-tack"—"Cat and fish the anchor"—"Haul out the spanker"—"Sheet home and hoist topgallantsails." But it is not necessary to explain these orders to the landsman,—and the sailor will not be amused by the elucidation. The principal sails being spread, and catching the full force of

"A breeze from the Northward free,"—

the ship began to feel the weight of her canvas; and, as the mainsail fell, a heavy ripple swelled beneath the bows of the Grampus as she gathered way. The men were now all called aft, to "splice the main brace;"—and you may be sure that no order is obeyed by the sailor with more alacrity than this—which, by a free translation, means the partaking of a stiff glass of grog.

"And now, for England-ho!" exclaimed Jethro Coffin, with enthusiasm, as the breeze freshened, and the ship heeled down to the wind.

"Ay—for old England—merry old England!" responded Seth.

The corners of the last available sail being stretched out upon the yard, the bustle of getting under weigh presently subsided. The ropes about deck were coiled up, and the sailors, one after another, as they finished their several tasks, disappeared from the deck, to arrange their kit in the forecastle. Before the night closed in, and ere a brilliant July sun sank in the western wave, to rise on the morrow with undimmed and undying lustre, the Grampus, holding an easterly direction, had "run down" the island; and its last visible objects, apparently growing out of the sea,—the new lighthouse, windmills, and all,—had sunk beneath the horizon.

"Farewell!" said Jethro, "farewell, brave little island!—all sand as thou art, thou hast nevertheless been bountiful and fruitful in my behalf!"

The musing of the captain was of a different cast. "By my right hand,—but she is a beautiful craft!" exclaimed he, while watching the log running briskly from the reel, by which he found nine knots indicated for her speed.

"Swear not, Seth," quietly replied Jethro. But while he thus admonished the captain,—as in duty bound,—a sly twinkle of triumph might have been detected in his eye. The doubting and half-unconscious skipper gazed over the tafferel, as if he questioned the truth of the log; but he saw the ripple and foam swiftly whirling past under the ship's counter, at a rate that he had seldom witnessed in other vessels, even when scudding before a gale. Jethro sat down upon the hencoop, and watched his captain with a silent, but gratified chuckle, while he appeared to be experimenting in the progress and facilities of the ship.

"Does she steer well?" demanded Seth, of his timoneer.

"Like a lily!" was the reply of the man at the helm;—"no use for the tiller-ropes, you see!"

"Let me feel how she behaves," said the captain, taking hold of the helm:—"thou sayest well;—a child might steer her with a thread."

But all speculation was ended in the course of a few days. After trying the ship by-and-large, her powers of sailing became well ascertained, and the novelty of the vessel wore away:—and when her rigging, which had stretched because of its newness, had been well set up, the seamen began to give signs of having nothing to do. Some listlessly stretched themselves about the forecastle, in sunny weather; others idly threw their bodies at full length, in some shady nook about deck, out of the way of observation, but within call at a moment's notice. The best sailor in the world will sometimes skulk in good weather;—but it is only your land-lubber, or some old jack-tar who has outlived his professional pride, that will attempt to steal away from his duty in a storm, or when danger menaces.

On a bright sunny day, when the voyage had well progressed towards its conclusion, some half dozen loiterers, sheltered from the sun by the friendly shade of the foresail, were gathered together, in the attitude of listening to a long yarn, spun out by an old weather-beaten sailor, who had seen service in the navy of England. Bill Smith, for that was the name of the tar, had knocked a great deal about in the world, and was now on his return to his native country, after an absence of many years, "to anchor at last," as he expressed himself, "among his shore friends and messmates, who, like himself, were past service." Bill's stories always told well among the crew:—and whenever he wanted a can of grog, or a plug of negrohead, he had only to signify his wants, and to promise a yarn, to obtain the gratification of rum and tobacco. A slender youth, apparently one of the crew before the mast, was always principal listener; and, it might have been observed, also, that he was always principal purveyor of those choice commodities of the sailor. The reader may presently surmise in what manner he obtained his supplies, and, in *tailor* phrase, may also give a shrewd guess as to whose stock *suffered* :—But all in good time.

"Come Bill!"—said the stripling—"grog and tobacco ahead;—come,—spin us a yarn, and then—dost see here?" The youth held up a replenished can, and the promised pigtail. The bait was tempting enough, but Bill always preferred being paid beforehand for speechifying.

"Nay—nay," said the boy—"thou gettest it not this time before the story is told;—thou hast tricked me more than once. Come!—the story, and *then* the grog."

"I'm damn'd if you do though," said Bill. "It's no go, d'ye see—You don't catch old birds with sich chaff. Tip us the can, my boy;—grog first, to set my recollection afloat,—and yarn afterwards."

Bill prevailed, as might be expected. He did not draw breath until he saw Moll Thompson's mark; and then, ramming a fresh quid of the boy's tobacco into his left cheek, he carefully deposited the rest in his seal-skin pouch.

"Well," said Bill, "come to anchor hereaway out of the sun, and you shall hear some of my young adventures. When I was a hop-o'my-thumb, about your size, d'ye see, I ran away from my good old parents—God rest their souls—they are dead now!—I ran away, d'ye see, and went aboard a man o'war. I was sick enough of that spree for a while;—but, presently, I changed all my metal buttons for horn;—soon learnt to tie my Barcelona in a 'damn-your-eyes knot,'—stuffed my spare toggery into a canvas bag;—got to liking lobscouse better nor any other dish, and fancied myself every inch a sailor. But—the fact o' the thing is, d'ye see,—I don't much like to talk over them times—for it makes me, some how, always feel queer about the eyes. I was a great fool—that's a fact—to run away as I did;—and, would you believe it, my old parents grieved themselves to death on my account; and, d'ye see, if you likes, I'll belay there, and tell you about the battle off Gibraltar, in which I sarved."

The eyes of the youth glistened with delight, in anticipation of a story of naval warfare, which Bill knew so well how to varnish up and deliver. He was glad, too, that the subject was changed; and he did not care to hear of the regrets of Bill's youthful days—for the boy, too, was a runaway!

"You must know," said Bill, "that Admiral Boscawen was sent out with a fleet in the year '59[*] to lick the French, d'ye see. We had been cruising in and out of the Gut for a long while, without making prize money enough to slush a parsnip;—when one day the man at the mast-head of the old

---

[*]See Hume's History of England.

Admiral sung out that a fleet was bearing down for us!—My eyes!—but that was jist what we wanted. It proved to be a heavy French fleet of twelve sail of the line, and some frigates, that had escaped out of the harbour of Toulon. Toulon, d'ye see, is in France, on the coast of the Mediterranean. Well, d'ye see, we were all lying at Gibraltar, refitting, d'ye see; for we had had a brush with some of the Frenchmen at Toulon, trying to cut 'em out; but they *wouldn't stay cut*,—d'ye see—and so, some how or other, we were *obliged* to haul off a little to repair damages, you know. Well, the old Admiral, d'ye see, weighed anchor in a jiffy; and the old America, and the Warspight, and the Newark, and a dozen others, more or less, followed of course. Down we smashed upon the mounseers, who set all sail for the Barbary coast,—thinking to lead us a dance, and then to run out of the Gut at night. But it wouldn't do, d'ye see. The old Admiral—as brave a heart as ever beat under a peajacket,—the old Admiral, d'ye see, in the Namur, was the first to come up with their hindmost ship;—but he took no notice of her, though she barked at him with a broadside or two as he passed;—but he didn't mind that, d'ye see;—and he passed on to take a grapple with the French Admiral De Clue in the old Oshong, (*Ocèan*),— it mought be about eight bells, d'ye see—"

"Forward, there!" shouted the first mate of the Grampus, in a tone which reached the ears of a dozen idlers upon the forecastle. The tale of marvel was cut short, and they started into view of the officer with a ready "ay, ay, sir?" Bill had indoctrinated the Quaker crew with good manners, as he called it, and taught them all to say "*sir*" to the officers.

The mate had been looking with the spyglass, and observed a sail to windward.

"Jump aloft, one of you who has good eyes, and tell me what you make out of that craft with the suspicious rake in her masts, on our weather bow!"

"Ay, ay, sir!" they again sung out, in full chorus; and away several scampered up the shrouds, pell-mell. Among the rest was perceived the slight figure of the lad, who ascended with remarkable agility, and left the others far behind. The mate could scarcely credit what he saw, and gazed aloft in amazement.

"What boy is that, steward," said the mate, "that runs up the rigging so like a squirrel?"

The dark complexioned functionary, who was thus addressed looked out at the corner of his eye rather sheepishly at the mate, and seemed debating with himself whether he should tell the truth at once, or practise deceit upon his superior officer. At length, after scratching his head, and looking aloft in well-pretended wonder, he answered—

"Don't know, massa—can't tell, I declare, who dat leetel chap be. My conscience—how he do run up de riggin!"

"Don't know!" repeated the mate:—"I'll be bound you *do* know who he is, and where he comes from. We had no boy on board, to my knowledge, when we left home. Who is he, sir?" demanded the mate, peremptorily.

Thus beset, the steward could see no means of escape, and answered—"De men, I believe, sir, stowed young Isaac Coffin away in de fo'castle; and I *guess* it be he:—I don't know 'zactly, but I tink it mus' be young massa Isaac."

"I thought as much, when I saw his peculiar spring upon the rigging. Here's a pretty kettle of fish!" said the mate, decidedly puzzled how to act in the premises. He was in doubt whether to convey the information at once to the captain, whose watch was at that time below, or to let him make the discovery for himself. He adopted the latter course.

"Maintopgallant, there!" hailed the mate.

"Ay, ay, sir!" replied Isaac, in as gruff a voice as he could muster for the occasion.

"What sort of craft is that to windward,—and how is she standing?"

"It is a small black schooner, all legs and arms," replied Mr. Maintopgallant; "and she is bearing down for us under a press of sail! Now she runs up a flag, which you can make out from the deck with the glass; and, by the flash and the smoke she makes, she has just fired a gun!"

Presently a dull, heavy report came booming on the breeze, and a thundering sound echoed against the side of the ship. The glass was bent upon the approaching schooner, whose hull had not yet entirely risen out of the water. Her flag was found to be French!

"Steward—call the captain!" cried the mate, in alarm: "Forward, there!—call all hands on deck—stand by to put the ship about."

"Ay, ay, sir!" echoed along the deck, and every sailor stood ready at his post for prompt action.

Seth and Jethro now appeared on deck, wondering not a little at the uncommon stir on board, and surprised to find every man ready, whenever the word should be given, to put the ship on a new direction.

"What does all this mean, mate?" demanded the captain; "why would'st thou change the course of the ship?"

"I did not intend to do so without your concurrence," replied the mate; "but I thought it best to have every thing ready for prompt manœuvring. We have a suspicious looking sail on our weather-bow, and she shows French colours. By the rake of her masts, I should not be surprised to find her a clipper, with a long-tom amidships; for she has given us a gun already."

"Rather a dangerous neighbour for us, surely," said the captain, "especially if she should prove one of those piratical rascals that sometimes cut up our commerce. Keep her away, and see if she follows us," continued he, lowering the point of his glass.

Away went the Grampus with a free wind, snorting, as it were, like a racehorse, and ploughing handsomely through the seas on her altered way.

"What!—Isaac *here?*" exclaimed Jethro, in amazement. He approached his son, who had, by this time, become thoroughly weary of remaining *perdu* in the forecastle, and was now as busy as the rest about the deck. "What art thou doing here? Where hast thou been? How camest thou here, I say? Surely I forbade thee coming on board the Grampus for this voyage; and thou hast dared to disobey me, boy! Thou hast been greatly and unpardonably disobedient, Isaac!"

"I know it, father," said Isaac; "but indeed I could not remain with safety where that Indian dwells. Knowing thee gone, he would have been the death of me on the first opportunity. Pity he had not been left alone, when I did the job for him in the water!—But Captain Seth *would* roll him upon the barrel, and he must needs bring him to life again!"

"Thy apology is not sufficient," said the father; "thou knowest that the Selectmen had agreed, before my departure, to send Quibby to sea in the first whale-ship that should sail from the island. Thou should'st have been content with that arrangement, and remained at home, to comfort thy mother. Go to, Isaac—thou hast done very wrong."

The conversation was not further prolonged, in consequence of the emergency at hand, which called every man to his duty; and Jethro walked aft, vexed and sorrowful; but eventually he acquiesced in gratifying the strong propensity of his son for the sea. Isaac, in the mean time, was much relieved, and felt lighter at heart, now that all had been discovered. He slid out of his father's sight among the sailors, who had anxiously watched the result of the interview. His unbounded and boyish joy showed itself by his cutting antic capers on the forecastle, and by his jumping on the backs of the jack-tars. In truth, he merited the rope's-end twenty times, in half as many minutes, for his tricks upon his companions. But Isaac was a favourite among the sailors, and they were all as glad as he, to find the first interview over, and no great harm done.

The Frenchman steered for and gained gradually and steadily upon the Grampus, and the event was most anxiously looked for by all on board. The ship, deeply laden as she was with oil, was of great value, and, as Seth thought, eminently worth preserving. But the Frenchmen were determined she should change owners,—for they managed their little craft with great skill, and altered their course in chase whenever Macy changed his. The breeze was brisk, and suited the schooner to a crack; while the laden ship, though the fleetest of her class, could not show her heels to advantage, without a stronger wind. Macy tried his vessel upon every tack—but escape was impossible—the wedge-like schooner gained upon him at every turn.

"Now would I give the half of our cargo," said Macy, "for a few guns to speak to that saucy little scamp in his own language!" and then turning to Jethro, he said, rather bitterly: "Dost thou remember, friend Coffin, what I told thee about the six-pounders, before we left port? I fear thou wilt pay dearly enough for not taking my advice.—There comes salute number *two!*"

A gun at that moment was fired from the Frenchman, across the bow of the Grampus; but the shot went wide, and was most probably intended merely as a warning to heave to. Seth paced the deck in great agony of spirit, muttering as he went words that sounded very much like "*damnation*" and the like. The sound may have been equivocal to the ear of Jethro, for he forbore to put in his usual caution of "*Swear not at all!*" as he was wont to do whenever Captain Seth used obnoxious words.

The Grampus was now kept off two or three points, and a foretopmast-studdingsail was about being set; but, in the hurry of the moment, by some mishap the tack got unrove. A couple of hands were ordered aloft to rig in the boom and reeve the tack anew. In an instant little Isaac, who had heard the order, put the end of the rope between his teeth, ran up the foreshrouds, crept out on the top of the fore-yard like a monkey, and then out upon the bare boom. But, before he had accomplished his task, the Frenchmen brought their long-tom, charged with small shot, to bear upon the yard, and let drive at Isaac; thinking, probably, that his labour might be the means of enabling the Grampus to escape. The little fellow was not disconcerted by this terrible salute, although the balls whistled like hail around him. He fearlessly and deliberately went on with his work.

"They are again charging the gun!" shouted English Bill. "Come down, my boy!—Creep in! creep in! Seize one of the halliards, and let yourself down with a run!"

"Ay, ay!" cried Isaac, as he finished reeving the tack. He then quickly gathered a few fathoms in his hand, threw the coil down upon the forecastle, and the sail was immediately hoisted. The long-tom was again elevated, and the gunner was in the act of applying the match; but Isaac stopped not for the additional peppering:—

> "The cords ran swiftly through his glowing hands,
> And, quick as lightning, on the deck he stands?"

"Hah !—my little younker!—my eyes, but you're a brave 'un!—You'll be an Admiral yet—d'ye see!" exclaimed English Bill, as he joyfully hugged the stripling in his brawny arms.

The prediction of Bill rang in the ears of Isaac for many year afterwards. It was like the prophetic sound of the bells to the hearing of Whittington:—

"Turn again, Whittington—
Lord Mayor of great London!"

The hasty strides of Seth were again arrested, by another shot, which passed through the sail over his head. He folded his arms—looked up at the rent sail—and drew up his form, as if some new purpose had taken possession of his despairing mind.

"By heavens!" said he, "I will not part with so fine a ship and cargo, without a deadly struggle!"

"Swear not!" said Jethro; "it will not help us in our strait. We may better yield quietly to the necessity. Put down thy helm, Seth, and bring the ship to."

"Yield quietly!—did'st thou say?—and did I understand thee aright, when thou bid me to bring the ship to?" The eyes of Seth glared wildly upon Jethro, and his nostrils distended like those of an infuriated wild bull at bay. "Put down the helm, indeed!—Pray, neighbour Jethro, who is the commander of the Grampus—thou or I?" demanded Seth, in high dudgeon. But he evidently availed himself of the first pretext to let off his anger, for he was waxing exceeding wroth.

Jethro answered calmly:—"*Thou*, surely, art her captain—and I yield all to thy discretion. Save the ship, if thou canst;—*but thou canst not.*. We have no means of defence,—and, if we had, it would not be justifiable to oppose with arms."

"Jethro!—My resolution is taken:—I will save this ship, or sink in her. What!—yield to that little gadfly—that gallinipper—that is scarcely larger than our longboat!"

Another shot, better directed than the other, splintered a piece from the mainmast, and wounded one of the crew.

"There, Jethro!—there are some of the tender mercies of the French pirate,—and an earnest of what we may all expect, if taken!"

"Yield thee, Seth,—yield thee! The longer thou dost delay, so much the more hazard to the lives of the people."

"Thou hadst better go below, Jethro—*I* must command here, Yield, indeed!—the ship shall sink first!" muttered Seth, as Jethro began to descend.

"Stand by there, men!" shouted the captain, in a voice that made every sailor start. It was evident to all that Seth had put off the Quaker, and that prompt obedience was necessary.

"Get the longboat ready to be launched at a moment's warning—clear away the quarter boats—and see all clear to lower them in an instant. Mate, take in all the small sails quickly!"

The manner of Seth was somewhat wild, but resolute and determined; and the men and officers, having done his behest, stood wondering what command would next be issued, and whereunto those would tend that had already been executed. The Frenchman was also at fault; for, mistaking the manœuvring of Seth for an intention to give up his ship, the schooner was hove to, and seemed to await the lowering of the boat from the quarter of the Grampus—even as the conqueror awaits the approach of an enemy subdued, who comes to yield up his sword. In rounding to, the schooner had given the advantage of the wind to the ship; and while the French crew stood agape at the management of the larger vessel, which they already looked upon as a prize, Seth seized upon the helm with his brawny hand. The men, scarcely needing the cautioning word, anticipated his intention as he put the helm hard up, and gave his impressive shout in a suppressed and peculiar tone, which was heard distinctly from stem to stern:—

"Let go all the braces and bowlines—slack off sheets and tacks—and square the yards quickly!" This was all done in the twinkling of an eye, and Seth shaped his course as though he would bring his ship under the lee-quarter of the privateer.

After making this demonstration, which was intended to deceive the enemy, her direction was suddenly changed, and her head was brought to bear directly apon the hull of the Frenchman! The crew of the schooner now discovered, but too late, the design of the Grampus; and confusion and dire amazement agitated the people upon her crowded deck. In their haste to remedy their oversight, the Frenchmen failed altogether to aver the threatened disaster.

"If thou dost intend to run her down," said Jethro to Seth, hurriedly, projecting his head for a moment from the cabin gangway,—"if—nay, hear me, Seth!—for the sake of humanity—if thou art determined to run her down, ease thy helm a little, and give them a chance for their lives!"

"Stand by to lower the boats!" vociferated Seth, stamping furiously upon the deck. A suppressed groan of horror escaped the crew, as they now more plainly conceived the design of their captain.

"The boldest held his breath for a time!"

The little schooner still lay to, in the trough of a deep sea,—her people running backwards and forwards in frightened confusion,—while the huge bulk of the Grampus mounted the last high wave that separated the two vessels.

"*Miséricorde!*" exclaimed a hundred voices.

A wild scream of despair—heard far above the noise of the element, and the dashing of the ship—burst from the poor doomed Frenchmen.

Down came the Grampus, thundering upon the privateer, and striking her with her plunging bow directly amidships! The frail schooner was cut directly in two by the shock; and her heavy armament, together with the irresistible force of the severing blow, bore both parts of her hull, with all her ill-fated crew of a hundred souls, beneath the wave.

"Down with the boats from the quarter—launch the longboat!" shouted Seth. But the command, though it could not have been uttered nor executed sooner with safety, came too late. The aim of Seth had been too fatally sure. The boats reached the spot, and narrowly escaped being sucked into the vortex where the schooner had gone down. The French crew were all sent to their long account; and the next wave left not a trace of the wreck nor a solitary human being to be saved from a watery death.

The ship and cargo were dearly ransomed, Jethro Coffin:—and, Seth!—thou didst sacrifice a hecatomb of human beings for thy preservation!

$\mathscr{C}$HAPTER FOUR.

Go, make thyself like to a nymph o' the sea;
Go—take this shape, and hither come in't.
The Tempest.

Old Ocean, hail! beneath whose azure zone
The secret deep lies unexplored, unknown.
Approach, ye brave companions of the sea,
And fearless view this awful scene with me.
The Shipwreck.

The play's the thing!
Hamlet.

IT was once-upon-a-time said, within our hearing, by a Cockney, in a boasting vein, that "Lunnun vent a-valkin out of town every day;"—and the saying was literally true. There are many old towns in England, whose population remains numerically stationary, and whose buildings are

199

never renovated. The end of the century finds all things about the same as when it had a beginning; and the people seem merely to come into life, to vegetate, and to become extinct, or give place to successors, on the same spot where their ancestors, from time immemorial, had done the same things, pursued the same callings, and had, finally, given up the ghost in the same quiet manner. It is not so, however, with the great city of London, and its eternally shifting people,—who increase and multiply, in a ratio which could not have been contemplated even by Malthus himself. From half a million inhabitants, (and that was not far from the number at the time we write of,) it has gradually gone on in its daily journey of "walking out of town," until its population has been tripled in little more than half a century. And who can say that that vast hive of human beings shall not, in fifty years to come, be again tripled in its people? But let that pass. We must shortly enter into some of the scenes of the great city, and carry a portion of our *dramatis personæ* along with us.

In good time the good ship Grampus found her way up the Thames. The fame of her recent exploit was soon talked of in high places and in low places; on the Rialto as well as in the pot-houses and beer-shops of the great metropolis,—insomuch that she became an object of the greatest curiosity to every body, who had the least particle of that pardonable failing to be excited. The deck of the ship, which exhibited in its construction the novelty of being *flush* fore and aft, or without obstruction from stem to stern, was crowded with the gay and the beautiful, the wealthy and the powerful, the high and the low,—not forgetting a goodly sprinkling of the real salt water English sailor, with his tar-glazed pauling, black Barcelona, clean check shirt, secured at the bosom by the bight of a bright-bladed jack-knife, and sporting his white duck trowsers, blue roundabout, with three rows of buttons on a side, and long-quartered pumps. It would not have been at all English, if, at any hour of the day, all this motley assortment of people of high and low degree, could not be seen passing and repassing upon the deck of the Grampus, and, as occasion served, evincing a deep interest in all that occurred worthy of note in the nautical or commercial world.

The English have always been "a nation of shopkeepers;"* and, necessarily, from their geographical position, addicted to commerce. Any improvement in naval architecture was, therefore, likely to attract attention. The new, and since that time approved model of the Grampus, together with the reputation she had obtained in sinking the French privateer, gained admiration on all hands;—and the names of Captain Seth Macy, and Jethro Coffin, the owner, were in the mouths of every body. Indeed, the metropolis being in want of a *lion,* or something new and strange for the town to talk about, the Grampus and her queer looking owner and commander offered themselves in the nick of time, as candidates for the high honour of being *the rage.*

The rival theatres, to wit, Drury Lane and Covent Garden, were then in the full blast of an *un-*successful experiment, in the financial way, as they have always been before and since the days of Garrick; and, even in *his* time, his treasurer was caught with "pockets to let" occasionally. The recent exploit of the Grampus was too good, and too likely to "*draw,*" to be passed without dramatizing. Old Drury first seized upon the bright idea; and forthwith the bills presented the following underlining in large letters, intended to forestall the theatrical market,—to wit:—

"The new Nautico-Pantomimical Drama of *The Devil and the Deep Sea,* or *The Nantucket Adventure,* founded upon the wonderful escape of the colonial ship Grampus, (now in the port of London,) from a French privateer, is in active preparation, and will shortly be produced, with new scenery, machinery, dresses, and decorations:—the part of the Sea-Enchantress by *Miss Nancy Dawson,* who will sing a new song, written expressly for the occasion by Dr. Samuel Johnson,—the music by Handel,—and will give an entire new exhibition, in character, called the *Padlock Dance.*"

All theatres have had their pet actresses in their time;—that is to say, females who, for some reason or other which it would be difficult, and perhaps impossible to ascertain, have become general favourites with the public, and who occasionally take the liberty to presume, egregiously, upon

---

*Napoleon Bonaparte

the good nature and the good taste of that same community. Of this class was the celebrated, and, we may add, notorious Nancy Dawson,—a *figurante* of the first water upon the London boards. She was truly a beautiful creature to look at; and that qualification, (we might almost venture, in these days of puff and paste, to call it accomplishment,) was her chief attraction. Of talent she had very little; but of tact a large cargo. "But," as the father of a celebrated American comic actor has said, "give me de pretty voman for de actrice, and d—n de talent. I shall bring much more *argent* to my theatre wis de bootiful female who vill not say von single vord, than you shall wis de best actrice in de vorld, if she is *not* bootiful—*bigar!*"

Nancy Dawson was a true English beauty, and a spoiled one to boot. She was rather over than under the middle size:—her form lusciously full and round, without any inclination to embonpoint; her eyes large, liquid, and laughing, and blue withal; her complexion, without the aid of cosmetics, was naturally what too many beauties strive to attain, by the aid of art,—namely, "pure red and white," as we Americans say,—and running so softly and so gently into one another, that the red, which predominated where it should be uppermost, on her cheek, faded away into alabaster whiteness about the forehead, neck, and bosom. Her bust was altogether faultless; and, though strictly feminine, her chest was broad at the shoulders, but tapering to a most delicately slender waist, which partook almost of ethereality. And such a heavenly swelling bosom!—

> "Hide,—oh hide those hills of snow
> Which thy frozen bosom bears,—
> On whose tops the pinks that grow,
> Are of those that April wears!"
> *Shakespeare.*

"And did Will Shakespeare write and indite that verse?"

"He did. But Johnson and Steevens, in their 'last *corrected* edition,' have taken the liberty to *cut* it. It has, very properly, been restored in a little volume of 'the Beauties of Shakespeare.'"

"Then, I say—Will Shakespeare must have seen Nancy Dawson at her toilet."

"Pshaw!—Listen to my description—will you?"

"I *have* listened till my mouth waters! But pray go on:—what sort of drumsticks had she?"

"Drumsticks?—oh—ah!—*trotters*, you mean.—Beautiful, sir,—beautiful—especially when she donned the male attire:—fine ample hips—small knee—tapering calf—delicate ankle—and a foot almost Chinese!—She was a speaking beauty—a very Venus de Medicis in every limb and feature. Ah, sir!—those bare arms of Apollo-Belviderean roundness—and that lady's hand of lily whiteness and chiselled perfection! But her nose and mouth were the prettiest things in the world;—and her teeth—fine, large, white pegs of ivory, regular as a regiment at evening parade; and not any of your baby teeth, sir!—She could sing and dance, and captivate a Stoic in a trice. Take her by-and large, she looked for all the world like—"

"No matter whom she looked like, sir;—I have her already pictured in 'my mind's eye, Horatio;' and, you may be sure, I have raised up an image there, that you will spoil outright if you attempt to give it a 'local habitation and a name.' Better leave it to the imagination, sir!"

But the play—ay, "the play's the thing."

The eventful evening came, at last, when Jethro and Seth's adventures were to be shown up at the theatre. The house was crowded from gallery to pit;—so much excitement had the doings of the Grampus created in the minds of the London multitude. The stage-box had been reserved—not for the critics, gentle reader,—but for Jethro Coffin, and Seth Macy, and the crew of the Grampus! It was an ill-advised location for the comfort of Jethro and his party, who were of course novices in theatricals: for much of the illusion of the scene is destroyed, by the position of the spectator in the stage-box, who, from necessity, is thus made the unwilling witness of many of the preparatory measures of actors and scene-shifters,—which it were better not to see. But the place had been chosen by the manager, because *he* thought it the best box in the house; and, like all other managers, he therefore believed that all the world must be of the same opinion with himself. It was so far the best upon this occasion, that the powerful blaze of the foot-lights enabled the audience to get a full and a better view of the Jonathan-looking boys, who had performed the bold action which was about being commemorated in mimic display on the stage, than if they had been placed in the front of the theatre.

Jethro and Seth were slowly pacing the quarter-deck of the Grampus in the London dock, when the (to them) strange message of the Drury Lane manager, couched, however, in becoming terms, and directed to "Jethro Coffin, Esquire," was handed to them. The messenger rather doubtingly gave the epistle to the man in the Quaker hat who answered to the name and superscription of "Jethro Coffin," but who peremptorily denied the "*Esquire*" at the end of it. He was about returning it as a misdirection; but the messenger was among the missing. The note ran as follows:

"To Jethro Coffin, Esquire, and Captain Seth Macy, of the good ship Grampus, of America.

"*Gentlemen*:—The manager of Drury Lane Theatre presents his compliments to Mr. Coffin and Captain Macy, and begs leave to inform them that the brilliant affair, in which they were the principal actors, and wherein the brave crew of the Grampus have covered themselves with so much glory, (at the expense of his Majesty's inveterate enemies, the French,) having been dramatized and got up at great cost, will, this evening, as they may have observed by the bills of the day, be represented at the theatre for the first time. The manager, although he has not the honour of being personally known to the gentlemen whom he thus presumes to address, takes the opportunity to enclose a printed bill of the entertainments of the evening, and also an order for the admission of Mr. C. and Capt. M., and all or any of the crew of the Grampus, who may have leave of absence from the ship for this occasion. An entire box has been reserved for the reception of Mr. Coffin, Captain Macy, and their friends, which will accommodate about thirty persons;—and it is at their service for the night. Permit the undersigned to add that they will confer an honour upon him, and the establishment which he controls, if they will deign to favour the place with their presence at the hour designated in the bill.

"David Garrick."

"What is the meaning of all this?" said Jethro to Seth, after a second perusal of the manager's epistle, and a most careful reading of the play-bill, both of which he handed over to the captain.

"It passeth my understanding," replied the captain, who had never before, probably, heard of a play or a theatre. "Let us look into it more narrowly, however;—perhaps it may be a letter of invitation from one of thy correspondents to spend the evening with him, and it may possibly make against thy fortunes if thou shouldst not embrace the opportunity of going."

"I have no correspondent of the name of Garrick; though, as he speaks of himself in the light of a 'manager,' he may, peradventure, be the principal clerk or agent of the house, and has forgotten to advise me of the name of the firm. The bill of parcels he speaks of is none of the clearest to my comprehension; and the items, whether on sale at his warehouse, or for shipment for America, do not appear to be arranged with that precision and brevity which betoken a well instructed merchant. Let me again look over its contents "

"'Sea-beach—Moonlight—Clouds in the distance—A heavy sea'—

"Why, Seth," continued Jethro, "these must be some paintings or designs—such as I have seen in Boston, in the picture-gallery of friend Hutchinson, the colonial governor: But let us proceed with the invoice."

"'Flourish of drums—beating to quarters on board the French rover— signal gun—French ensign—long-tom amidships—heaving to—ship bearing down—Captain Shadbelly—'

"I cannot make out the import of this farrago," said Jethro to Seth; "but to be on the sure side of the question, it may be well to call up the crew at the hour spoken of, and take them to the place appointed. We shall be strong enough to look down the London cut-purses, who are numerous, if they should have planned the cunningly devised fable to despoil us of our property. It may, after all, be meant as a neighbourly civility to ourselves and the crew;—so even let them have their beards shaven, Seth; and a clean shirt a-piece will not be amiss in anticipation of Banian-day."

Long before the drawing up of the curtain at Drury Lane, the house began to fill rapidly; and when Jethro, piloted by some good-natured

citizen to the place, gained the entrance of the lobby, followed in good
order by Seth and his crew of thirty men, the bystanders tittered outright;
and the English tars, who were crowding the house to witness the nautical
display, saluted each other with various exclamations, indicative of
surprise at the sight of the Quakers.

"My eyes, Bill, what chaps them be!" said one old sailor to his
neighbour: "Did you ever see sich queer toggery?"

At this moment the ears of Jethro were assailed by the noise from the
orchestra, where the musicians were tuning their instruments; and the
catcalls of the gallery, answered by those of the crowded pit, in not very
gentle echoes, struck him all a-back. He hesitated, and thus held
communion with the captain:—

"I misdoubt much, Seth, but that we are in the house of the dragon!"

"As how?" demanded the captain; who, having heard of the "*wild
beastesses,*" as the Cockneys call them, that were kept in the Tower, was
trying to force his ideas by a circumbendibus, as he afterwards said, so as
to associate the "*dragon*" spoken of by Jethro, with the scene and the
throng of well-dressed people before him.

"Yea, friend Seth," continued Jethro, "the house of the dragon—the
very temple of Sathanus—the playhouse of Beelzebub!"

"Dost think this grand building, which is large enough to lodge the
king in, is what people call the playhouse? In America, thou knowest, we
have no playhouses;—and, therefore, Jethro, since we *are* here, I should
like to look at one. If we do not see some of the sights of London, we shall
have nothing to tell of in the long winter evenings at home. Let us enter,
and see the upshot on't."

"I fear me, Seth, that thy curiosity will be the means of causing me to
break through one of my established rules of life,—namely—that when
abroad, my conduct shall be such precisely as it is at home, both in word
and deed. I would not be reproached at home, by the brethren, for my
conduct abroad. Nevertheless, since we *are* here, as thou say'st, and as
men of established character, such as thou and I, do not run much risk of
defilement in a place we know so little about, I agree to remain for half
an hour with thee. But remember, Seth, the morality of the people of the

Grampus is in thy keeping; and thou must render an account to friends, if thou dost suffer an abuse to creep in upon their conduct."

The box-keeper, who had heard a portion of this conversation. being instructed to afford those who should hail from the Grampus a fitting reception, ostentatiously led the way to "*Box No. 1;*" and with mock parade stowed away the crew, while he chuckled inwardly at the oddness of the costume of both master and men. Great care was taken by the wicked box-keeper, to place Jethro and Seth in the front row, so that their broad beavers—much broader than those of the crew—should shadow forth conspicuously and to advantage.

The ancient Friends of Nantucket, whether eating or worshiping, and particularly upon public occasions, declined removing their hats—"upon *principle.*" We have never heard a better reason given for the principle or the custom, than that assigned by Jethro, to his neighbour in the next box, whose sight was obstructed by his inconvenient drab sombrero. Politely tapping with the end of his rattan upon Jethro's crown, the stranger gave the admonitory cry of "*hats off!*" as is the custom in some of the theatres: but the admonition was unheeded by Jethro, until the assault upon his head was repeated, with a direct request to remove his hat.

"Friend," answered Jethro, sternly, "I have always found my head to be the best of pegs whereon to hang my hat! Take thine own off, if thou find'st it inconvenient; but mine shall remain where thou seest it, unless forcibly removed;—and in that case, my body must remove with it."

There was a spice of the devil in Jethro's eye as he made this speech; and his dander or his Ebenezer was evidently up. Making example from Jethro, not a hat was removed from the heads of the thirty-and-*odd* men in the box, and they sat the sitting out with their beavers on.

The attention bestowed by the audience, upon the costume of the Grampus's crew, naturally led the spectators to inquire who the strange animals were that were crowded and huddled together, like so many sheep, in the fashionable stage-box. The manager, who was earnest and sincere in his civilities, had taken care that their names and quality should be correctly given to all such inquiries; and "for this night *only,*" (as the playbills have it,) it may reasonably be inferred that the actors on the stage received less notice, and less applause, than the visitors in the stage-box. When it came to be known about the house, that these were the brave and hardy people, whose bold and surprising action the audience were assembled to see performed again in miniature, cheer followed cheer in quick succession, and they were greeted, with much good will, by various demonstrations of hearty applause. It is true, the uproar was sometimes occasioned as much by the singular appearance of the strangers, as by the enthusiasm created by the wonderful feat of the Grampus; but, in the main, the audience wished to testify their respect to the Americans.

It came to pass, however, that Miss Nancy Dawson felt aggrieved by the attention bestowed upon the people in the sidebox, which drew off a large share of the admiration that she had been accustomed to receive from the playgoers. Vexed at this division of applause, between herself and the *drabs*, in which the larger proportion was given to the latter, she swore a woman's oath, and eventually took a woman's revenge on Jethro, to the great and uproarious amusement of pit and gallery; and she afterwards became a greater favourite than ever in consequence thereof.

"The green curtain was "rung up;" and the orchestra played "God save the King;" in which the actors on the stage, and the audience, uncovered, (all but Jethro and his party,) joined heartily, and with an earnestness and seriousness that appeared quite devotional. When it was finished, and the bustle had subsided, Jethro turned to Seth, and observed that—"Though string-ed instruments were an abomination, yet this display was not so *very* bad;" and he added, "I shall speak more reverently of the fiddle for ever hereafter, for the noble music it hath made to my ears to-night. But what have we here?—What a waste of oil, Seth?"

The glare of the foot-lights elicited the last remark of Jethro.

"Ay, neighbour," said Seth,—"but the extravagance brings grist to our mill; and therefore e'en let them burn oil by the cask, or by the cargo, if they will."

A blaze of powerful light, reflected from a thousand lamps, and most painful to the unpractised eye, was thrown upon the stage, illuminating the tinsel scenery of a rich background, resembling a coral cave, with piles of glittering conchs, and the natural treasures of the deep sea, with which the story books fill the caves of mermaids and water-nymphs. The side scenes represented the green water, with well defined goldfish, and fanciful sea-monsters, so admirably delineated by the painter as almost to deceive the critical London pit and gallery, who are up to all sorts of traps of this sort. A round of hearty applause rewarded the painter for his skill; and it was never better merited. And now commenced the "Nautico-Pantomimic Drama of the Devil and the Deep Sea, or the Nantucket Adventure."

First there was heard a chorus from invisible water sprites, and then a response from the head she-dragon of the cave, warbled at the wings by Miss Nancy Dawson, whose clear ballad-voice was heard distinctly in every part of the house. As the chant ceased she made her entrance upon the stage, bedecked and bedizened after a style peculiar to those *artistes* who assume to be Mermaid-milliners, and who, of course, consider the greatest approach to nudity the nearest approach to the perfection of their art. Pirouetting to the music, and displaying a well-shaped leg, which, as her over-dress was looped up, she took no care to conceal, she waved her silver band gracefully over her head, beckoning to her mates,—and then by various equivocal contortions of the body, calculated to display the charms of her person to advantage, she gently turned her back to the people, and peered languishingly over her bare shoulder at the audience, which she scanned in the most *nonchalante* way imaginable.

Jethro cast his eyes to the earth. It appeared to him not the most modest exhibition in the world—and indeed bordering on the lascivious. But still there was fascination in the scene. Had Jethro lived to witness the short *commons* and the other short comings of the Parisian dancers now passing current in America, he would have remembered Nancy Dawson, the actress, as a personification of modesty itself in the contrast! The other grot-fairies pirouetted also, and sidled in, and along, and about, until they formed a brilliant semicircle behind their queen:—and a queen she did look like and would have illustrated the description given of the majestic appearance of Calypso among her nymphs; excepting that, perhaps, Miss Nancy Dawson had rather more of the "dainty Ariel" cast of form, than Fénélon has vouchsafed to bestow upon his magnificent island goddess.

The "*Tempest*" of Shakespeare was drawn upon heavily, this night, for more things than a "dainty Ariel;" and well would is be if that incomparable model of the Bard of Avon should be drawn upon oftener,—even to the enactment of the entire original, when submarine caverns, and doings beneath the "deep sea," are planned by managers.

Suffice it to say, this prelude of "spirits of the vasty deep" was intended to represent to the audience certain preparatory rites around the altar of David Jones, Esquire,—the Neptune of the sailor,—at whose shrine the spirits of a hundred Frenchmen were doomed to do penance, after their bodies had been sacrificed to appease his wrath. Old Neptune, towering in a mighty passion, at the invasion of his realm by a French cockboat, was shown up in good style to the audience, who, being mostly British, were hugely delighted with the conceit, which the artist or the author had arranged to represent in the august person of Neptune, the tutelary genius of Old England, having exclusive command and dominion over the seas. A most sonorous curse was pronounced by the water-god upon the heads of the "*Mounseers;*" and his altar was thereupon lit up with red and blue fires, to the great annoyance of Jethro's olfactory organ;—and then the scene and the actors vanished together.

It is a sight worth witnessing, to observe the effect of a well-managed scenic display at the theater, upon the mind and muscles of a novice. Jethro Coffin was astonished and bewildered at all he saw. His eyes swelled out like saucers, and his nether jaw hung down in wonderment, wide enough to have taken in a half peck loaf; while his hands were grasped like a vice to the handrailing of the box, and the perspiration rolled like peas down his forehead.

"Didst ever see the like!" exclaimed Jethro, as the scene vanished from the stage.

"Powerful,—powerful!" responded Seth. With a sly wink to his chief mate, who sat in the rear of Jethro, Seth ventured to hint to his patron that the half hour was fully up, although the glittering scene had seemed but a minute in passing. "It is time to go on board," said Seth.

"Nay—I protest," said Jethro; "and I move for another half hour—and then—"

"Thou wilt move for another," thought Seth.

The second act commenced, and the old-fashioned sixpenny waves of Drury did their best, and wallopped about, under a canvas blanket representing the sea, and dashed against the rocks and tall cliffs of the scene to admiration. Thunder and lightning, and guns and drums in the distance, did their best, too. Presently a gallant ship, manned and rigged, bearing a broad streamers with the word "*Grampus*" painted in its field in large letters, dashed furiously in upon the stage. And there *she* wallopped and banged about, until Jethro, jumping up in his place, could hold in no longer:—

"Down with your helm there,—or you will be upon the rocks!" shouted Jethro, from his box. The command was heard far above the noise of the mimic tempest.

"Ay, ay, sir!" instantly responded the sham skipper from her deck, through his speaking trumpet; and he put the ship about.

The audience entered into the scene; and there came a roar of laughter and applause, and three hearty rounds from the John Bulls. You may be sure the salute was none of the gentlest; for it came from mouths used to converse in storms, and from horny palms redolent of tar and pitch.

"Three cheers for Jonathan and the Grampus!" shouted a Herculean jack-tar, raising his burly form in the midst of the crowded pit, and swinging his tarpauling high up into the air.

"Go it, Tom;—my eyes!—give it to 'em!" was echoed from the gallery: and away *it went*, round and round again, heavy as the explosion of a broadside from a seventy-four.

On came a cockleshell of a privateer, in chase of the Grampus;—up went the French flag—and deep rolled a gun, intended to bring the merchantman to. Then came the manœuvring, and dodging, and backing and filling—and finally down went the Frenchman through a trapdoor in the stage. and Jonathan's ship gallantly rode over the spot where the little craft had disappeared! Another shout, and another hurrah were rung out for the victory of brother Jonathan.

"My eyes! Bill!—but that's the go!—The Mounseer can't do a hooter to huz—can he?" said the gallery.

"Shiver my taupsils, if he can!" said the pit.

"You lubbers in the cockpit, pipe up the physic!" resounded from many quarters at once, as the curtain fell upon the second act. The *physic*, or the *music*, which, in a theatre, are synonyms with the sailor, thought proper to obey at once, and struck up "Rule Britannia." The sailors, who were not a few in number, now took *their* turn at wallopping and rolling about, and made free to chime in with the band *a la Boréas*.

The scene now changed to the sparry palace of the god of the deep sea. He was discovered seated on his throne, in the background, with his forked trident *rampant* in his hand, surrounded by—

> "A thousand fearful wrecks,—
> A thousand men that fishes gnawed upon;
> Wedges of gold, great anchors, heaps of pearl,
> Inestimable stones, unvalued jewels,—
> All scattered in the bottom of the sea!"

A portion of the wings represented the wreck and the armament of the privateer, and the drowned bodies of the Frenchmen, descending to the caverned regions of Neptune. The truth of the transparencies seemed to give the force of reality to the gorgeous and fearful spectacle.

"Shiver my timbers, Bill—but that's too bad!—Couldn't save 'em, eh!— Well, well;—Jonathan couldn't help it, I s'pose:—There they go—poor fellows—eaten by the fishes, and devoured by the hungry sarpents of the sea!" Such were the exclamations of the old sailors, while the rolling scenery exhibited, from time to time, pieces of the wreck, and now and then the body of a French sailor, with muscles relaxed, pitching head foremost; while his limbs were mutilated by ravenous sharks, which, as the scene trembled in its descent, seemed alive and busy at their horrid work. All this was seen slowly descending to the ocean depths, to the apparent satisfaction of the grim god who presided over the scene of destruction. Honest, briny tears, moistened the cheeks of some of the old tars at the sight: and this trait of generous feeling exhibited at the hard fate, even of an inveterate national enemy, was not unworthy of a sailor. Jethro Coffin was also much affected, and he shaded his eyes; and Seth took an opportunity of lowering his head upon the railing, under pretence of renewing a quid of tobacco.

But, presto—change!—What have we here?—A coral grotto, brilliant as Neptune's regal palace of spar, burst upon the audience. Jethro was shocked at the by-play which he witnessed at the side scenes—no less than Miss Nancy Dawson coquetting with a noble favourite, who sported a star upon his breast! Oh, shocking! Jethro Coffin's under-jaw dropped again and he communed with himself upon the morality of the house of the dragon.

"Do you see that stupid old hunks in the stage-box?" demanded his lordship, as he encircled the slender waist of Nancy with one arm, and pointed with the gloved hand of the other at Jethro. "How inquisitively he stares at us!"

"I have been vexed the whole evening at him," replied she: —"Garrick says he is the owner of the American ship, whose avail with the Frenchman we have been rehearsing. He bothers me so, when I am on the stage, by his impertinent gaping and staring, that he sets the people in an uproar—the cause of which, so annoying to me, he appears to be totally unconscious of."

"Jonathan all over!" ejaculated his lordship.

"I'll be even with him yet," said Miss Nancy; and she trotted on the stage, as the orchestra began playing the symphony to Dr. Johnson's song,—in the pauses of which she essayed parts of her new "Padlock Dance," in the character of goddess of the sea, to the infinite delight of the sailors.

The MERMAID'S SONG, by Dr. Samuel Johnson, as sung by Miss Nancy Dawson, in the "Devil and the Deep Sea:"[*]

---

[*]In 1737, Johnson and Garrick, master and pupil, went together to London in search of employment; and, though suffering many privations and disappointments in their career, they toiled on for the prize of their several callings, and eventually gained an enviable immortality. When Garrick became manager of a theatre, in company with Lacy, Johnson

O, gather round me, mermaids all,
To give our welcome to the Gaul,
To give our welcome to the Gaul,
    Sent hither by the Grampus:
Come! since her work's so bravely done,
Without the aid of pike or gun,
We'll burn our light on altar stone,
    And raise our pæan chant thus:—

The singer waved her wand, and a flood of light was poured in upon her crystalline grotto, adorned with a magnificent altar of variegated spar in the background. The attendants danced around the chief goddess of the water, waving their wands, while the symphony played, and the rolling transparent side scenes continued slowly to bring down pieces of the wreck and the bodies of the drowned. The song then proceeded:—

See, to our realm the foeman wends,
His barque upbroken, too, descends,
His barque upbroken, too, descends,
    And sea-dogs round are prowling,
To seize the prey, now sinking slow,
Down deep in silent depths below.
Where ne'er is heard the threat'ning blow
    Of Boreas roughly howling.

---

occasionally wrote for the stage, under the patronage of his former pupil. Some of his lighter pieces are preserved in manuscript;—and, among the rest, mediocre as it is, the song of Nancy Dawson, as it was introduced in the above mentioned play, is still extant. Handel, in his day, was for a long time composer for several of the theatres, and commenced his career in London in the Haymarket. In 1773, Garrick assumed the entire management of Drury Lane, and continued in it until 1776, when he took his farewell of the stage. He died in 1779. It was not until 1775, when his literary reputation was well established, that Johnson received the degree of LL.D. from the University of Oxford. He died in 1784. Johnson and Garrick were inseparable friends in life; and in death they were not much divided. Their remains are deposited near each other, in Westminster Abbey; and the British nation has shown its respect to the great moralist as well as to the player, by erecting monuments to their memories.

'Tis meet that thus the conquered come,
Who dare invade the sea-dog's home,
Who dare invade the sea-dog's home
    Upon the erected water,—
To bow around old Neptune's throne.—
That throne now glittering like the sun,
High raised, and built of sparry stone
    Deep dyed with human slaughter!

Come!—dance and sing, my mermaids all,
O'er bodies of the conquered Gaul,—
O'er bodies of the conquered Gaul,
    Fast to our realm descending:
'Tis thus we triumph o'er the foe,
'Tis thus we greet them down below.
While spirits brave do upward go,
    Our wat'ry realm defending.

As this verse terminated, some wild, rapid and discordant music was thrown off by the band, indicative of sudden interruption; and the water-sprites scattered in most admired disorder, on the entrance of a huge bellowing sea-dog, with a chain about his neck, denoting that he had escaped from confinement. The chief water-nymph, perched upon a clustered tuft of fan-coral, where she had taken refuge, began to exorcise the apparition in no very gentle manner, and with such sudden breaks in the music, that one could hardly have believed it to be the same smooth air which had been sung to the foregoing verses. The exorcism ran thus:—

Thou com'st the mermaid's enemy!
But hence! huge beast, nor let me see—
Hence—hence! huge beast—nor let me see
    Thy dragon form appearing!—
Now, by old Ocean!—thou shalt feel
Within thy jaws this clog of steel,
Of which do I, thy doom to seal,
    Condemn thee to the wearing!

A mighty flourish was given with horns, and trumpets, and fiddles, and kettle-drums, which might have inspired a host to the onslaught. But the sea-dog stood his ground, and roared like a bull, and rattled his ox-chain like a blacksmith. Nancy Dawson, as intimated in her song, here caught up a huge padlock, such as might serve to lock up a giant, or an ogre at the least;—and opening the hasp, she ran towards the beast, and made a demonstration as if she would fain have fastened it to his mouth. But the animal was apparently restive, and seemed not to relish her kind intention of putting a stopper so soon upon his roarings.

"Smite him on the nose!" loudly, but unconsciously, exclaimed Jethro, who well understood the manner of killing the seal species at a single blow:—"Smite him on the nose," repeated he, "and thou'lt do the job for him effectually, I warrant thee!"

The audience again indulged in unrestrained laughter and obstreperous applause. Nancy Dawson needed but this to cap the climax of her vexation, and to determine her mode of action in the premises. She paused a moment, looked at the padlock which she still held in her hand, and darted at her *naive* tormentor "like a streak o' lightnin'." Ere he could shut his gaping jaws, she inserted the hasp in Jethro's mouth, and closed the lock upon his cheek![*] And there he stood dumbfoundered, before a Drury Lane audience—the laughing-stock of thousands,—with an immense padlock dangling from his face; while the shouts, and the claps, and the loud merriment of the Londoners, and eke of his own crew, were absolutely deafening. Nancy's revenge upon Jethro was complete; and after skipping and dancing around the stage to her entire satisfaction, she suddenly stopped before him, and made a profound curtsey, exclaiming, in affected simplicity—

"Oh la, my dear sir!—let me relieve you from that inconvenient burthen about your cheek. I beg pardon—I protest I did not mean to be so rude. Shall I take it off, sir?"

"Do—I beg of thee," replied Jethro, leaning forward; "I find it an unseemly ornament in this goodly presence."

---

[*]Fact

In a twinkling the spring was pressed which had secured the cheek-lock immovably to his face, and Jethro stood bolt upright again, and laughed with the audience, and good-naturedly forgave the spoiled theatrical pet for her sin against propriety.

But there was no more playing that night. The audience would hear no more of the "Devil and the Deep Sea," after Dr. Johnson's song and the wonderful feat of the padlock; and Nancy retired amidst the deafening shouts of the house, and was received at the wings in the arms of her noble lover, with the endearing salutation of "You wicked little devil!—you have made a hit to-night that will make your fortune!" And so it turned out. Nancy Dawson was the favourite of the stage for many years; and, ever after, the sailors, who remembered the scene of the padlock, used to greet her appearance with broad grins and shouts of "Nancy Dawson forever!"—while the well remembered melody of her song, known afterwards only by her own name, was danced by learned horses at the circus, and whistled along the streets by the sweeps and lazaroni of the gallery, until it became as common in the mouths of the vulgar, as the beautiful airs of Cinderella and Masaniello now are after their fiftieth night.—What an immortality!

CHAPTER FIVE.

A plague on *both your houses!*

Romeo and Juliet.

I do not weep!—the springs of tears are dried—
And of a sudden I am calm, as if
All things were well.

Byron.

THE barque of Jethro had scarcely lost sight of the island, before the first imaginings of Miriam's ambition began to be developed. She surveyed the humble range of apartments constituting her dwelling;—projected alterations and improvements;—and finally abandoned them, after counting the expense, and coming to the prudential conclusion that it would cost more to pull down, and refit, and rebuild, than it would to erect a new mansion from the foundation. She therefore sent for the chief builder of the town, and requested him to make out plans of a building, upon a scale of magnificence then unknown upon the island. At first he suggested a barn-like pile, with the usual tumble-down roof, and broad, unsightly gable to front the street. It was an approved pattern with the generality of the inhabitants, which admits of incontestible proof even unto this day. But Miriam, who had seen other houses abroad, seized her pen, and astonished the architect with her readiness at design. She first showed him the front of a double house, and gave him a sketch of the mouldings, and pilasters, and the well-imagined ornaments of the time, which were then in vogue upon the main:—and *this* front, she said, should face the street.

Here was an innovation that caused the honest builder to stare! The plan of the roof, too, was to him an absolute marvel. With two strokes of the pen, Miriam indicated to him the fashion of the roof, which resembled the letter A,—only not quite so steep. The very simplicity of the design astonished the builder. What!—not have the roof to slope off behind, with a gradual concavity, until all the outhouses in the rear were covered by it, and its extremity should come almost in contact with the ground?—And were the complex, triple pitches of the roof, on the other side, to be discarded for a single descent? Monstrous!—Yet Miriam *would* have it so, or not at all. She selected a pleasant site on the margin of the bay, which threw the front of the building to the North.

"Gadzooks!" said the builder;—"place the front towards the North!—who ever heard of such a thing before?"

The accommodation of looking out upon the bay was nothing. The prevailing fashion of fronting towards the warm South, (even though sand-banks should intervene to shut out the prospect,) was everything. Miriam prevailed; and the builder acquiesced. But he had his misgivings as to her sanity. Her prudence, at any rate, he believed to be clean gone. The mansion was, nevertheless, built under the eye of Miriam; and a lapse of more than half a century still finds it one of the best-looking architectural designs upon the island. But its fine water prospect is cut off, by the multitudinous dwellings and warehouses that have since grown up between it and the shore; and you must now ascend to its "*walk*," or terrace upon the roof, and take your station by the side of the pole supporting the weather-cock, if you could look forth upon the sea.

If the Moslems have their minarets at the tops of their dwellings, from which to call their neighbours to prayer at mid-day,—so have—or rather *had*, the Sherburne people their "crow's nests" at the tops of theirs, to look out upon the deep in every direction, and from whence to convey the first news of a homeward-bound ship to the people below. All the ancient buildings of the town still display these convenient look-out places.

Simultaneously with the building of her magnificent town house, Miriam had determined to erect a country seat, a luxury never before thought of on the island. It was a piece of extravagance that no one could comprehend. But her mystery was her own, and she permitted no one to penetrate it. Miriam had ulterior designs:—and the signs of a political storm, which her foresight predicted would shortly break forth were, in fact, her chief inducements for selecting the distant and lonely spot, whereon to place her country mansion.

A long and narrow bay, navigable only for small vessels, but connected with the main harbour of Nantucket, runs up towards the eastern part of the island. Near the extremity of this bay were the remains of an ancient Indian settlement, close upon the margin of the estuary; and the place still bears the Indian name of "*Quaise.*" The Indians had once planted their wigwams upon the little knoll of land that overlooked the water; and upon this same hill did Miriam determine to build the foundation of her house. The land declined gently to the borders of a small pellucid lake, in which fishes of many varieties sported, as yet unharmed and unvexed by the angler. Altogether the location was inviting, and preferable to any other within the same distance of the town; and it was, besides, approachable by water without exposure to the sea. From the hill a broad blue expanse of ocean was visible, shut out by a long low bar of sand that embraced the bay. To the eastward, at the extremity of the harbour, on another gentle declivity, stood, at the time, the little Indian settlement of "Eat-Fire-Spring," with its circular wigwams. These were the only habitations of human beings within sight of Quaise. The back-ground was a vast heath, broken only here and there by a slight undulation in the plain. The romance of the island is in its water prospects; there is none in its heathy plains and stunted bushes.

The progress of building the country-seat,—its details of stone and mortar, and timber and shingles, we will not inflict upon our readers, for to them, as to us, they would be uninteresting. Suffice it, that the country-seat,—a splendid thing of its kind,—was built at great expense, and was long afterwards familiarly known as "Miriam's Folly." When last we saw it, time and exposure to storms had covered it with a mossy coating, and it was occupied by an industrious farmer and his family, who seemed to take a pride in speaking of its origin and its peculiarities.

A peaceable lodgment being effected in the town house,—which had been garnished anew with furniture, conforming in splendour to its outward finish,—a party was projected under Miriam's auspices, who were to go in calêches to take formal possession of, and to regale themselves at, the country mansion,—which had also previously been comfortably and even elegantly fitted up with all that was necessary for its occupancy.

A train of one-horse, two-wheeled, springless carriages, was got ready to the number of half a dozen, which were seen emerging from the outskirts of the town on a pleasant morning towards the close of September, 1774. The van, as was fitting, was led by Miriam and her daughter, under the escort of Grimshaw, who took upon himself to be charioteer for the occasion. Three high-backed, rush-bottomed chairs, were lashed with cords to the sides or gunwale of the cart; and being spread over with some soft covering (a checkered coverlet, or a figured counterpane)—the riders were as well accommodated as the outward indulgence in the luxury of the times would warrant. There were then no carriages with springs—no gigs,—nor stanhopes,—nor coaches with luxurious seats. It was many years after this before even a chaise was tolerated on the island; and when two of these, with wooden elbow springs, were introduced by some of the wealthier families, the hue-and-cry of persecution was set up against them; and their owners were fain to abandon the monstrosities, and betake themselves again to their calêches. One chaise, however, was allowed to be retained by an invalid: but it is related that even he was not permitted to keep and to use it, unless upon all proper occasions he would consent to lend it for the use of the sick.

Next in order came the vehicle of our somewhat neglected friend, Peleg Folger, (the kinsman of Miriam,) and his daughter Mary: and these were attended, merry and mercurial as ever, by the fashionable Imbert in his red coat and powdered wig. But Imbert and Mary,—who by this time had arrived at much familiarity of speech and intercourse,—had all the talk to themselves;—interrupted, to be sure, once in a while, by "minnows and mack'rel!"—the peculiar phrase of Peleg, as he chided and urged on his fat horse, from a lazy walk to a still slower jog-trot, over the smooth and almost trackless heath.

Cars, holding some of the wealthy townspeople, came next. These guests had been invited by Miriam to take a share in the social jaunt; but although this was held forth as her ostensible design in asking the company of her neighbours, she secretly wished to observe the effect of her splendour, and what she believed to be her first approaches to greatness, upon her companions.

On arriving at her mansion, Miriam descended quickly from her calêche and entered the new dwelling. When her visitors had disengaged themselves from their travelling paraphernalia, she was found ready at the door of her country seat to welcome them. She gave them a reception which was thought, at the moment, to be rather formal and grandiloquous, for one who had been accustomed to the plain mode of speech and manner, peculiar to those professing the unsophisticated ways of the Quakers; but this was soon forgotten by her visitors, or remembered but slightly, amidst the earnestness with which she pressed her hospitality upon the wondering islanders.

The guests were received in a carpeted drawing room, furnished and adorned with luxuries which strangely contrasted with the plain and scanty articles of household garniture, that they had left at home in their own houses. Allowing a proper time for refreshment, as well as for indulgence in curiosity, Miriam led her guests to other parts of the building, whose appointments excited equal wonder with those of the reception chamber.

The grandeur of the hostess showed itself somewhat after the manner of the sailor, who had seen and admired the vest of his Admiral,—the facings of which had been manufactured of costly figured silk-velvet. The jack-tar, being paid off on his coming into port, forthwith sought out a fashionable tailor and contracted for a similar waistcoat, whose linings, as well as facings, should alike be made of the rich material. Meeting the Admiral in his wanderings, he stripped off his roundabout and displayed his vest fore-and-aft, exclaiming, in the pride of his heart, as he made a complete revolution on his heel—"No *sham* here, you see, Admiral!— Stem and stern alike, my old boy!" It was even so with Miriam. From the garret to the kitchen every thing was complete. Her upper chambers were arranged with a neat display of all that was convenient as well as ornamental. The parlour was by no means furnished at the expense of the sleeping chambers or the kitchen; and Miriam felt a matronly pleasure in giving occular demonstration of the fact. There was no *sham* there;—stem and stern—fore-and-aft, were alike admirable.

Her half-brother Peleg surveyed the whole in mute astonishment. When he had, as he thought, seen all within, he proceeded to the kitchen and lit his pipe:—and thereupon he sallied forth to take an outward view of the premises. Here, as his mind became completely filled and running over with wonder, and after making a due estimate of the prodigal expense, he was observed to take his pipe from his mouth, and to puff out a long whiff of smoke.

"Minnows and mack'rel!" said he, slowly, as he footed up, and comprehended, the vast outlays which his sister had incurred, for nothing in the world but to indulge in the unheard-of vanity of a country mansion.

Peleg had never heard of Anaxagoras; but he meant precisely the same thing, at this time, by the above peculiar exclamation, as did the philosopher, whose opinion had been asked in relation to a costly imperial monument:—"What a deal of good money," said Anaxagoras, as he gazed at the pile, "has here been changed into useless stone!"

"Why, Miriam!—Miriam, I say!" shouted Peleg, at the top of his "tin-pipe voice," as he finished his survey of the wonders of Quaise.

"I hear thee, Peleg:—thou speakest to every body as if they were thick of hearing;—what would'st thou, Peleg?"

"I am sorely amazed, and troubled at thy extravagance; and I have called to thee aloud to tell thee so. I will uplift my voice in reproof, *in* season and *out* of season, against such shameless waste of thy husband's property;—and I take these good people to witness, that I cry aloud, and spare not!"

"Go to, Peleg," said Miriam: "we have enough of the world's goods to spare, and shall not miss the trifle that thou would'st cry so loud over. I have built this pleasant dwelling, out of town here, as much to set such close-handed misers as thou an example of spending money worthily, as to furnish a retreat from the close air, and the dust, and the turmoil of the town, in seasons when enjoyment may be had abroad."

"Dust and turmoil, indeed!" said Peleg; "and talkest thou of close air in the town!—minnows and mack'rel! who ever heard of such downright nonsense? The air is as free and untainted in the settlement, as it is hereaway among the rotting seaweed of this choked harbour of Quaise, and the swamps of the stagnant ponds in the neighbourhood."

Miriam did not much relish the freedom of Peleg's speech, whom, heretofore, she had always found a pliant echo of her own opinions;—but then she forgot that her former actions and performances were the results of wise counsels and profound calculation; and she did not sufficiently credit Peleg for independence of opinion about matters with which he was familiar. The building of a costly house, and that house, too, so far away from town, was the height of folly in Peleg's eyes. His opinion remained unchanged after he had resumed his investigations; and more closely inspected the interior. He found, by accident, a range of small apartments, curiously leading from one to the other, with doors unnecessarily opening in several directions, and having bolts, and bars, and ponderous fastenings, incomprehensible in their use. He lost himself in the labyrinth, by following a flight of steps, that led from one of these mysterious closets to hidden places beneath the house; and he stumbled along a dark vaulted passage, and up another flight of steps, which led to a small trapdoor concealed among some bushes, and opening near the water of the bay. Peleg whistled outright as he emerged into the light of day, and with more than his usual emphasis, he ejaculated—"Minnows and mack'rel!—the woman's crazy—stark, staring mad!"

Miriam had lost sight of Peleg in his wanderings; but she caught a glimpse of him just as his head peeped through the trap-door from beneath the ground. He had seen more than she intended should be disclosed to any of her visitors; and she hastened, with real anxiety, to put a stopper upon his speech, before he should let others into the secret. It was no easy matter, however, to lead Peleg away from a subject upon which he could discourse so eloquently, as the extravagance and waste which his eyes had beheld, and of which his kinswoman had been guilty;—and she was right glad when it was proposed and voted that the whole party should walk over to the Indian settlement at the Spring. Miriam forthwith took the arm of Peleg, and walked briskly forward; and she thus effectually secured her plans from further exposure. The other members of the company paired off with one another, and strolled after them at their leisure.

Imbert was absent when the party set out; but his absence created no uneasiness, nor elicited any unusual remark. He might be in pursuit of game, or fishing in the bay;—at all events, he could easily discover their route, and would doubtless follow as soon as he should ascertain the absence of his friends.

The ceremony of knocking at a neighbour's door, previous to entering, was not much practised at Nantucket; and it is not, even now, held at all necessary by the older people. Miriam, therefore, entered the hut of Tashima without sign or announcement. There was no person to be seen in the outer chamber; and she was proceeding, without ceremony, to explore the premises, when she was met at the doorway of the inner apartment by Manta. There was some confusion in the manner of the Indian girl, as she hastily closed the aperture, and motioned Miriam and Peleg to seats. A man's step was heard within; the curtain was withdrawn, and Imbert carelessly entered the apartment where Miriam was sitting! Manta cast her eyes to the ground; while Miriam,—suspicion flashing over her mind,—scanned the face of Imbert with a quick and searching glance. His design, if he had any in being there alone with the Indian-girl, was impenetrable. He was the same smiling, bold, gay Lothario that he had always appeared, and saluted the new comers with the utmost unconcern!

"Minnows and mack'rel!" said Peleg; "there have we been hunting and *helloing* all over for thee, and lo-and-behold thou art here!—Come, come, daughter of Tashima, thou needst not look as if thou wert blushing, at being found alone with friend Imbert. 'Efags! when I was a young man like him, I used to have many an innocent romp with the Indian maids."

The allusion of Peleg seemed to create still greater confusion in the manner of Manta; but she was soon relieved by the arrival of the rest of the party, and by the general conversation that ensued. The beverage of the unrivalled spring beneath the solitary willow, was, as usual, tasted and admired for its purity; and then the company paid their respects to the veteran Tashima in his school-room, where he daily toiled on in his laborious vocation. He welcomed them, as usual, with hearty, but sedate cordiality, and in due season they departed, filled with pleasure and surprise at his success with his Indian pupils.

Imbert contrived to linger behind, where the others were paying their visit at the school-house. He took the almost lifeless hand of Manta in his, and led her from the door to a seat. The fire of her eye, and the elasticity of her form were gone. She sank heavily upon a settle, and covered her eyes with her hands, and sobbed aloud.

"Why do you weep, Manta?"—asked Imbert, soothingly.

"Ask me not why I weep," said she; "it is an idle question for you to ask, who know so well the cause."

"But these tears are out of place now:—come—cheer up, and do not betray yourself to these people. You did not see *me* wince under the curious gaze of that Argus, whom they call Miriam Coffin, when I was unexpectedly discovered here by her. Fie, fie, Manta;—put on the smiles again with which you used to greet me, when I have stolen away from the town to visit you."

"Ah!—those fatal visits have been rare of late. Indeed, indeed, I am very sorrowful. I will not upbraid you—for I love you too well. Ah me!— it was blindness—or madness—or both, perhaps, that hindered me from seeing consequences. How foolish, not to know that the dark skin of the Indian maid would prove the impassable barrier to my happiness! I see it all now;—and yet I did not run headlong into the snare: I was urged,

Imbert, and you know it;—I was over-persuaded by you! May the Great Spirit,—he that is your God as well as mine,—forgive you all! Ah, my heart—my poor heart!"

Scalding tears trickled through her long dark fingers, while she sobbed convulsively. But the reader needs no further description of a most painful scene, whose cause can be so easily apprehended. It is enough to say that the daughter of Tashima had been betrayed.

"Come, my good girl," said Imbert, withdrawing his head from the doorway, "dry up your tears;—they are coming this way again. Fie, Manta!—cheer up, child, for heaven's sake, and don't expose yourself thus. Go to your chamber, Manta, and leave me to manage these unwelcome visitors. There is a kiss for you, my girl;—go in—go in quick!—or we will be again discovered together."

"You shall see no more of this weakness," replied Manta, with a convulsive sigh, as she suffered herself to be led passively to her chamber. "I have given way too much to nature: you shall see me exert the self-command peculiar to my race.—There! I am calm now, and my heart shall throb no more. See, even my tears are restrained at your bidding."

"It is well," said Imbert; and he hastily retired, unperceived, through the little garden,—his form being sheltered by the clustering shrubbery. He sprang over the fence, and, by a short turn among the huts, he came out upon the party just as they finished taking leave to Tashima. Not the least indication was apparent, in his manner or conversation, that he had, but a moment before, been looking upon the ruins of a generous and confiding woman, the source of whose consuming tears was in her breaking heart!

Imbert succeeded, without betraying his design, in drawing his companions away from the hut of Manta, and contrived to send them all on the road towards the mansion they had left at Quaise.

In the main, the party had been a pleasant one; and nothing worthy of note occurred to mar the general festivity. The grief of Manta, and the anxiety of Imbert, were unknown to any but themselves; and Peleg's usual exclamation, as he shrugged up his shoulders, while looking for the last time, and railing upon the extravagances at Quaise, was unheeded by everybody, and most especially by Miriam, after she had seen him well deposited in his calêche. Miriam's purpose had been so far accomplished, that she knew her visitors would not rest until the whole town should be made acquainted with the magnificence of her country establishment: and she also knew that in proportion as she affected magnificence, so she would excite the envy of the people; and that, in fact, by her assumption of superiority, it would eventually come to be a thing conceded,—and she would thus, by degrees, lay the foundation of her greatness among her townsmen.

CHAPTER SIX.

Not Ocean's monarch shall escape us free!
Masaniello.

Soon to the sport of death the crews repair:
Redmond, unerring, o'er his head suspends
The barbed steel, and every turn attends;
Unerring aimed, the missile weapon flew,
And, plunging, struck the fated victim through,
Awhile his heart the fatal javelin thrills,
And flitting life escapes in sanguine rills!
Falconer.

WE must now change the scene. Among the indentations of the coast of Western Africa, the bay of Walwich may be traced upon the chart. This bay was much resorted to, in years past, for the right-whale, or the species that live by what whalers call *"suction."* The bay contains good anchorage ground, and shelter for ships; and, at some periods of the year, known to

231

whalefishermen as the season for feeding, the coast along its margin is visited by these huge animals in pursuit of food, which consists principally of peculiar kinds of small fish, that keep in shoal water about the bay, and herd or school together in countless numbers. Thousands of the mullet, the roman, the stonebream, the harder, the mackerel, and many other varieties that abound in African bays, together with myriads of the Medusan race, are *sucked* in by the right-whale for a breakfast, through the vertical bars of whalebone that stud its mouth, like the gratings of a prison window, or the palings of a picket fence.

There are but few persons who do not know the difference in the formation and habits of the two principal species of the *cetaceous* tribe— the *mysticetus* and the *cachalot*—which are the object of pursuit of the whale-fishermen. They are called the *right-whale* and the *spermacetti*. The former has immense jaws of bone, without any well-defined teeth, but with a groove of dark fibrous material within its huge mouth, called whalebone, through which to strain its food;—keeping mostly in shallow water, and living upon small fry; disappearing from the surface at short intervals; remaining under water but for a few minutes; breathing, or ejecting from its blow-holes, columns of water, in two perpendicular streams, or *jets d'eau*, on rising to the surface, and producing inferior oil. The latter, to wit, the spermacetti, has tusks of ivory on a huge, dropping underjaw; blunt, clumsy head, and broad tail; frequenting none other than the deepest water; diving deep and perpendicularly; staying long out of sight, and, on rising, blowing or spouting in a single jet, or stream, which inclines to the horizon; and producing a better quality of oil, though in smaller quantity according to its bulk, than the right-whale. The spermacetti yields, in addition to its oil, a valuable matter called *sperm*, which is highly prized as an article of commerce; and also produces that rare aromatic drug, called *ambergris*.

Jethro, with his son Isaac, remained in London, intending, when his business should be finished there, to take passage home in some merchantman bound for the colonies.

The Grampus set sail from the Thames. The place of her rendezvous with the Leviathan had been appointed at Walwich bay. The Grampus, without any remarkable incident, arrived first upon the spot, and had waited for her consort for several days. Some forty whaling vessels, of all nations, were riding at anchor within the bay, waiting the expected visits from the whales. Day after day—week after week—had glided away, since the arrival of the major part of the fleet, but not a solitary animal had as yet made his appearance. The Grampus was fitted out for the sperm-whale fishery, and had taken in her three years' provisions at London. Her captain and crew, who had been some time idle, now longed for sport; and they cared very little,—since wait they must for the good ship Leviathan, in order to double The Horn in company,—whether the invitation to amusement should come in the shape of a right-whale, a spermacetti, or a razorback;—the last the most dangerous and least productive of all.

Africa has a burning, sultry coast. The sun was sending a lurid glare upon the sea, which heaved long and sluggishly in the bay, without a breath of air to curl the crest of the swell. The crews of the assembled ships were at their early breakfast, and the officers and men on the lookout were lazily gazing upon the mirrored surface of the water, or listlessly walking to and fro upon their posts. In many of the whale-ships,—particularly in those that had previously been in Northern latitudes,—a crows-nest, or a sort of sentry-box, surrounded, breast high, by canvas stretched as a protection against the weather, and covered with an awning,—was perched on the maintopmast, or at the topgallant-mast-head. In these places of look-out, a man is always stationed to observe the approach of the whale, and to communicate his motions to those on deck. But in the Grampus,—destined as she was for temperate latitudes in the Pacific,—no other accommodation was provided for the sentry, than the bare maintopgallant cross-trees, where for hours together the lynx-eyed watcher sent forth his anxious regards upon the ocean, and deemed his station a post of honour,—as it always proved of extra profit, if he should be the first to discover a whale within pursuing distance.

"Dull work!" said Seth, slowly pacing the deck;—"dull work,—by my hopes!—in this accursed climate, where scorching airs blow from the great Afric desert:—and as for *amusement*,—we may feast our eyes, if we like, by looking upon armies of naked Hottentots, 'capering ashore,' smeared with slush, and surfeiting upon tainted blubber!—who mock us in our commands, as we coast along the bay,—repeating, as they follow us, our very words like an echo—and mimicking our minutest actions, when we attempt to make ourselves understood by signs. Poor brutes! The Creator has smitten their continent and their minds alike, with barrenness; and has given to the one its arid plains, which defy the hand of cultivation,—while the souls of the people are unblessed with the refreshing dews of intelligence. But what boots it?—they are happier, in their ignorance, than we who boast of knowledge, but who are restless in our desires

'——As the Ocean—
In one unceasing change of ebb and flow.' "

The reflections of Seth, upon the blessings of ignorance, were interrupted by a thrilling cry from the mast-head.

"Flooks—flooks!" was the welcome salutation from aloft. The half-eaten meal was broken off,—and the rush to the boats was tumultuous. It was like that of an army of practised gladiators, in the arena of the Coliseum. The alarm was heard by the crews of other vessels; and the intelligence spread like wildfire that a whale was entering the bay. Four boats were lowered—manned and put off from the Grampus, in less than half a minute after the cry was uttered aloft. A hundred other boats were instantly in motion, and bearing down upon the animal. Some, however, took the precaution to separate from the rest, and thus divided the chances of capture. None could count with certainty upon striking the prey, for his course was irregular while in pursuit of his food. The whale is not a vicious animal, unless wounded; and, if not frightened, will move off sluggishly from his pursuers, and appear and disappear at regular intervals: —so that, if the direction is well observed when he sinks, (or shows his *flooks*, or forked tail, as he dives,) a pretty accurate calculation may be made as to the place of his reappearance.

The whalers in the boats that had scattered, had their share of excitement in turn; while those who had headed the whale, when he sunk from their sight for the first time, saw with mortification, by the indication of his flooks, that he had already deviated largely from his first course. As a score of others were already near the spot where he would next rise to blow, the first pursuers naturally lay upon their oars;—but they were watchful of the event of the chase.

Macy, with his two mates, and an approved boat-steerer, had each command of a separate boat. The selection of the crews for these boats, is in fact a matter of taste or favouritism with these officers of the ship. The captain has the first pick of the whole crew;—and, if his judgment is good, he chooses those of the most powerful limb and muscle, quickness of apprehension, and readiness of execution. The next choice falls to the first mate;—the second officer's turn comes next;—and the siftings of the crew fall to the boat-steerers. It may readily be believed that Macy, who was an experienced whaler, was altogether discreet in his choice, and had a crew of oarsmen who might be pitted against any other crew of the whole fleet. To say that they were Americans, and experienced whale-fishermen, is sufficient assurance, of itself, that they were competitors for all whaling honours, against the whole world. It is still, as it was eminently then, altogether un-American to admit of superiority in this business. It was, therefore, with deep chagrin that Macy saw the game escape him; for thus far he had led the van of the attack; while the whalers in some fifty boats in the rear, if not altogether content that he should be their leader, were at least satisfied, that to be beaten by *him* was no dishonour.

The Englishman, the Dane, the Dutchman, the Swede, as also representatives of other European nations, were Macy's ambitious competitors, for the honour of killing the first whale of the season:—the long and the strong pull was exerted to carry off the prize, and fair words of encouragement were offered, and enforced in the blandest and most persuasive manner, by those who controlled the boats. Some, uselessly enough, where so many were engaged, pulled after the animal in his devious course after food; while others rested on their oars to watch the result, and to take advantage of his wanderings. The scene was most animating—and but a few minutes served to scatter the boats in every direction;—to sprinkle the bay with dark moving spots;— to people it with life—sinewy life;—in short, it was an exhibition of the noblest of God's creation, both animal and human, waging a war of extermination, and threatening death and destruction by collision.

The noble animal,—for it was a right-whale of the largest class,—held on its course up the bay, scooping its food from time to time, and annihilating its thousands of small fish at a dive;— leaving the boats far in the rear. and darting off in new directions, until those who were most on the alert, or rather those who pulled the most constantly, were fain to give up the chase and to lie on their oars. The whale approached the anchorage ground of the ships; and its speed was increased as it shoaled the water, in proportion to its eagerness after its flying victims. The small fish, driven before their huge devourer, clubbed together, and concentrated in schools of such immense magnitude, that the ships were surrounded, as it were, with a dense mass of animal matter, huddling together for common safety, or flying in swarms before their common enemy, like the multitudinous and periodical flowings of the herring from the Greenland seas.

Intent upon his prey, the whale appeared unconscious of the dangerous vicinage of the ships, and played among them with a temerity which evinced a tameness, or perhaps an ignorance of its danger, that plainly showed he had never been chased by the whaler, nor hurt by the harpoon. His eager pursuit after food may, however, account for his recklessness; for, generally speaking, the instinct of the whale is sufficient, upon all occasions, to avoid an unusual object floating upon the water; and at such times the nicest strategem of the art of the whaler is required to capture him.

The persecuted tribes have been chased so often,—pursued so relentlessly, from haunt to haunt, that they must not be unnecessarily scared;—for, if they are, the pursuit may as well be abandoned first as last. No crew can row a boat, for any length of time, to keep pace with a frightened and fugitive whale.

The animal, gorged with its fishy meal, at last commenced its retreat from the bay; and the boats manœuvred to head him off as he retired. Obeying the instinct of his nature, he now showed his flooks and vanished from the sight, before the boats could get within striking distance. A calculation being made where he would next appear, (for beneath the water the whale does not deviate from a direct line in his horizontal progress,) a general race ensued; and each strove, as if life were on the issue, to arrive first upon the spot. Some twenty minutes' steady and vigorous pulling found the foremost boats a full mile behind the whale, when he rose again to breathe. Several boats were unluckily ahead of Seth in the chase, as their position at starting enabled them to take the lead, when the animal began to push for deeper water. But Seth's men had been resting on their oars, while nearly all others had exhausted their strength, in following the whale among the ships; and the captain judged rightly, that in darting after his tiny prey, he would lead them all a bootless dance. He had determined to wait for the retreat, and then hang upon the rear of the enemy. There were others, however, acquainted with the soundings of the bay, whose tactics were scarce inferior to Seth's; and the advantage gained over him by several boats was proof of this, or at least of the superior accuracy of their calculations. It was a long time since Seth had given chase to an animal of the right-whale breed;—he had grappled, of late, only with the spermacetti;—and, therefore, it was not to be wondered at, at this time, and under the circumstances, that some of those around him should beat him in manœuvring in the bay. But, in the steady chase, he knew that he could count upon the speed and bottom of his boat's crew, and he was now resolved to contest for the victory.

"We have a clear field now, my boys—give way steadily—we gain upon them—give the long pull—the strong pull—and the pull together: keep her to it—heave ahead, my hearties!" Such were the words of Seth, as with eyes steadily fixed upon a certain point, and with his steering oar slightly dipping at times, he guided the light whale-boat unerringly towards the place where he expected the whale to reappear. One by one he had dropped his antagonists by the way, until three only remained manfully struggling between him and the prize. The whale again breathed at the surface, and the distance between the headmost boat and the animal was found to be diminished to half a mile—while the ships in the bay were run "hull down." The pursuers were now out upon the broad ocean.

Those who had abandoned the chase in despair, were slowly returning to their ships. The rigging of the vessels was manned by anxious spectators, watching the motions of the tiny specs out at sea, with beating hearts. The whale again cast his flukes in the air, and sank from the view of his pursuers. Now came the tug of war.

"You must beat those foreigners ahead," said Seth to his men, "or crack your oars: they are of good American ash, and will bear pulling," continued he:—"Give way with a will?—Pull—pull, my lads;—that whale will not sink again without a harpoon in his body:—and 'twill never do to tell of at home, that we allowed men of other nations to beat *us*. Keep your eyes steadily on your oars; mark the stroke of the after oar, men—and give way for the credit of the Grampus!"

Here Seth braced himself in the stern-sheets—seized the steering oar with his left hand, and placed his right foot against the after oar, just below the hand of the oarsman.

"Now pull for your lives!" said he, "while I add the strength of my leg to the oar:—Once more!—Again, my boys!—Once more—There,—We pass the Spaniard!"

"*Diabolo!* " exclaimed the mortified native of Spain.

The additional momentum of Seth's foot, applied to the stroke oar had done the job;—but two more boats had to be passed,— and quickly too,— or all the labour would be lost.

"At it again, my boys!—steady—my God, give way!—give way for the honour of the Grampus.—One pull for old Nantucket! and—there—we have shown a clean pair of heels to the Dutchman!"

"*Hagel!—Donder and blixem!* " said the Hollander.

"There is but one boat ahead," said Seth;—"It is the Englishman!—We must beat *him* too, or we have gained nothing! Away with her—down upon him like men!—One pull for the Grampus, my boys!—another for old Nantuck——"

The American now shot up alongside of the English boat: but the honour of the nation, too, was at stake, and they bent to their oars with fresh vigour. Five athletic Englishmen, each with a bare chest that would have served for the model of a Hercules,—with arms of brawn and sinew,—swayed their oars with a precision and an earnestness, that, for a minute, left the contest doubtful. The English commander, seeing how effectually Seth managed the stroke oar with his foot, braced himself in a similar attitude of exertion;—and his boat evidently gained upon the Nantucketer! Seth saw the increase of speed of his rival with dismay. The whale, too, was just rising ahead. The bubbles of his blowing, and of his efforts at rising, were beginning to ascend! It was a moment of intense anxiety. The rushing train, or vortex of water, told that he was near the surface. Both commanders encouraged their men anew by a single word; and then, as if by mutual consent, all was silent, except the long, measured, and vigorous stroke of the oars.

"For old England, my lads!" shouted the one.

"Remember old Nantucket, my boys!" was the war-cry of the other.

Both plied their oars with apparently equal skill;—but the hot Englishman lost his temper as the boat of Seth shot up again, head and head with him—and he surged his foot so heavily upon the after oar, that it broke off short in the rowlock! The blade of the broken oar became entangled with the others on the same side, while the after oarsman lost his balance, and fell backward upon his leader.

"I bid thee good bye!" said Seth, as he shot ahead.

"*Hell and damnation!*" vociferated the Englishman.

"Way enough—peak your oars!" said Seth to his men. The oars bristled apeak, after the fashion of the whale-fishermen. The harpooner immediately seized and balanced his weapon over his head, and planted himself firmly in the bow of the boat. At that instant the huge body of the whale rose above the surface; and Seth, with a single turn of his steering oar, brought the bow dead upon the monster, a few feet back of the fin. Simultaneously with the striking of the boat, the well-poised harpoon was launched deep into the flesh of the animal.

"*Starn all!*" shouted Seth.

The boat was backed off in an instant; and the whale, feeling the sting of the barb, darted off like the wind! The well-coiled line flew through the groove of the bow-post with incomparable swiftness, and it presently began to smoke, and then to blaze, with the rapidity of the friction. Seth now took the bow with his lance, exchanging places with the harpooner, and quietly poured water upon the smoking groove, until it was cooled. The oars were again *peaked*, and the handles inserted in brackets fixed on the ceiling of the boat beneath the thwarts—the blades projecting over the water like wings; and the men, immoveable, rested from their long, but successful pull:—and much need did they have of the relief,—for a more arduous, or better contested chase they had never experienced.

The line in the tub was now well nigh run out; and the boatsteerer, with a thick buckskin mitten, or *nipper*, as it is called, for the protection of his hand, seized hold of the line, and, in a twinkling, caught a turn around the loggerhead, to enable the man at the tub oar to bend on another line.

The rapidity of the animal's flight the while was inconceivable. The boat now ploughed deeply and laboriously, leaving banks of water on each side, as she parted the wave, that overtopped the men's heads, and effectually obscured the sight of every object on the surface. The swell of the closing water came after them in a heavy and angry rush. The second line was now allowed to run slowly from the loggerhead; and a *drag* or plank about eighteen inches square, with a line proceeding from each corner, and meeting at a point like a pyramid, was fastened to it, and thrown over to deaden the speed of the whale. Another and another drag were added, until the animal, feeling the strong backward pull, began to relax his efforts:—and presently he suddenly descended, though not to the full extent of the slackened line.

It now became necessary to haul in the slack of the line, and to coil it away in the tub carefully; while the men pulled with their oars, to come up to the whale when he should rise to the surface. All things were soon ready again for the deadly attack.

The ripple of the whale, as he ascended, was carefully marked; and when he again saw the light of day, a deep wound, close to the barbed harpoon, was instantly inflicted by the sharp lance of Seth. It was the death blow.

"*Starn all!*" was the cry once more,—and the boat was again quickly backed off by the oarsmen.

The infuriated animal roared in agony, and lashed the ocean into foam. The blood gushed from his spout-holes, falling in torrents upon the men in the boat, and colouring the sea. The whale, in his last agony, is a fearful creature. He rose perpendicularly in the water, head downwards, and again writhed and lashed the sea with such force, that the people in the retreating boats, though ten miles distant, heard the thunder of the sound distinctly. The exertion was too violent to last long:—it was the signal of his dissolution. His life-blood ceased to flow, and he turned his belly to the sun! The *waif* of the Grampus floated triumphantly above the body of the slaughtered Leviathan of the deep—and the peril of the hardy crew was over.

CHAPTER SEVEN.

"Here lies the body of John Gardner, who was born in the year 1624,
and died A.D. 1706, aged 82."

THE above is the substance of a simple inscription, on the only headstone,—in fact the only memorial of any kind,—which points out the spot that once served for the burial-place of the ancient inhabitants of Nantucket. It stands on the road or slight wheel-path, leading from the present town of Nantucket to Mattekat harbour, at the western end of the island,—around whose waters the first Anglo-American inhabitants erected their settlement of houses. But no vestige now remains of the old town of Sherburne, as the place was called, from which the early inhabitants sallied forth on the broad Atlantic, in their first rude and imperfect essays to entrap the whale. The harbour was found too much exposed, and far less convenient for shipping, than that which is, at the present day, known as Nantucket harbour; and by degrees the new town of Sherburne, (now Nantucket,) was built and peopled, while the ancient

243

site was deserted. Many of its houses,—hauled overland upon rollers and skids, and placed upon their new foundations on the northern side of the island,—were made to follow the current of population, while others were suffered to go to decay.

The ancient burying-ground naturally shared in the neglect of the settlement to which it appertained: and places more contiguous to the new town were selected to deposit the dead. The headstones of the first fathers, rudely sculptured, but venerable for their antiquity, became moss-grown and ruinous. The inscriptions, however, were obliterated as much by desecration as by the crumbling touch of time. The fences and little grave enclosures were carried off piecemeal, and served for firewood or kindling stuff for the poor, in seasons of rigour or scarcity. The gravestones, in time, one by one, disappeared, from the wanton mutilation of unthinking boys, or were upturned by browsing cattle, or by the effects of the severe frosts of the high Northern latitude, which loosened and finally ejected them from the bosom of the earth. A few sad memorials only remained at the commencement of the revolution, tottering to decay, and clustering around the sole monument of other times, which, at this day, [1834,] remains, deep-bedded in the ground,—standing alone, like the last warrior at the Pass of Thermopylæ, after all his fellows had been hacked down to the earth. It was the only one whose inscription was legible when the following scene occurred; and, though more than half a century has since passed, it still bears the name of "*John Gardner*" distinctly carved upon it. It owes its preservation to the induration and unyielding nature of its material,—which is of a dark silicious texture,—and to the depth of its setting in the ground. This stone seems to have given the name to that ancient receptacle of the dead. It was then, and is still called the "Gardner Burying Ground." It has had many a pilgrimage to its shrine, made alike by all ages and classes, who, escaping from the labour of the day, or wrapped in their own reflections, were desirous of strolling in loneliness upon the heath. It was the only spot on a long route over the treeless and uncultivated plain, calculated to attract the attention of the passenger;— in fact, it formed the end of a long walk, in that direction, which, having been attained, the stroller turned upon his steps.

Towards this secluded spot Imbert and Grimshaw took their way on a Sabbath afternoon, when the month of October was in its wane, and while the inhabitants of the town were at their several places of worship.

Unlike as these gallants were in their temperament—the one mercurial, and the other cold, sedate and calculating—yet there was a fellow-feeling between them—a sympathy inexplicable in its nature,—which bound them to each other. They were young men "pursuing fortune's slippery ba',"—looking to the future, which appeared all smiling to their view:—but the one recklessly trusted to the adventitious development of that future, without prudence in the management of the present;—while the other cautiously and selfishly laid his plans, and laboured incessantly to influence the attainment of his fond desires. Few words passed between them, until they arrived in sight of the place where the ashes of Gardner reposed. Imbert had lost his usual buoyancy; and Grimshaw, naturally taciturn, forebore to interrupt the silence.

The sight of the gravestones seemed to recall Imbert to his speech. He had evidently been revolving in his mind some unpleasant subject. He bit his nails with impatience; his gestures were sudden and inexplicable, while, now and then, he would utter some hasty exclamation, that appeared to have no connection with any subject.

"You are in a queer humour to-day," said Grimshaw.—"What's in the wind now? Upon my soul, you are all at once a most dramatic and agreeable companion."

"I am about to leave you," said Imbert; "and that little cluster of quaint-looking headstones reminds me of the cause. I must in reality part from you in a few days—and I fear you will say I am bound on a Tom Fool's errand!"

"You are, as usual, playing upon my credulity," said Grimshaw: "You will not, surely, leave me to plod on alone, uncheered by your presence, on this 'sand bar?'"

"You mistake, my friend; I was never more serious," replied Imbert: "I shall shortly be a dweller among the Antipodes;—and if you have any message to send to the world's end, or to the Anthropophogi who dwell in unknown regions beyond, and wear their heads, as we do our fan-tails, beneath their arms, I advise you to make up your dispatches forthwith. I am bound for the Pacific Ocean!"

"Enough of this, Imbert;—you have had your joke," returned Grimshaw: "and now tell me how you speed with the daughter of Peleg."

"Pe-leg!" repeated he, slowly, and somewhat scornfully.

"Ay—Peleg Folger,—the great admirer of 'minnows mack'rel!' Is it not a good name to conjure with?"

"Pshaw!" ejaculated Imbert, impatiently.

"Well, then, if *his* name does not suit, and the mention of his daughter Mary displeases you, in God's name unfold to me the mystery of your words frankly and fully. To the point—"

"To the point, then, it is," said Imbert: "You have conjured successfully with the name of the daughter, and you shall hear. I know not what attraction there is in yonder spot—but it was there," (and here Imbert pointed to the little clump of gravestones on a slight eminence ahead,) "it was upon that spot,—holy or accursed, as it may be—I know not which,— that I yesterday declared myself to Mary Folger."

"Aha!—Sits the wind there?"

"Hear me, Grimshaw, and you shall judge. There is a witchery about that girl that I cannot withstand. There is heaven in her luscious blue eyes,—elysium is perched upon her rosy lips,—innocence and truth are enthroned upon her countenance—"

"Hoity toity!" said the unmoved Grimshaw, "you *are* in love, forty fathoms deep:—or are you mad?"

"I think the latter, upon my honour," said Imbert, seriously; "I have even calculated the moon's age, to ascertain her influence upon the mind:—but no more of that. I invited her to walk with me yesterday, and we sauntered thus far together. I observed an unusual sadness in her manner, that appeared to me unaccountable. I exerted every little art of conversation and remark that I was master of, to dispel the melancholy that evidently hung about her, but to no effect. When we arrived here, a tear stole into her eye, and she turned away from me. I could see that she applied her hand to her eyes; and her manner, so gentle and so winning as it always is, evinced, upon this occasion, a pensiveness of expression that to me was truly distressing.

"'Dear Mary,' said I, 'tell me the cause of your distress. If one, no longer a stranger to you, may presume to inquire what grieves you, I entreat you to confide in me. I will sympathize with you, if I cannot relieve your sorrow.'

"She turned her moist blue eyes upon me, beaming, as I thought, with gratitude,—and attempted to speak; but her utterance failed her, and she only pointed to this dark gravestone displaying the name of 'Gardner.' A thought flashed upon me:—there is a shy lover of hers who bears that name, and he has crossed my path more than once, since I have been here. I have fancied that a speaking devil lurked in his eye, warning me to 'beware!' It may have been only the incipient feeling of jealousy, so nearly allied to love, they say, that it attends upon it close as a shadow to the substance that projects it.

"'What may I understand by your action?' said I;—'these are but the mouldering relics of people of a past century: these rude monuments cannot surely conjure up any remembrance of them; the memory of the entire generation is extinct; and nought lives to preserve them from utter oblivion, but

'These frail memorials, still erected nigh,'

to tell their names,—their birth,—their age,—their death. Can any recent association with these have excited unpleasurable feelings?'

"I paused a moment to observe the effect of my words upon her. She answered me timidly—but with an eloquent gush of natural feeling, that went to my heart of hearts.

"'Though the dead that lie here,' said she, 'are incorporated with the earth, and, 'dust to dust,' are no longer partakers of mortality,—yet—nay, let us pass on,' continued she, with strong emotion, 'this is no fitting place for me now.'

"'Nay, dearest,' said I, gently detaining her, 'I would behold the image that has been conjured up in your mind. I entreat you to tell me—'

"'There is a name engraved there,' said she, 'which is also deeply impressed here,' and she laid her hand upon her heart as she spoke.

"'Gardner!' repeated I.

"'Thou hast spoken it,' said she.

"'Ah, now I discern the cause,' replied I; 'the young man departs within a week for the South.'

"'He does,' said she, and sighed deeply: 'There is an indefinable something that tells me misfortune will befall him, and that he departs never more to return. He was the companion of my childhood, and I cannot tell why, but melancholy forebodings whisper to my heart that a tragical end will be his. The name upon the tombstone is that of his ancestor. He was the first of the name known to our island. I grieve to say that I am the principal cause of Harry's going to sea;—and I may not retract. Suffice it to say, that it is in pursuance of a custom of the place:— it is to fulfil the duties of a species of knight-errantry imposed upon him. It is not meet that I give further explanation at this time.'

"Mary delivered this with much hesitation. An awkward pause ensued, which my wit failed me to break in upon for a while: But the time was come for me to unfold myself, for the melting mood in woman invites to tales of love. Bitterly did I find, however, that my confident calculation, in possessing her entire partiality, was a deception;—or, at best, that I could only count upon a reversion of her affection. Deeming her, heretofore, securely my own,—and all my own,—whenever I might choose to demand the boon, I had carelessly omitted opportunities to prefer my suit;—but, when I found the prize likely to slip from my grasp, I cursed my own folly, and eagerly sought to retrieve my lost advantage. My experience, you will perceive has thus made me sensible of the truth of the trite saying, that riches, when on the wing, seem far more valuable in the eye of the loser, than when in absolute possession.

"'I had fondly hoped,' said I to Mary, 'that I might claim an interest in your heart, and ask to have *my* name engraven there:—but alas!—you have chilled my hopes—your words have blasted my fond anticipations. Not knowing the cause of your grief, I offered to share it with you: but believe me, dear Mary, I have now a greater need of *your* kindly sympathy.'

"She looked at me in doubt. I could plainly perceive the revulsion in her feelings, in the play of her face; and I hastened to follow up the advantage so unexpectedly gained.

"'Grieve not, my dear Mary,' said I, while I took her passive hand in mine;—'the mishaps that you anticipate are but the dreams of a waking fancy, and do not deserve a moment's serious consideration: Grieve not for the departure of Gardner—or, at most, let me hope you will send after him only such regrets as a *friend* may indulge in; and that *my* assiduity may be rewarded, eventually, by a smile of approbation.'

"A faint smile dwelt for a moment on her countenance, and I observed that her tears had ceased to flow. They had passed away like a summer's cloud. If ever I believed in my own infallibility, and felt the full force of my vanity in the effect of my power over women, it was then. I had taken her grief by storm;—no—it was not altogether by storming—I summoned the citadel, and it capitulated:—But some unpleasant conditions were annexed, which I could ill digest, yet eventually was obliged to accept."

"And those conditions were—?"

Grimshaw's question was interrupted by Imbert, who replied—"You shall hear them in good time. In the ardour of my protestation, I demanded of Mary what I should do to prove the sincerity of my love, and challenged her to name a thing possible to be performed, and declared that I, her most devoted admirer, would attempt its execution, in the hope of one day calling her mine. This was, as the event turned out, running a mile beyond the winning post to be sure of the race. It was over-doing the matter: and I fear this extravaganza engendered doubt of my entire sincerity in her mind. Gentle and confiding as Mary appears, she is shrewd withal. I, however, managed to draw a confession from her which placed the cause of her recent grief in its true light, and relieved me somewhat of my shooting pangs of jealousy. It turned out, that although her partiality for Gardner had originated in childhood, it had by no means matured into downright love. The tears I had seen shed were an indication of the progress of her affection, and I had come in time to nip it in the half-blown bud. No absolute engagement exists between them, as I could learn; though there seems to be a tacit understanding among their relatives that he will, at some future day, claim her for his bride; and, until I made my declaration, I am of opinion that she had never seriously thought of any other alliance. Indeed, from my free-and-easy, and perhaps cavalier manner of deporting myself in her presence, until yesterday, she could never have been led to believe that I intended more than appeared in my conduct. She was then undeceived. I was vain enough to think that I should be looked upon as rather higher game than common, and that it would be the easiest thing in the world to eclipse Gardner. This was another grand mistake.

"There is an accursed association of women here," continued Imbert, "who control the young ones, and make them promise to favour none but such suitors as have pushed their fortunes upon the sea, and performed the delicate operation of letting blood from whales. It has finally come to be a settled thing, that the daughter of a whale-fisherman loses *caste*, and degrades herself in the eyes of her acquaintance, if she unites her destiny to a landsman! This is a damnable prejudice—and I swear not only to be the means of eradicating it, but to hunt the institution itself down! But to return:—Gardner was long ago given to understand, by some means that I cannot comprehend, that Mary's favour was to be propitiated, only, by a successful exhibition of his talent in the branch of surgery to which I have alluded; and he goes, nothing loath, to gain for himself the name of a fearless whaler—*an exclusive*—before he will be allowed to indulge in hope. Well!—Mary, with a determination of manner that has nettled me, and that, to my notion, plainly enough said, 'I have caught you at last—but I doubt your sincerity'—or perhaps for the pleasure of having two strings to her bow,—has contrived to impose the same pilgrimage on—*me*!—Julius Imbert, M.D.,—born a gentleman—"

"With a silver spoon in his mouth, I suppose," dryly observed Grimshaw.

"A fair hit," said Imbert; "but, my dear fellow, egotism between us, is not boasting, you know."

Imbert proceeded in his narration:—"I pressed my suit with her, as I thought, successfully; and went so far as to demand some love-token which I might keep as a testimonial of her favour. I was about to imprint a kiss upon her cheek, to seal, what I thought, a good understanding between us, when she interposed her hand and said—

"'Hold, friend Julius!—I fear this has proceeded too far already. I cannot allow thee to ratify a contract that I have not yet entirely approved on my part, and, whose conditions may perhaps need further consideration on thine. Thou knowest that I am young in years, and lack experience; and thou shouldst not call on me to act on the spur of the moment. Thy declaration is as sudden as unexpected: and yet thou hast already asked of me a pledge of constancy, and seemest to look upon it, as a thing of course, that I should at once comply with thy demand. Beshrew me, but thou art over confident. Young as I am, I know the privilege of my sex:—it is for *me* to demand the token from *thee*, as a pledge of thy sincerity and constancy.'

"'Name the boon!' said I.

"'Thou hast already asked of me,' said she, 'to name a task to be performed, as a test of thy purity of intention towards me. Dost thou wish to retract the offer?'

"'No, by heaven!' exclaimed I.

"'Swear not,' said she, 'unless thou would'st have me to doubt thy truth. Thou dost promise obedience then?'

"'I do.'

"'Listen to me, Julius. I am the youngest member of a certain female association, whose rules I have promised to observe. What those rules are, I may not tell thee;—but I would not, for a kingdom, be the first to break through the regulations that I have subscribed to—for, if I did, I should lose my own self-esteem, and perhaps meet with the scorn of my associates. I will not further discuss the question whether my adherence to them is wise or unwise: suffice it to say, I am a fast-bound member, and so I must remain. The conversation between thee and me hath proceeded to that extent, that I deem it proper to say thus much to thee:—I cannot, under my vow, accept thee as a suitor of mine, until thou hast well and truly proved thyself worthy of alliance with a whale-fisherman's daughter.'

"'And how can I best prove it to you?' demanded I.

"'By going upon the long voyage, and killing thy whale!' answered she.

"'Why Mary!—what folly is this?' exclaimed I, vexed at her words.

"'Thou must do it!' said Mary, with energy, 'and return to me a whale-fisherman—and a brave and skillful one to boot,—or the hand of Mary Folger shall never be thine. My heart is yet free;—but there are those who have already undertaken to win it in the way now proposed to thee.'

"'But, Mary,' said I, 'I have a reputable profession already—and is not that enough? To possess a knowledge of the healing art, is held most honourable among all nations;—and does *my* profession pass for nothing at Sherburne?'

"'I will not argue the question with thee;—thou may'st take back thy vaunted promise. I thought it would prove, upon the test, a vainglorious boast,—words—mere *words,*—when thou didst volunteer it. Nay—scowl not at me—thou hast forced a bashful maiden to confession, and hast caused her to throw by a portion of the natural delicacy of her sex. We now understand each other; and it is well that thou hast learned, at the outset, that thou canst neither flatter me out of my 'mind's propriety' with a smile, nor scare me from my 'mental pyramid'[*] with a frown.'

"'Mary!' said I, surprised at this trait of firmness in her character, 'my promise shall be kept—and your command shall be performed to the very letter. I did not, it is true, relish your imputation of deceit;—but I *will* go, and win a title to your favour by enacting prodigies upon the seas;—and if I do not succeed over every rival—for I have rivals, it seems—and prove myself entitled to tell the 'biggest fish-story' of them all, I will be content to resign my interest in the prize for which I contend.'

"So now you have heard all, Grimshaw," said Imbert; "and you will confess that I am in a fair way to spend some three years abroad, at the command of a mistress, whose knight-errants must poise the lance skillfully, or be disgraced. I could not, as a true knight, back out from any thing that Gardner is willing to undertake to show his devotion. 'None but the brave deserves the fair,' you know;—and the bravest upon this occasion wins."

---

[*]Fairfield

"And are you not, Julius Imbert, M.D., &c., with all your ready wit, a most egregious blockhead—an irreclaimable idiot, to listen for one moment to such folly? By the bones of Thomas-a-Becket,—or of the sainted, puritanic John Gardner, aged 82, beneath our feet—you are either fool or hypocrite—and I suspect the latter. I know you of old—there is more in this than you have dared to tell. You would circumnavigate the globe to win that girl—and then abandon her, as you have the Indian maid!"

"Hush—not so loud!—lest even the gravestone of old Gardner should hear you. It has witnessed one of my follies already; let it not get wind of another, which the censorious world might call equally reprehensible. But be careful how you trench upon private property, my boy. My actions and my after-intentions are my own—they may not be descanted upon thus freely, even by my friend.—Poor Manta!" continued Imbert, musing; "was ever being so devoted—the love of Pocahontas was nothing to it! To confess the truth," said he, aloud, "I care not if I absent myself for a season, until the anticipated effects of my *liaison* at Fat-Fire Spring shall cease to be the town talk. It must all be blown shortly, and my departure is to me the less irksome on that account. I should prefer a shorter trip to the continent, however; but the pleasure of tantalizing my rival with my presence will, of itself, prove no small gratification—and so I'll e'en take to the sea. But, by heaven, you say truly!—I *will* win that girl, and in her own way;—and though three years servitude, consorting with greasy whale-killers the while, is an apprenticeship a thought too long,—yet it is not without precedent in holy writ. Jacob's period of servitude to win Rachel, the daughter of Laban, you know, was twice seven years—but mine, to win the daughter of Peleg, will be a mere bagatelle in the contrast. There is comfortable doctrine in the text:—'See *Genesis* xxviii. 20 *and* 30,' as the man in the pulpit has it. Yes!" continued he, speaking to himself, "I will *win* her—but dearly shall she pay for the biting sneer which goaded me on to this Quixotic expedition:—

'Though that her jesses were my dear heartstrings,
I'd whistle her off—and let her down the wind
To prey at fortune!'"

"And what ship," said Grimshaw, to whom the last remark of Imbert was inaudible,—"what ship will have the honour of 'bearing Cæsar and his fortunes?'"

"The Leviathan," answered Imbert; "I have rated myself a landsman on board of her already."

"Were I captain of the Leviathan," said his companion, "methinks I should have chosen one of the hardy Nantucketers in your stead."

"The captain was pretty much of your opinion, I believe," replied Imbert: "It was not without some difficulty that Captain Jon-a-*thing*, as they call him, consented to my going with him. A red coat and smalls, silk hose and fan-tail-beaver-macaroni, were not the best passports for shipping on board a whaler."

"And how did you manage to creep into favour with the skipper?"

"Before my intention had time to cool, I made personal application to him yesterday. I found him on board the ship, superintending her outfit.

"'Captain,' said I, 'I have a notion of trying my fortunes upon the sea:—can I have a berth with you?'

"'In what capacity;' demanded he, in some astonishment; 'we have no occasion for a surgeon;—he would be of no more use to us than a spare pumpbolt,—as our simple mode of living secures to us good health and a long life—barring accidents. Thou dost not surely wish to become *accoucheur* to such 'delicate nurslings'[*] as we have to deal with upon the whaling ground!'

"'Nay, my good sir,' I replied, humouring the joke, 'I do not come to offer professional service,—and least of all to those producers of bantling twelve-foot babes, that you speak of. I wish not the *increase* of the species, heaven knows; but desire rather to thin the tribe, and to try my skill with the exterminating lance of the whaler—exchanging therefor the lance of my profession, which is likely to grow rusty for lack of use. The people are most distressingly healthy here, sir.'

"'Ho—ho!' snorted the captain; 'come,—that last joke is a good one. But, let me tell thee—if thou art serious that it is a wild scheme;—it would

---

[*]Professor Leslie

be sheer madness in one, such as *thou*, to attempt it. Be advised, and think no more of pursuing the freak. Why, doctor, what under the sun could'st thou do at sea amongst the whales? I cannot imagine what good service we could put thee to. Thou canst neither hand, reef, nor steer;—pull an oar—slush a mast—climb the rigging—nor—'

"'Stop there,' said I, 'and look you here—'

"With this, being somewhat of a gymnast, I made a spring at the fore-stay, and ascended, hand over hand, to the round-top, without touching the rope with my feet; and descended to the deck in the same manner, by my hands alone, on the inner side of the ratlins.

"'There!' said I, 'if any of your crew can beat that, or do any thing else that *I* cannot do, I will agree that I might possibly prove a useless appendage to your ship.'

"'Thy delicate skin and lady-hands belied thee,' answered he: 'They are, in good sooth, no recommendation to the whale-fisherman. But I see there is metal in thee, and we will soon give them the opportunity of acquiring a substantial coat of brown. Thou may'st come aft and sign the articles, if thou likest. Odds fish!—What will the people say to my having shipped a tippy lobster-coated doctor before the mast?'

"And now, Grimshaw," concluded Imbert, "you have the upshot of the whole matter. But if you imagine that I am going to pine away with useless regrets—or that I cannot put on the manners of a sailor the moment I don his round jacket, you were never more at fault. I have that in me which people call versatility of character; and, let me go where I will, it is an easy thing to accommodate myself to circumstances. It is not now *in* character, to be sure, to troll a sailor's song, and make gestures 'to match,' in this fashionable toggery—and upon a Sunday, too—but *n'importe;*—we are alone—and you shall hear:—so here goes—

> When the anchor's weighed, and the ship s unmoored,
>   And landsmen lag behind, sir,
> The sailor joyfully skips on board,
> And, swearing, prays for wind, sir:
>   Towing here—yehoing there—
>   Steadily, readily, cheerily, merrily—

Still from care and thinking free,
Is a sailor's life at sea.

When we sail with a freshening breeze,
　And landsmen all grow sick, sir,
The sailor lolls with his mind at ease,
　And the song and the can go quick, sir:
　　　Laughing here—quaffing there," etc.[*]

---

[*]From an early number of the "*Port Folio*," published originally in Philadelphia.

$\mathscr{C}$HAPTER EIGHT.

—By all heaven's powers,
Prophetic truth dwells in you!
Venice Preserved.

AN American whale-ship is fitted out with more than ordinary care. The health of the crew is of paramount importance, and their food and clothing are generally selected with reference to the variation of all climates. A heedful commander will display as much anxiety in culling and packing his sea-biscuit, as a careful matron in stowing away her three years' supply of poundcake, in jars of stone. For the better keeping of the hard bread, casks that have contained ardent spirits are sought after with avidity; and sometimes, when these are not to be had, new barrels are prepared with a coating of the spirits of turpentine between the joints of the staves, as a protection against the worms that are generated in the biscuit and peas of the sailor, when put up for long voyages. The beef and the pork must be packed in the best possible manner; and such vegetables

257

as can be preserved for any length of time, are picked over and over again upon the voyage, and used with rigid economy. The potato is a luxury at sea, and is held in high estimation as an antiscorbutic. It is sometimes grated by the sailor, like horseradish, and eaten raw with vinegar. Prepared in this way, he finds it a delightful condiment to the salted provisions, of which he is obliged to partake, day after day, for months together, after the live stock, with which he is plentifully provided at first, is exhausted. Other provisions are also procured with an especial eye to preservation and the comfort of the crew. Flour, and meal, and molasses, and vinegar, and all necessary things, are laid in of the best quality; and that commander would be regarded as criminal in his conduct, who failed to inspect with his own eyes, and to select with his best judgment, whatever is intended for his crew, who are invariably destined to undergo hardships and privations upon a long whaling voyage, that are not dreamed of by landsmen, who go not "down to the sea in ships," but quietly stay at home, and enjoy the comforts of a snug chimney-corner while the storm rages abroad.

The women, too, in those places that the whale-fishermen call their home, are ever watchful of the comfort of the crews. The expected departure of a whale-ship is, to them, a season of anxiety and preparation. Mattresses and bed-clothing, trowsers and jackets, stockings and shirts, pea-jackets and storm-coats, are carefully overhauled, and the rents in the garments made whole. New supplies of clothing are added, to suit all weathers; and a thousand little nicknacks and keepsakes are stowed away in chests and clothes-bags, that betray the tender consideration of woman for her sailor-kindred.

It is only by attentions like these, that our race of the bravest and best seamen in the world is preserved. Neglect these precautions, and you may be sure that the privations consequent upon their omission would send home your crews mutinous and dissatisfied; and that the hazardous but exciting trade itself would soon be neglected, and come to a natural decay.

There are other things of equal importance, that are looked to with a critical eye by the experienced whaling captain; and the success of his voyage often depends upon them, as much as upon an active and willing crew. The ship must be well found in spars and rigging; the clinker-built whale-boats must be light and buoyant; the oars well balanced, and of the toughest material; the lines well spun, and the harpoons, and lances, and blubber-spades, made of tough and pliant irons and laid with the best of steel. With preparations such as these,—with fearless hearts, strong hands, and steady eyes—success is almost certain. But the perils of the trade, and the many casualties of the profession, often render the best preparatory measures nugatory, and the voyage disastrous.

A whaling captain, in the very best sense of the word, was Jonathan Coleman, the commander of the Leviathan. He was a light-hearted, merry fellow, and loved his joke; but his profession was, notwithstanding, a passion with him. He had, with constant assiduity, overlooked the storage of his provisions and his oil casks;—picked his crew from the young and hardy men of the island;—paid frequent visits to the forecastle, and pried, good naturedly, into the preparations of the seamen; and, where it was necessary, gave them good advice for their future welfare: and he sometimes insisted, pertinaciously, upon an additional blanket, or a better bed,—a new pea-jacket, or an additional flannel shirt. If means were lacking for a proper outfit, his hand and his purse were open to supply the purchase, either as a gift or as a loan.

"Darn your skins!" said he, "you must trust to an old whaler in these matters:—there must be no grumbling on board my ship—no shivering with cold—no short allowance:—I am determined you *shall* be comfortable. But mark!—when we get upon whaling ground, every one must do his duty. I should almost be tempted to pitch a man into the sea, if I saw him blench, or even wink at danger. Plenty to eat, and plenty to drink,—but no skulking, my boys!"

The reader will not think it strange, if such a man as the captain of the Leviathan was a favourite with his crew. His motto was—"business first, and pleasure afterwards."

"Come, my lads!" said he, when he saw the ship ready for sea, "our labour for the present is done. The remainder of the day is yours:—trundle yourselves ashore, all who wish—and say farewell to your friends—kiss your sweethearts—and be jolly for the hour,—for to-morrow we set sail. So away with you all!"

The hint of the captain was obeyed by more than half his men;—but there were some interdicted from a participation in the leave granted to go ashore;—and these were a boat's crew of five or six Indians, most of whom, for some offense, had been compelled to enter on board the Leviathan. They were large men, and, as usual with the Indian, strong and muscular; and for that reason had been chosen by Coleman to man the first whale-boat—an honour that was frequently granted to length of wind and dogged endurance, in preference to general activity. The trouble of collecting these fellows again,—for it was believed they would not voluntarily return,—was the reason assigned for the denial to them of a few hours' liberty ashore. They formed a mess by themselves. Quibby, as the reader is aware, had been placed on board by the Selectmen. He did not, however, partake of his meals with the rest, but was observed to keep aloof, and to brood over his confinement with a grim expression of visage that was anything but pleasant to look upon.

Among those who most eagerly availed themselves of the proffered leave of absence, were Starbuck, Gardner, and Imbert.

"I know Harry's object in going ashore, well enough," said Imbert to himself; "and wheresoever he goes—provided Mary be there—I will most assuredly be present. There must be no more 'last words' between them, or I may run a chance of being defeated before I have set out upon my pilgrimage to whaling-land. No, no, my boy!—you don't catch me sleeping now:—no more tears, nor kisses, nor love-tokens, without I have a share therein!"

Harry and Thomas went to their homes for the purpose of brushing up a little, before seeing their mistresses for the last leave-taking; but Imbert steered directly for the house of Peleg. He was rigged out in his sailor clothes; and, like all sailors, was somewhat perfumed with tar. He found Mary melancholy and alone: but the unexpected sight of her visitor, in his blue sailor jacket, which became him well, brought a smile to her features, and revived her spirits. She had made up her mind that the busy affairs of the ship, now on the eve of departure, would prevent the possibility of her again seeing either of her suitors, before their distant return from sea; but she was glad to be thus disappointed. On seeing Imbert she was sure that Harry would not be long behind him.

"You see, Mary, that I have fairly undertaken to execute your cruel commands," said he;—and he then added in playful badinage, "pray how do you like my new costume?—It is every inch a sailor's—isn't it? It is not half so cumbersome as Don Quixote's coat of mail, in which he assaulted the windmills;—but its wearer, I fear, is going on an expedition equally foolish."

"Oh, say not so!" said Mary, while a momentary shade came across her countenance: "Thy dress becomes thee much—thou wert surely born to wear a sailor's jacket—"

"For three years at least," answered Imbert; "by which time I hope to prove an accomplished seaman and whale-killer to boot, for your sake, Mary. Why, I am more than half a sailor already. I have learned the names of all the ropes about the ship, and can point them out, and handle them, as readily as a starved apothecary can find out his drugs by the labels on his boxes and gallipots. I have had my hands in tar too, as you may perceive; and have turned the laugh upon some of my knowing shipmates, more than once, when they have ventured to suspect me of ignorance. I won the heart of the captain by climbing up the forestay, without the assistance of my feet; and have made my brother sailors believe that I think a tub of lobscouse the most savoury dish in the world. The only man I have not been able to make my friend, is Harry Gardner; and as I am sure he will shortly be here, to assist me in taking a most lachrymose leave of you, I hope you will urge upon him the propriety of showing a better temper in my presence for the future. To end the history of my 'pilgrim's progress,' I will give you a short imitation of myself, and show you the way in which I amuse my fellows when off duty:—Listen, Mary, and don't laugh, while I thunder forth a verse of my favourite sailor's song,—'suiting the action to the word, the word to the action:—'

'When the sky grows black, and the wind blows hard.
      And landsmen skulk below, sir,
   Jack mounts up to the topsail-yard,

> And turns his quid as he goes, sir;
>   Hauling here—bawling there—
>   Steadily, readily, cheerily, merrily;—
> Still from care and thinking free,
> Is a sailor's life at sea.' "

The vapours of Mary entirely gave way before the rattling nonsense and jack-tar imitations of Imbert; and she burst forth into a fit of loud laughter. In the midst of her cachinatory exercise, Harry Gardner entered the room.

He was thunderstruck at finding Imbert there before him, and Mary indulging in such unseemly levity, at a time when decent sighs and tears should have been the prevailing fashion. He hesitated a moment at the doorway, and appeared bewildered at what he saw. His first resolution was to retreat;—the next to remain—and he thereupon formally took a chair.

"I am glad to see you so merry!" said Harry at last, while his countenance gave the lie to his words.

"Ah, Harry, I have been melancholy enough, for a week past, to be pardoned a harmless laugh at the drolleries of this new-made sailor. He tells me that you are to be companions on the voyage, but complains of thy distant and captious conduct towards him on shipboard."

"And did he show *me* up as a subject to excite your merriment, just before I entered your presence?" demanded Gardner, fiercely. Imbert returned the defying glance of his rival with interest.

"Nay, nay—thou art all too hot in thy suspicions:—I was but laughing at his imitations of a sailor, while he sang a verse of a sea-song."

"Then, as I have interrupted the merriment, I will withdraw," said Harry, rising from his chair, hurt,—he scarcely knew at what.

"Nay—thou takest not leave of Mary in such guise," said she, extending her hand to him. Harry's anger was chased away by a smile. Mary extended her other hand to Imbert, and beckoned him to approach.

"Come hither, both of you," said she, drawing Harry gently into the room again—"there is a hand for each of you, as a pledge of my friendship. It becomes me not to question the reason why you get angry at each other:—but—mark me, both;—he that hereafter first gives cause of quarrel to the

other, shall forfeit that friendship for ever. You are to be companions—
messmates—for three long years;—remember,—he that is most for-
bearing—he that is bravest, and truest to my injunction, may count upon a
smile of recognition from Mary when he returns." Mary blushed deeply
when she had uttered this, fearing she had exceeded maidenly propriety
in thus interfering to secure a permanent courtesy between the rivals.

"I know not, Mary," answered Imbert, "whether, by placing your left
hand in mine, you intended me to understand that I am held nearest your
heart;—but I will quit its hold, to offer Gardner the pledge of that hand
which has held yours, as a warranty, on my part, of the faithful execution
of your commands. Will you meet it, sir?" demanded Imbert, extending
his open hand.

"I will," replied Gardner, "and pledge you honestly and fairly."

"Minnows and mack'rel!" exclaimed Peleg, entering at that moment:
"What does all this mean?—Bidding farewell—hey?—what a shilly-shally
set the young men are now-a-days!—Give the girl a smack, and off to sea
with a light heart, my lads:—that was the way when I was young!"

Neither of the young men dared to obey the command of Peleg;—
though either would most probably have attempted it, if he had been
alone with Mary. The scene was becoming somewhat awkward to manage;
and both the young men, as if by mutual consent, motioned to depart.
There was a shaking of hands, however,—and a farewell, faintly uttered by
Mary—and then the rivals disappeared, and walked off together.

Thomas Starbuck, had, in the mean time, gained admittance to Ruth.
He was ushered into the grand parlour of Miriam, where he found Ruth
and her mother, and the stick-plaster, 'Squire Grimshaw. Ruth placed a
chair for Thomas. A long silence ensued, which Miriam and Grimshaw
were determined should be sufficiently irksome, so far as they could
prolong it by their presence. Ruth and Thomas had a mighty strife within,
for words to commence a conversation; but they died away upon their
lips, or stuck fast in their throats. At last, from sheer pity, and to end the
long agony, Miriam spoke up.

"So, neighbour Thomas," said she, "I hear thou art going to sea in one
of *my* ships to-morrow."

"I am," said he.

"And thou comest to say farewell, I suppose," continued she.

"I do," answered he.

"Well, Thomas, few words suffice for leave-taking," added she, by way of hint for him to be jogging.

"Madam!" exclaimed Thomas, starting to his feet, in a hurry to be gone.

"Mother!" exclaimed Ruth, turning red with shame, and starting to *her* feet. Ruth went immediately up to Thomas, and gave him her hand, with a frankness altogether at variance with her previous embarrassment. "If thou hast come to bid us farewell," said Ruth, while her voice faltered— "take my best wishes with thee."

"I will remember your words," said Thomas, moving towards the door.

"And, Thomas," said she, in a husky whisper, "do thou be true and brave, and when thou returnest, thou shalt find that Ruth has remembered thee.—Fare thee well!"

"Fear not me, dearest Ruth, if I may call you thus:—although your mother's coldness fell like an icicle on my heart, the needle cannot be truer to the pole than I will be to you.—Farewell, Ruth!"

Miriam bustled towards the door, in order to cut short all further parley; but she found Thomas already gone, and Ruth straining her eyes after him from the doorway.

"A three years' absence will cure thee of this childish dream," thought Miriam;—and, thinking so, she forbore to inflict upon her daughter the observations that were rising to her lips.

Harry and Thomas met each other in the street, soon after making their adieux to their mistresses, and related their various success: and, although the former was not altogether pleased with the share which Imbert appeared to hold in the affections of Mary, he was obliged to be content for the present. Thomas had no cause of complaint whatever against Ruth, and by this time he had half forgotten Miriam's rude treatment. He knew the inflexible determination of Ruth, and that she would prove true as steel. He sighed, however, when he thought of his lowly fortunes; but he was cheered when he reflected that he was in the same road to improve his estate that others had successfully trod before him.

It is a trite and oft-repeated saying, that sailors are superstitious. It is true in the main; and our young whale-fishermen were not exempt from the failing of their brotherhood. The eve of the sailing of a whale-ship from Nantucket was always a prolific time for the fortune-teller. The hut of Judith Quary had already been secretly visited by many of the sailors of the Leviathan, who had crossed her palm with silver coin, and had good or ill fortune bespoke for them, according as they were generous or niggard in their gifts. Gardner and Starbuck, half rejoicing that the Herculean labour of paying their farewell visits had been got through with, and the "farewell" said, without the usual inconvenient "blubbering," as they termed it, agreed to meet each other after nightfall at the hut of Judith, when it was most likely they would be unnoticed by the curious—for, seamen as they were, and, of course, somewhat superstitious, they were not insensible to the world's dread laugh, and therefore chose to consult the fortune-teller secretly.

At the appointed hour they were at the door of the hut, in the midst of the dark heath. They knocked loud and long, but were unanswered. Listening attentively, however, they heard a suppressed conversation going on at times within; and, being vexed at the delay in answering their summons, they uttered some vague threat of violence upon the door, if it were not instantly opened to them. This had the desired effect, for Judith, in total darkness, withdrew the fastening, and commenced scolding the young men for their unseasonable hours.

"Ha!—Judith!" said Thomas, disregarding her threats, "have we started you at last!—Mother Judith, be satisfied that we have come in good faith, and will not trouble you again for three years to come. Strike a light, good Judith, and turn us up a lucky voyage—and, by the way, tell us something about our sweethearts:—Come! that's a good mother!"

"How coaxing they all are, when they want good fortunes told to them," said Judith, "and vastly polite withal;—but that over, Judith may starve, for aught they care. Well! continued she, fumbling for her tinder-box, "if I must, I must;—pence are not so very plenty now-a-days, that I can afford to turn customers away. You should have come earlier, though—for the night is apt to prove unlucky. There is the light—come in.''

The young men entered the gloomy hut, and sat down. She looked at them closely, holding the lamp up to their faces. She then examined their palms. The result, apparently, was not a pleasant one, for she shook her head, and looked grave and mysterious. These were common tricks of her art, however, and passed for nothing with the young sailors; they had seen such manœuvres before.

"Speak out, Judith," said Harry;—"but, by the bye, friend Thomas, we have forgotten to unloose her tongue.—There, Judith, is your fee for both." A half crown rolled upon the table, which she eagerly snatched up and pocketed.

"That round piece of silver, with a king's head upon it, should buy you a good and prosperous voyage," said she, "for it is a more liberal fee than people are in the habit of giving me:—but faces and palms will sometimes deceive; and these, to-night, have not spoken well for you."

"Try the cards, then," said Thomas.

"No," answered she, "they are deceptive, too, at times; but the cup has never failed me."

"The cup then be the trial," answered Starbuck;—"and if that corroborates what the face and the palm have shadowed forth,—why, E'en let us hear it, be it good or bad.''

The woman poured some tea-grounds into a cup, and turned it several times, bottom upwards, on a platter. She looked at the interior a moment, and her whole soul seemed breaking forth from her eyes. She tried the experiment again; and the result, judging from her actions, was evidently similar to the first. Her frame trembled, and cold drops of perspiration hung upon her forehead. Panting with affright, at the image she had conjured up, she convulsively dashed the tea-grounds from the cup, and repeated the trick for the third time. Her hand rested for a moment on the cup, before she ventured to lift it. She turned it slowly to the light, and exclaimed, horror-struck—

"There is death in the cup!"

The attention of the young men was excited to the highest pitch. They demanded of her to tell them further.

"Seek not," said she, solemnly, "to unravel more:—go home, young men,—and, if you are wise, go not to sea. More I wish not to tell."

"Tut!—and is that all? There is not an old woman in all the land that would not advise the same thing, for the sake of tying her darling to her apron string," said Thomas, with a sneer in his accent. "You said there was death in the cup!—it may come to either of us as well on the land as on the sea."

"It will come to both," answered she, "if you go to sea tomorrow."

"It never rains but it pours," said Thomas; "good luck or ill,—it comes in immoderate showers, when sent by you, Judith. Two deaths on the same voyage?—That is rather bountiful, good Judith!"

"Thrice have I sought to change these figures in the cup, and thrice have they come up the same!—Say you there is nothing in that?"

"Ay!—there is nothing extraordinary in the disposition of the leaves in that cup," said Harry Gardner. "Come—come, my good woman, you don't scare us so easily."

"Unbeliever!" exclaimed she, "you would not credit the prophecy of your grandsire, were his ghost to rise from the grave to deliver it!"

"Certainly not," said Harry, "if he used such means as this to prophecy with.—Hist!—what noise is that?"

A slight but prolonged groan was distinctly heard by all. The young men turned pale; but Judith took advantage of the circumstance, to impress her auditors with her skill in her vocation.

"Speak not irreverently of the dead!" said she.

"It was you that raised the ghost," said Harry, "and not we—that is, if so be it *was* a ghost that spoke. But go on, and explain the figures that you pretend to see in the cup."

"Why, look you there," continued Judith,—"see you not that monster with open jaws?"

"Ay—there is something like a whale, to be sure," answered Thomas, with an awakened interest in his countenance.

"I do not see it," said Harry; "it is but a mass of tea leaves."

"It concerns not you," said Judith, in answer to Harry's observation— "but it deeply concerns him who can most easily make it out."

"But what of the whale?" demanded Thomas, with additional eagerness.

"Seest thou not a small object projecting from its jaws?" said Judith.

"I do;" answered Thomas, "it is the only thing that disfigures the outline of the whale."

"It is the half swallowed body of a man!" exclaimed Judith.

Thomas was for a moment thoughtful and sad; but he rallied himself, and pursued the questioning of the fortune-teller. She proceeded—

"Do you see that ship at anchor, with her sails furled?"

"I cannot distinguish the outline," said Thomas.

"But *I* can, though, and quite distinctly," interrupted Harry; "what does the ship import?"

"It imports to *you* much," replied the fortune-teller; "for you are able to distinguish the figure. There is great confusion on her deck: she has just returned from an interrupted and disastrous voyage: there has been a foul deed done on board—it is *murder!* "

Harry shuddered as she uttered the dreadful word.

"There is a gallows on that hill," said she, pointing with her finger to what indeed looked like that contrivance to stretch human beings upon. Judith continued: "Ha! I should know that form!—it is an Indian's!—it is—it is *he!* "

Judith dropped the cup, and the pieces jingled on the floor. Another groan, as of one in a disturbed sleep, succeeded. The young men jumped to their feet in an instant, and rushed together to a neighboring closet. Judith sprang after them—but it was too late to prevent discovery. They dragged forth the half inanimate body of Quibby, who had escaped from the ship by dropping silently into the water, and swimming ashore. The liquor he had found in the closet proved too potent for his faculties; and it was he who had groaned in the stupor of his maudlin sleep.

"Harm him not!" exclaimed Judith, "but depart, and leave him with me."

"It may not be as you command," said Thomas: "He goes with us."

"Go hence, young men,—but take not him,—nor venture upon the seas with him, as you value your lives. If you despise my warning, beware of the consequences! The fate of Jonah, without his deliverance, shall be the lot of one of you, among the first brood of whales that you encounter: and as for the other—I would, at least, that I might avert the fate of the other—for the prisoner you hold must suffer for the deed! Let Quibby go free, and all may yet be well. I beg the boon of you; for, persecuted as he is by those in power, he is the only person who of late has been kind to me."

"Away! witch!" exclaimed Thomas, "it is folly to heed you longer:—and, but for the passing of an idle hour, we had not provoked you to such silly speech as you have contrived, though but for a minute, to deceive us withal!—We part not with Quibby, neither: he has escaped from the vessel we know;— his wet jacket testifies to the fact: and we should be wanting in duty, as well to our captain as to the magistrates of the town, were we not to restore him to the ship."

"Fools that ye are!" said Judith, "to rush upon your fate!—Go, then;" continued she, as they departed, closely guarding the runaway between them; "and may my malison be upon you   for you are doomed men!—

'Mischance and sorrow go along with you!
Heart's discontent and sour affliction
Be playfellows to keep you company!
There's two of you;—the devil make a third—
And threefold vengeance tend upon your steps!'"

CHAPTER NINE.

The time is out of joint!

Hamlet.

Cease, rude Boreas, blustering railer!
List ye landsmen all to me:—
Messmates, hear a brother sailor
Sing the dangers of the sea.

Old Song.

WITH the rising sun the Leviathan tripped her anchor, and took her departure for the place of rendezvous at Walwich Bay. Before her sails were loosed, with extraordinary punctuality as to the time appointed, two boats reached the ship, containing the shoregoing part of the crew, of whom we have spoken, accompanied by the captain, who had gone ashore with a determination to be prompt in supplying the place of any man who should unnecessarily linger beyond his hour. He was not a little surprised to find Quibby among the rest; for as yet he had not been missed from the ship.

271

The sulky Indian was duly delivered over by his captors, and compelled to aid in pulling himself back to the Leviathan. The manner of finding him was honestly detailed to the captain by the young men; and every word and circumstance of the fortune-teller's prophecy minutely recapitulated. Good-natured and careless of speech as Coleman was generally,—inspiring life and activity in his crew by his own cheerfulness,—he could not resist the solemn impressions that stole over him, upon hearing the circumstances of the interview with Judith recounted.

Taking the cue from the captain, who was unusually taciturn for the hour, the two boats had rowed off to the ship in silence, side by side; and scarcely a word, except occasionally a slight command from the coxswain, was breathed by the crews. The misty advance of the dawn, and the deep, blood-red, refracted sun, struggling through the thick atmosphere at his rising, were in unison with the chill silence of the oarsmen, broken only by the long and measured stroke of the oars, which gave back a melancholy sound, much like the cheerless ticking of a clock, in the still hour of midnight. A few sea-gulls hovered over the boats, screaming, at times, loudly and unpleasantly. The scene was painful to all; but nothing occurred to interrupt its awkwardness, until the boats touched the side of the ship, when the men, glad to escape from the unnatural coventry to which they had subjected themselves, scrambled eagerly up to the deck.

"This is anything but a merry parting," whispered one. "Long faces are the fashion with all hands!"

"It's a bad omen!" said another.

"There must be a Jonah aboard!" exclaimed a third.

"True!—that infernal Indian is here!" responded a fourth.

The lynx-eyed captain saw his men gathering into small groups about the deck, and conversing in mysterious whispers. The scene at the fortune-teller's was rehearsing among them, with variations and additions, as he judged by the sober faces of the men. An hour's conversation upon such mysterious subjects, at a time like the present, he knew would be fatal to the voyage: for some of the men, unwilling to abide the witch's augury, were already hinting that they would fain return to the shore. There was a movement made by several towards the quarterdeck; and Coleman thought he could read that in their faces which betokened a determination to be liberated from their engagements. The superstitious belief of some seamen is, in fact, their religion; and its promptings are matters of conscience. The most skillful tact is, therefore, required to counteract its baneful influence over the minds of a crew. The captain bethought himself of an expedient. His luggage was still in the boat alongside, and he hastily called two or three of the malcontents, in his wonted cheerful voice, to jump into the boat and pass up the articles lying in the stern-sheets; while, in the same breath, the mates were ordered to loose the sails and heave up the anchor. This had the desired effect; for the bustle that followed, was in consonance with the sailors' notions of the spirit-stirring scene of getting under weigh. The cheering sound of *"ye-ho-heave-o!"* was responded to by the men upon the forecastle, tugging lustily at the windlass; and the men upon the yards began to feel in their element once more, as they briskly executed the quick and peremptory orders of their officers. The captain still kept his eye upon the boat at the side, giving the disheartened men upon luggage duty no time for a moment's consideration.

"Bear a hand there, Jenkins, and pass up the can containing the morning's grog:—be careful, man, and don't spill the kritter—unless it be down thy own throat:—so!—all's safe!"

The serious face of Jenkins was lit up with a faint smile at the attempted joke of the captain, and he tugged the more earnestly at his work,— passing up in succession all the nick-nacks and small stores that had come off in the boat. At last, packed away at the bottom of the stern-sheets, a curious box was discovered, that drew forth a silent chuckle from the men in the boat, as it was lifted up to the captain.

"Aha!" shouted Coleman, as he seized upon the circumstance to say something encouraging to his men, "be careful of that box, boys; there's fun and frolic packed up there;—it's my favourite child,—and he squalls terribly with bad usage: but a good nurse and delicate fingering delight him overmuch. Come up here, thou king of *fiddles!*—and let me try whether the dews of the morning have affected thy smooth voice!"

The captain immediately strung the instrument, and, apparently in a careless mood, as if to try the fiddle, but in reality with deep anxiety, he dashed off upon some rattling tune, that reached the ears of all on board, alow and aloft. He furtively watched the effect upon the men, and was not disappointed in the result. A grin of satisfaction, and a knowing nod of the head passed from one to another, and good humour was restored. He put the cap-sheaf upon his manœuvre by piping the men to grog.

"Avast heaving there!" said the captain; "Let all hands come aft. Steward, pass the horn round, and see that the mainbrace is set up taut:— a cold morning this, boys—fill up—fill up, the liquor's good, and plenty of it!"

There were no more sober faces that day; and the occurrences of the morning and of the previous evening were soon forgotten. The Leviathan held on her course steadily, and, in due season, entered the bay of Walwich. She there found her consort; and, as she anchored abreast of the Grampus, the crews saluted each other with three hearty cheers. Boats rapidly passed from one to the other; and news from home, and many kindly greetings, were given and received; and a day of merry indulgence crowned the happy meeting. The fiddle of Jonathan was put in requisition, until the cramped fingers of the player could hold out no longer.

The wondering Hottentots crowded the shore as usual; and, seeing the sailors jigging it away, the huge bronzed natives of the woolly tribe commenced cutting their capers too, in close imitation of their white visitors; but they danced without motive, and without feeling a particle of the enjoyment or spirit of the scene. The Hottentots carry no *soul* into their amusements. They are a languid and gluttonous race, and are devoid of energy or enterprise. Those now assembled upon the shore, were waiting for the *kreng*, or carcass of the whale, the prize of Seth, which had been towed to the anchorage of the Grampus, and was undergoing the operation of "*flinching*" or "*flensing*," which deprives the mass of its outer coating of blubber. Temporary try-works or oil kettles had been set up on board the ship; and, when the Leviathan arrived, a hundred barrels of oil had been tried out; and, in the course of the day, the huge carcass, deprived of all that was valuable, was cut loose, and launched into the bay, before the longing eyes of the hungry natives. It soon grounded on the shore, and, when the tide receded, the feast of putrescence was greedily commenced by the locust multitude of dainty ebony gourmands.

The ships now left their anchorage, and bore away for The Horn.

The passage round this promontory is made by all navigators, except our own, with dread and apprehension. The "Stormy Cape,"—the bugbear of the Spaniards—has ceased to scare the Americans, as it should all other nations. With us, there is no longer any foolish preparation of spars and rigging while doubling this cape; and, from our fearless example, we may shortly hope that, forgetting the nursery tales of Patagonian giants and storms, all navigators will cease to look upon "The Horn" as a "*Cabo des los Tormentos,*" and that they will regard it, with its prominent brother of the other continent, and for similar reasons, as a "*Cabo di bon Esperanza.*" Much of ideal security or of danger is made to consist in the presence or absence of the means of relief and support: and, perhaps, if a friendly settlement, capable of yielding supplies, were established at or near Cape Horn, as at the Cape of Good Hope, the exaggerated dangers of the former would never more be dreamed of.

It has fallen to the lot of our Nantucketmen to pilot the way here, as it has, in many other instances, to be pioneers amidst nautical dangers—amidst reefs and quicksands, rocks and currents, in distant and unexplored seas. Whilst the Island of Nantucket is their sea-girt place of rest, in which all their joys and affections centre, their secondary home is upon the broad Pacific. Distant as it is, it is their own ocean. It is their fishing-ground; its perils, and its sources of wealth and enjoyment are theirs. Hail, mighty water!—thou hast been generous to brave men, and we would speak of thee proudly, and as thou dost deserve to be spoken of!

Upon emerging into the Pacific Ocean, and coming into more temperate latitudes, arrangements were made by the captains for recruiting after the long voyage. A large portion of the oil of the whale caught in Walwich Bay was transferred to the Leviathan; and Coleman bore up for one of the South American ports, with the design of exchanging or disposing of it for fresh provisions. The Grampus held on her way to the Gallipagos Islands, to lay in a supply of the delicate turtle which abound there in inexhaustible numbers.

The Gallipagos turtle, or terrapin, which lives only on land, and differs in that respect from the green turtle, is a peculiar and luscious food. These animals are found in no other place than these islands; and hence the name of the cluster. They may be stowed away in the hold of a vessel; and, without being fed, can be preserved alive for more than a year, without any sensible diminution in their weight. They carry their own supply of water about them. Their flesh is a luxury from which the appetite never turns away with satiety; and every whaler will dilate upon the dainties of the dish with irrepressible fluency. "*Toujours perdrix*" never applies to the uncloying terrapin food of the Gallipagos.

The rendezvous of the ships was appointed at one of this group of islands, and a fortnight from the time of separating was fixed for their reunion. No whales had yet appeared. The season for the spermacetti, in this latitude, had not yet come. Indeed, whole months are sometimes passed without falling in with a solitary animal, in some of those seas; while in other parallels they may be found in abundance. The experienced whalefisherman will accommodate his cruising latitudes to the known seasons of their appearance; while the novice will keep all sail set for months together, and be as likely to run away from their haunts as to approach them. When the sperm whale is met with, however, it is not singly, nor in pairs; but whole troops go together, consisting sometimes of females and their young, led on and protected, as it were, by a single enormous patriarch of the male species. A skillful commander among a troop of these, aided by expert officers, will contrive to thin their ranks of some half dozen, before his day's work is complete; and if the young ones are first singled out, the mothers generally fall an easy prey to the pursuer, from indulgence in that affectionate principle, implanted in all natures, brute as well as human, which prompts the female to protect her young.

While the voyage of the Leviathan was successfully made, so far as to get into a Spanish port without accident; and while Jonathan is chaffering for the sale or exchange of his oil, we must follow the Grampus in an unexpected turn of fortune.

The latter vessel was within a few days' sail of the Gallipagos, when she was arrested by one of those tremendous hurricanes that sometimes blow up suddenly in heated equinoctial regions, and carry everything before their irresistible power. To contend against the gale that now blew upon the Grampus was worse than useless. There was hardly time to hand the sails, and put the vessel before the wind under bare poles, before the strength of her spars was tried, by a rushing blast that made all crack again. The ship behaved well, however, and sustained her previous reputation for a capital sea-boat. Nevertheless, she was careering on, with unmeasured speed, before the hurricane, until Seth had gone over many more degrees of longitude than he had ever before ventured to traverse in the present region.

The ship was constantly leaving the American coast, before a strong gale from the north-east. Macy knew that all or nearly all the islands in the Pacific were laid down, upon the common charts then in use, imperfectly; and that others were growing out of the water, from day to day, by the slow but sure process of deposit of that *building worm*, to which the coral islands in the Pacific owe their origin. He found himself dashing in among these numberless isles, without the power of controlling his noble ship, except in keeping her steadily driving before the wind. The perils of these seas at such a time are great and inappreciable. The heart of Seth was dismayed:—but the crew, who never troubled themselves with the intricacies of navigation, were as yet unaware of the extent of their danger. They were active and on the alert, and quick to obey every command about the deck; but no man dared to ascend the shrouds. Indeed, Seth would sooner lose his masts than his men. The spars might possibly be preserved by running with the wind; but it was sure destruction to the individual to order a man aloft. He could control nothing—remedy nothing;—for the masts and spars bent and quivered like the leaves of the aspen, while the cordage rattled to and fro, as if swayed by a thousand furies.

For two days the gale held on in its turbulent fury, lashing the ocean into foam, and forcing the billows mountain high. Island after island was passed, of that countless number that stud the Pacific;—some barren, some covered with verdure and trees,—but all so low as to be but just verging above the water. Some were peopled with naked inhabitants, who ran along the shore, and clapped their hands in wonder at the strange sight of the ship, which they mistook for some huge animal rushing by with inimitable speed. No haven appeared in sight to which to fly for shelter; and the seamanship of every man was tried to the uttermost, in manœuvring to escape shipwreck upon these inhospitable shores. The stormsails were tried; but before they were well hoisted they were torn to ribbons, and the flapping shreds became knotted, like thongs, in an instant.

The night of the second day set in. The crew by this time had become acquainted with all the dangers of their fearful progress. The first day had been passed without meeting with many islands; but, with the experience of the second, they now saw nothing but the horrors of death before them at every plunge. Still they were bold and courageous, and blenched not. They were ready to use all human means for their preservation; but they were deeply impressed with the belief that their time was come, and that all exertion would be unavailing, among the dangerous archipelagos through which they were forced to thread their uncertain way. The night was dark; and the look-out, upon the bows, while endeavouring to pierce the gloom, declared from time to time, as he was hailed in the pauses of the storm, that he could not distinguish the end of the bowsprit. Thunder and lightning now accompanied the blast. The roar of the one seemed to give notice that all Pandemonium was let loose, while the vivid lightning, so terrible and impressive at other times, was now a relief to the terror-stricken men, who eagerly strained their eyes in the direction of the ship's course, whenever it sent forth its strong lurid coruscation upon the waters. Flash after flash gave them a momentary reprieve, and showed them, as yet, clear sea-room ahead.

The night was considerably advanced when the fierce tempest began to lull. Hope, for the first time, sprung up in the bosoms of all. The ship was now brought with her side to the wind, and her speed to leeward was consequently greatly diminished. Sails were about being set to keep the ship in her position, when a strong flash of lightning brought a renewal of all their dangers.

"Land on the lee-bow!" resounded from twenty voices.

"Let go the anchor!" shouted the captain: but before the order could be executed, the ship struck and became immovable.

The shock was not severe, but seemed to produce a sort of grating sound, as if the keel was running like a sleigh-runner over the ground.

After the first confusion subsided, it was discovered, by the flashes of the lightning, that the ship, after being brought to the wind, had worked herself, by the aid of a strong current, around a projecting point of land, and had grounded, at some distance from the shore, on the lee-side of a high island. As yet it could not be discovered whether the situation was dangerous, or whether the ship could be got off at a favourable state of the tide. It was with great joy, however, that the pumps were sounded, and no leak appeared. The ship, in a few minutes, gently heeled over, and showed that the tide was receding. It was determined to wait for the dawn of day, and for the reflux of the tide, before any measures should be taken to relieve the ship. The eyelids of the sailors were, by this time, almost glued together with watching and fatigue. They had been constantly and fearfully occupied for more than two days, without a wink of sleep; and deep anxiety had deprived them of all appetite for food. Now all was comparatively safe, and they were fain to seek nourishment, and repose for their worn bodies. The captain alone slept not. He continued walking the deck until morning. The storm had by that time ceased altogether.

As the day broke, the situation of the ship became apparent. Her keel was found to be slightly sunk in a yielding bed of coral branches, and the vessel lay about two miles from the shore of a well-wooded island, of large dimensions. By sunrise the tide was on the flood, and all hands were called to assist in constructing a raft of the spare spars, in order to lighten the ship of such heavy articles as could be got at readily. The longboat was launched; and that, as well as the quarter boats, were filled to overflowing with provisions and water casks, whose contents had as yet been undisturbed. The raft, too, groaned under its burthen; and everything was got ready to heave the ship off when the tide should be at its height.

When all was prepared, Macy caused a spare boat to be manned, and carried off a small kedge anchor to a suitable distance from the ship, where, carefully dropping it, the warp was hove taut on board, and kept ready to take the first advantage when the ship should float clear of the reef. He now heedfully sounded the passage by which he had entered upon this dangerous ground, and noted the bearings and distances of the crooked channel. At times, shoaling the water upon the steep sides of the coral banks, he ordered his men to rest upon their oars for a minute, to enable him to look at the brilliant scene beneath him.

Columns and spires of variegated coral shot up from the bottom of the sea, assuming the appearance of architectural regularity, which, with but little stretch of the imagination, might have passed for gothic ruins of spar, changing the hues of its material as the bright sun darted its rays directly or obliquely upon its varying surface of stone and adhering shell, until all other colours were blended with the green of the water in unfathomable depths. Here and there the bright-hued tropical fish would dart across the eye, or gently swim out from the recesses of the rocks, or carelessly approach the surface, as if to flaunt its surpassing beauty of intermingled tints of gold and silver, in the strong light of the sun. No comparison between the rich, sparkling dyes of the fishes that play between the glowing tropics, among the ever-changing coral reefs of the Pacific, can be instituted with those of the piscatory tribes of any other seas. Their colour and loveliness are rich, in the gorgeousness of their splendour, beyond the power of language to portray. Well might the poet ask, when looking upon such a scene—

"Who can paint like nature?"

Yet *one* poet has painted a scene like this, and that poet is our own inimitable PERCIVAL, who, to the deep regret of his friends, holds himself, we are told, retiringly in the shade, while he is capable of sending forth finished pictures, burnished with gold, and studded with diamonds, like the following:—

"THE CORAL GROVE.

"Deep in the wave is a coral grove,
    Where the purple mullet and gold-fish rove,

Where the sea-flower spreads its leaves of blue,
That never are wet with falling dew,
But in bright and changeful beauty shine,
Far down in the green and glassy brine.

The floor is of sand, like the mountain drift,
    And the pearl shells spangle the snow:
From coral rocks the sea-plants lift
    Their boughs, where the tides and billows flow:
The water is calm and still below,
    For the winds and waves are absent there,
And the sands are bright as the stars, that glow
    In the motionless fields of upper air;
There, with its waving blade of green,
    The sea-flag streams through the silent water,
And the crimson leaf of the dulse is seen
    To blush, like a banner bath'd in slaughter;
There, with a light and easy motion,
    The fan-coral sweeps thro' the clear deep sea;
And the yellow and scarlet tufts of ocean,
    Are bending, like corn on the upland lea;
And life, in rare and beautiful forms,
    Is sporting amid those bowers of stone,
And is safe, when the wrathful spirit of storms
    Has made the top of the wave his own;
And when the ship from his fury flies,
    Where the myriad voices of ocean roar,
When the wind-god frowns in the murky skies,
    And demons are waiting the wreck on shore—
Then far below, in the peaceful sea,
    The purple mullet and gold-fish rove,
Where the waters murmur tranquilly,
    Through the bending twigs of the coral grove."

We know not that the poet ever looked upon the reality of what he so eloquently shows up to our wondering eyes; but this much we do know, that had he been present during the whole of the voyage of our ship, he could not better have grouped his figures from nature. The truth and aptitude of his picture were so striking, that when the "*Coral Grove*" first met our eyes in the columns of the "Charleston Courier," it revived this scene of our by-gone days, and restored reminiscences of the sea, and of real life, much older than himself. As we cut the gem from the musty folds of the newspaper, we could have sworn, in earnestness, that its author had been one of our crew of the Grampus, and had looked, with us, upon "life in rare and beautiful forms," and upon growing "bowers of stone," that may, at no distant day, emerge from the great valley of the Pacific, to form the substratum of an immense continent like our own, and become instinct with human life.

But to return to our story. Macy had scarcely completed his surveys, when he espied a stealthy gathering of natives on the shore, and a launching and mustering of warlike canoes, with javelins and missiles bristling above the heads of the savages as they put off towards the ship. The whale-boat was instantly put in motion, and a race for life commenced. The natives manœuvred to cut Macy off,—but the sinewy rowers bent to their oars with Herculean vigour. The boat reached the ship, and the last man sprang into the chains just in time to avoid the stroke of a well-poised lance, which was aimed to pin him to the side of the vessel.

The ship was now surrounded with savages of fierce and frightful aspect, and forms of gigantic mould. Already were the natives clambering up the sides of the vessel; but the crew of the Grampus were prepared for their reception. They had observed their hostile approach, and hastily mustered their harpoons, their lances, and their blubber-spades,—tools always kept in order by the whale-fishermen,—gleaming with brightness, and trenchant as a well-tempered razor. As the assailants showed their ferocious heads above the bulwarks, they were pricked off with the ready weapons of the crew, and forced, repeatedly, to loose their hold and plunge into the water. But they were undismayed by this species of resistance, which was nearly allied to their own mode of warfare of clubs and javelins, slings and arrows, and mace-hammers of stone—all of which the savage of some of the South Sea islands wields with inimitable skill. They are missile implements with which his hand is made familiar from his childhood.

Again and again the dark warriors returned to the assault; and as often were repulsed by the active crew, who handled their weapons with as much dexterity as their assailants, but with far less exposure—being protected by the thick planking of the ship's bulwark. But this defensive warfare served only to exasperate the savages, who were spared by the American crew from motives of sheer humanity. If wounded at all, they were only slightly pricked by the harpoons and lances of the Nantucketers.

By this time, however, the number of war-canoes and natives had become greatly augmented; and they were skillfully arranged in several formidable divisions, for the evident purpose of making a simultaneous attack upon various parts of the ship. Two divisions drew off upon the bows, and an equal number took their positions under the quarters; while the sides of the ship were menaced with a countless multitude, that advanced in an array that would do credit to the tactics of an experienced commander.

Macy hastily made his dispositions to anticipate the assault, and stationed his men under cover of the various points which it was presumed would be attacked. The captain then harangued his men with few, but impressive words:—

"We must now fight," said he, "in good earnest, my boys, or be murdered and eaten by those horrid cannibals. I, for one, will not be captured alive. If there is a man among you that shrinks from the battle, or from the sight of blood, let him go below, and not encumber us with his presence. There must be no more pricking: every stroke must be a home thrust; and every thrust we give with our irons must let daylight through a savage. We must, from necessity, kill without remorse, or be, ourselves, crushed in a twinkling!—Who goes below?"

"Not I,—nor *I*,—nor *I!*" was responded by every man of the crew, as they clutched their weapons with earnestness.

"Will you all stand by me, then, and follow my example?"

"Ay—to the death!" was the united reply.

"Be ready, then; and the first savage that touches the deck—pin him with the harpoon,—in short, bleed him as you would a whale—and be sure to strike home!—There will be no more children's play, or I miss my guess as to the intention of their present preparations."

Macy now headed up an empty cask near the mainmast, and quickly collected all the spare weapons. With one stroke of the cooper's adz he stove in the head, and planted his sharp irons therein, as a sort of arsenal, or arm-chest in reserve, ready to be resorted to by any of the crew who might lose his weapon in the conflict.

The native armament came boldly on, in the most approved order, but in perfect silence. Suddenly the sound of a single conch was heard, and the savages instantaneously rose in their canoes, brandished their spears, and shouted their formidable war-cry! The men in the Grampus rung out a shout of defiance in return. But they had no sooner shown their heads above the rail of the bulwark, than the savages poured in upon them a cloud of stones and arrows, that seemed almost to darken the air with their flight. No damage, however, was done to the crew, as, after giving their shout, they anticipated the action of the assailants by covering themselves immediately. The natives waited for some answer to their fire; but perceiving no demonstration of its being returned from the ship, they pulled up to her sides, and sprang into the chains and rigging. They had no sooner effected a lodgment there, than some two score of them, who were gathering themselves for a spring upon the deck, were obliged to loose their hold, and they fell backwards into their canoes, or into the sea. Before they touched the water, they were dead. They were pierced with the weapons of the whalers, and their life-blood dyed the sea with crimson.

The savages of those far-off isles of the sea are not, however, daunted at the sight of suffering or of death, when it comes in a way that is comprehensible to their obtuse faculties. They saw their fellows fall by weapons similar in shape to their own, and they were, of course, accustomed to that mode of warfare. They beheld thousands of their warriors still alive and full of eagerness for the fight; and they had been accustomed to see the tribes of other isles yield only when the power of physical resistance, numerically speaking, was nearly annihilated. They saw, also, that the numbers of their enemy were as but a drop to the bucket, when compared to their own host of warriors, and that their foothold was upon a diminutive spot, growing, as they imagined, out of the sea, in the shape of a contemptible islet.

The signal for assault was again sounded, and the war-whoop swelled upon the air in discordant shrieks. The canoes suddenly and vigorously pulled up to the ship again, and the natives seemed to vie with each other for the honour of scaling the ramparts. But the barbed weapons of the crew met them as their breasts were elevated above the bulwark, and they were transfixed on the spot. Some of the lances and harpoons were secured to the ship by whaling lines attached to belaying-pins; and, as the sable victims fell beneath their deadly touch, their writhing agonies were horrifying. But humanity could not now be propitiated. Self-preservation, which is declared to be "the first law of nature," was the uppermost consideration. As the savages fell alongside, the smooth lances withdrew from their bodies, and were quickly regained by the crew. Not so, however, with the harpoons. The bodies of some of the slain hung, upon the barbed steel, by the side of the ship, and frequently the irons could not be recovered by those who had wielded them, without exposure to the constantly projected missiles of the assailants.

Resort was now had to the arsenal of Seth; but the weapons of the cask were soon put *hors de combat* in the same manner, and only a few lances and blubber-spades remained in the hands of the defenders. Each of the harpoons that hung over the sides of the ship held the body of a dead savage suspended midway, serving for the foothold of fresh assailants to ascend. The cords were cut from necessity, and the carrion-carcasses dropped heavily into the water.

The means of defence were greatly exhausted by this procedure, and the sailors were becoming weary in their active and alarming labour. But the voice of Seth rose, encouragingly, above the din of battle.

"Fight on, my brave boys!" shouted Macy: "fight on! We have already slain our hundreds—and, thank God, not a man of the crew is hurt! Strike boldly—kill—kill the black brutes!—Drive it home there on the lee-bow! Repel the savages from the larboard quarter! Slay the rascals at the weather gangway! Bravely done, my lads! Now follow me, my boys, to the forecastle—away with them, before they gather their limbs to use their weapons. If we give them foothold we are gone! Aha! That swoop was well executed! Follow me once more!—down with the savages from the starboard quarter! God!—they are pouring over the bow again! All hands rush to the forecastle, while I sweep with my single lance, the few that are clambering over that taffrail!"

Macy could not be everywhere; and though he was well imitated in the business of extirpating nearly a whole savage generation, he found his devoted ship assailed at so many points at once, that his hopes began to flag. With one broad sweep of his lance-blade, similar to that by which a mounted dragoon would mow down a whole rank of infantry, he cleared the starboard quarter rail of some half dozen heads that were rising into view; and jumping to the larboard quarter, he performed the same service to as many more, While every individual of his crew was bravely battling for existence along the waist and on the forecastle.

Suddenly a giant-savage made a spring over the bows; and, seizing the first mate from behind, hurled him to the deck instantaneously, as if he were but an infant in his grasp. He raised his stone hatchet over his head to despatch the faithful officer. Though Macy's body did not possess the power of ubiquity, his eye was everywhere. He had just sent his last harpoon through the carcass of a desperate native, and, as it fell over the quarter, he caught sight of the prostrate mate. With one bound from the quarter-deck Macy reached the arm-cask at the mainmast, and seized the only instrument remaining. It was a blubber-spade. Quick as thought the keen instrument was balanced in his right hand, and it darted, gleaming in the sun like a lightning-flash. Before the mace of the savage commenced its descent towards the skull of the mate, the head of the brute, cleanly severed from its trunk, rolled upon the deck, "grinning horribly a ghastly smile!" The unerring spade, having done its office, pitched upon the deck beyond, and its sharp blade entered a full inch into the planking.

"Mate! thou art redeemed from the very jaws of death!" shouted Seth.

"I thank thee for the well-aimed blow," replied the mate. He rose on the instant, and threw the headless body over into the sea, and hurled the head after it high into the air. It descended into the canoe of the chief, and as he held it up by the hair before his followers, a shout of fury and revenge was raised by the savage host.

It was plain, by the conduct of the savages that they were more than ever infuriated at their repeated discomfitures; and it was equally apparent to Macy that it would be unavailing to wage war much longer. His means of defence, all but a few well-tried lances, were exhausted; and he discovered several of his harpoons in the hands of his enemies, which had been cut loose from their fastenings, and withdrawn from the bodies of the slain.

The act of the mate, in throwing over the head of the decapitated warrior, had unexpectedly created a diversion among the natives; and they ceased, by common consent, from their attack upon the ship, to listen to an angry harangue from their chief.

Macy descended to his cabin. He reappeared in a moment with a weapon in his hand, heretofore forgotten. It was a musket, (and the only one on board,) which he had occasionally used on former voyages for a fowling piece. He had barely time to charge the gun, and to slip a bullet into the barrel, before the war-whoop was again raised.

"They come once more!" cried Macy. "To your posts, men,—and quail not. Look to your irons—and be careful to keep them well in hand. We have lost too many already: but by the favour of Providence,—who hath written that 'the battle is not always to the strong,'—we will send a hundred more of the cannibals to their long account before we yield!"

"Ay, ay!—never fear for us!" shouted the men cheerfully.

"Brave hearts!" said Macy. "Your day's work has been a bloody one: may God grant us deliverance from this unlooked for danger! And now," said Macy, addressing, unconsciously, his solitary gun, "fail me not in this strait—for thou hast never failed me yet, even when pointed against the swift sea-fowl on the wing!"

The canoe of the chief led the van of the attack, this time; and his followers, seeing the immense number of their slain brethren floating round them, and that no impression had as yet been made upon the ship, although her sides bristled with arrows, were fain to avail themselves of his experience and encouraging example.

Macy now showed his body over the railing of the quarter. The chief instantly stood up in his approaching canoe, and, elevating his long javelin, he shook the pole of his lance in the air, in a menacing attitude, as if trying its elastic strength before hurling it at the unprotected body of Seth.

The captain suffered the canoe to come within half musket-shot of the ship when he levelled his piece with a steady aim. It flashed!—and instantly the savage chief, in the act of speeding his lance at Seth, fell dead into the arms of his attendants. The ball had entered his heart. The report of the gun, and the unaccountable condition of their leader, appalled the invaders. Many of them jumped tumultuously into the water, to escape the vengeance of the lightning tube, and the displeasure of their deity, whose interposition, and whose warning voice, they believed were exerted against them.

The panic-struck savages fled to their island in confusion, uttering horrid shrieks, and shouting their dissonant war-cries in disappointed rage.

The coast was now clear, and no time was to be lost. The kedge was tried; and, to the unbounded joy of all on board, the ship yielded slowly to the pull upon the hawser. She floated once more freely in her element!—Her sails were set, and a light breeze wafted the stately vessel safely through the channel of coral rocks, and away for ever from these inhospitable shores.

$\mathcal{C}$HAPTER TEN.

—Where is that loved one now,
Who should redeem his plighted vow?—
Lo, there! the monster's gaping jaws
Show a deed of blood
Far—far o'er the flood!

The Prophecy: Chap. vii., vol 1.

IT took many days for the Grampus to regain her lost ground. She had been driven so far to the Westward, and had wandered among so many isles unknown to the navigators of the day, that her commander deemed it prudent to return by slow stages; and at night either to heave to, or to arrest her ordinary progress, by shortening the canvas to the fewest possible sails. He was thus necessarily obliged to feel his way among those groups that, at a subsequent day, appeared upon the charts under the names of "the Navigators," and "the Society Islands," and "the Marquesas." By the time that Seth was able to work his ship into the harbour of Charles' Island, (one of the Gallipagos,) the time appointed for his meeting Coleman had expired. It was, therefore, with much gratification that he found his consort had arrived before him, and was still waiting at anchor within the harbour;—for much of his whaling apparatus, and all his best provisions, were exhausted, and he was running short of water. The supplies from the Leviathan would be welcome and seasonable; and what with the expected grunters, and fowl, and vegetables from the coast, and the terrapin from the island, the captain of the Grampus hoped to furnish the means of refreshing his men, after their long and arduous toils, and to recruit them thoroughly for whaling operations. It was his intention, therefore, after dividing the provisions between the two ships, to remain at anchor for a few days, to allow his crew time for recreation, as well as to take in a supply of turtle.

Upon hailing the Leviathan, as the Grampus dropped her anchor, Seth had been answered by the mate of the former, and duly informed that Jonathan was on board and well; but to his inquiries about provisions, the mate made some unsatisfactory reply, and desired Seth to come on board the Leviathan. The anchor of the Grampus was no sooner cast, than Macy manned his boat and boarded the Leviathan. To his surprise, when he mounted the deck, he found that Jonathan was not there to receive him, nor to offer those little courtesies, and make those inquiries after his welfare, which are usual upon such occasions, and especially between those who consort together in their business.

There is but little ceremony in whale-ships; but Macy at least expected, from his previous intimacy with Coleman, and from the fact that he had been so long and unaccountably away, that the latter would be anxious to ask after the particulars of his voyage. Seth walked aft, and was about to enter the cabin, when the well-remembered tones of Coleman's violin struck upon his ear. It might be nothing more than a freak of his brother captain, who, as we have elsewhere hinted, had the reputation of being an *odd-fish*. But Seth was still more surprised when he found Jonathan snugly stowed in his berth, sawing away in his recumbent position, and not deigning to notice his visitor. Macy stood motionless for a time, but at last his patience gave way, and he hailed the violinist rather crustily in the midst of his performance.

"Hello!"—no answer. "Jonathan!"—still no reply. "I say, Captain Coleman!"

"I hear thee," said Jonathan, at last; but the fiddle still went on.

"What the devil is the meaning of this foolery!" exclaimed Macy.

"Don't interrupt the symphony, and thou shalt hear directly," replied Jonathan.

Hereupon Jonathan accompanied his violin with words which seemed to Macy to have been composed for the occasion, to carry out one of Coleman's dry and puzzling jokes. The stave, uplifted, ran as follows:

> "We sailed for the shore,
> And North-east we bore,
> And drove a tremen-di-ous trade."

"Aha!" interrupted Macy, while his eyes brightened, "thou hast been successful then;—but what provisions did'st thou bring?"

"Thou marrest the music, friend Macy;—listen to the end, and thou wilt be duly enlightened," replied Coleman, and he again sawed and sung away:—

> "The oil is all sold
> And the money's all told,
> And a d—l of a v'yage we have made!"

"Well, well—enough of that," said Macy:—"Come, tell me in plain prose about the provisions."

"I shall never be able to instruct thee in the melodies and the harmonies, if thou dost not refrain from interrupting me. The stave must always be sung over from the *repeat:*—

> "The oil is all sold,
> And the money's all told,
> And a d—l of a v'yage we have made!"

"There!" continued Jonathan, "since thou hast heard me out, thou shalt now learn the particulars of our fresh provisions."

"Well!—what hast thou got that is fresh and good?" demanded Seth, while his mouth watered in expectation.

"T*a*rrapin!" replied Jonathan.

"Oh, that of course!—but I don't mean that sort of food, for we have it here at Charles' Island, for the trouble of picking on't up.—What else!"

"T*a*rrapin! " repeated Jonathan.

"What!—no hogs—no fruit—no potatoes—no—"

"No!—T*a*rrapin, I say again;—and nothing else but t*a*rrapin wilt thou find on board the good ship Leviathan, in the shape of fresh provisions."

"What!" exclaimed Seth, in blank amazement.

"All true as a book!" replied Jonathan; "The steward shall swear to it on the almanac, or on Napier's Book of Tables, if thou think'st the oath improved by it, and doubt'st the truth of my affirmation."

"In heaven's name, Coleman," said Macy, "thou must be joking;—thou had'st forty barrels of oil, and thou hast disposed of it ?"

Jonathan struck up, in answer—

> "The oil is all sold,
>> And the money's all told.
>> And a d—l of a v'yage—"

"The joke may be a good one to thee," interrupted Seth as he began to ascend the cabin ladder: "and I will leave thee to enjoy it alone. I have heard of *Nero* fiddling while Rome was on fire; and thou remindest me of his criminal unconcern in the midst of the people's calamity.—But thou wilt, of course, account to the crews and to Jethro for the oil?"

"Thou never spoke a truer word in all thy life:—the forty barrels of right-whale oil at the market-price, are already logged against me, by my own direction," replied Jonathan.

"But what became of the avails?" demanded Seth.

"That is my own secret;—and it must remain so," said Coleman.

"So be it," said Seth, "thou hast only delayed the commencement of our operations for another month. To-morrow I shall set sail for some port on the main, and lay in my own provisions. Thou must, hereafter, find thy own means to furnish thy ship. Spare oil is too precious, at the present moment, to allow of my offering to share again with thee."

"Nay," replied Jonathan, "and if thou goest to-morrow, I will go with thee. I have a hold full of tarrapin, which I will willingly divide with thee; and thou knowest they are worth all the grunters in the world;—but the vegetables, I grant thee, are somewhat scarce, just now."

"Thou wilt consult thy own pleasure about leaving the anchorage:—but, mark me!—I will not share a single shilling's worth of oil, nor an ounce of provisions with thee," said Seth, seriously, and in a determined manner.

Hereupon Seth stepped over the gangway into his boat, which he found loaded, almost to the gunwale, with terrapin, and his men busied in knocking down the heads of the brutes with the oarblades, as they attempted to crawl over the side. The mate of the Leviathan had placed the seasonable supply there, in conformity with the secret ordering of Jonathan;—and Seth, finding how matters were, could not help casting up his eye, by way of inquiry; but, seeing the quizzical phiz of Coleman peering over the quarter, he could not avoid laughing aloud at this most acceptable manner of repairing damages. Seth pushed off, in renewed good humour; and in an hour's time his crew were feasting sumptuously, and in a way that they had not feasted before for many a day.

The secret of Jonathan's failure to supply provisions, was well kept for a time; but, eventually, it leaked out, that he had been entrapped, by complaisant and accommodating sharpers, on shore; and there was something said about the bright eyes and the ruby lips of his entertainers, and the drugged quality of the circling wine. But we will draw the veil, in all charity. No man passes through the world without his *faux pas;* and the misfortune of Jonathan served only to accumulate the proofs that human nature is weak,—and liable, in the best families, and even among Quakers, to accidental besetments.

Seth Macy was true to his word. The meridian sun of the next day saw him clear from the currents and under-tows of the "Enchanted Islands," as the Gallipagos are called by some navigators, because of the difficulty of escaping from the powerful eddies and counter streams, that whirl with peculiar force and rapidity among the volcanic cluster. The barque of Jonathan was not behind the Grampus. When Seth loosed his sails,

Jonathan's were loosed also; and when the anchor of the Grampus was heaved up, that of the Leviathan was tripped as soon;—and they sailed forth again upon the broad Pacific together.

It was, in those days, a glorious sight to see two such noble ships spreading their canvas upon a sea, which, with but few exceptions, so eminently deserves the name of *Pacific.* Its storms and severe gales are far less frequent than those which are felt upon any other sea. Its climate is more equable and pleasant, and its resources far more prolific, than those of any other water bearing the title of Ocean. Its natural riches, even unto this day but partially known and explored, are mines of wealth to whole nations; and its incomparable islands, with their varied and inexhaustible fertility, are, of themselves, adequate to the support of an increase of people equal to the present number of inhabitants on the globe.

The heads of the ships pointed to Valparaiso, upon the South American coast. The bright, burning sun of the Equatorial seas had set and risen again, since they had taken their departure; when, at a long distance in the direction they were steering, the man at the mast-head descried tiny moving specs upon the ocean, which seemed occasionally to appear and disappear. The ships and these uncertain objects approached each other steadily, until they were made out to be a vast school of spermacetti whales, sporting and gamboling, and blowing and diving, as if, in truth, they were the school of a pedagogue let loose from thraldom, and rejoicing in their liberty.

The information from aloft set every thing in motion on deck. Boats were cleared, irons prepared, lines coiled; and the men stretched themselves, as if rousing from inaction, or from the lethargy or weariness; and the laugh and the joke, which had been somewhat scarce of late, were bandied about in the utmost glee. The landmen's hearts beat tumultuously, in anticipation of their first feat among the giants of the water. The approach of danger, and the hope of success, swayed their minds alternately; and it was difficult to say whether they most coveted the opportunity of grappling with such mighty antagonists, or whether they would not willingly have deferred the encounter. To them it was a moment of anxiety, like that preceding the approach of two hostile squadrons.

The feelings of the veterans were different. They were as eager for the moment of attack as slot-hounds to be loosed upon their prey. Feeling confidence in their skill, and in the superiority which art gives over the exertion of mere brute power, they hailed the prospect before them with feelings approaching to boyish enthusiasm.

There was one, however, on board the Leviathan, who, amidst the animated bustle which precedes an attack upon a school of whales, did not partake of the cheerfulness of his fellows. We need scarcely say that the individual was Thomas Starbuck. There was a determined soberness in his face and demeanour, from the moment the cry from the mast-head was uttered, which, at first, drew upon him the bantering jibes and jokes of his messmates; but he heard them without resentment, and he turned oft their ill-timed jests with unangered answers. There was a deep gloom preying upon his spirits; and while all others seemed to be in high good humour, and "eager for the fray,"—*he* was listless and desponding. The fortune-teller's words had been forgotten, until now;—but the sight of the approaching whales, and the active, noisy preparation for attack, brought all she had said afresh to his memory.

Starbuck, who was harpooner to one of the boats, and a most important man in that capacity, was ashamed to show the white feather upon the first occasion that had been presented for signalizing himself upon the voyage;—but the words of Judith rang in his ears, and he felt that he could not lightly disregard the omen. Stepping aft to the quarter-deck, as much to ask the advice of the captain, who was aware of the prophecy of the fortune-teller, as to obtain permission to remain on board for the time, he held a few brief words with Jonathan.

"Captain," said he, "I feel an unaccountable presentiment that the words of Judith Quary are about to be fulfilled. I would fain disappoint the prophetess, if she be one; and, though I know my duty, and have heretofore acquitted myself sufficiently well to be named one of your boat-steerers, yet I am unwilling to go out upon this expedition without your positive commands. In short, I lack confidence to-day; and I come to ask you to appoint one of the crew as my substitute."

"There is no time to argue this thing now," replied the captain, "or I might give thee convincing proof that fortune-tellers cannot look into futurity. I respect thy feelings, Thomas, however thou may'st have come by them; and, therefore, I will neither urge nor command thee to go. Let it be as thou wishest:—if thou decline, I will appoint another in thy stead."

Thomas Starbuck retired, with a heavy heart. He saw that he had relinquished all chance of distinguishing himself for the day; and the dishonour of staying on board at the approaching crisis, with a troop of whales in sight of the ship, could probably never be wiped away. The thought, too, of what Ruth would say to his conduct; when he should return home, and, above all, the certainty of the imputation of cowardice, which might be cast in his teeth by his companions, made him half repent the steps he had taken.

The crew had witnessed the interview of Starbuck with the captain, and guessed at the import of their conversation.

"So!" said one of the men, within earshot of Thomas, "we shall not have Starbuck's company to-day, I s'pose. He's begged off, I'm sure, or he'd be taking his place at the for'ard oar. I wonder who's to be harpineersman for our boat, if *he* don't go?"

"A faint heart never won fair lady," said another, who had heard of his attachment to Ruth; for secrets of that nature get whispered about among a ship's crew, especially if they all come from a small place like Nantucket, where everybody's business and motions are likely to be known and canvassed by his neighbour.

"He has reason to be chicken-hearted to-day," observed a third, "about that fortune-telling affair. Do you remember the morning we pulled off from Sherburne? For my part, I'd a notion of going ashore again, for everybody looked so solemncholy that I knew we'd have a misfortunate voyage. I'm glad he don't intend to go; I never knew Judith Quary to fail in her prediction."

The whales were now near enough to lower the boats, and the crews jumped in and were ready to push off, in order to scatter themselves among the approaching animals, and thus multiply the chances of striking them, when they should attempt to escape. Four boats pulled away from the Grampus, and instantly three more followed from the

Leviathan. The fourth boat, commanded by one of the mates, still lay alongside, waiting for the complement of oarsmen, (to be made from those whose duty it was to remain on shipboard,) to supply the place of Starbuck. Imbert was one of this crew, and was assigned to pull the after oar. He felt, as every novice feels, who, for the first time, is about to approach an animal so huge and dangerous as the whale; but he was devoid of childish fear, and rather courted the sport than otherwise. He had made himself a favourite with the whole crew, except Gardner, who could not divest himself of the thought of his being his rival, and, as he thought, a successful one: but, on most occasions, they treated each other with respect, though cool and unfamiliar in its nature. Gardner was harpooner for another boat, and had managed to get rid of the company of Imbert, by assisting one of the mates to pick the crew, to the exclusion of his rival. The chance of Imbert, to exhibit his prowess, was small, as, being a new hand, his task was merely to pull a steady oar, for the first voyage; and, until some lucky opportunity should offer, he could not expect to signalize himself, nor perform any prodigy to boast of.

"On deck there!" bawled the impatient mate, from the whaleboat.

He was answered by one of the crew, from the gangway, who had been designated to supply the place of Starbuck.

"Be quick!" said the mate, "or all the sport will be over, before we can get a chance at the whales. Hurry, man!—hurry! Jump in—jump in!"

Thomas now came to the gangway; and his irresolution gave way, as he saw his substitute about to let himself drop into his place in the bow of the boat. A flush of pride came into his face at the moment;—his resolution came back from very shame;—he seized the man by the shoulder, and drew him into the ship, and then rushed over the side, in an indescribable agony of mind.

"Let life or death be on the issue" said he, as he pushed off desperately from the ship, "I *will* go! It shall never be said that Thomas Starbuck disgraced his name, or his calling, by skulking dishonourably at a time like this.—Pull, boys, pull!" said he, aloud, to his comrades, while he madly surged upon his oar, with a strength equal, at the moment, to that of all the other oarsmen. The energy he exerted infused a spirit of emulation into his companions; the lingering whale-boat soon caught up and passed the others; and it was now leading the van. His shipmates in the other boats, who were acquainted with his intention of remaining on board, and with his reasons for so doing, saw in his flushed face, as he dashed by, that he had left all his superstitious fears behind; but they shook their heads at each other in sorrow, for they were all more or less imbued with the notion that he was rushing on to his fate, and that the super-human strength he was exerting was but hastening on the catastrophe.

The fearless whale-fishermen now found themselves in the midst of the monsters;—some turning *flooks,*—some rising to the surface to breathe, with their young upon their backs;—others spouting their cataract streams high into the air,—while some, in play, or to dislodge, by the shock, the barnacles and tantalizing suckers, that fastened, like vermin, to their sides, came jumping into the light of day, head uppermost, exhibiting their entire bodies in the sun, and falling on their sides into the water with the weight of a hundred tons, and thus "*breaching*" with a crash, that the thunder of a park of artillery could scarcely equal. It was a fearful and thrilling sight to the new-comer;—but, to the practised whale-fisherman, a scene that he delighted in, though full of imminent danger.

The commander of each boat immediately singled out his whale, and gave chase with steady earnestness. The ships, in the mean while, followed the course of the whales and of the pursuing boats;—a sufficient number of hands being left on board to work the vessels.

Macy and Coleman, with a promptness that is the peculiar recommendation of veteran whale-fishermen, fastened at once to their whales, taking the first that came in their way, without regard to size. They proved to be young ones, that were still under the protection of their mothers. This was fortunate for the fishermen, for they fell an easy prey; and their mothers, too, keeping close to their dead bodies, in a few minutes more paid the forfeit of their unalienable affection. The other officers showed no lack of skill; and, in less than an hour, six spermacetti whales, of various sizes, were the fruits of the victorious assault .

The mate of Coleman was more ambitious than the rest, and was determined, if possible, to strike the leader of the troop. He was of prodigious size, and worth any two of the others; but he was wary and watchful, and led his pursuer a tiresome chase, far away from his mates; and then, by a circuitous route, he came back again to his scattered convoy. Still did the baffled mate return to the charge, endeavouring to head his stupendous antagonist as he should rise to blow.

At last, the bubbling ripple from below indicated the approach of the animal to the surface; and a few vigorous pulls brought the boat to the spot where it was judged he would rise to its side. The oars were eased, and the word given to the harpooner to *stand up.*" The bow was turned to the spot;—the oarsmen rested on their oars, ready to back off;—and Starbuck stood erect, cleared his line, and balanced his iron. He placed himself in the posture for striking, and was bracing his knees to the bow, when the hump of the monster emerged from the water. It was a moment of indescribable anxiety;—but to none more than to the harpooner. But what was the consternation of all, when the head of the animal suddenly turned over! It is a motion made by the sperm-whale, preparatory to using his teeth upon an object floating upon the surface of the water. His huge underjaw, armed with immense ivory tusks, parted with the rapidity of thought. The bow of the boat struck suddenly against his jaw, and poor Thomas, in the act of launching his harpoon, lost his foothold, and pitched, headlong, into a living tomb! The jaws of the monster closed upon his body, leaving the legs of his victim projecting from the mouth!

The frightened mate lost his presence of mind, and omitted to give the word to back off. He held his steering oar without the power of motion. But Imbert, new as he was to the scene, seeing the opportunity to be avenged for the loss of his companion, seized the sharp lance of the mate, and plunged it to the hilt in the body of the whale, as he turned to escape. In an instant the boat and the crew were driven into the air, by a stroke of the animal's tail. The frail barque was shivered into a thousand pieces; and the men, bruised and lacerated, fell into the broad ocean.

All that had thus transpired was seen from the ships, and boats were despatched forthwith to the relief of the wounded crew. Some had seized upon fragments of the wreck; while others sustained themselves with pieces of broken oars, supported beneath by the strong saline buoyancy so eminently peculiar to the unfathomable depths of the ocean.

The unfortunate crew were rescued in time to witness the last agonies of the desperate whale, which, like Samson crushing the temple in his might, dealt death and destruction on all sides, while he himself was overwhelmed in the general ruin.

The animal, blind with rage, and feeling the sting of the death-wound in his heart, whirled round the ships, in irregular circles, for a short time, and then descended. The crews lay upon their oars, watching where he would next appear, while the ships were hove to, to await the result.

Suddenly, a mighty mass emerged from the water, and shot up perpendicularly, with inconceivable velocity, into the air. It was the whale;—and the effort was his last expiring throe!—He fell dead;—but, in his descent, he pitched headlong across the bows of the Grampus, and, in one fell swoop, carried away the entire forepart of the vessel!

The crew escaped, by throwing themselves into the boats alongside, and rowing quickly off. The gallant ship instantly filled with water, and settled away from their sight.

CHAPTER ELEVEN.

But yesterday the word of Caesar might
Have stood against the world: now
None so poor to do him reverence.

Julius Cæsar.

"——Shall I then fall
Ingloriously, and yield?—No!—
Though you were legions of accursed spirits,
Thus would I fly among you!"

———

No more!—Betake thee to thy task at home:—
There guide the spindle, and direct the loom.

Hector to Andromache.

A FULL year had passed since the departure of Jethro Coffin from Sherburne, and no tidings had, as yet, been received, intimating his intention to return. His protracted absence did not, however, create uneasiness in the minds of his friends; for, it must be borne in mind by the reader, that arrivals from England were, at that time, few and far between. There were not then, as now, regular days of departure for packets, and almost as regular periods of arrival. A year intervening, between the embarkation and return of an individual to the colonies, was therefore almost a certainty,—no matter how trivial may have been the business, or the object, that called the voyager from his home. It is different now-a-days. The sixth part of that time is sufficient to make a passage to Europe and back again, and yet leave a reservation of a portion of the time, for the transaction of business, or the pursuit of pleasure. It is, with us, an age of fleet ships, skimming steam-boats, and flying rail-road vehicles, that almost annihilate time and distance. It is a mechanical age—an Augustan era, prolific in the development of mechanical genius.

Soon after the ships of Jethro had doubled The Horn, hostilities commenced between the mother country and the colonies. It was, for the time, the death-blow to the prosperity of Nantucket; and the distress which fell upon the people, as much from their isolated situation as from any other cause, was severe beyond measure. Their ships were swept from the ocean; their trade with the continent annihilated, and, consequently, their supplies cut off. They were without the power of resistance, or of self-protection. They were subject alike to pillage from either party; and their flocks were carried away by both friend and foe. A fishing smack, with a single gun, could at any time lay the unresisting town under contribution. Each arrival from a whaling voyage, instead of furnishing the means of support to the inhabitants, was the cause of lessening their stores, by the introduction of an additional number of consumers. Interdicted, as they were, from intercourse with the continent,—without grain, without bread, and without fuel—in short, without the common necessaries of life, but with abundant pecuniary means under other circumstances, the islanders were reduced to a condition so straitened, that it was not only sad to contemplate, but appalling to think of.

It was in the midst of this general distress that the genius and cupidity of Miriam Coffin shone forth, to the unfeigned astonishment of the islanders. Foreseeing the advantages that must naturally accrue to her, by the course she had almost immediately adopted, she despatched one of her husband's smaller vessels to New-York, with a letter to Admiral Digby, who commanded the squadrons cruising on our coast. In this paper she was careful to express her devoted loyalty to King George, and, with well-turned phrase, to represent the extremities to which the people were reduced. Miriam concluded her epistle by humbly asking permission to send her vessels to New-York, and the privilege of trading between that city and Sherburne.

To this arrangement the Admiral assented, and granted a free passport, running in the name of Miriam, to trade to and fro: But (as she had insinuated in her letter, that by far the largest portion of the people were rank whigs in principle) he gave her to understand that the privilege was the meed of her loyalty alone, and not a boon to the people; and therefore that she; above all others, should enjoy a monopoly of the trade.

This decision was precisely what Miriam aimed at. On the other hand, in order to prevent supplies from being introduced by the Americans, she took care to have the false information spread abroad, upon the neighbouring continent, that the islanders were all thorough-going tories, and adhered to the Crown. In this posture of affairs there was, of course, no sympathy for the Nantucket people, either from whig or tory. She thus succeeded in her plans, and for a considerable time the source of supply was confined to herself alone.

In a short period after these successful arrangements had been effected, it was observed that the warehouse of Miriam was groaning, not only with substantial provisions of every sort, but even with such luxuries as the islanders had been accustomed to purchase in the days of their brightest prosperity. Her small vessels were constantly employed between the two ports; and riches, without bounds, flowed into her coffers. For her merchandise she would receive, in the way of barter, the oil and the candles of the island traders, at a large and ruinous discount to those who held the commodities; and when these were exhausted, she dealt with them for their ships at the wharves, and for their houses, until she became possessed of property, or the representatives of wealth, at least, in mortgages, to an amount exceeding her most sanguine dreams of abundance.

By and by, however, it came to pass that Miriam could no longer furnish the ready and tangible means of exchange for foreign merchandise, when the oil and candles that she had received in barter were all shipped off and exhausted. Her liens upon ships and houses were not a medium current with British merchants and shopkeepers at New-York. Such securities were considered too precarious in their value to be objects of speculation to the foreigners. The ships and the houses, though the undisputed property of one party to-day, might change hands to-morrow, by the right of invasion and conquest.

Miriam, therefore, bethought herself of another scheme to give permanency to her operations. Her mercantile credit, arising from the largeness and punctuality of her dealings and payments, was in good repute among the commercial dealers of the city;—and she opened a negotiation in New-York, for a permanent supply of all needful stores and merchandise, upon her individual responsibility. She took the precaution, in order to prevent suspicion of her incompetency to act in the premises, to cause certified copies of her power of attorney to be circulated among her creditors there; but it was scarcely necessary,—for her previous success in trade had already established her good name with the principal dealers in the place. These, as we have hinted before, were mostly British merchants, who received countenance and protection from the commander-in-chief of the British forces, whose head-quarters were established at New-York. In place of her former exchanges of oil, which, being exhausted, could no longer be the circulating medium for Miriam, she deposited her own bonds (in the shape of judgment securities, that could be enforced at any moment,) with her merchant creditors; and, for a season, they were as current, for the amount expressed upon their face, as if they had been exchequer notes.

Not satisfied with the monopoly of a trade that was comparatively legitimate in its nature, Miriam opened a traffic with certain contraband dealers, whose smuggling shallops, and privateering operations, were the source of much anxiety and vexation to the officers of the revenue, on various parts of the coast. While her dealings with New-York were carried on openly, those with the free-traders, or "South Sea Buccaneers," as the jealous inhabitants spitefully called them, were transacted in secret, and with a mystery which the shrewd and prying islanders could not penetrate. It was, in fact, mainly for the better prosecution of an illicit trade, that Miriam had built her country-house; although, ostensibly, she pretended to have constructed it for purposes of retirement. She had even had dealings with the smugglers before the war broke out.

Small craft were seen hovering around the island, from time to time, whose suspicious manœuvres were regarded with alarm and dissatisfaction by the people. Boats, gunwale-deep, had been seen to land, in the dusk of the evening, upon the beach in the vicinity of Quaise; and their crews were observed to flit hastily and stealthily to and fro, carrying small burthens in the direction of the mansion, and then disappearing unaccountably among a clump of bushes, from which they would shortly emerge and retrace their steps, without seeming to enter the building. The vessel, which awaited the return of the crew, would then spread her sails, and stand out from the bay.

It was remarked, too, that a wing of Miriam's town-house underwent a great alteration about this period. Two large rooms, that before had been used as parlours, were thrown into one, and shelves and counters were arranged for the reception of merchandise; and the capacious cellar was partitioned off into curious but commodious bins. By degrees the shelves were filled with costly dry-goods and cutlery, and rare fancy articles from France and other European countries; while the bins were stored with wines and liquors, which, it was suspected, were not brought into the island by the ordinary course of importation.

The wealth of the Indies seemed to be at the command of Miriam; and the gorgeousness of her establishment, which she took all opportunities to flaunt in the eyes of the people, showed forth like the stately pile and liveried household of a grandee of an empire, while all around was misery and wretchedness, and betokened poverty and decay.

The exorbitant prices demanded and received by Miriam, for all the supplies furnished to the islanders, finally took the semblance of barefaced extortion. If people complained of the dearness of her commodities, she would coolly replace the goods on the shelves, and advise them to go where they could be furnished at a cheaper rate; nor would she again deal with the individual who dared to question her prices. The inhabitants, becoming almost desperate from the inadequacy of their means, and tantalized by the daily exhibitions of plenty, temptingly placed before their longing eyes by Miriam, but which their exhausted means could not compass, began to feel that want and starvation would be their portion, even in the midst of abundance, if this alarming state of the times should continue.

A shadow of a revenue office was still kept up in the town, the officers of which were in the pay and interest of the British government. The great mass of the people were, however, decidedly republican in their feelings and principles; and, in total disregard of the authority which the few officers of the crown still exerted, a meeting was called at the Town-House, to deliberate upon the means of relieving the general distress that prevailed. Some of the speakers openly hinted at the unfair practices of Miriam, and denounced her oppressive course in no measured terms. It was, among other things, deemed proper, as a preliminary measure for counteracting the approach of future and greater evils, that a new board of Selectmen should be chosen; and, of course, in acting upon this motion, those in power must necessarily be deposed. The old magistracy were of the tory interest; and, as such, the adherents of Miriam, and the connivers at, if not the participators in her unheard-of extortions. A new board, of whig complexion, was thereupon organized, and its first act was to petition the American Congress for relief.

A messenger was forthwith dispatched, who explained, in moving terms, the forlorn condition of the islanders to the assembled Congressional delegates. But that patriotic body, although deeply and sincerely commiserating the distress or the people, were alike too poor and powerless to afford efficient succour or protection. The only measure that could be adopted in this extremity, involving a probability of efficacious relief to the suffering community, was the unanimous recommendation and consent of the Congress, that the Nantucket people should declare themselves neutral in the pending contest, and represent their condition to the British commander-in-chief. This suggestion was immediately acted upon; and indeed it was quite consonant to the peaceful religious doctrines of the people, who were all more or less imbued with the tenets of the Quakers, the prevailing sect, as we have elsewhere said, of the island.

A new life seemed to invigorate the desponding inhabitants, at the prospect which now opened upon them. Combinations were immediately formed for the purpose of retaliating upon their oppressors. Like the patriotic women of the continent, who refused to partake of imported teas, the islanders thereafter utterly abstained from dealing with Miriam. Her goods rested upon the shelves, without a customer. Her provisions were thenceforth untasted; and a few scanty vegetables, laboriously grubbed by the inhabitants, were made to supply the place of her high-priced breadstuffs.

While negotiations were going on at New York, and with the naval commander of the station, the incensed Nantucketers undertook a secret expedition against Miriam's "South Sea Islanders." A party of some twenty resolute individuals, armed with instruments to which their hands were best accustomed, to wit, the lance and the harpoon,—lay in wait, night after night, around the country seat of Miriam, with the determination of intercepting her contraband supplies. At night-fall the conspirators, if we may so call them, might be seen straying singly, and without any apparent purpose, near the outskirts of the town; but the Mill-Hills once passed, there was no further occasion for concealment, and they rapidly congregated at a given point, where their instruments of warfare were secreted among the bushes. Here, marshalling their forces, and every man being made acquainted with the signal for onslaught, the party took up their line of march for Quaise; and each one, secretly and silently ensconced himself behind some stunted bush, or projecting object, awaiting the moment of attack.

Again and again were the party foiled in their anticipated capture;

and the smugglers escaped unaccountably, inasmuch as they made no visible entrance or egress into or from the house. Regularly as the night would come, a small sail might be observed laying off and on; but as the dusk of the evening would gather, she would run in towards the shore and entering the small bay that leads to Quaise, heave to opposite Miriam's house. It was sometimes observed that she would depart without lowering her boat;—some private signal, probably, being omitted, which was necessary for encouragement to land. At other times it would boldly put off, and figures might be distinguished walking on the beach. Whatever was their object in landing, it was observed that the silence of the night was unbroken by noise or bustle of any kind; and again they would leave, as they came, observing a profound stillness in all their operations.

The men from the town thought there must be something more in this, than the mere pleasure of coming into the bay and departing; and they determined to array their forces differently. Instead of closely investing the building as formerly, on the next evening they enlarged their circle, and planted sentinels near the landing place for closer observation. The night was fitful, and dark masses of clouds obscured the moon at intervals, which, for the time, entirely concealed the approach of objects. The wind blew in gusts, and the surf tumbled in upon the outer beach with more than its usual commotion.

"Hark!" said one of the sentinels, approaching his neighbour; "heard you nothing just now?"

"No," replied his comrade; "nothing but the roar of the surf. I fear the night is too dark, and the wind too high for the purpose of the smugglers."

At this moment a loud noise was heard above the monotonous roar of the sea, like the violent flapping of a sail; and the moon, bursting suddenly forth from behind a dark cloud, displayed a small vessel in the act of coming to the wind. The boat, as usual, was lowered; and after a short detention alongside, during which a number of men appeared to be engaged in stowing away bundles and packages in her bottom, she shoved off from the shallop. Three men employed themselves in rowing the yawl towards the shore, with oars muffled, while a fourth stood up in the stern-sheets, and controlled her motions.

A low whistle was heard to pass from sentinel to sentinel upon the shore, which, without being understood, would have passed to stranger ears for the chirping of a cricket, or the tremulous note of a disturbed sea-bird. The band instantly contracted their circle at the signal, but left a wide opening for the smugglers to enter, if they should decide upon landing.

The boat struck the shore; and the men, jumping quickly out, hauled her up the beach The sailors set to work to unload the yawl of the various packages, and silently deposited them in a heap upon the dry sand, near a little spit or eminence, around which a small gully, or pathway, led to the upland. Directly over the brow of the slight hill, but at some distance to the right and left of the path, several of the townsmen were posted, with their bodies thrown flat upon the earth, but with eyes eagerly glaring over the little precipice upon the motions of the crew. The boat, being entirely unladen, her *kellock*, or little kedge, was brought forth and planted in the sand, for the better security of the yawl, whose stern was washed by a rising tide.

"Tom!" said one in a whisper, who appeared to direct the motions of the others; "mount the hillock and see if the signal is still there."

As the man ascended, the eyes of the ambushed islanders followed his steps, and glanced in the direction of the house. A faint light, heretofore unobserved, was perceptible from a thick bull's-eye of glass, placed in one of the shutters. All the rest of the building was enshrouded in darkness. The man descended, and in a low voice uttered the simple monosyllable—"*Ay.*"

"All's right, then!" replied the leader, in the same subdued tone:—"Bear a hand, men, and lift these packages. Take care to follow me, and stick close; and, d'ye hear?—on your lives utter not a single word, whatever you may see or hear. Come,—be lively now; this infernal cloudy night came near playing the devil with our little craft: we must hasten back to make sail upon her, or the wind will drive her ashore."

The moon gave out her flickering light for a moment, as the sailors advanced. The proper place of deposit appeared to be gained, and the leader ordered the men to halt.

"There!" whispered he, "throw down the bundles on this spot, and let us return for the others."

"No thee don't, though!" exclaimed one of the sentinels, while his companions rushed in to his aid. The driving clouds hid the moon again, before the assailants could reach the spot where the smugglers stood; and when she re-appeared, packages and crew had vanished! Not a word had been spoken by the assailed; but the foremost assailant declared he had heard a slight rustling noise as if the branches of some bushes, near at hand, had been parted. The harpoons of the invaders were thrust in among them in vain. The smugglers were unaccountably gone, but where to look for them was a mystery. They could not have escaped over the clear heath, for the circle of the watchers had been so suddenly and regularly contracted, that it was not possible they should have passed without being observed.

The pursuit after the fugitive crew was soon abandoned; and it was thereupon determined that a portion of the persons present should board the craft in the bay, and carry her by a *coup de main,*—while the remainder should enter the house of Miriam, and explore some of its mysteries. It was thought that the boat's crew must have taken refuge there, by some means of entrance unknown to those who had invested the building.

Four persons, well armed, answering to the number that had come ashore in the boat, were selected for the purpose of taking possession of the sloop; and some eight or ten others attempted to gain entrance into the house,—leaving a sufficient number on the outside, guarding all the passages of egress, to prevent the escape of the indwellers.

The outer doors were tried, but did not yield to the pressure from without. A slight rap upon the door, such as might announce a neighbourly visit, was then given; and instantly the light from the bullseye was withdrawn. A door was almost immediately opened by an Indian domestic, who, the moment she saw the array of armed men, attempted to close the door in their faces.

"Nay,—thou must not shut the door upon us," said the leader of the troops. "We would enter the house."

"What for?" demanded the woman.

"Thou wilt see directly. Come, stand out of the way there,—or we must put thee gently aside."

"I will *not!*" said she. "I am commanded not to admit strangers at this hour of the night."

"Thou wilt not?"

"No."

"Then take the consequences."

Saying this, the assailant drew back, and, with a heavy drive of his foot, stove the door off its hinges, and the servant rolled upon the floor of the entrance.

An inner door was instantly opened by some invisible hand, and a strong light came into the passage. The men rushed, rather tumultuously, into the room; but the foremost had scarcely taken three steps into the apartment, before he recoiled upon his followers, at the sight of a woman!—It was Miriam Coffin. She stood at the upper end of the apartment, in perfect self possession, and regarded the intruders with an eye of severity. Her stately form was drawn up to its full height, and displayed the commanding port of Majesty. As soon as the confusion among the men had somewhat subsided, they took courage and came forward.

"Well, gentlemen!" said Miriam, sarcastically, "to what fortunate circumstance am I indebted for this kind and neighbourly visit?"

The men looked at each other, without replying. No spokesman volunteered to apologize for their rudeness.

"What!" exclaimed Miriam, "will no one speak;—Brave men, like you, who can exert your hearty prowess upon the door of my mansion, should surely be able to find words to address a lone woman withal! Come in, and take possession, since you have battered down my doors!—or shall I hand over the keys of my closets and my drawers to you? Here," continued Miriam, releasing a small bunch of keys from her girdle, "take them, *gentlemen*, and make free at the house of Miriam Coffin:—This is the key of the drawer containing my silver spoons;—this one unlocks the chest, wherein you will find the silver plate that my mother gave me on the day of my marriage;—and this one will put you in possession of a hundred silver crowns. What!—not take them?—Beshrew me, gentlemen, he that will assault and batter down the outer door of a private dwelling, should not hesitate to lay his hands upon the spoils within. I took you for some brave band of brotherly associates, of the Agrarian order, whose creed is the equal division of property. I cry you mercy; —I have mistaken your object, *gentlemen!*"

Here Miriam courtesied slowly to the floor, with deep ceremony, while a curl of contempt sat upon her lips. The men, unable, as they afterwards declared themselves, to stand before the searching fire of her eye, hurried from her presence without making a word of reply. There was not a man among them that would not sooner have grappled with a whale, than encounter a woman's tongue; and especially if that woman was Miriam Coffin.

In the mean time, the four men had descended to the beach, and launched the small boat. The sloop was an easy prey; for only two persons, and those but half-grown lads, were remaining on board. They were not sensible of any danger, until the strange faces came aft, and their unusual costume became visible by the light of the binnacle. The frightened youths rushed for the boat, but were seized at the gangway by the brawny hands of the Nantucketers, and forced to remain in custody. The boat was sent back again to the beach, and the townspeople were brought off, together with the packages remaining on the sands. Sail was instantly made, and the cold stomachs of the captors were warmed with some good Holland, which they found on board, and broached, no doubt, at the expense of Miriam. An hour's sail brought the craft safely into port; and, as no one appeared to claim her, she was declared forfeit to her captors.

Soon afterwards the envoys to the British authorities returned with favourable reports. The Nimrod, brig of war, anchored in the offing, and a twelve-oared barge, bearing her commander, and a white flag, in token of amity, approached the shore. The starving inhabitants crowded to the landing place to receive the messenger; and, as in duty bound, they conducted him, with every demonstration of respect, to the Town-House. Silence being obtained in that ancient hall of reception, the magistrates of the town arranged themselves in their places. A duplicate set of Selectmen, however, presented themselves, and contended for precedence:—the whigs, on the one side, believing themselves to be the choice of a majority of the sovereign people, and the tories on the other, who had plucked up courage to make a show of loyalty to the crown, countenanced, as they supposed they would be, by an officer of his majesty.

The commander of the Nimrod approached the table, which divided the factions of the houses of York and Lancaster, and, in a prefatory speech, declared himself the humble messenger of his majesty's government, to inform the inhabitants that their wish to remain neutral, in the pending contest, had been acquiesced in. He further went on to say, that the people would be allowed freedom of trade to all parts of the continent, so long as that privilege was not abused, by succouring their countrymen, the rebels; and that license was granted for their whale-ships to come and go freely. He finished by laying his dispatches upon the table, and then retired a few steps to await their reply.

The despatches were directed, in their superscription to the *"Worshipful Magistrates of the Town of Sherburne and Island of Nantucket."* The unyielding manners of the old Nantucketers were never more conspicuous than upon this august occasion. A formal argument, but carried on with all the quaintness and propriety which distinguish Quaker debates, was here entered upon by the speakers of the several factions. The ex-Selectmen declared it their high privilege to receive and open his majesty's despatches, and cited the words of the superscription as an argument that the packet belonged to them exclusively. The whig party, who had abjured all titles of this nature, contented themselves with the simple designation of *"Selectmen,"* and publicly denounced the sounding dignity of *"Worshipful* Magistrates." The literal construction of the superscription was, therefore, likely to prove a bone of contention between the parties, to the great detriment of their constituents. But the whigs, though they would not break the seal of the paper themselves, from a too nice regard to etiquette, were determined not to yield the important document up to their opponents.

Meantime the packet remained untouched. The gallant commander of the Nimrod became uneasy, at the unnecessary delay which the far-advanced and still waxing debate occasioned him, and thought proper to put in his oar.

"Since," said he, "the liberality of his majesty's government is so little appreciated, although granted at your earnest prayer;—and, as I perceive such a perversity of disposition here, which, it seems to my poor comprehension, you would sooner indulge in till doomsday, and suffer the people to starve, than concede supremacy one to the other,— I will retire, and report what I have seen and heard. I must, however, since no one will receive it, restore this packet to those who have commissioned me to bring you relief:—but I must say, it strikes me as in the highest degree singular, and out of place, that amidst distress, such as prevails here, you should stand upon ceremony in breaking the seal of these important despatches, addressed respectfully to the magistrates of the town."

"Minnows and mack'rel!" exclaimed Peleg Folger, who belonged to the whigs;—"I am a convert to thy eloquence, and am inclined to think pretty much as thou dost in this matter. By thy leave, I will settle this dispute, in the twinkling of a bedpost. There!" continued Peleg, "let those who please, quarrel about the envelope and its worshipful designation;—for my part, I will, for one, take a peep into the interior, and pick the kernel out of the shell, without longer giving heed to the palaver of the S'lackmen."

"*Slack* enough, in all conscience!" said the officer to a bystander.

Peleg tore off the cover, which he mischievously handed over to the leader of the tories. He thereupon read aloud to the rejoicing people, the warrant of their release from privation and want. He then held up the papers in triumph and the people shouted aloud as he descended from the rostrum.

"Let us home to our families, and spread the good news;—and do thou, neighbour Peleg, hold fast of the document," said a townsman of Peleg.

"Ay—minnows and mack'rel!—that I will—and the worshipful blockheads may remain behind, and talk about the inviolability of the anointed magistry, as they call it, until they grow black in the face for lack of something to eat!"

The crowd followed Peleg, and the hall of audience was cleared of all but the wordy belligerents,—who, seeing themselves abandoned by the people, soon grew ashamed of their puerile debate, and went upon their several ways; while the captain of the Mighty Hunter, finding that his mission was at an end, took to his barge again, and departed the coast.

The monopoly that Miriam had so long enjoyed was now at an end. Supplies came pouring into the neutral port of Sherburne from every quarter, and in less than a fortnight's time the inhabitants were effectually and abundantly relieved. But this was not all. The reaction against Miriam commenced. The wheel of fortune, which is always turning, had carried her to the top, while it had, at the same time, crushed a whole people. She was now on her downward career, and the bruised and contemned were taking their turn upwards. The remembrance of her conduct had been treasured up against her; and, sooth to say, the means of bringing about her downfall were plotted industriously and without remorse. The springs of mercy and the milk of human kindness were dried up, for a time, in the breasts of her opponents. The owners of the ships and of the houses that had been mortgaged to her, bethought themselves of an expedient to redeem their pledges at small cost, and they hesitated at nothing to compass a wide revenge. They clubbed together their funds, and pledged their credit with their numerous friends upon the continent for additional means, for the purpose of buying up the judgment bonds of Miriam, which were floating about among the merchants of the city of New-York in large amounts. They were but too successful in their designs. They came back upon her with their demands, like an overwhelming flood. She found, too late, that she had not only overreached herself, but had been overreached; and that in accumulating riches, by unfair and exorbitant means, she had created a host of enemies, who were now as implacable in their prosperity as she had been inexorable in her demands and extortions, while they were needy.

Miriam, however, was game to the last. She looked the danger that threatened her steadily in the face, and took her measures promptly, but not warily.

"Since my enemies will have it so,—let them have war to the knife— let it be a war of extermination!" exclaimed she, with energy as she called for Grimshaw, her confidential adviser, and gave directions to foreclose every mortgage which she held, and to put every demand in suit in the Colonial courts.

"But, my dear madam," replied Grimshaw, "this will be the means of creating a more determined opposition in your enemies. Trust me, discretion is the better part of valour now; for you cannot fail to see the advantage of holding these liens *in terrorem* over their heads, while they are proceeding against you."

"Talk not to me of temporizing:—I will be obeyed;—put them all in suit forthwith, and crush the hornets in one nest together! They clamorously demand payment of my bonds, and will take nothing but silver and gold. I have neither, and they know it: but they shall be paid in their own coin;—bond for bond—ruin for ruin! I am not a woman to ask favours of the world; and least of all will I bend to this white-oak race of unmannered cubs.—No! Miriam Coffin is as unbending as the best of them!"

It was done as Miriam directed, and an internal war, more ruinous than has ever visited the island before or since, was carried on between the powerful and all-grasping Miriam Coffin, on the one part, and a whole community on the other. The fortunes of Miriam were prostrated in the struggle; but she would have been victorious in any other place upon the main, of equal size and resources. An isolated spot, like Nantucket, is favourable for mercantile combinations; but, on the continent, free competition renders most attempts of this nature nugatory. As it was, however, Miriam saw herself standing alone, in opposition to all the people of her little world.

Whenever she attempted to sell their property, by virtue of the mortgages which she held, as she was compelled to do to raise funds to meet her engagements, her debtors, by agreement with one another, stood by and saw ship after ship, and house after house, knocked down to a single bidder in their interest for a nominal sum. The rightful owner, it may be supposed, never suffered by these forced sales, but enjoyed his own again at Miriam's cost. And again: whenever portions of her own or her husband's property were seized, by virtue of the bonds enforced against her, her goods and chattels, houses and lands, by reason of the same combination, which she had provoked in the pride of her prosperity, were sacrificed for the tithe of their value. Even her splendid town-house was sold, over her head, for a sum less than half the cost of the stone foundation.

The strict morality of this proceeding, on the part of a people generally fair and upright, was, perhaps, never canvassed. The war, so far as carried on by Miriam, was looked upon as one of aggression; and the defence and retaliation regarded in the light of self-preservation.

In the midst of this state of things, Jethro Coffin returned to his home. He found himself a ruined man. Like a true philosopher, be set himself about repairing his shattered fortunes; but in the end was enabled to scrape together only a few fragments of a magnificent wreck. He placed great reliance, however, on the return of his ships from their whaling operations to resuscitate his mercantile name and credit; but the reader has already been made acquainted with their ill success and their misfortunes, and may therefore judge of the keen disappointment of Jethro, when he found his hopes entirely blasted.

Jethro could never be brought to look upon Miriam's splendid designs, which had ended so disastrously, with anything like patience or complacency.

"Had it not been for this," said Miriam, after she had finished giving her husband a faithful relation of her transactions,—"Had it not been for *this* misfortune,—and *that* accident;—if things had gone *so*—and *so*—as I had good reason to expect,—we should, as thou seest, have been the wealthiest family in the colonies."

"Nay," answered Jethro, "I do *not* see as thou seest;—thy unchastened ambition, not content with reasonable gains, hath ruined thy husband, stock and flook!—Get thee gone to thy kitchen, where it is fitting thou should'st preside:—Go—go to thy kitchen, woman, and do thou never meddle with men's affairs more!"

Miriam's proud heart was humbled: it was almost broken, at this reproof from her husband. But she obeyed; and, in time, put on the show of content, and seemed to the eyes of the world at least, to accommodate herself, without murmuring, to the humble pursuits which suited her decayed fortunes. But that world never knew of the volcanic fires, burning with a smouldering flame in her bosom;—nor of the yearnings for power;—nor the throbbings, struggling to be revenged upon those who had brought her house to its ruin. She was—

> "——Like Etna;—
> And in her breast was pent as fierce a fire."

$\mathcal{C}$HAPTER TWELVE.

These days—these months—to years had worn,
When tidings of high weight were borne
    To that lone island's shore.

Walter Scott.

O fortunate, e ciascuna era certa
Della sua sepoltura.

Dante.

MUCH bustle and speculation were created in the town of Sherburne, by the appearance of a large ship, riding at anchor off the harbour, early one morning, shortly after the return of Jethro Coffin to his native place. She showed no flag, nor displayed any signal. Her sails were furled; and the stillness of death seemed to reign over her decks. Not a single form could be detected, even with the glass, moving on board; and her dark hull swung, broadside to the town, steadily and motionless, as if her keel were imbedded in the sands.

319

As the sun rose, a single boat put off from the ship and approached the shore. It was a whale-boat, full-manned; and the helmsman, as usual, stood erect in the stern-sheets, while an extra man occupied the bow. The latter seemed, by his squatting position, to cower beneath the gaze of him at the helm, and to be desirous of escaping from observation. As the boat approached the pier, many of the inhabitants, anxious to ascertain the name of the ship, gathered at the expected point of debarkation. There was an object, carefully covered from the sight, that reclined in the stern near the helmsman, which from its shape and peculiar position, attracted the curiosity of the by-standers. The boat sheared up, and displayed faces long familiar to the islanders.

"Can it be possible," exclaimed they, "that it is Captain Seth Macy so soon returned?"

"You do indeed see him before you," answered he.

"And is that vessel riding at anchor thy ship?"

"No:—It is the Leviathan."

"And where is the noble ship Grampus?"

"At the bottom of the Pacific Ocean."

"And the crew—where are they?" demanded a breathless spectator.

"Safe," answered Seth,—"all safe, on board the ship in the offing. I would that I could say as much of her own crew."

The eager curiosity and deep sympathy of the auditors, who surrounded Seth upon the wharf, compelled him to repeat the painful story of his misfortunes; and the recital was listened to with silent attention. When he spoke of the manner of young Starbuck's death, a shudder thrilled the assembly, and they shed tears;—and when he described the awful suddenness of the catastrophe which befell the Grampus, there was unfeigned sorrow depicted on every countenance. Seth continued thus:—

"You see, my friends, that all, save poor Starbuck, escaped. It was the providence of God that saved us, and provided us with the means of escape. It was with heavy hearts that we reached the Leviathan, for we had lost our all; and we mounted her deck without a single change of clothing. We were now nearly a hundred souls in all; and the ship, of course, was encumbered with a double crew. After deliberating on our condition, and thinking over what was best to be done, we came to the conclusion to put the ship about and return home. Our voyage seemed to be accursed. Thus far we had had nothing but accident and misfortune, and vexation upon vexation. Every thing went wrong, and even the elements conspired against us. Having determined to return to port, we set about gathering our few slaughtered whales together; and in a few days, after securing all that was valuable of the animals, we left the Pacific. We arrived off the harbour late last evening, and cast our anchor where you now see the ship;—but, as if Heaven had not yet emptied its vials of wrath upon us to the very dregs, it must visit us with murder!—Nay—start not, my friends, it is true to the letter. Cain was the first murderer in the human family, and I bring you the first ever known to our peaceful island. Behold him there!"

The auditors of Seth recoiled in horror, as they looked upon the dogged countenance of the murderer. He still sat in the bow of the boat, without attempting to move.

"It is that accursed Indian!—it is Quibby!" exclaimed one, as he called to mind the features of the brute.

"Nay, fear him not," said Seth, observing the bystanders shrink from his presence, as if the angel of death were before them; "Fear him not," said he, "for he is manacled; his power of harming is past; and, if the laws of the land are enforced, he will shortly take his last look upon the face of men, and appear for judgment before his Creator, whose image he has marred, in the person of the young and gallant Harry Gardner!"

Seth uncovered the body of the murdered young man, and displayed his pallid face to the horror-struck islanders. The Indian shuddered as the corpse met his eyes. There was a deathlike stillness in the audience, interrupted at times by sobs and groans. Not a word was spoken: but the eyes of many overflowed with tears. The scene was most painful to behold, and was the more shocking to the people, because they had never even dreamed of witnessing such inhuman violence in their exemplary and peaceful community.

There were some of the young men of the town present, who were intimate friends of Harry, and had grown up from childhood with him. When the first burst of grief had in a measure subsided, another feeling seemed to take possession of the minds of the younger part of the spectators. A slight movement was observed in the crowd, and a few whispers passed among the youthful part of the assembly. Suddenly, a powerful young man jumped from the wharf into the boat, and seized the culprit. He was thrown out upon the quay as if he had been a bundle of cork, and was surrounded in an instant by a guard of young men, who had already matured a plan of revenge upon him, for the death of their comrade. It was time for Seth to act.

"What would you?" exclaimed he, springing to the side of the Indian: "would you commit murder, as *he* has done, and take his life without the sanction of law?—Shame!—shame, young men—thus to forget yourselves! Leave him to the law, and to his punishment hereafter. Back!—back, I say!—Murderer as he is, I will protect him for the present, until he is delivered over to the authorities. Friends!—I call upon you all, to aid me against this offered violence, which nothing can excuse."

There was a stir in the crowd, which plainly indicated that Seth was seconded. The middle-aged, and the elder portion of the people, came forward, with serious faces, to the assistance of the captain; and the excited young men retired, abashed, before this strong exhibition of the force of right moral feeling.

The Indian, who seemed to be in considerable pain, from a wound received in the thigh, was led slowly towards the Town-House, and the crowd gathered after him as he proceeded. The body of Gardner was, in the mean time, conveyed to the house of his afflicted relatives; while such magistrates as Nantucket boasted of at that period, assembled to take cognizance of the case. A universal gloom spread over the town at the report of the death of Harry, who, upon the eve of landing among his friends, was thus cut off by the hand of violence. The misfortunes of the ships, and the manner of Starbuck's untimely end, added, if possible, a stronger shade to the sadness which prevailed. A deep and unbroken silence was preserved after the magistrates had taken their seats; and the prisoner was arraigned to undergo his preliminary examination. When questioned, however, he would answer nothing; and he maintained his taciturnity, with the inflexible gravity and tact of an old offender. It became necessary, therefore, to summon other witnesses; and Imbert, who had seen the whole transaction, was called upon by name, and stood forth. He told the sad story in few, but impressive words.

"We had cast anchor last night," said he, "and our sails were furled, before the tragical event took place. The deed was done in the forecastle. I had thrown myself in my berth, after the fatigues of the day, and my example was followed by nearly all the crew who were not on duty. A lamp, suspended from a beam in the middle of the forecastle, was left burning. I had scarcely closed my eyes when I was disturbed by a noise of several of our Indians, who appeared to be quarrelling, for some cause which I did not understand. Among others I distinguished Quibby, the prisoner now before you. He had been a sulky, quarrelsome fellow, during the whole voyage, and grumbled at the most reasonable duty. The noise of a general fight among the Indians awakened others of the crew, and several leaped from their hammocks, and interfered to part the combatants. I saw Harry Gardner dragging Quibby from the prostrate body of his antagonist, and the quarrel ceased; but Gardner had scarcely loosed his hold from the collar of the prisoner, before Quibby buried the blade of his jack-knife in the breast of the young man. Harry spoke not a word afterwards, but fell dead upon the floor. The prisoner made a spring for the ladder to escape,—which possibly he might have done, being a capital swimmer;—but there happened to be a lance standing at the side of my berth, which I had been putting in order,—and, without a moment's reflection, I let it drive at him, and pinned him to the bulk head. He is wounded, as you perceive, in the fleshy part of the thigh. I have nothing further to add, except to say that the whole scene took place in less than half the time that I have occupied in relating it."

Imbert ceased. A buzz of approbation of his conduct ran through the assembly, and the young men of the town, especially, applauded him in their speech to each other. He became a favourite, at once, with all classes and ages; and when his entire conduct at sea, among the whales, and in the last melancholy affair, was better known to the people, there was none who stood higher in their general esteem, than Julius Imbert.

The Indian was ordered into confinement, to take his trial at a future day, before a high Colonial tribunal.

It was thus, sadly and disastrously, that the voyage of the young men terminated; and thus, that the high hopes of Jethro Coffin, and his captains, were blasted. The predictions of Judith, the half-breed fortune-teller, were fearfully realized.

CHAPTER THIRTEEN.

See the cypress wreath of saddest hue,
The twining destiny threading through;
And the serpent coil is twisting there—
While, regardless of the victim's prayer,
The fiend laughs out o'er the mischief done,
And th' canker-worm makes the heart his throne!

The Prophecy: Chap. vii, vol. 1.

—I could wish
That the first pillow whereon I was cradled
Had proved to me a grave.

Ford.

TIME rolled on:—Time,—that lays his hand gently upon us,—that softens sudden affliction, and strews roses over the tomb of the ardently beloved.

The shock of the melancholy tidings, brought by the returned whale-

ship, was severe both to Ruth and Mary. Tears took the place of smiles;—
and solitude, for a time, that of the common gayety of youth. But the
sorrow of no woman is immortal. There are but few modern instances of
lasting grief, equal in duration to that of the peerless Artemisia of old,
whose tears flowed, and whose frame was enveloped in sorrowful weeds,
even until Scopas and Briaxis, Leoshares and Timotheus had built up
the renowned tomb of Mausolus; and until the powder of his ashes,
swallowed in morning bitters by his queen, had found a resting place in
a living sepulchre!

Imbert, as in duty bound, presented himself before Mary soon after his
arrival, and told the story of his wanderings; but he forbore to press his
suit, until the effect of his tragical relation had somewhat worn off. He
was not, however, disappointed, when he proposed himself in form, to
find a ready acquiescence in his wishes. He had been obedient to the
commands of his mistress and had voyaged for whales at her behest; he
had given the death-blow, at least, to one unwieldly monster—and that
monster the destroyer of the devoted admirer of Mary's companion, Ruth
Coffin. He had borne himself bravely, and had come back a thorough
sailor in nautical knowledge, and had forgotten none of the
accomplishments which had made him acceptable in the drawing room.
He had behaved honourably with his rival;— and had, in his last
extremity, secured the culprit who committed the murder. Imbert took
care that all this should be well understood by Mary, before he ventured
to claim her hand as the reward of his devotion. The heart of Mary and
the promise of her hand were yielded, in maiden confidence, to one who
appeared so true and so honourable; and she looked forward to a life of
happiness with her admirer.

Ruth Coffin possessed a mind of less elasticity than the gentler Mary
Folger; and the loss of her lover sank deep into her heart. Grimshaw had,
as yet, never declared himself to Ruth; but he always looked as if he was
just on the point of doing so. There was something in her manner that
froze up the words in his throat, and he dallied on from day to day. Ruth,
from sheer spite, or perhaps for mischief, had given him many
opportunities for making known the height and depth of his tenderness,

for the wicked purpose of having the pleasure, once for all, of flatly denying him, and putting an end to his suit for ever. But he could never be brought to cross the Rubicon: he never told his love. He had lately risen somewhat in her favour, however, by the patient and active assiduity which he brought to bear in the entangled affairs of her mother, who, if anything, had heretofore marred his suit, by always trumpeting his praises in the ears of her daughter. The death of Thomas Starbuck was the summing up of her youthful afflictions; and it was many months before she regained her wonted cheerfulness, or allowed herself to mingle again with her young companions in public.

The day was fixed for the wedding of Imbert and Mary. The only reluctance that Peleg manifested to the match, arose from the fact that they could not be joined in wedlock in the usual way, in the meeting-house of the Friends. Imbert had not a drop of Quaker blood in him. But that great difficulty being obviated, by the perseverance and expedients of the lovers, every thing else went on smoothly. The cake was made;—the dresses were bought; the priest selected, and the guests invited. Those indispensable attendants, the groomsman and bridesmaid, were not forgotten; and Grimshaw was nominated by Imbert, being his early friend,—while Ruth, of course, was the selection of Mary.

The wedding night came. The tapers of sperm blazed upon the mantel; and the guests, old and young, came forth in their best attire. The bustling Peleg welcomed all with hearty good will, and cracked off his "minnows and mack'rel!" in return to the sly jokes of his friends. A wedding is a legitimate season for jokes, and all sorts of good-natured innuendoes and insinuations. Grimshaw, too, was busy among the throng, and did his best to put every one at his ease. The clergyman came, and was ushered into the parlour among the guests. The appearance of a clergyman is always a damper upon the auditory, be it at a wedding, or at any sort of feast or ceremony. where is a natural feeling of respect towards the cloth, manifested in all civilized societies, which effectually curbs the tongue of its license, and suppresses the rising jest. The strongest bond of society is religion; and its ministers are properly regarded as things holy. They are vessels sanctified to a holy use; and it speaks volumes for the morality of that community, where children are early taught to pay becoming deference to the ministers of the peaceful doctrines of Christianity.

The bride and her maid were yet in their chamber, awaiting the coming of the groom. The lovely Mary needed no adventitious aids to heighten her charms. A simple upper robe of white satin, well adjusted to her slender form, at once declared her good taste in preparing her bridal dress. Her hair flowed over her shoulders in natural ringlets, and was confined about the brow by a plain band of white ribbon, that contrasted but slightly with the marble clearness of her forehead. Ruth, with similar good taste, had arranged her own costume in the most becoming simplicity; but there was a pensiveness in her manner that spoke of an aching heart. The preparations for the ceremony of giving away her friend, and for the banquet that would succeed the ceremonial, revived the sadness of her own condition, and tended to bring back the memory of her faithful Thomas with painful recollections. She sighed as she surveyed the charming Mary, "beaming all over with smiles," while she indulged in the buoyant anticipation of the wedding scene. Ruth's dark eyes melted into tears as she took the hand of her companion.

"Peace and prolonged happiness be thine," said she, "for thou dost deserve the choicest blessings of heaven!—But for *me*—"

"Talk not sadly upon this occasion, I beseech thee," replied the gentle Mary: "there are happy days in store for *thee* too. Come, come, Ruth!—must *I* play the comforter now, when thou know'st it is the fashion for the bride to claim all sympathy? Seest thou not that I am trembling with affright?—and hark!—that hearty laugh in the parlour is surely at my expense;—for brides and bridegrooms are considered fair game with the guests, upon wedding days. But, dear me!—where does Julius loiter so long? He was ever punctual in his engagements; and now, when there is most occasion for his presence,—when I most need the encouraging influence of his cheerful words, he lingers:—Ah, that quick step upon the stairs is his!"

Mary flew to the door to meet her betrothed; but her countenance fell with disappointment, as her father entered, and demanded the reason of her delay in appearing below among the guests.

"All is ready," said he, "but, minnows and mack'rel! where is the groom—where is Imbert? Eh—not come yet?—what can he mean by keeping us waiting so long!"

The ever-moving Peleg flung out of the room impatiently, and mingled again among the people below. By and by, hints began to be thrown out, by his friends, that it was time the ceremony should commence: some smacked their lips in the ears of Peleg, in anticipation of the feast; and the minister gravely pulled out his watch, and remarked that time was flying apace. All this Peleg understood as direct allusions to the delay which had taken place; and he was worried into an agony of vexation. The thunder of a loud rap, upon the outer door, smote upon his ear; and he rushed from his tormentors into the hall. He opened the door, and the light within fell upon a man whose form was muffled up in a cloak, and whose hat was partially drawn over his features. Peleg believed it to be Imbert, and hastily called to him to enter.

"Come in—come in!" said he, in his peculiar quick tones—"minnows and mack'rel, man!—we have been waiting for thee this whole hour past!"

"Not for me, I presume," said the stranger, while he held out a letter to Peleg.

Peleg took the letter, and turned it over and over in stupefied wonder. He approached the light to decipher the superscription; and when he turned towards the door again, the messenger was out of sight. The paper was addressed to Mary, and was carefully folded and sealed. He quickly ascended to her room, and put it into her hands. While she hastily broke the seal, it was observed that a strong tremor agitated her frame. It seemed to her, coming as it did at this peculiar juncture, a messenger of woe. She opened the paper, and gave a reluctant glance at its contents. The letter dropped from her hand, and a deathlike hue overspread her countenance. Her eyes closed, and the poor girl fell senseless into the arms of Ruth.

An anxious outcry from Peleg brought many of the guests up into the chamber, and the letter which had caused the mischief was passed from hand to hand. It ran as follows:—

"To Mary Folger:—

"When this letter is put into your hands, I shall be far distant: but be not surprised when I tell you that I am resolved never to return to claim you as my bride. If you would know my reasons for this determination, I have only to refer to our past intercourse. The blame must rest with yourself, and with that unnatural society to which you have given your pledge, and which has forced me, against my will, to assume a character foreign from my nature, and to play the hypocrite in order to win you. I confess that I have also had many misgivings as to the possession of your affection; for the woman who can so far forget herself as to play upon the feelings of her lover, and put him to unnecessary tests, such as I have undergone, for the mere gratification of whim or caprice, must be guilty of duplicity, to say the least of it. You will now reap the harvest of your folly. From the moment I knew of your determination that I should go to sea, and thus sink my profession to the level of uneducated whalers, I made up my mind to win you against the world, and make an example of you for the benefit of others. I have accomplished my purpose;—but I will not possess you. I would have gone to the world's end to compass this just revenge; and it pleases me the more that it will be felt, through you, by other members of that hateful association of women, who, in imitation of the men, must have their secret societies, but without the merit of their good intention. The fertile brain of some women, I know, delights in mischief;—but the reaction is ofttimes a merited retribution for their indulgence in their wayward fancies. Remember, you would have rejected me, had I refused to comply with your commands. I determined to obey them, to the very letter, in order that I might have the satisfaction of healing my wounded pride by rejecting you in turn. I have now turned the tables upon you, and am revenged in full. I have contrived that this letter shall be handed to you upon the evening which was intended to be our wedding night. It will be placed in your possession when the guests are assembled:—I have arranged it so, in order that my retaliation may be the more complete; for you will be surrounded by many that have been the upholders of your conduct towards me, and who will thus have an opportunity of witnessing the effects of their folly, and the injurious tendency of their association.

"Farewell for ever.

"JULIUS IMBERT."

The blow was tremendous and overpowering to poor Mary. The restoratives, which her friends applied, were ineffectual for a long time. She revived at last for a few minutes; but the interval was passed in piteous moans and wild, incoherent ravings. Her maddened brain whirled and her tortured heart sent up prayers to her lips, asking for death.

"Hide me, father, from this deep disgrace!" said she, and again relapsed into convulsions.

Peleg hung over his daughter with paternal solicitude, and at times vented maledictions, in his peculiar way, upon all flaunting coxcombs who lay snares to entrap the hearts of females, for the mere pleasure of outraging them afterwards. Ruth remained by the bedside of Mary, an anxious spectator of her sad condition. She failed not to soothe her with all the kind and endearing language, that a sister might bring to her aid, upon such an occasion; but it was many weeks before her faculties were restored to their natural and healthful play.

It is needless to say that the frightened guests hurried from the house of Peleg; and that the cause of their premature dismissal created a deep and lasting sensation in the little town of Sherburne.

CHAPTER FOURTEEN.

——Last scene of all,
That ends this strange, eventful history.
Shakspeare.

To sum the whole—the close of all.
Sterne.

WE have now brought our story nearly to its close. It remains for us, only, to satisfy the reader in a few particulars, by disposing of our characters in a manner befitting their several stations, and consonant to the parts they have sustained in this drama of Real Life.

The war of the Revolution, which at first affected the people of Nantucket most disastrously, was much softened in its rigour after the neutrality of the island had been recognized by the contending parties; but it was not until peace was restored, and the colonies became Independent States, that its trade thoroughly revived and flourished again. Many families, at the beginning of the war, removed to the State of New York, and settled themselves at a place they called "The Nine Partners;" and the flourishing city of Hudson, at the head of the deep water on the river of the same name, owes its origin, in a great measure, to the whale-fishermen of Nantucket, who peopled it, and afterwards sent out their whaling ships from the port. The second war between the United States and Great Britain, affected the island in the same way as that of the Revolution. Its commerce was annihilated—its ships in the Pacific captured—and its local distresses were equally great. In this last war, similar arrangements were entered into with the contending powers, from absolute necessity; while many of its people, abandoning their ancient homes, were scattered over the interior of the country. Some three score families, in one body, moved off to the far West, and settled in and about Cincinnati, in Ohio; and, at this day, names known at the beginning of the Revolution, as appertaining to Nantucket alone, may be found dispersed over the continent in all directions.

Vast accessions have since been made to the island population from abroad; its ancient manners are greatly altered; its shearing days, though still kept up, are shone of their former splendour and conviviality; the Quakers have ceased to predominate; and other religious denominations are establishing themselves in their ancient stronghold. The whale-fishery, once the sole monopoly of the island, is pursued with equal vigour in other parts of the country; but the fame of the Nantucket commanders has not abated a jot, and they are still preferred over those of the whole world besides. Education flourishes, and mercantile and mechanical operations of all kinds have been introduced and are successfully carried on upon the island. Musical societies and dancing associations thrive apace. Every good and eke almost every evil known to other places, are now as common here as elsewhere. Lawyers alone have, as yet, scarce an abiding place in Nantucket; and the jail—the follower, the very jackal of civilization,—is tenantless! The enterprise of the place has undergone no change, except, perhaps, for the better. Thrift and prosperity, and hospitality, and politeness, and amenity of manners never prevailed more generally than now, when the rigid manners of the ancients have given way to the refinements of polished society.

But let us return to the characters of our tale.

Jethro Coffin, a worthy and honourable representative of the name, and a direct descendant of the *"first Trustum Coffin,"* lived to a good old age, respected by every one who knew him; and, when well stricken in years, he died, as he had lived, an *honest man,* and in charity with all mankind.

Miriam Coffin, who was a woman of strong passions and ambitious to the last degree, from the period of Jethro's return till his death, devoted herself to matronly cares; but it was with a great deal of secret discontent that she witnessed the triumph of her enemies, and saw them build up their prosperity upon her ruin. She contrived, however, though at a late day, to put the disarranged affairs of her household and her previous business operations in a fair train of equitable adjustment; and she compelled many to make restitution for the wrongs she had sustained at their hands. She was a being of fierce mind and great force of intellect; but the softer shades of female character were absent in her composition. She was a woman that one might easily fear, but never thoroughly love nor admire. In her reverses she was more anxious than ever that her daughter should unite her destiny with Grimshaw; and she urged so many good reasons in that behalf, and pestered her so incessantly with the theme, that a reluctant consent was finally wrung from Ruth, and the marriage rites were shortly afterwards performed.

The wedding day was not a joyous season to Ruth; and her heart almost sank within her, when she pronounced the vow of love and obedience at the altar. But Grimshaw, though naturally selfish, was not the worst of men. He had no positive vices—and his outward morality was unimpeachable, and in the main he made a good husband. That he was strongly attached to Ruth was certain; and though his first design may have been to unite himself with her in order to better his estate, by coming into possession of her promised dowry, yet, when misfortunes overwhelmed her house, he did not suffer his ardour to cool, nor his attentions to flag. It was an honourable trait in his conduct towards her, and she did not fail to perceive and appreciate it. In the course of their wedded life, if there were no very strong symptoms of love, neither were there any remarkable outbreakings of angry and quarrelsome tempers. It was, in this respect, rather a happy union than otherwise; for their lives flowed on with an even tenor. Ruth reigned undisputed mistress of her mansion; and Grimshaw,—good, easy man,—never strove to thwart her inclinations. He was, in short, a memorable sample of Yankee perseverance; and content with obtaining his ends, he never very scrupulously canvassed the means by which he had gained them.

The country-house of Miriam was one among the few things of her former possessions, which did not fall into the hands of the Philistines. The newly-married pair chose it for their residence, and it suited the natural indolence of Grimshaw passing well. There was fishing and fowling in abundance in its neighbourhood;—and these facilities, so close at hand, eventually confirmed Grimshaw in the habits of the sportsman. The house has passed into other hands, and some sixty years have gone by since it was thus inhabited; but even to this day, among other things associated with Miriam Coffin's name, the iron hooks upon which 'Squire Grimshaw's fowling-piece used to hang, are pointed out by the present occupants to strangers, as a sort of curiosity belonging to another age, and especially as giving evidence of the propensities of the son-in-law of that far-famed woman.

The explorer after antiquities will, however, look in vain for the smugglers' vaulted passages under ground, which opened among the clump of bushes that we have more than once referred to. At the command of Ruth, that singular communication with the house was cut off; and every vestige of the covered way removed;—so that there are now no remains which indicate its extent, or give evidence of the uses to which it had been applied.

Young Isaac Coffin proved to be a worthy son of a worthy father. His fearless conduct on board the Grampus, when attacked by the French privateer, gained him the notice and approbation of his father's friends in London,—among whom there were several who were influential with the government. Seeing Isaac's inclination for a seafaring life, they procured him a midshipman's warrant in his majesty's navy; and Jethro, after much persuasion, yielded his consent that his son might accept it. We cannot now detain the reader by tracing the various turns of his fortune in naval life; but must sum the whole up by saying that he arrived, at last, by the regular steps of promotion, to the highest rank in the service, and was fortunate enough, through life, to merit the favour and approbation of his adopted sovereign. In youth he sailed and associated with the present "Sailor King" of Britain; and, in his old age, he was not forgotten by the promoted scion of royalty. The prophetic words of Bill Smith, the English tar, were never forgotten. *"You'll be an admiral yet!"*—were sounds that were interwoven with all his dreams of ambition, and seemed to him to be echoed in every gale. In his manhood Isaac returned repeatedly to the land of his birth;—and in scattering his munificence, and spreading the lights of knowledge among the people of his name and the countless kindred of his family, he has earned a civic crown that has rivaled the glory of his professional career. When time shall lay him low, there will be hundreds of living beings here to say, in sincerity—

> "Green be the turf above thee,
>   Friend of my early days!
> None knew thee but to love thee,—
>   None named thee but to praise." *

Peleg Folger lived to an advanced age; and, in his latter years, took to writing the history of his times. He embodied, in an antique dress, many curious incidents and stirring events of the day. In turning over his notes, to which we have had access, we came across one sentence that struck us as particularly faithful. It was,—that "The females of Nantucket are good looking, and some of them even beautiful!"

Well done, Peleg!

We have heard that after labouring hard at this gallant sentence, for half a day, Peleg got upon his legs, and, snapping his fingers, shouted— "Minnows and mack'rel!—what will posterity and the brethren say to *that!*"

The overclouded morning of Mary Folger's life was followed by sunshine; and the noontide of her years was spent in happiness. She gave her hand in marriage to a man of exalted worth, who loved her for her virtues and amiable qualities. Her gentleness and personal beauty—her

---

*Halleck

goodness of heart and purity of mind, were jewels in the crown of a fond and excellent husband. Of their passage over the down-hill of life we have no authentic information; but no woman ever deserved to be happier in her earthly lot than the gentle Mary Folger.

Of Julius Imbert, whose unworthiness we have seen in his reckless conduct towards Mary and the Indian maid, there is not much more to be said. His career through life was a tissue of deceits; and female ruin and desolation tracked his steps. He was last seen in one of the West India Islands. Remorse for his early irregularities and wanton criminality, was then making sad havoc with his manly beauty; and, at the age of forty, the dissipation in which he indulged to drown the whisperings of a goading conscience, had covered his head with premature whiteness, and his brow with deep furrows. His speech had become morose and offensive, and the sparkle of his eye was gone. His day of enjoyment was over; and reflection had come to dash his cup with bitterness. There is a period in the life of every man, when it is consoling and rejoicing to the heart, to be able to look back upon an honourable and well-spent life. Such, however, was not the lot of Imbert. He was gay and boldly designing in his youth, and preyed upon innocence; but his latter days were burthensome to himself, and were passed in unsatisfactory and unavailing retrospection.

The reasons assigned by Imbert, in his letter, for the desertion of Mary, gave the death-blow to that extraordinary association of women upon Nantucket, whose secret doings took the semblance of Free-Masonry. At any rate, the members were never known to assemble afterwards in secret conclave; and though some of them may still be living, and may possibly meet at each other's houses to talk over their former exploits and reminiscences, yet it is believed that they never attempted further to make proselytes, or to receive candidates for membership.

Benjamin Tashima was gathered to his fathers in the fullness of time. He was preceded, however, by his daughter Manta, who, overwhelmed by shame, was hurried to her grave by the silent grief that preyed upon her heart, and the utter desolation of her condition. The secret of her betrayal, or the name of her betrayer, never escaped her. But Miriam Coffin, at the last interview of Imbert and Manta, at her paternal wigwam, had seen enough to convince her how matters stood between them; and she, alone, of all Manta's acquaintances, was able to account for the fatal calamity that probably shortened the days of both father and daughter. They were buried, side by side, with their heads pointing to the west, in the circular burying ground of the tribe, near the head-waters of Lake Miacomet, and within sight of the present shearing-pens of the islanders. The little grassy hillocks, piled over their graves, are still visible; and there,—too,—undisturbed by the hand of desecration,—

"The rude forefathers of the hamlet sleep."

The departure of Tashima was the signal for unlimited license among the Indians; and the tribe soon sunk into nothingness. The settlements of Eat-Fire and Miacomet went to decay; and nothing now remains, to indicate their locality, but deep beds of ashes, mixed with sea-shells, which unerringly point out the hearths of the wigwams of the Indian.

The fate of Quibby, the murderer, remains to be told. He was arraigned and tried before the High Court of the Colony, over which the celebrated Governor Hutchinson presided as chief justice. The session was held at Sherburne, and was conducted with all the imposing forms and solemnity, which were calculated to impress the auditors,—especially the Nantucket people, to whom the sight was altogether new,—with awe and veneration. After a protracted and impartial hearing of the case, he was brought in *"Guilty"* by the jury, that, for greater fairness, was composed of an equal number of whites and Indians. The presiding judge then addressed the criminal, and pronounced the sentence of death. The muscles of Quibby's face never moved from the commencement of the trial to its end, and the feeling address and sentence of the court had no visible effect whatever upon him. He was reconveyed to prison, to undergo, at a future day, the penalty of the law. But repentance came not to soften the hardness of his heart. It remained flinty as the nether millstone, to the last;—and, as if to set the power of the law at defiance, and to convince the world that one murder was not sufficient to satisfy his blood-thirsty propensity, he lifted his hand once more against the life of a fellow creature. An Indian companion, who had been confined in the same building, for some trivial offense against the law, was found dead in the chamber of Quibby, on the morning of his being brought forth for execution. They had quarrelled over night, and Quibby had seized him by the throat, and choked him until life was extinct!

The day of expiation of this doubly-dyed criminal came at last. A gallows was erected upon the common, to the eastward of the town; and at the hour appointed, it was surrounded by thousands of people, who, though generally opposed to the Mosaic doctrine of "blood for blood," were, in this instance, reconciled, in a great degree, to the mode of punishment which the law pointed out for the offender, who now stood before them with the halter dangling over his head. The miserable culprit was launched into eternity, without a pitying tear from the bystanders. The gallows upon which he was executed stood in the place where it was planted, for many years afterwards; and it was never passed by any of the inhabitants without a shudder. It finally disappeared, during a scarcity of fuel, in a pinching winter. The last house in what is called the "New Town," on the road leading to the "Bug Light," now marks the spot where the gallows was erected.

The body of Quibby was claimed by Judith Quary, who, in all his confinement, and in his last moments, appeared to be the only friend he possessed upon the island. It was yielded at her request; for the authorities believed, with the celebrated John Wilkes, that a man is of no further use after he is hanged. She caused it to be carried to her lonely hut, where she enveloped it in decent habiliments, and dug his solitary grave with her own hands. The tie, that bound Judith to this Indian, was even stronger than death;—crime itself could not sever it. The offspring of Quibby, and the half-breed, Judith Quary, is still living upon the island, and is a man quite advanced in years. As the name of Quibby was odious to the people, he took that of his mother, which he still bears. He is *the last* of the Indian race that once owed allegiance to Tashima. Without a known relative upon the face of the earth, he wanders about the island an object of curiosity possessing all the peculiarities of the Indian developed in his mind and person. The lineaments of his face are those that a painter or sculptor might choose to copy after, with the certainty of transmitting to posterity an accurate and strongly marked specimen of the aboriginal countenance.

Quibby is the only murderer that has ever disturbed the peace of Nantucket, since its settlement by the whites;—and his execution is the only capital punishment that the exemplary islanders have had occasion to inflict.

In disposing of the characters who have had an active agency in our pages, we must not forget our sea-captains. Seth Macy and Jonathan Coleman are both favourites with us, in their way, and do not deserve to be left unaccounted for. After their return to the island, on the termination of their disastrous voyage, they were both made to feel the privations of the war, in common with their townsmen. When peace was restored, Jonathan again put to sea, and mended his fortunes among the whales. His light heart, and buoyant mind,—always looking to the bright side of the future,—carried him happily through the world; and, in the winding up of his professional career, he enjoyed a green old age upon his native island, to which he clung with the fondness of a first love. There was no place like Nantucket to him. It was a haven of rest for Jonathan, more lovely and inviting than all the world beside.

It was not so, however, with Seth Macy. He would go to sea no more. He was frequently offered the choice of the ships in the harbour; but he could not be tempted. He had spent most of his life away from his native place, but always longed for the fireside pleasures of home. When teased with the importunities of the oil-merchants, who knew his sterling worth, he would often reply in a strain similar to that of a modern bard—

> "'I hate your hoary face—gruff sea!—
> 'T were vile hypocrisy in me
> To say I love you.—If I do,
> May I be d—rowned!' *

"No!" continued he, "I will leave ploughing the ocean, and betake myself to ploughing the land. My mind is made up, and I will gather my traps together, and move off to the West."

---

*Byron

Macy redeemed his promise, and settled in the "new countries," as the interior of the "Empire State" was then called. His days, thereafter, ran smoothly on, and he enjoyed himself in the midst of his family, and became an independent farmer,—the most satisfactory occupation in the world, where one looks to the productions of the soil for returns for his labour, and places his dependence upon his own personal skill and industry, and the protecting smile of Providence. Macy held to "the use of means;" and put his own shoulder to the wheel, while he called on Hercules for aid. "Paul must plant, and Appollos water," said he; "and Heaven will give the increase." Macy was a happy man, and fortunate in his worldly speculations; and his children grew up around him, and flourished, and became estimable citizens of the peerless and glorious State, which their father had adopted for his residence in his declining years.

Sherburne has since taken the name of Nantucket; but by what process it was brought about, or for what reason, we are unable to declare. It bore the former title as late as the time of Dr. Franklin, who commenced a poetic epistle thus, while sojourning upon the island:

> "From *Sherburne*, where I dwell,
> Your friend who means you well," etc.

The well-conducted newspaper of the town, which has had more than the usual influence of the press in this country, has doubtless been the greatest and most powerful agent in affecting a change in the manners and habits of the islanders. As some evidence of this, as well as of the progress of refinement there, let us take a few modern extracts from its columns. What unmeasured innovation do they show upon the old-fashioned, primitive ways of the people!

"On Monday evening next, the lecture of Mr. A—— on Dramatic Literature, with illustrations from Shakespeare and the old dramatic authors, (which was received, on Friday evening last, with unbounded applause, by a numerous and fashionable auditory,) will be repeated at the Town-Hall, by particular desire."

"On Tuesday evening the regular monthly Oratorio of the Handel and Haydn Society, will take place at the —— church. The selections are principally made from the old masters, interspersed with some of the brilliant compositions of Rossini. Miss B—— will preside at the organ."

"The Greek and Latin classes of the Coffin School will be submitted for public examination on the afternoon of Wednesday next, at the academy. Mr. C——, the principal, respectfully invites the patrons of the school to be present."

"Mr. D—— respectfully informs the ladies and gentlemen of Nantucket that his Quadrille parties will commence for the season on Thursday next. For terms of admission, &c., apply at the rooms between the hours of twelve and one, when Mr. D. will be in attendance."

"Miss F—— has removed her academy for music and drawing, (which she is happy to say has been more than ordinarily encouraged this season,) to No. 5 ——Street. Charge for use of musical instruments extra."

"The Philosophical lectures will be resumed, at the Hall of the Athenæum, on Friday evening next. Mr. F—— will lecture on Chemistry and Natural Philosophy as applied to the arts; and Mr. G—— will continue his course on Natural History."

"Saturday. Arrived, steam-boat Telegraph, with three hundred passengers, who visit us to participate in the hospitalities and amusements of our annual festival—the Sheep-shearing. Same day, arrived U.S. Revenue Cutter Alert, Capt.——, who saluted the town with a battery of thirteen guns, which we would have been most happy to return, but for the lack of the one thing needful—*ordnance!*"

"Sunday. A riot occurred among the blacks in the quarter of the town called Guinea. One person, in attempting to interfere, was severely injured by the dirk of a negro, who came to the island yesterday. We are happy to say the wounds of the sufferer are not likely to prove dangerous. The high sheriff immediately took the offender into custody, to answer for his assault at the next term of our court of Common Pleas. A tumult of this nature is of rare occurrence here:—indeed, we have had no parallel since the days of Quibby, the murderer. The town was thrown into commotion and consternation by the report of the outrage."

"The post-coach for 'Sconset will hereafter depart at the hour of 10 in the morning."

Shades of the Ancients! How would your bodies wriggle and turn over in their graves, could you but listen for a moment to the recital of some of these monstrosities. Music and dancing! Steam-boats and theatricals!— But we have done.

Sixty years have passed, and are numbered with those beyond the flood, since the enactment of the various scenes constituting the groundwork of this tale; but in that time what changes have come over the whole country, as well as Nantucket! We have, in the time, sprung into existence as a nation; and our population is more than quadrupled. We are now leading the way among nations.

Fiction has but little to do with our pages. The incidents and the manners of bygone times, which we have shown up to a new generation, are faithful pictures of a past age, and are drawn from materials, which, if not altogether matters of record, still live fresh in the memory of a few persons, whose day of nativity dates near the middle of the last century.

If we have succeeded in conveying a useful moral, and in showing the young and inexperienced female where the true sphere of her duties lies;—if we have enabled her properly to appreciate the butterfly acquirements of flippant dealers in mere compliments and insincere protestations, which proceed from the tongue outwards, and have no origin in the heart;—if we have, in any way, contributed to give to the world a just representation of the character and hazardous pursuits of the daring Whale-Fishermen, who form a race of mariners of whom we are proud;—in short, if we have afforded the reader but a moiety of the pleasure in perusing some of the simple annals of Nantucket that *we* have experienced in tracing them,—we shall be satisfied that our time has been spent to some good purpose:—for we have been both instructed and amused, while collecting and putting together the various parts of this tale. And here is the

END OF THE "WHALE-FISHERMEN."